Four Brothers In Sickness

Book 7

JEL JONES

(Sequel to Four Brothers In Love)

Copyright © 2018 by Jel Jones
All rights reserved. No part of this book may be reproduced, stored in a retrieval system or transmitted in any form or by any means without the prior written permission of the publishers, except by a reviewer who may quote brief passages in a review to be printed in a newspaper, magazine or journal.

First Printing

All characters in this book are fictitious, and any resemblance to real persons, living or dead, is coincidental.

ISBN 978-1-387-56953-3
Published by Lulu

Lulu Press, Inc.
627 Davis Drive – Suite 300
Morrisville, NC 27560
www.lulu.com

Chapter One

    Time hadn't soften Sabina's misery as an entire hour had gone by since Sabrina confronted Britain at Courtney's house. She cried silent tears in her room and realized she was home alone when she noticed the entire family and all the staff were off the premises. She was filled with too much anguish, shock and disappointment to think clear to remember that the family and staff were all out of the mansion at the fundraiser where Starlet was scheduled to sing, America.
    Sabrina felt hopeless as she paced back and forth in front of her bedroom fireplace, then it startled her when she heard the doorbell. She grabbed her face with both hands and shook her head in anguish and disappointment. It dawned on her that if she didn't answer the door there were no staff around to answer it. She had second thoughts about leaving her room and heading downstairs to answer the door. She was in no condition to face anyone. Plus, she figured it would be Britain showing up to try to explain himself. She was too disappointed and upset with him to confront him. Therefore, she made no attempts to head downstairs to answer the door. She continued to pace back and forth in front of the fireplace until soft knocks begin at the front door. Standing in the middle of her bedroom floor, she placed her hands over her ears and closed her eyes. She was wishing the knocking away, when suddenly the knocks stopped but the doorbell sounded repeatedly. Sabrina tried to fade out the ding dong as she continuously held both hands over her ears. Nothing mattered, she was numb with anguish.
    Moments later, the ringing of the doorbell and the knocks at the front door ceased. Sabrina swallowed hard and took a deep breath and stood still in the middle of her bedroom floor hoping to hear the sound of a car engine starting up and leaving her driveway. But as she stood there in tears, she

didn't hear the start of a car engine leaving the driveway. She wondered if Britain had given up on trying to get her to answer the door. Crushed with heartbreak, she dropped down on the side of her queen size bed and grabbed her face in her hands. She felt drained and exhausted as she fell over on her back and stared up at the pink ceiling. She couldn't shed anymore tears as her eyes were red and felt sore from her flow of tears. She was lying there trying to make sense of what had just happened nearly an hour ago at Courtney's house. But suddenly, she sat straight up in full alert from the sound of footsteps headed down the long marble hallway toward her room. She sat there on the side of her bed motionless looking toward her open door when suddenly Britain walked up and stood in the doorway with bright confused eyes staring at her.

"Sabrina, I know you're upset about something."

"If you know I'm upset, why are you here?" she exclaimed.

"It's obvious you're upset," Britain calmly said. "However, you and I really need to have conversation."

"Now is not the time. Please leave," she stressed.

"Sabrina, I have no intentions of leaving here without having a discussion with you. We both need to find out what just happened at Courtney's," he said frustrated.

"Britain, please leave."

"Sabrina, are you listening to me? I'm stressing how much you and I need to talk."

"I can't talk to you right now," she sadly said, pointing toward the door.

"I can see how upset you are."

"Yes, I'm very upset," Sabrina sadly mumbled.

"I'm sorry you're upset," Britain assured her. "I'm not upset. But I'm frustrated and somewhat confused; and know we really need to talk."

"But I don't want to talk to you. Besides, there's nothing you can discuss that I want to hear," she sadly uttered, looking in his eyes. Then it dawned on her, he had gotten inside without her answering the door.

"Sabrina, I promise I will leave after you hear me out," he assured her.

"I'm not interested in hearing you out."

"I don't think that's fair," Britain said. "How can you get a clear picture of what just happened if you won't hear me out?"

"I already have a clear picture."

"But you really do not."

"I think I do. I know what I saw and what I heard," Sabrina sadly said.

"What you saw and what you heard is not the clear picture, believe me. So, I know you're really upset. But I really need you to talk to me," Britain suggested.

"Britain, maybe later. But you need to leave now," she strongly urged him. "I wasn't going to let you in. So, how did you get in?" she curiously asked. "There's no one else here that could have let you in."

"The front door wasn't locked. I rang the doorbell a few times and knocked and when you didn't answer, I grabbed the doorknob and turned the knob and the door opened. I guess you forgot to lock it when you got here."

"Maybe I did. You have me out of my mind with your sneaking around," she tearfully fussed.

"My sneaking around?" Britain asked. "What do you mean by that statement?" he asked with confusion in his eyes.

"You know what I mean," she glumly mumbled.

Somehow just seeing his face choked her up and brought forth overwhelming irritation and disappointment. She hopped off the bed and threw up both arms. "Britain, why are you standing there staring at me as if you have no clue why I'm so upset with you?"

"Maybe, because I have no clue what's going on in this house or Courtney's?" He pointed toward the window.

Sabrina shook her head. "You know plenty. I'm the one who's in the dark. So, please don't insult my intelligence by standing there looking innocent. Besides, I'm really disappointed in you and I have asked you to leave, but you're being rude by ignoring my wishes," Sabrina sadly stated, looking in his eyes.

"Listen, Sabrina," Britain said frustrated. "You're not listening to me it seems. I'm trying to tell you that I have no idea what you're distressed about. I know you asked me to leave, and I'm not purposely trying to be rude, but we're both adults and we need to get to the bottom of why you're peeved at me and why you think I also know why you're peeved."

"I don't want to talk about it," Sabrina said looking toward the floor.

"Maybe you don't want to talk about it; and I still don't know what you don't want to talk about. Nevertheless, we seriously need to have a discussion before I leave here. We can't just leave things up in the air," he calmly suggested. "Besides, I feel if we have a discussion, we'll be able to get a clear picture of what's going on and why you're upset with me."

Sabrina didn't comment as she continued to look toward the floor with her arms folded around her chest. It dawned on her how sincere he sounded about not having a clue about why she was upset with him. She knew how honest he was and wondered if she was making a mistake by thinking what she was thinking.

Britain noticed how she kept looking down as he looked toward her. "Listen, Sabrina. I'm confused and I'm sure you are too. That's why we need to talk about it. Is it okay if I come inside your room?" he softly asked.

Sabrina looked toward Britain and shook her head. Looking in his face irritated her more and made her relive the image of seeing him in Courtney's bedroom. That image was carved in her brain as the shock of her life. Therefore, suddenly the thought of her thinking she had made a mistake quickly vanished from her mind. Suddenly, all the sad feelings rushed back; and she was beside herself with heartbreak of him visiting Courtney's house and ending up in Courtney's bedroom. It made Courtney's words about going with him appear true in her mind.

"I thought about it. But I have decided I just don't want to talk right now," she softly said. "I just want you to leave," Sabrina said in a choked up voice. "Why did you bother coming over? You didn't have time to spend with me earlier! So I don't have time to spend with you now," Sabrina snapped.

Britain propped an elbow on the doorframe. "Maybe I should leave because you're just not listening to me; and right now we're getting nowhere with a lack of much needed communication. Plus, you have me at a disadvantage since I'm in the dark about whatever it is that you're supposedly irritated with me about," Britain calmly said as he slowly walked across the room and grabbed both of her hands in his. He looked at her with serious eyes. "We need to talk and get to the bottom of what put you in this mood."

"Britain Franklin, don't you pretend you don't know what I'm upset with you about! I'm sure you know what I'm talking about?" She pulled her hands from his and turned her back to him.

"Please turn around and look at me, Sabrina," he humbly suggested with confusion in his eyes and frustration on his face. He was in complete wonder about her upset behavior.

She turned around and looked at him with solemn eyes. "Britain, you're acting oblivious to all of this." She held up one finger. "But allow me to refresh your memory. Does a one o'clock appointment ring a bell?"

He stood there bewildered by her anguish and was too disturbed by her touchiness with him to put the dots together that she was upset about his visit to Courtney's house.

"Sabrina, in order for me to properly offend myself, you need to explain the issue you're upset with me about," he very calmly and politely suggested.

"I think you already know my issue with you; and if you don't, you should," she softly mumbled, grabbed her face with both hands and cried silent tears.

"I'm on the level. I don't know what you're getting at. Just tell me already," he strongly suggested. "I'm confused but mostly I'm concerned about you and how whatever this is that have gotten you in such an emotional state. So, what's the matter?"

"The matter is quite clear to me. You cancelled our lunch plans in order to keep your one o'clock appointment, remember?"

Britain stared at her trying to process what she was referring to and when he didn't reply she felt she had him redhanded.

"No comment now? After you cancelled our lunch so you could be on time for your visit to see Courtney Ross at one o'clock!"

Britain raised an eyebrow and gave Sabrina a surprised stare before he spoke. "Is that what you're upset about, my visit to Courtney's house?" Britain asked surprised.

"Don't try to deny it, Britain Franklin. I was there too and I saw you in her bedroom! Remember! You showed up at Courtney's house at one o'clock on the button!" she fussed.

"Sabrina." He raised one hand. "I'm not denying it, I'm just trying to be clear about why you're so touchy with me. I'm surprised you would be so peeved and bent out of shape with me due to a visit I made to Courtney's house?" he confusedly asked. "But is my visit to Courtney's house the reason you're so touchy and irritable? Is that what you're upset about?" he asked.

Sabrina didn't answer as she stood there looking in his eyes. She didn't know how to feel or what to believe. He seemed so casual and calm about his reasons for visiting Courtney's house.

"Sabrina, are you going to answer me? Is my visit to Courtney's house the reason you're in such an emotional state? You didn't speak to me, you just ran out of Courtney's house as if the place was on fire. You wouldn't let me say one word. You just ran to your car and drove off."

"Of course, I ran out and drove away. I was stunned to see you there. Why were you there, Britain? I know I shouldn't have been there. But she dared me to show up at her home at one o'clock," Sabrina tearfully admitted and then grabbed her cheeks with both hands, standing there staring at him as tears rolled down her face.

"Courtney dared you to show up at her house at one o'clock?" Britain asked with a surprise expression and a puzzled look in his eyes. "Sabrina, I guess I'm not following you. Please, calm down and explain yourself."

"I wasn't there because I thought you would come to her house. I was there because I was sure you wouldn't show up. I wanted to prove to her that she was lying when she announced you would be dropping by her house to pay her a visit!" Sabrina sadly explained. "But you did show up just as she said you would!"

"Let me see if I'm following you correctly," Britain said and pointed toward the settee in her room. "Is it okay if I be seated over there?"

"Sure, why not," Sabrina mumbled as she walked across the room behind him and took a seat in a chair near the settee. She folded her arms in her lap and looked toward Britain.

He looked toward Sabrina with a serious expression on his face as he took a seat on the settee. "Sabrina, you're upset with me and torn up inside because I paid a visit to Courtney Ross's house?"

Sabrina nodded. "Yes, that's why I'm upset."

"You're upset because I showed up at Courtney's house, but you thought I wouldn't show up there. You only showed up because you wanted to prove to her that I wouldn't show up. But I did show up and you're beside yourself with distraught and I cannot remember a time when you were touchier and so unwilling to listen." He held up both arms. "Nevertheless, I'm still lost because I don't know why you're so distressed that I paid a visit to Courtney Ross's house," he said to her. "The young woman does work for me. Granted, she had a crush on me and may still do, but that's in the past. Besides, Courtney mentioned that you two are friends now," Britain told her.

Sabrina frowned. "Courtney Ross is not my friend," Sabrina admitted.

He nodded with surprised eyes. "Okay, she's not your friend. However, I accepted her at her word about the friendship since I have seen her coming and going paying you visits at the Taylor mansion a few times."

"Courtney is not my friend and what she felt for you is not in the past!" Sabrina relayed strongly. "Courtney Ross still loves you. So what was I supposed to think when you showed up at her house just as she said you would?" Sabrina softly asked.

He looked at her lost for words since they were both dealing with two different realities. He thought Courtney was a new friend of Sabrina's and had moved on from him. Now he's being told she's still in love with him and is not Sabrina's friend. Plus, he's thinking about the odd situation that occurred at Courtney's house.

"Sabrina, you are visibly trembling and I can see tears in your eyes as if the world is ending. Your irritation is centered at me when frankly I'm not sure I get a clear picture of what's going on between you and Courtney.

Clearly, there's some bad blood between you two that I'm probably not aware of. However, we'll get to the bottom of this particular situation!" He assured her as he got out of his seat and hurried across her large room toward her open bedroom door.

Sabrina looked at Britain wondering what he was doing as he stepped out into the long hallway and looked to his right and then called out.

"Kenny, could you please come upstairs to Sabrina's room and bring your sister with you! Just come straight down the hallway to the first open door."

Sabrina grabbed her face with both hands in shock. "You mean Courtney Ross is here in my house?"

Britain looked toward her while standing in the doorway waiting for Kenny and Courtney.

"Yes, I brought them with me and we all came inside together."

"Why would you do that?" Sabrina asked not pleased.

"I had my reasons for bringing them along," he politely told her.

"Maybe you had your reasons, but why didn't you tell me you brought them with you? You should have told me that Courtney and Kenny were downstairs in my living room." Sabrina shook her head in distress. "You have no idea the things she said to me this morning. I don't want Courtney Ross in my house. Believe me, she is not well."

Britain glanced toward Sabrina and nodded. "You don't have to convince me of that. That's why I asked Kenny to come and bring Courtney along. I felt something was off with this whole situation; and I'm right. Something is very off but I intend to get to the bottom of it just as soon as Kenny and Courtney makes it upstairs," Britain assured her.

"Britain, this isn't going to work. You want answers from them. But you still haven't given me any answers about why you were visiting Courtney. All I have is her explanation which is too revolting and despicable to repeat. So, I definitely do not want her in my house; and without an explanation from you, you should leave as well," Sabrina sadly urged.

Propped with his back against the doorframe with his arms folded, Britain looked toward Sabrina with warm eyes. "Sweetheart, whatever you think I have done is just a big misunderstanding that will be cleared up soon. When Courtney and Kenny gets upstairs, hopefully we can get some answers out of them and get to the bottom of this bizarre afternoon," he said and then glanced toward the end of the long marble hallway wondering what was keeping Kenny and Courtney. It had been enough time that they should have made it upstairs. Looking toward the end of the hallway, Britain realized

Kenny hadn't answered him when he first called to him. It dawned on Britain that Kenny and Courtney probably couldn't hear him from the location of the second level middle ways the solid hallway. Therefore, Britain figured he needed to walk down to the edge of the hallway and call out to them. But before doing so, he looked around the doorframe at Sabrina. "I'm sure they didn't hear me the first time. I'm going to the edge of the hallway and ask them to come up," Britain said and headed down the hallway.

Chapter Two

Britain stepped back into Sabrina's room and nodded toward her. "They're coming upstairs now. But I just want you to know. I'm deeply sorry that you're going through this and I respect your wishes that you want me to leave; and I also respect your wishes about not wanting Courtney in your home. Nevertheless, Sabrina. Just sit tight until we get to the bottom of this disarray. I need to find out why you're so dismayed with me. Something tells me, it has a lot more to do with than just the fact that I showed up at Courtney's house."

"Britain, of course, you're right. It does has to do with a lot more than just that. But I'm disappointed and upset about all of it," Sabrina sadly mumbled.

"I don't know what you mean by that," Britain said, filled with frustration but he kept his composure. "However, I intend to get some more answers from Courtney and Kenny," he said. "I heard you and respect the fact that you no longer for whatever reason want her in your home. Soon as I get some answers from her and vindicate myself in your eyes, Courtney Ross can leave," Britain humbly assured her. "I'll also leave after I get my answers if that's what you want," Britain respectfully relayed to her as he stepped over to one of her bedroom windows, pulled the curtains back and looked out.

Before Sabrina could reply, she and Britain clearly heard Kenny and Courtney's loud voices fussing their way down the long hallway toward Sabrina's bedroom. Britain exchanged looks with Sabrina and she nodded.

"Its okay, show them to my room and ask your questions," she hesitantly mumbled.

Britain nodded at Sabrina and then hurried across her bedroom floor to stand at the door. He saw them down the hallway and they were clearly unaware of which room belonged to Sabrina as they headed toward the first door on the left.

Britain called out to them. "Kenny, bring your sister this way," he said, beckoning them to continue down the hallway to Sabrina's room.

When Courtney and Kenny walked into Sabrina's room, Sabrina screamed out and grabbed her mouth and held it tight with both hands. Bloodstains were splattered all over Kenny's white shirt. The left side of his face was slightly swollen. He looked like he had been in a fight with someone who had gotten the best of him. But when Sabrina eyes caught Courtney, she screamed louder. Courtney looked worse than Kenny. Her clothes were ripped and torn, her long shoulder length hair had been chopped to the ear length and she had two black eyes and a swollen lip.

Sabrina felt the nightmare wouldn't end. She was home but none of her family or staff were there. It dawned on her that they were all still at the fundraiser. Observing how shaken Sabrina appeared, Britain stepped near her and put his arm around her waist. She didn't push him away as she trembled in her tracks as a cold chill ripped through her. Something told her Britain was a victim too.

"Start talking, Kenny!" Britain demanded in a firm tone.

Kenny stood there staring at Sabrina with confusion in his sad eyes. He held up both hands and shook his head.

"I said, start talking, Kenny! What are you waiting for?" Britain strongly urged, with a serious look on his face.

"Sure, I'll start talking," Kenny said with a crushed look on his face. "But like I was telling you earlier, I'm halfway in the dark here myself."

"Just tell us the part where you're not in the dark," Britain calmly demanded.

"I don't know where to start." Kenny grabbed the back of his neck with his right hand and paused up at the ceiling for a moment; and then looked at Britain. "So, where do you want me to start? I agreed to come over here and I dragged Courtney with me because I wanted to clear up that closet incident that you punched me in the nose about. But I'll be damned if I know anymore about what's going on than you do! Courtney is the only one who really knows what this was all about!" Kenny pointed toward his sister. "But look at my spaced out sister. She's completely off her rocker. She's in no condition to answer any questions. I have to get her back home and stay there with her until Trina or Mom gets home. She has to be admitted that's for sure. Man, after what we just witnessed, there's no doubt in my head that my sister has cracked up and lost touched with all reality."

Britain nodded in agreement with Kenny, but he still wanted to clear the air with Sabrina and needed Courtney to explain to Sabrina why he had visited her. Britain rubbed his chin and then paused looking Kenny in the eyes.

"Kenny, to be completely honest, I feel sympathy and compassion for what has happened to Courtney and her state of mind. It's sad and rips at me to see her like this," Britain compassionately stated. Nevertheless, my main priority at the moment is to clear the air with Sabrina. It's becoming apparently clear that Courtney has connived and manipulated Sabrina in some way and I want to get to the bottom of it!" Britain glanced at Courtney and shook his head. "What a difference a few months can make," he said sincerely and then looked toward Kenny. "Your sister was a completely different young lady when we first hired her at the company. She was smart and polite and all the customers loved her," Britain said. "She had a bright future ahead of her."

"Then she hit the bottle again," Kenny solemnly added. "Suddenly she started being sneaky and untruthful and went straight downhill from there," Kenny said with deep disappointment in his voice. "Now it deeply pains me to say my sister has reached the bottom." He held out both hands. "But she brought all this chaos and misery on herself!"

Britain nodded. "It's obvious that she's quite ill and needs to see a doctor. But she has managed to single-handedly push all of our buttons! She has all three of us at each other's throat! Sabrina is upset with me! I'm pissed at you, and Courtney had a hand in it all," Britain said disappointedly.

Kenny agreed. "You're hundred percent correct about my messed up in the head, devious, scheming, calculating sister. She surely had a hand in it all!" Kenny said firmly. "But you both should take a good look at her." He pointed toward Courtney. "You can see how she has flipped out. I need to get her back home and to a doctor as soon as possible. Don't you think? She's in no condition to talk or explain anything," Kenny told them.

"You're absolutely correct. She does need to see a doctor as soon as possible," Britain agreed. "Nevertheless, a few minutes here isn't going to make that big of a difference. Therefore, before the two of you walk out of this room, Courtney needs to open her mouth and do a little explaining to Sabrina!"

Kenny understood Britain's request, but he felt his sister was in no condition to comply. "But she's in no condition to communicate or explain herself; and as you suggested, I drove her around in my car with the windows down for nearly an hour and supplied her with three cups of coffee. But you know all of that because you trailed us. You felt we should try to sober her up before we met over here to face Sabrina. But as you can see, none of that helped. She's still out of it. Maybe water will help," Kenny suggested.

Britain glanced at Sabrina and she reluctantly nodded. "You'll have to wait here while I fetch her a bottle of water from the kitchen, all the servants are out."

"You don't have to do that. Faucet water will do," Kenny suggested.

"Okay, I'll grab her a cup of water from my bathroom," Sabrina said as she headed across the room toward her connected bathroom.

She returned and handed Kenny the cup of water and a few minutes after she gave Kenny the water for Courtney to drink, Courtney was still mostly dead weigh hanging on Kenny's shoulder. He had only gotten her to sip a fourth of the cup of water. "I'm sorry, Britain. She is still incoherent and I need to get her home. Clearly, she has experienced some kind of mental break," Kenny urged.

Britain nodded. "I can see that you are most likely correct; and I deeply sympathize. However, I will not back down. It's crucially important that Courtney corrects this colossal misunderstanding that she set in motion," Britain seriously relayed to Kenny. "I can see she's mostly out of it, but I need her to at least attempt to explain herself; and make herself just clear enough to take back whatever untruths she planted in Sabrina's head," Britain firmly insisted. "It's obvious that she manufactured some scheme to get Sabrina to her home and upstairs in that closet," Britain heatedly stated.

Kenny exchanged looks with Sabrina; and then Kenny and Sabrina looked toward Britain who continued. "Your little sister who you say is in no condition to talk or explain herself, asked me to come over to your home today to see her at 1:00 o'clock. I never would have bothered, but she said she wanted to make amends and throw Sabrina a surprise bridal shower," Britain explained. "Why she needed to see me if she wanted to throw a bridal shower for Sabrina, I wasn't sure. But at the time her request sounded like a worthwhile effort. But I was in the dark to what she was really up to. I was also under the impression that she and Sabrina had become friends."

Sabrina jaw dropped as she grabbed her face with both hands. She realized how Courtney had conned Britain into playing into her game as well. Suddenly her heart sunk and she knew she had no reason to be upset with Britain. She immediately felt ashamed of herself for her ill behavior toward him, which he hadn't deserve.

Chapter Three

    They stood there in silence for a while as Kenny debated in his mind how he was going to approach Courtney to get her to explain her actions and own up to her scheme in front of Sabrina. But as Kenny tapped Courtney on the shoulder she just continued to stare into space as if she was in another dimension. Kenny knew it was hopeless in trying to get his sister to cooperate to give Britain the explanation he wanted Sabrina to hear from Courtney. Kenny shook his head and held up both hands. "I hear you talking, but I can't make her talk or sober her up. Besides, I'm sort of worried about her at this moment. Something is deeply wrong with my sister. I just need to get her out of here and to a doctor," Kenny strongly suggested.

    Britain nodded with compassion in his eyes. "Kenny, I can tell you are restless and need to get Courtney home and to a doctor as soon as possible; and I won't hold you long." Britain inhaled sharply and exchanged looks with Sabrina. "Because from the way she behaved earlier, she has lost all logic of reality," Britain said sincerely as his eyes glowed with sadness. "I sensed something was off when I first arrived at your house and walked inside. Courtney immediately wasn't herself and started talking fast and acting strange right off," Britain explained. "She said something bizarre about getting it on later, which really went over the top of my head. It didn't dawn on me at the time that she was saying things for the sole purpose of having Sabrina overhear her. She wasn't being logical or making any sense and before I could process the fact that something was really off with her behavior, she had hurried me along by the arm up the short stairs to her bedroom. Enroot to her room while I was trying to figure out why we were headed upstairs to her bedroom, I could clearly see the open door to her room and we had stepped into her room before it registered with me that something wasn't right,"

Britain calmly explained. "Nevertheless, I didn't comment as I stepped inside her room. However, once we were inside her room, the only thing she wanted me to know and I quote: "It's not a good time to talk." Therefore, when she looked at me and said that, it dawned on me that what she had said didn't make any sense," Britain explained. "She had just went to the trouble of taking me upstairs to her room, and the moment we stepped into her room she tells me that. I just looked at her waiting for her to explain herself. I thought it was odd that she led me into her bedroom to say such non sense. But, once again, I brushed aside how odd her behavior seemed and turned to head out of her room. But just as I reached the door, she shouted loudly that she had something she wanted me to see. Before I could anticipate about what the something could be, she pulled open the closet door and there stood you and Sabrina! For a moment I was speechless as Sabrina tore out of the closet and headed out of the room. Stunned, I stood there for a moment trying to collect myself as my brain went into overdrive trying to figure out what had just happened. I looked toward Courtney who was propped against the doorframe holding both cheeks, bent over laughing as she watched Sabrina run out of her room crying. When I headed out of the room to chase after Sabrina, Courtney grabbed my shirt and stopped me. She shouted that she had really wanted me to drop by to catch you and Sabrina in the closet making out."

Kenny raised both arms and shook his head but kept silent as Sabrina stood holding her face with her mouth open.

"I regretfully lost my poise when she screamed such an outrageous accusation in my face," Britain looked apologetically toward Kenny. "You stood there speechless, that's when I lost my composure and punched you in the face," Britain said remorsefully with much regret. "Kenny, I want you to know I'm deeply sorry and I'm not pleased with myself one bit for striking you, especially when you were innocent to Courtney's trumped-up story," Britain said humbly. "Even if you were not innocent, violence is never the answer and something I'm totally against and frown upon. Nevertheless, I struck you before it dawned on me everything she said were lies. Therefore, Kenny, once again I apologize and can't stressed enough how sorry I am."

Sabrina walked over to Britain and threw her arms around him. "I'm the one who's sorry. I'm deeply shamefully sorry," Sabrina said in tears as she touched Britain's face. "It's partly my fault. I know Courtney and should have known she was scheming and playing a sick game. I should have been stronger and not allowed myself to fall into her web of all those lies! She told me that the two of you were lovers and that you had been making out with her for months," Sabrina sadly told Britain.

Britain looked at her with disbelief and shock in his eyes. "My goodness, I had no idea Courtney had reached such a level of manipulation. Something is seriously the matter with that young woman," Britain sadly admitted.

Sabrina wiped a tear from her left eye with her fingers. "She told me you spent the night together. She said I could see the both of you together today at her house with my own eyes at 1:00 o'clock if I dared to show up," Sabrina sadly explained. "Courtney lies bothered me and knocked the wind out of me. I knew she was lying. Yet, I made a huge error in judgement when I decided against my better judgement to see her scheme through."

"Her untruths were so outlandish, how could you have given them an ounce of credence?" Britain asked. "Just the mere accusation that I spent the night with her. It's all too unreal and not me. I love you like no tomorrow and we're engaged and about to be married very soon. Besides, even if we were not about to me married. It's still not in me to do what she accused me of."

Sabrina stood there facing him with no real good explanation of why she allowed herself to get swept up into Courtney's web of lies. She was ashamed to say she wanted to catch Courtney in a lie, which was her real reason for playing along with Courtney's game. Therefore, she stayed mute as they all felt duped by Courtney, trying to figure out what was going on in Courtney's mind.

"Sweetheart, this is turning into a real live nightmare," Britain said to Sabrina. "But I must admit, I'm thrown that you played into her web," Britain admitted. "Especially, if you knew she was lying, which you just said you knew she was lying. I have to ask, what made you go over to her house to be a part of such a farce?" Britain calmly asked.

Sabrina humbly looked Britain in the face. "Honestly, I'm ashamed of why I followed through with her invitation. I did it because I knew deep down that she was lying and I needed to prove to her face that she was lying. The way I expected to do that was by you not showing up after she told me you would," Sabrina softly explained.

"By saying deep down you felt she was lying, that indicates that you were not one hundred percent sure of her lies," Britain inquired.

Sabrina nodded. "I deeply apologize for my moment of doubt. It was just a sliver of a moment," Sabrina regretfully admitted.

"A sliver of a moment is a lot when there should be zero doubt between us," Britain firmly stated. "We're about to be married. "There's no room for doubt in our relationship. It pains me that you had even a sliver of doubt."

Sabrina grabbed his arm. "Please, forgive me for getting myself caught up in such a bizarre mess, making you think I doubted you in any way."

"You did just say you had a sliver of doubt toward me," Britain told her.

"I know I said that. But I don't doubt you even a sliver. I say that because the doubt I felt wasn't real. It was under false pretense. Remember earlier when you came over and wanted to grab a quick sandwich?" Sabrina asked.

"Yes, I remember. What does that have to do with this?"

"It has everything to do with this. It ignited my false doubt since the incident caused me to lose some of my faith when you came over and suggested a quick sandwich because you had an appointment at 1:00 o'clock. I'm only human and when you told me that you had an appointment at the same time Courtney had said you would be at her house, my imagination went crazy and I lost my composure and thought all kinds of ridiculous thoughts. I didn't want to believe her, and as I said, deep down I didn't really believe her. But I drove to her house and you showed up just like she said you would. Being in the dark of her setup, what else could I believe? She manipulated me just as she did you and Kenny. Furthermore, she darned me to show up. I had to go to her house to prove to her that she was a liar," Sabrina tearfully told him. "So, please believe me." Sabrina held up both hands. "I know you deep down in my soul and I would trust you with my life and the life of everyone dear to me. I know you are the epitome of what a gentlemen should be and there's not a splinter of doubt in my heart about your impeccable character," Sabrina said with conviction.

Britain nodded and then shook his head as he stepped up to Sabrina and grabbed her in his arms and kissed her on the lips. He pulled away and looked at her. "I believe you and would like to offer my apologies for questioning your belief in me. Things are just a bit intense right now. I'm disappointed Courtney won't speak and admit she orchestrated this whole charade. I know you believe me. But I would like for you to hear her admit she set me up."

"I knew she had issues, but I didn't think she would go this far," Sabrina admitted. "I was trying to help her by being her friend. I should have known my friendship wasn't what she really needed. She needed professional help and that's what I should have encouraged her toward," Sabrina admitted.

Kenny looked at Sabrina and shook his head as he hit his fist in his hand. "Don't feel sorry for her. She didn't feel sorry for us. It's clear how devious my sister turned out to be. She manipulated and played us all for fools," Kenny firmly reminded them, as his expression went from concern to disgust. He took both hands and shoved Courtney away from leaning on his shoulder as he continued with distress in his voice. "She is certifiable, and with everything you two have just said, and the lies she told me to get me inside the house, I wouldn't put it past her to be faking it right now! Maybe she's pretending to keep from facing the music," Kenny angrily suggested.

Britain and Sabrina exchanged looks, knowing his suggestion could be true. But they both could see how spaced out and out of touch with reality she appeared as she stood there as if she didn't know where she was.

Kenny grabbed Courtney by the shoulders and placed her back firmly against the bedroom wall. "Let us know if we are right about you! We want to know if you're faking it girl?" he yelled angrily in her face.

Courtney had a blank look on her face as if she didn't understand him.

"Don't just stare at me as if you have no clue," Kenny angrily yelled. "Open your conniving mouth and answer me! I want to know if you're completely finished with your scheming lies!" He released her shoulders and walked away from her.

Kenny paced back and forth in front of Courtney with both hands holding the back of his neck. He was shaking his head with disgust since it had just occurred to him how she had constantly lied to him for weeks. He stepped back up to Courtney and gripped her shoulders again. "Who are you anyway? It just dawned on me that you have lied to me for weeks! Feeding me that garbage about Samantha having a thing for me, and to think I bought into your lies when you said Samantha was inside the house and wanted to see me.

Courtney still didn't speak as she stared at Kenny with half shut eyes as if she was about to fall asleep.

"I know you hear me. You are just pretending to be out of it," Kenny heatedly yelled. "You might as well start talking because I'm not buying into whatever you're trying to pull right now. As a matter of fact, I will never buy into anymore of your lies. Especially since I was a bigger fool than you to buy into your lie about Samantha! But you knew exactly what you were doing! You played on my weakness! Knowing how I have always felt about Samantha." Kenny exchanged looks with Britain and Sabrina and shook his head.

Kenny looked toward the floor for a moment, then he stared at his sister and angrily stated. "Damn you, Courtney! You schemed and lied and played on my feelings and emotions to set all three of us up! I'm ashamed to call you my sister!" Kenny roared angrily in her face, giving her a slight shove in the chest as she stumbled about with a dazed look on her face.

Courtney started talking to herself. "Britain, I know you love me, but I understand the situation you're in. You can't let Sabrina know how much you want me. Sabrina might find out. But we can't let her know."

Sabrina clung tighter to Britain and looked toward Kenny.

"What happened to her face and hair?"

"She happened to her face and hair! Nobody laid a finger on her. She flipped her lid when Britain threw a punch at me, and then looked at her and told her he didn't buy her lies. She ripped her own clothes and cropped off her hair; and then went as far as to punch herself in each eye with her own fist," Kenny sadly confessed.

"Why would she do that?" Sabrina asked.

"Why does she do any of the whacked out stuff she does?" Kenny pointed to her head. "She's hitting the bottle again heavy, but it's more than the liquor this time. She went too far and has clearly lost touch with reality. She's completely off her rocker," Kenny sadly admitted, choked up with disappointment. "Her plan was to frame Britain for rape."

"Kenny, are you kidding?" Sabrina asked stunned. "Is that what she told you that she intended to frame Britain for rape?" Sabrina sadly looked at Kenny. She could see from the sadden expression on his face and his anxious manner how crushed he was from Courtney's behavior and actions.

Kenny nodded. "Yeah, it's what she told me. I'm not pleased to say, but that was her plan after Britain didn't buy into her garbage after you ran out of the house," Kenny shared. "But after her well-played frame-up, there was a minor problem she hadn't considered."

"And what was that?" Sabrina asked.

"It was me. I was a witness to her madness."

"This is all so unbelievable," Sabrina grabbed her cheeks and looked toward Courtney who seemed lost in another world. "And to think, I thought she was my friend for awhile. But I finally caught on." Sabrina grabbed her head and looked up at the ceiling in disbelief. Then she looked at Britain, shaking her head in disbelief as she took her fingers and continued to wipe tears from her eyes. "When you two first walked in here I was so beside myself about the issue Britain and I was trying to resolve until I didn't really fully notice her face and hair. I'm stunned by what she did to herself. "Is this really happening? Is that really Courtney?" Sabrina pointed toward Courtney.

Britain sadly nodded. "This is really happening and it's really Courtney."

"This is all so sad that it had to come to this." Sabrina eyes watered. "I'm highly upset by her treachery. But I'm more upset by her condition. I hate this happened to her. It's obvious she has suffered a breakdown. When Kenny walked in and mentioned a breakdown, I wasn't sure he was sure. But just observing her behavior, there's no doubt in my mind. She needs to see a doctor as soon as possible." Sabrina grabbed her face, shaking her head. "I'm deeply sorry about her condition, aren't you Britain?"

Britain held Sabrina tight and nodded with sad eyes. "Yes, of course, I'm sorry about her condition. She is obviously sick and need professional attention. I guess we all missed the big picture. If we had seen the serious signals, other than just assuming she was filled with vodka, we could have helped her get the help she needed," Britain compassionately stated.

"It's so sad to see her in such a state. I remember when you and I first met, you were telling me how nice and polite Courtney was and I remember back when she was dating Rome for a while," Sabrina recalled. "She was like night and day from the woman I'm looking at now. It was as if overnight, she became jealous, scheming and manipulative," Sabrina said, squeezing her hands together. "When before she was so nice and sweet; what happened to that girl? People don't just suddenly lose their minds overnight."

"It didn't happen overnight," Kenny quickly weighed in. "I noticed a change in her right after the holidays."

"I noticed a change in her also at work," Britain added. "I couldn't put my finger on it, but her behavior wasn't what I had remembered it to be."

"I noticed the same," Kenny agreed. "I remember how depressed she became right after the Christmas holidays when your brother stop seeing her and she lost her job. Your company rehired her back with a job offsite but she still didn't perk up. It was only after you eventually gave her a job back onsite that she seemed a little less down. But Courtney never seemed like herself again after all that," Kenny shared. "I didn't think too much of it because I just figured she was grumpy and upset with herself for messing things up with your brother. I figured she would get over it. But I guess she never did. I think she has been headed downhill since the first of the year. She started back to drinking heavy around that time and she also started behaving somewhat indifferent about stuff around then as if nothing really mattered. Trina also mentioned how Courtney wasn't eating or sleeping well," Kenny shared. "Thinking back, I recall that Trina also mentioned how she had noticed a shift in Courtney's behavior before I moved from home into my own apartment. But again, when Trina mentioned her insight on Courtney, I didn't give it any credit. I chalked it up to be mostly about the heavy drinking and figured she would soon get off the booze as she had done in the past," Kenny respectfully explained. "But it blows me away that she ended up this way. The folks always held Courtney up as an example for me and Trina. They felt she would be the one to make something out of her life; and that Trina and I would just be in her shadow," Kenny told them.

"That's a tough pill to swallow," Britain commented. "Your parents should have just made all three of you feel like number one. That was always my parents' mode." Britain stepped over and patted Kenny's shoulder. "Sorry, you felt like your parents had you living in your sister's shadow."

Kenny nodded. "That's just the way it always was in my household. Courtney was their favorite because of her smarts and good looks mostly. They always said Trina and I were always just average in everything; and that's probably because she's the one who dated and had the love of a rich Franklin," Kenny explained and paused. "I know I'm referring to your family, but there's no way around it. Because it is your family," Kenny said, as if his mind was in deep thought. "Trina and I never had a chance with a Franklin. She once had a slight crush on Sydney, who never knew about her slight crush and I have always been in love with Samantha and never had a chance with her. However, Courtney was different; she could have who she wanted but she just didn't have the good sense to keep that person," Kenny sadly stated, and then looked at Courtney and shook his head. "Let's get out of here, Courtney. I need to get you home so we can get you to one of those mental facilities."

"Kenny, I know your family cannot afford medical treatment for Courtney at one of those facilities. So, please, have your mother take Courtney to the facility of her choice and my family will foot the bill," Britain assured him. "Your family won't have to worry about the medical cost."

Kenny paused and stared at Britain for a moment. "I thought she had employee health coverage with Franklin Gas?" Kenny inquired.

Britain shook his head. "We offer it with a ten dollar deduction from each paycheck. She declined the health coverage. Nevertheless, we'll cover it."

It was a moment of silence after Britain offered to foot Courtney's medical care at any mental facility of her family's choice. Kenny was pleasantly surprised and pleased with Britain's unexpected generous offer.

Kenny exchanged smiles with Sabrina and then nodded at Britain. "Thanks Britain. I'm overwhelmed with gratitude and I know my mother will be as well. It will take a huge financial burden off of my mother's shoulders." He held out both arms. "However, I can't believe your generous donation to foot Courtney's medical bill. That's more than generous of you, considering the scheme Courtney just pulled on you and Sabrina today."

"I know. It was unfortunate the game she played. We're all disappointed and upset with her, but we can afford to be compassionate since we're not the ones ill. We have to keep in mind that she's not herself. She's a very sick young lady," Britain reminded him.

Chapter Four

Courtney leaned her back against the dresser with her head lowered as Sabrina gave Kenny permission to use her bathroom. Sabrina and Britain noticed how Courtney held her face with both hands looking toward the carpet the whole time Kenny was in the bathroom. When Kenny stepped back into the room, Britain nodded toward him.

"Get her home and to a doctor. She's quite ill."

"Of course, you're right," Kenny agreed. "My mind just haven't processed it all. I can't get over how pissed I am at her for duping us into this mess. But I will get her home so we can get her the medical attention she needs," Kenny said as he gripped her arm to lead her out of the room. "Courtney, let's get out of here and get you home," Kenny said as he started to head out of Sabrina's bedroom.

Courtney resisted and wouldn't follow along with him. "Kenny, get away from me!" Courtney angrily shouted and jerked her arm away.

Kenny grabbed her arm again and gave her a slight nudge toward the door. She staggered and landed up against the doorframe. Colliding against the doorframe seemed to unleash another personality from within her. Suddenly, Courtney looked wildly about the room and then slowly reached into her bosom and pulled out a switchblade. Before Kenny realized her state of mind, she quickly charged up to him and sliced his hand.

"I said get away from me and I meant that Kenny Ross!" She angrily shouted at the top of her voice.

Kenny jumped back, grabbed his hand and yelled. "You really have gone mad!"

"Stay where you are!" Courtney shouted toward the three of them, pointing and swinging the switchblade.

"Don't worry guys! I don't plan to hurt either one of you! It's that skinny bastard Sabrina I'm after!" Courtney angrily shouted. "Her luck just ran out! She has to pay for taking Britain from me!"

"You need to put that knife away before you really hurt someone," Kenny managed to say as he held his hand in burning pain.

"Shut up! I'm talking and I'm not playing," Courtney yelled at Kenny. "This one." Courtney pointed toward Sabrina. "She has some nerves to think she can sail into this town and take my man without a fight or any efforts on my part!"

Kenny shook his head as he exchanged looks with Britain and Sabrina. Then he shouted at Courtney. "You need to put that knife away now!"

Courtney eyes were burning with anger as she stared at her brother with contempt. "Are you nuts are what? I said shut up. I just cut your hand and I'll cut the other one if you don't be quiet while I'm talking."

Kenny swallowed hard from the look on Courtney's face and the sound of her voice. He sensed she was too far gone from reality for either one of them to reason with her.

After a moment of silence, Courtney laughed. "That's better." She stared at Kenny. "I'm glad you got my message to put a sock in it. Because I'm trying to get a point across to this skinny bitch." Courtney pointed her switchblade toward Sabrina. "You have another thought coming if you think I'm going to let you walk into the sunset with my Britain. You backstabbing witch!"

Courtney was totally out of control. They didn't mumble a word as they all exchanged shock looks with each other. Kenny had disbelief on his face and tears in his eyes. His expression told Sabrina that he was just moments from tackling his sister and her knife head on. Then he made a couple steps toward her and she swung the blade at him and sliced his other hand. Now he stood there with blood gushing from both hands, spilling out on Sabrina's plum bedroom carpeting. He was obviously in a lot of pain as he dropped to his knees in the corner of the room.

Britain made one step toward Courtney, and Sabrina grabbed his arm. "Don't go near her. She's mad and out of her head. She'll cut you too."

Britain nodded and said firmly. "Just be calm. I'll be careful, but Kenny needs medical attention. My cell phone is in my jacket in the car. Where's your phone?"

"It's in my purse on my dresser," Sabrina said, pointing toward the dresser.

Courtney looked at Britain with the look of a sick love gone mad. For a moment, Sabrina thought Britain would get through to Courtney, but as

Britain headed toward Kenny to check on him and to try to step toward the dresser for Sabrina's purse, Courtney shouted. "Don't make another step toward that damn dresser or my deceitful ass brother! Don't you touch that disloyal bastard! I don't care if he bleeds too death!"

"You don't mean that, Courtney," Britain pleaded calmly. "Just put the knife away, Courtney! Everything is going to work out, but right now Kenny needs a doctor. You need to let me help him, or at least let us call 911. He's losing a lot of blood!"

Courtney didn't reply. She just stared at Britain in somewhat of a daze as if her mind was a million miles away. Britain walked closer, waved both hands across her face, and then took another step toward her, but just at that moment she snapped out of her daze and swung her switchblade toward him, trying to cut him.

"Don't come any closer! You just lied to me! Nothing is going to work out! And how can it as long as Sabrina is in the picture! She is the reason for all our pain! You know that, Britain. I have no other choice but to make her pay! I should have followed my first mind and gotten rid of her right after Christmas! Why was I such a fool to wait all this time, allowing her to get her hooks so deep in you? But it will all work out now because I plan to finish her off!"

Sabrina grabbed her mouth and screamed. "This nightmare is getting worse! If you can't get through to her, nobody can!"

Britain glanced around at Sabrina and touched her face to comfort her. "It's going to be alright," he said, trying to assure her.

Sabrina covered her face and shook her head. "Nothing is going to be alright. She just cut her own brother. I doubt if she's going to hesitate to do the same or worse to you and I," Sabrina strongly suggested.

Britain glanced at his watch. "Where is everybody? The house seem deserted. I remember you mentioned when you fetched that cup of water for Courtney that all the staff was out," Britain anxiously inquired.

Sabrina nervously nodded. "Yes, the house is deserted. It's never completely deserted like this, but Father, my grandparents, Starlet, Samantha, and all the staff are out at the WJJ Theater for that fundraiser to hear Starlet sing." Sabrina grabbed her face. "It had slipped my mind earlier, but that's where they all are. If I hadn't overslept, I probably would have called and cancelled our lunch to attend the fundraiser. Then I wouldn't have ended up in this jam."

"That's right, my house is empty as well," Britain recalled. "I recall mother mentioning the fundraiser and that all the staff would also attend to hear Starlet sing. I had informed her that you and I had other plans," Britain said.

"That's too bad. Both homes are empty while we're on our own trying to talk down a mentally ill person," Sabrina said as she trembled with frightened nerves.

Sabrina screamed when they both looked toward Courtney just in time to see her pull a small silver pistol from her bosom. Sabrina grabbed her mouth with both hands and stopped her scream as she swallowed hard. She and Britain exchanged looks with each other and stared at each other for a moment. They were stunned and at a standstill. Then Britain called out to Kenny who was down on his knees near the bed in obvious pain.

"Kenny! You have to do something! You have to try to get through to your sister! She has a gun!"

Sabrina shook her head as tears filled her eyes. "Britain, what can he do? Kenny is in too much pain to help us. He'll probably go into shock and pass out if we can't call an ambulance and have him rushed to a hospital soon."

"I know you're right, but we have to think of something. We need to get through to Courtney so she'll allow us to grab your purse from the dresser to call for help for Kenny. He needs to be rushed to an Emergency Room now!" Britain urgently relayed.

"But she won't listen to you, Britain," Sabrina cried. "What do I have to lose, maybe she'll listen to me," Sabrina said and then stared at Courtney with humble eyes. "Courtney, please, let us out of here! Your brother needs medical attention." She pointed toward Kenny. "Can't you see how he's bleeding out on the carpet? Do you want him to bleed too death? What has happened to you? Where is that girl who used to hang out at Franklin House months ago? I would see you there and you were nice and quiet. Be that girl again and open your eyes to what you're doing right now! I beg of you!" Sabrina pleaded.

Courtney laughed. "You're one to talk about Franklin House. What a short memory you have! I'm no longer hanging out at Franklin House because you put an end to that! That's why I plan to put an end to your little sweet life now!" Courtney laughed and waved her gun in the air.

"Courtney, open your eyes to what you are saying and doing! Something is wrong with you! You need professional help!" Sabrina strongly suggested. "What you're doing is not just wrong, it's criminal. You're committing a crime by holding us in this room against our will! You'll also go down for murder one if Kenny doesn't make it!"

"Who cares if a disloyal traitor doesn't make it?" Courtney angrily shouted.

Sabrina shook her head in dismay. "I finally put two and two together and figured out that you're manipulative, conniving and untruthful. But I never figured you would go as far as to cut or shoot someone!" Sabrina cried.

Britain had a solemn look on his face as he caressed Sabrina's shoulder to calm her down. "Sabrina, she's over the edge. She's not going to listen to reason."

"He's right, you know! I would never listen to anything out of your mouth! You gullible silly fool! You might as well save your breath." She kept waving the gun in the air over her head.

Sabrina could feel her legs shaking with her heart in her throat. She kept hoping and praying Courtney would snap out of it and come to her senses. But with each passing minutes the possibility of Courtney facing reality seemed slimmer and slimmer.

"I don't know who Britain is trying to fool but I know he's not really into you, Miss Sabrina Taylor. How could he be into someone like you? You're too bony and whiny, crying every minute. Why cry, just face your fate and be done with it." Courtney glanced in the corner at Kenny and stared at him for a moment as if she was noticing his wounds for the first time. Then she glanced away from him with a robot stare straight at the gun in her hand.

For a moment it seemed as if reality hit Courtney and she wondered what was happening; and within that moment, Britain and Sabrina noticed her behavior and held their breath at the possibility of her coming to herself. And what seemed longer was only a split second before she focused her spaced out, cold piercing eyes back toward Sabrina and Britain. "I'll tell you right now!" she shouted. "Calling me all those disgusting names like manipulative and conniving won't get you any mercy from where I'm standing!" Courtney bitterly shouted, slightly rocking from side to side. "How stupid can you get? I have the gun with my finger on the trigger and you have the nerve to call me bad names! You are one dense billion dollar baby!" She bent over laughing before she stared at Sabrina and coldly shouted. "Oh, well, I guess it doesn't matter since your dense days are over!"

"Why is that, Courtney?" Sabrina trembling with nerves asked.

"I'll tell you why your dense days are over, Sabrina Taylor! They are over because you have a snowball's chance in hell of leaving this stylish pink room alive! You couldn't give up Britain, now you have to give up yourself!"

Sabrina reached out and grabbed Britain's shirttail, pulling him back near her. She was trembling as Courtney spoke with such bitterness and demented anger. They knew she meant every word and definitely wanted Sabrina dead.

"Britain, I'm so scared right now. I feel we're trapped by her. What can we do? I know she's just that far gone to shoot me."

"Don't worry, sweetheart. I love you more than anything! She'll have to get through me before she can harm you. She can only fire one bullet at a time. When I approach her and she fires, I want you to run out of this room as fast as you can," Britain demanded in a deeply worried voice. "Don't stop anywhere in the house to use the phone, run to your car and drive away. Then use your car phone and call for help."

"But, Britain, I can't let you throw yourself in front of a bullet. You could lose your life. I won't do it. I would rather die than see you killed. I can't do it. I won't do it," Sabrina firmly stated between tears.

Sabrina and Britain were standing not far from the corner of the bed where a weak injured Kenny was bent over on his knees in excruciating pain. Nevertheless, after hearing Sabrina's defeated words that she would rather die than see Britain killed, those words miraculously gave Kenny incredible roaring strength that he didn't even know was within him. He sprung swiftly to his feet. His eyes were sad and wet and he was in obvious agonizing pain, but with the determination and added strength of three men, he wrapped his wounded hands around himself.

"Sabrina, you won't have to watch Britain sacrifice himself for you!" Kenny yelled with conviction. "My screwy sister might be packing a piece, but it won't stop me from stopping her whacked out ass!" Kenny assured them with conviction. "This show is over!" He roared angrily and charged into Courtney quicker than she could blink. He caught her off guard as her back landed hard against the bedroom wall. She stumbled, almost losing her balance.

"Get out of here guys!" Kenny hollered toward Britain and Sabrina.

Britain and Sabrina tore out of the bedroom, but by the time they made it down the hallway to the staircase and across the enormous living room floor; they paused in their tracks when they heard a shot. Sabrina looked back, but Britain swung open the front door and pushed her through it. Then there was another shot just as Sabrina ran through the door and across the front porch and down the front steps. Sabrina glanced over her shoulder and didn't see Britain. She paused and turned to head back up the steps, but just as she did, she caught the third bullet from Courtney's gun. She fell backward off the steps into her family's big front yard.

Chapter Five

Sabrina eyes blinked opened to find herself lying on the ground. She was lying flat on her back with her eyes half open. Courtney walked up and stood over her. Sabrina could see clear enough to see that Courtney was bending over laughing. It reminded her of the scene in the cemetery a month earlier. She wish she would have seen Courtney for the mentally ill young lady she was during that eerie bizarre episode. She figured Courtney deserved a break. Now Courtney had broken them all with a mental break.

"Sabrina Taylor! Can you hear me? You aren't dead yet! But soon you will be! Just as dead as a doorknob! And you know what? It does my heart good to look down at you suffering and crying as your life slips through your fingers. There isn't a damn thing you can do about it! Yes, Sabrina Taylor! You had it all. You had good looks and lots of friends! But most of all you had the love of my man! Britain Franklin was my man and you strolled into town and stole him! That wasn't right. I had him first. He was mine. But you stole him and made me a loser! But now, who's the loser? Who's lying flat on their back holding on for dear life by the skin of their teeth?" She yelled down at Sabrina.

"You little sucker! From the moment I first knocked on your door and pretended to be sorry about the loss of your mother, it was all a scheme!" She laughed. "It's unbelievable how easy it was to pull the wool over your eyes. I thought you had more brains. But I guess you consider yourself smart. You better think again. You're closer to dumb than most. You think I'm loony but not even I would have fallen for all the cons I pulled on you," Courtney bent over laughing. "Britain is the best looking, smartest man in this town. I don't blame him for hooking up with a dummy like you! He just made a mistake. He was taken with you not realizing how brainless you are," she bitterly roared.

"If you were so damn smart, you wouldn't be lying flat on your back right now in your own front yard. You were so easy to con, so now here you lie; a goner!"

Courtney paced a bit and then kicked a nearby bush. She was silent for a moment staring into space, and then she turned around and looked down at Sabrina with even more rage in her red, wet eyes.

"It's a shame two other people had to lose their lives because of you, Sabrina!" She screamed down at her, kicking her in the ribs and shoulder.

The pain was unbearable as Sabrina lay there silently screaming inside. Sabrina could only grit her teeth and frown in excruciating pain, but it didn't seem to matter. Courtney had taken Britain's life. Now Sabrina suddenly felt numb and indifferent as if her entire world had crushed down around her. Deep down inside she felt as if she wanted to die too. She was extremely weak as she was going in and out of consciousness and she felt each second was bringing her closer to death and closer to being with Britain and her two mothers. Somehow that thought gave her peace and took away her fear.

"I hate you so much, Sabrina Taylor! I should shoot you again in the middle of your forehead and put you out of your misery! But I have no compassion for you, none! It was you who forced me to put a bullet in Britain! Poor guy! He was such a blind fool to hook up with you. He would have been so much better off with me, but he couldn't see that! So now he's stone cold too. I didn't want to do that to my Britain. I tell you, it seems like such a waste to take the life of such a perfect man. You know what I mean. You saw it with your own damn eyes. He left me no other choice. He didn't stand up for me. He stayed right by your side and looked at me like I was the plagued or a monster! So I killed him. Sorry, but life's a bitch and then you die, especially if you try to play me! He had no right to look at me like that. He was supposed to look at me with love in his eyes. I just want you to know that's why I killed him." Courtney grabbed her head with one hand and screamed. "Oh! No! That means he's gone! That's not what I wanted! Only you were supposed to die! Not my Britain," she yelled in a dazed, wiping tears with her torn dress.

"Kenny, on the other hand, he had it coming! He got in the way too many times. Over at the house he wouldn't back up my stories. Then the fool tried to take my gun! Can you believe the nerve of that damn lush! Some big brother he turned out to be! You would never know he has me by three years since he has peanuts for brains! I've always been the smarter sibling. Where was his loyalty when I needed it? I hope he rots in Hell!"

Courtney dropped down to her knees beside Sabrina and placed the little pistol against Sabrina's head. Sabina didn't blink as she laid there staring up at the bluest sky ever observed. There wasn't a cloud in the endless view of space. It was clear peacefulness in the air as the sun was very bright. She could smell the cedar bush near her head that she watched the gardener plant right after they moved there. Sabrina could smell the evergreen near her feet. With all the familiar smells of home, her front yard seemed unfamiliar to her.

"Sabrina Taylor! If I had more than one bullet left in this gun, I would put a bullet right between your eyes and watch as your brains spilled out on the lawn; and I would watch you die a horrifying death!" Courtney angrily shouted as she stood to her feet. "But you'll just have to die slowly and painfully because this last bullet is for me. You didn't think I was going to hang around in this poor, pitiful world without Britain? Did you? No way! As much as I hate you and would love to plant this last bullet in your brains, I must refrain myself because I must be with my Britain."

Courtney placed the gun on her stomach and pulled the trigger. She fell on the ground beside Sabrina. Blood scattered from Courtney's gunshot wound onto Sabrina's arm. Sabrina trembled beside Courtney's injured body as she felt herself becoming weaker and weaker. Her heart would soon stop, but she had to try and make her way up the front steps and get inside to see Britain and kiss his beautiful face before she took her last breath.

Sabrina grabbed her right side and rolled herself over on her stomach. She looked toward the front steps that were only a few feet away, but they seemed to be miles from her. "I'm too weak," she cried. "How will I manage to get to Britain? I have to see his face one last time."

Sabrina dropped her face in the grass and noticed that it was just long enough to grip, but she wondered could she find the strength to grab onto the grass and pull her own weight? She thought to herself and knew that deep down somehow, she would have to find the strength to get to Britain; and she knew her determination wouldn't fail her. She knew she had to get to Britain no matter how much pain and suffering she had to endure. She reached out both hands as far as she could and gripped two handfuls of grass and started crawling on her stomach. Inch by throbbing inch with each agonizing breath she took, she made it closer to the front steps. Then, between her heavy breathing and sobbing, she heard a car passing down the exclusive street. It dawned on her why would they stop when they had no idea there were two people lying dead at huge estate and two more slipping away swiftly.

Sabrina had come to love their elite estate tucked away off the main road in a secluded affluence section with other priceless homes. The area mirrored immaculate landscaping with shapely evergreen trees and bushes; and while Sabrina laid surrounded by all the exclusiveness of her home, she thought how she was in unbearable pain lying helpless in her own front yard, thinking that each breath would be her last. Her mind flashed back on when her parents purchased the Taylor mansion and how she instantly fell in love with the estate. Now lying on the front lawn fighting for her life, she wondered if anyone was home at Franklin House or the Coleman mansion. Her hopeful thoughts faded when it dawned on her all of Franklin House and the Coleman mansion were likely at the fundraiser, otherwise someone would have rushed to their rescue after hearing the gunfire.

She gripped another fistful of grass, and pulled herself right up to the steps, between her heavy breathing and sniffling, she heard a squeak noise.

Her left hand gripped the bottom step as she paused to listen. This time all she could hear was an airplane in the distance. Her right hand grabbed the other edge of the step and she struggled in excruciating pain to pull herself up the bottom step, but she couldn't muscle up enough strength from her painful weak body. She laid her face on the step and tried to catch her breath.

"Britain, I'm trying," she cried out in a low weak voice. "God knows I'm trying. I love you, Britain; and I just need to see you one last time. Then I'll give up and let the suffering stop," she cried in a low feeble voice.

"Sabrina, Sabrina, is that you, my darling beautiful Sabrina?" Britain asked in a low weak voice. "Are you okay?" he said breathless.

It was Britain's voice and it meant he was still holding on. Sabrina's weak heart raced with joy from the sound of his voice. Hearing his voice was like a voice from Heaven to her as her half closed eyes sparkled with esteem from the thought of him being okay. "Sabrina, I need to see your face. I need to hold you just one last time," Britain called in a low weakened voice.

Knowing he was still alive and holding on gave Sabrina instant strength to move. She screamed inside with each breath she took as the horrific pain ripped through her as she pushed herself. It was pure determination up against horrendous pain. She closed her eyes with a tight frown as she somehow gathered up enough strength to push herself up the bottom step. Then she opened her eyes, and through her cloudy, wet eyes, she saw his magnificent face. He was crawling on his stomach through the front door. Agonizing pain and determination showed on his face.

He managed to crawl almost to the edge of the porch, reached one hand, fully stretched out to Sabrina. Her hand managed to reach his. He grabbed her hand and gripped it with all his strength. He had no more strength to crawl. She had no more strength to move. She laid at the bottom of the steps with her hand in his. He laid across the porch with his hand in her's.

He gripped her hand tighter as he managed in a weak voice, "I love you."

Sabrina managed with her last ounce of strength. "Britain, I love you."

Chapter Six

The scent of red roses and pink carnations mixed with the scent of rubbing alcohol and expensive perfumes were the scents that filled the air as Sabrina eyes blinked open that Sunday morning. Her eyes were cloudy as she scanned the room. She could see fresh flowers throughout the room, sitting on windowsills and on each table top in the room. She laid there and rubbed her eyes to get a clearer view of her whereabouts. She had a confused expression on her face, rubbing both eyes trying to figure out where she was as she constantly blinked her eyes, stretching them wider trying to focus on the faces of Samantha, Starlet and her father. They were all standing over her looking down with smiling faces. For a moment, as Sabrina took her fingers rubbing both eyes, their faces were foggy, then as seconds passed, her vision focused sharply to crystal clear.

Sabrina head rested on two pillows as she stared up at Samantha, who reached down and touched her forehead with the back of her hand. After touching her sister's forehead, Samantha nodded and exchanged looks with Starlet and their father. "She's awake. Isn't that great," Samantha said, smiling as she gently rubbed Sabrina's cheek.

Sabrina eyes appeared weak as she glanced from side to side, but the confusion that saturated her mind and overwhelmed her as she first opened her eyes had ceased with the realization that she was lying in a hospital bed and very much alive. She was amazed that she had survived what appeared to be an un-survivable twisted confrontation with a mentally irrational Courtney.

"Finally, you open those bright eyes," Samantha smiled. "We have been waiting all night and most of the morning for you to open your eyes," Samantha said with tears of joy, as she smoothed Sabrina's hair from her face.

"We know you're shaken by all of this. But the good news is, your doctor told us you're going to be okay. He also told us, you're healing well, and headed toward a full recovery. They removed that bullet from your side successfully," Samantha softly shared with her.

Sabrina nodded at Samantha, then grabbed her face and started crying.

Charles was immediately concerned and wondered if she was in pain. "Get a nurse, Starlet," he quickly suggested.

But Samantha didn't sense that Sabrina was in physical pain as she shook her head toward her father. "No, Father. Wait Starlet." Samantha held up one finger. "I don't think she's in pain."

"Well, maybe we should get a nurse anyway," Charles said. "She's not crying for no reason."

"I know, father," Samantha said as she exchanged looks with her father and Starlet. Then she touched Sabrina's shoulder. "You're not in pain right now, are you?" Samantha softly asked.

Sabrina shook her head. "You're right. I'm not in pain."

"If you're not in pain, why are you crying, dear?" Charles asked.

Sabrina stared at her father and her two sisters, but didn't immediately comment as she continued to wipe tears from both eyes with her fingers.

Samantha touched her cheek. "Do you feel like talking about it?"

"We know it was probably a nightmare of what happened," Starlet said.

Charles nodded. "If that's why you're crying. Try to keep your mind off of that horrific incident."

Samantha nodded in agreement. "Father is right. Just try not to think of what happened. We're all so sorry we didn't get home sooner," Samantha told her. "My advice is to push those awful images from your mind when they creep in your thoughts," Samantha suggested. "All will be okay now!"

"No, Samantha. You're wrong. Nothing will be okay!" Sabrina cried.

"What do you mean?" Samantha alarmingly asked.

"I'm talking about my life and how it's now destroyed."

Charles grew concerned by Sabrina statement. "Listen, sweetheart. I know it will take some time. But eventually you'll come to terms with that awful incident. It won't consume you and destroy your life."

"Father is right, in time those horrible images will become more bearable," Samantha assured her. "Your life will be fine."

Sabrina looked at Samantha with serious eyes. "My life will not be fine because everything has changed." She paused, exchanging looks with Samantha, Starlet and her father. "I know you don't want me to focus on that horrifying incident. But I'm consumed with what happened. I cannot get the images out of my head. The sound of the gun shots are constantly ringing in my ears," she sadly explained. "I have no idea why I pulled through to face this distress?"

"You pulled through because you have so many who love you and we were all praying for you," Starlet softly said.

Sabrina shook her head. "I'm sorry to say this because it sounds so ungrateful. But honestly, I didn't want to pull through!" Sabrina cried.

Samantha exchanged looks with her father and Starlet, and then Charles stepped closer and patted Samantha's shoulder. Samantha stepped aside as Charles pulled the bed cover up to Sabrina's neck.

"Why are you crying, sweetheart?" he asked. "What did you mean when you said you didn't want to pull through?" Charles asked with urgent concern.

"It just seems useless that I did."

"Sweetheart, why would you say something like that?" Charles passed her a box of Kleenex from the bedside table.

"Father, I'm sorry. But it's as I said. I feel my life has been destroyed.

"Sabrina, I really don't want you to entertain such negative thoughts," Charles seriously said. "I realize that ordeal was horrendous and no doubt you'll need some counseling to help you through the dreadful memories of that incident. But now you have me worried and quite concerned by what you just said. You need to come to terms that your life has not been destroyed," Charles assured her. "You're on the road to recovery and in time, those horrific memories will fade from your mind. Therefore, try to explain to us why you think your life has been destroyed," Charles stressed strongly as he stood there waiting for her to explain what she had said.

Sabrina looked up at her father in silence for a moment, then spoke. "Father, I'm talking about Britain." She wiped a tear with a tissue.

Charles exchanged glances with Starlet and Samantha. "I don't follow, sweetheart; what do you mean? What about Britain?"

Sabrina looked up at her father in silence and slightly shook her head without answering him as she wiped tears from both eyes.

Charles repeated. "Sweetheart. What about Britain?"

"It's too painful to talk about. But I'm talking about my life and what's left of it; and how it's not going to mean that much without Britain! I'm wondering how I'm going to get through the rest of my life knowing I'll never see him! It's a nightmare!" Sabrina cried. "Father, how can I survive this pain, knowing I have lost my mother and the man I love? It's too much to bear! It's just too much to bear!"

Charles, Samantha and Starlet exchanged looks and slightly smiled at each other as Samantha gestured to her father that she wanted to answer Sabrina. Then Charles touched Sabrina's cheek. "You will survive. Everything is going to be fine. Your sister have something to tell you," Charles said, then stepped away from the bed and took a seat in a nearby chair as Samantha stepped over to Sabrina's bedside and touched her cheek. "Sabrina, we were just about to tell you the good news."

Sabrina's eyes widen with curiosity. "Good news? Is it about Britain?" She glanced across the room and caught her father's eyes. "Is Britain okay?"

Charles smiled and nodded toward her, then Sabrina looked at Samantha and Starlet happily as she grabbed her cheeks with both hands.

Samantha smiled and nodded down at her. "Yes, Britain is going to be okay. He pulled through."

Sabrina looked across the room at her father with happy tears as Charles spoke. "Yes, your young man is going to be okay. He was taken into emergency surgery at the same time as you, and a bullet was removed from his upper stomach. He's a very weak and sick young man, but his doctor said he's going to be just fine," Charles said with a smile.

Sabrina took a deep breath as a permanent smile formed on her face. She looked at Samantha speechless for a moment before she spoke. "Oh, my God, I can't believe it's true. I'm so happy it's true," she excitedly cheered as tears instantly flooded her eyes. "This is the best news and the best medicine I could ever get. It's like waking from a horrible nightmare."

Samantha nodded. "It was an awful nightmare what happened. But we're all so blessed that you and Britain are going to be fine."

"We are blessed. I'm so glad," Sabrina said, as she slowly held out her left hand and glanced at her engagement ring. Then she looked at Samantha. "I'm assuming they brought us to the same hospital. Is Britain here also?"

Samantha smiled, nodding. "Yes, he is. He's on the third floor."

"What floor is this?" Sabrina asked, looking toward the open door.

"This is the fifth floor," Samantha answered.

"I'm so thankful we're both okay. Now we have a second chance." She looked toward the door. "I wish he was on this floor. I just want to see him."

Samantha discreetly glanced over at her father and he shook his head.

The gleam in Sabrina's eyes faded as she observed Charles shaking his head. "Father, I just need to see him to make all of this real."

Charles frowned. "Listen, Sweetheart. You're a very sick young lady. You need to concentrate on getting your strength back and nothing more."

"I know, Father. But I'm worried about Britain also. I just need to see him to know he's okay."

Charles nodded with sympathetic eyes. I do understand how you feel Sweetheart. Your need to see Britain. Nevertheless, I wouldn't advise it. You're still quite weak and you need to stay put to get your strength back."

Sabrina stared disappointedly at her father without commenting.

"You need to give it a little more time," Charles adamantly suggested.

"Father, I know I have a lot of healing to do. But I feel strong enough, and with a little bit of help I can get out of bed." Sabrina glanced from her sisters to Charles. "Besides, I'll be in a wheelchair. I could be wheeled to his room." She stared at Samantha.

Samantha stared at Sabrina with sympathetic eyes. But didn't comment.

"Please, can any of you understand how I feel? I just want to see with my own eyes that he's okay. It's not going to feel real in my mind that he's okay until I see him," Sabrina urgently explained.

Charles nodded. "Sabrina, we do understand how you feel. We know you want to see Britain and I'm sure he wants to see you as well. But considering your weak condition, I just don't think you should get out of bed to travel about in this hospital so soon after your surgery," Charles explained in a sympathetic voice. "Besides, I'm sure Veronica and Catherine along with his brothers are doing all they can to keep Britain stationary in his hospital bed. He probably has the same idea as you. But hopefully Veronica can keep him in bed. Neither does he need to travel to this floor trying to check on you. You both just had major surgery and need to give yourself time to heal."

"Father, I hear you and I know you're right." Sabrina grabbed her face with both hands. "But my need to see him is overwhelming. It's hard to lie here in this hospital bed knowing he's in this hospital, and not be able to see for myself that he's okay," Sabrina sadly mumbled.

"We know that," Starlet nodded. "But father is right. You're just too weak to get out of bed and travel around in a wheelchair right now. You have stitches and too much moving around could hinder your healing process. Major surgery is something you need to take it easy from."

"That is correct," Charles agreed with Starlet. "It's not advisable for you to move around too much. Your condition is too fragile to make visits to that young man's room; and as I said before, he's also too weak to make any visits up here to the fifth floor. You both just haven't been out of surgery that long. You kids just need to give yourselves a little more time to get your strength back before you start traveling from one floor to the next to see each other," Charles seriously suggested.

"Father is right, you know," Starlet agreed. "Sabrina, you need to just stay in bed and gather your strength back. Britain also needs to do the same."

Samantha smiled over Starlet's shoulder as she walked over to pull the heavy hospital draperies open. Sabrina carefully turned to her left and looked toward the window, out at the clear sky and immediately felt blessed to be alive. She reflected on how she had survived such a horrible ordeal. She knew her father and sisters were right. She and Britain needed to stay in bed to recover. She looked at her father and nodded. "Father, you are right. All of you are right. I know I need to be patient and gather my strength before I travel to Britain's room to see him," she humbly admitted with a smile. "I'll just settle for phone calls until we both gather enough strength to travel back and forth to each other's rooms," she said, as she smiled at the bright sun pouring through the open draperies of her hospital room.

Samantha glanced around and looked at Sabrina while standing at the window. "Is that too much light for you?"

"No, Samantha. That's fine, she said, smiling.

"I'm glad the light won't bother you. It's a clear day outside."

"Thanks for letting the sun in," Sabrina said. "Seeing the sunlight lets me know I'm alive and all is well," Sabrina said spiritedly as she stared out at the clear day through the tall wide window of her spacious hospital room.

The warmth from the sunlight filled the room and suddenly she felt such relief to be alive and to know Britain was alive.

"It's good to see you smile," Starlet said, exchanging looks with her father and Samantha. "What happened was unreal." Starlet shook her head. "I know Courtney was behaving strangely yesterday morning, but it never occurred to me that she was completely mentally ill." Starlet grabbed her face and paused for a moment. "She had suffered a mental breakdown and if I had paid closer attention, maybe I would have figured something majorly was wrong and could have prevented what happened," Starlet sadly reflected.

Charles quickly weighed in. "Starlet, your sister is in a better mood and I don't think we should dampen it with the details of yesterday event," he seriously commented. "I know it helps to discuss and we all have questions and want to talk about it, but now isn't the best time."

Samantha and Starlet exchanged looks and nodded in agreement at each other as Charles continued to speak.

"Let's get this one home and back on her feet, and then we'll have plenty of time to put the pieces together and figure out what went wrong with Miss Ross that led to yesterday's dreadful tragic event," he said as a nurse stepped into the room and handed him a bottle of water.

The tall, middle age nurse dressed in all white handed a bottle of water to Starlet and Samantha as well and then she turned and left the room. She returned minutes later with a clear plastic pitcher filled with iced water and placed on Sabrina's bedside table. After the nurse left, Starlet pointed to the pitcher and Sabrina nodded. Starlet poured a cup of water for Sabrina and handed it to her.

"Father is right; we need to talk about more uplifting subjects. And I know just the subject that will cheer you up," she said, smiling. "We," she pointed to herself and then to her father and Samantha." She paused for a moment with a big smile on her face. "We paid a visit to Britain earlier."

Sabrina's eyes lit up as she lay propped against two pillows with the white linen up to her shoulders. "The three of you went to his hospital room? How is he? Did he get bruised up at all?" She grabbed her face and shook her head. "I hate to think of the pain and suffering he went through."

Starlet nodded. "Yes, the three of us went to his hospital room because we had to see for ourselves that he was okay, and we needed to be able to let you know how he was doing," Starlet said to her. "The moment you were resting peacefully in your room after your surgery, the three of us went down to the hospital cafeteria to grab some dinner. After dinner, we looked in on you and you were still sleeping. Father insisted we go check on Britain who we knew had been taken to emergency surgery at the same time as you."

Sabrina looked toward her father. "Thanks Father."

Starlet continued. "When we walked into his large hospital room there were hardly anywhere to walk since the floor was cluttered with gifts and bouquet of flowers. Mrs. Franklin said workers from Franklin Gas had dropped off carloads of gifts and flowers after they heard the news of what happened," Starlet explained.

"She's right, so many gifts and flowers," Samantha added. "Those Franklin guys are loved by so many because they're so loving."

Starlet nodded and pointed to her chest, then pointed to Samantha and then to Sabrina and smiled. "We're all blessed to have such honorable men in our lives."

Sabrina wiped a tear. "I never knew how blessed I was until today," she humbly stated. "I thought all my happiness had been ripped away from me. Nothing has ever shaken me more. It opened my eyes and I'll never take what I have with Britain for granted again. To think I broke up with him for a while. I was so not thinking straight to do such a foolish thing. I'm so thankful that's behind us and we found each other again." She wiped her tears with a tissue.

"Wipe those tears," Starlet smiled. "When we walked in Britain's room last night, he was lying there in his bed looking the picture of health. He didn't look like a man who had just been shot and wounded, recovering from emergency surgery. Although, he had a solemn look on his face lying there surrounded by family. He didn't have a bruise on him," Starlet shared.

"That's good to hear. But he'll still need someone to care for him for a while the same as me," Sabrina said. "My body is so sore until I can barely move. He's probably in the same condition. I need help to get out of bed and to walk to the bathroom, I'm almost helpless right now and I'm sure Britain is in the same condition," Sabrina stressed tearfully.

Charles nodded. "I'm sure you're concerned but there's no need to worry yourself about that. You'll have a round the clock nurse at your side once they release you; and I'm sure Veronica will have no less for Britain," Charles stated seriously said, and then smiled. "Knowing Veronica, she'll probably have two nurses at Britain's bedside. You definitely will not have to worry about that young man getting the care that he needs."

Samantha nodded. "That's for sure. Mrs. Franklin doesn't half do anything. She's a smart, powerful woman and she'll make sure Britain is situated with every comfort possible during his hospital stay and when he gets home. While we were visiting Britain last night, Mrs. Franklin said, she's not leaving Britain's side until he's completely healed and back at work: the whole nine yards. She said regardless of her busy schedule, she or his Aunt Catherine would be at his bedside along with the regular nurse at all times until his last day of hospitalization," Samantha said with conviction. "There you have it. You don't have to worry about Mr. Britain Franklin."

Sabrina smiled, "Thanks for reassuring me, but it's silly of me to even think he would have anything but the best care after he arrives home. I already know how methodical and thorough his family is."

"During our visit to Britain's room in between all the chatter and flowers being delivered, he did ask about you," Starlet gladly shared.

Sabrina smiled because if she couldn't see Britain, the next best thing was to talk about him. Starlet news was just what the doctor ordered. Sabrina wanted to hear whatever Starlet had to say about Britain.

"What did he say?" she asked, smiling.

"He asked how you were and asked me to give you a message."

"He told you to give me a message?"

Starlet nodded. "That's right. He wanted me to tell you, you're in his thoughts," Starlet said, and then bent over to kiss Sabrina's forehead.

Chapter Seven

Sabrina drifted into a light sleep for about ten minutes before the ringing of her hospital desk phone. Starlet was standing near the bedside table and quickly answered the phone. It was Amber and Rome calling to check on the progress of Sabrina. Starlet shared that Sabrina was healing well and was in good spirits. But also mentioned that Sabrina was taking a nap. Therefore, Amber and Rome didn't lingered on the phone that long. They asked Starlet to give Sabrina their love and prayerful thoughts and then they ended the call.

Starlet softly hung up the phone, but by then Sabrina was covering her mouth in a yawn. "I could have spoken to Amber and Rome. I'm awake now. I guess the medication I'm on is keeping me drowsy and sleepy."

"It probably is," Starlet agreed, as she stepped aside as Samantha and Charles stepped over to the bed.

Starlet, Samantha and Charles discreetly exchanged looks with each other as they each had serious expressions on their faces.

Samantha touched her father's arm. "We should tell her now, Father," Samantha sadly mumbled.

Starlet nodded. "Yes, Father, we should tell her now before she turns on the TV and hears it on the news," Starlet sadly agreed.

By now Sabrina mouth was open and she had surprise and sadness in her eyes waiting for whatever news they had to share. She took her right hand and gripped the rail of her bed as she braced her back against the mattress.

Charles looked at Sabrina with solemn eyes as he stepped closer to her hospital bed and took a seat on the edge. He reached for her right hand and he placed it in his, as he held her hand in silence for a moment before he humbly said. "Courtney survived her surgery. But she's still in critical condition."

Sabrina closed her eyes and shook her head as she gently removed her hand from her father's. She grabbed her face with both hands and started crying. Starlet and Samantha stood at her bedside speechless as she got out a good cry. "She hates me but I don't want her to die. I didn't want any of these nightmares. I wish I could wake up and find it was all a horrible dream," she cried. "But it's not a dream. Courtney Ross is in critical condition and I don't know if I'll be able to handle it if she doesn't make it. She blamed me for all of her problems. She told me I destroyed her life when I moved to town," Sabrina cried. "What if I'm really the cause of her breakdown?"

"That's enough, Sabrina," Charles firmly stated. "I will not sit here and allow you to blame yourself while you're lying in a hospital bed healing from a gunshot wound that young lady inflicted on you. It's not your fault and I will not allow you to take the blame for that young lady's madness. We all know now how unwell she was and how distorted her thinking was," Charles seriously stressed. "Therefore, of course, no questions asked. You're not the blame for that young lady's breakdown and actions."

"Father, I know you don't want me to blame myself, but I have so many emotions right now until I don't know what I should or shouldn't feel. Besides, Father. You don't really know Courtney Ross," Sabrina cried.

Charles nodded at Sabrina as he sat motionlessly on the edge of her bed. "You're right, sweetheart. I don't know the young lady well. I have only seen her a few times coming and going when she would show up at the estate to visit you. Nevertheless, I wasn't in the dark on her background. I have heard a few things about her troubles with Rome and Britain," Charles casually told her. "However, regardless to whether I know the young lady well or not, it's obvious she was ill. Therefore, anything she said to you was questionable."

"But Father, in the back of my mind, I keep thinking I'm the reason for what happened to her and why she did what she did," Sabrina sadly mumbled. "I presume I feel this way because all her anger was aimed toward me."

Charles raised both hands. "Okay, listen, Sweetheart. You feel the way you feel and no one can tell you how to feel. But in time, counseling will help you sort through all that happened and find some perspective. But right now, Sabrina, you need to realize that none of us really know what happened to that young lady and what made her do what she did," Charles reasoned with his daughters.

Sabrina tearfully nodded. "You're right, Father. Nobody knows what really happened to Courtney. She just somehow slipped over the edge while we were all watching," Sabrina sadly mumbled.

Samantha nodded with sad eyes as her thoughts seemed far away. "You're right, Sabrina. Its like we all watched that girl go through some kind of conversion." Samantha grabbed her cheeks, overwhelmed with sadness. "And her transition from just an average girl to someone unrecognizable all happened in such a short amount of time," Samantha sadly reflected.

Charles shifted in his seat on the edge of the bed. He was uncomfortable with the discussion of Courtney Ross critical condition and the events of yesterday. He wanted his daughters to drop the discussion for a later date or never. "Samantha, must the three of you discuss that young lady at this time. It's all so distressing. It makes everyone sad and miserable. Let's pray she makes a full recovery and just drop the subject for now," Charles suggested.

"Father, we all know it's distressing and sad, but I think it actually helps to talk about it. It's too hard to keep something like this inside and not discuss it," Samantha said, standing at the window staring out into space.

"Well, maybe you're right at that." Charles looked at the water bottle in his hand, twisted off the cap and turned the bottle up to his mouth for a long sip. "I guess I was thinking like your mother for a moment, that I could spare your pain." He took another sip from the water bottle. "Go right ahead with your discussion if it helps to sort things out for you girls," Charles consented.

"Thanks, Father, for understanding how it seems to ease our stress discussing yesterday and Courtney and everything that happened," Samantha said as she stepped toward Sabrina's bedside and took a seat in one of the bedside chairs next to Starlet.

Samantha held her face in her hands for a moment and then she exchanged looks with Starlet. "It's all so unreal. You had just talked to Courtney that morning. How did she seem to you?"

Starlet rubbed both hands down her hair and took a deep breath. "As I said earlier, she seemed somewhat odd when I opened the front door for her yesterday morning. She was behaving slightly odd. It wasn't anything that I could put my finger on; I just sensed that something was off about her in an alarming way." Starlet took her fingers and wiped a tear that rolled down her left cheek. "Plus, it was so odd that she had shown up at the house at the crack of dawn while we were all still in bed. That should have been a big enough red flag by its self," Starlet sadly uttered, filled with frustration.

Samantha reached over and patted Starlet's shoulder to comfort her. "I know you wish you could go back and look inside of her head so that you could have prevented the dreadful episode of yesterday," Samantha humbly said. "But we can't roll back the clock and see or fix what we couldn't see or fix at that time. We can only go on and try to learn from our mistakes."

"That's a good mature, levelheaded choice of words," Charles agreed. "Those are my thoughts exactly. We all must go on and learn from our mistakes," Charles said and nodded. "I see your sister sitting there." Charles looked toward Samantha. "But just now, hearing her words and calming grace is just like having your mother in the room." He turned his view to Sabrina. "That's exactly what your mother would have said. Therefore, that's exactly what the three of you need to do. Try not to focus on the darkness of yesterday and the horrendous events and how that young lady spinned out of control. But focus on the positive of how blessed and lucky this family is that Sabrina is going to be fine; and that Britain is going to be fine and that it wasn't as devastating as it could have been," Charles humbly explained.

Sabrina reached out and touched her father's hand. She nodded and smiled. "Father, you are so right. We're all so blessed; and I know I'm so humble and graceful for our blessings that God spared me and Britain." She grabbed her chest. "I will take your advice to heart and try to focus on the positive," she softly uttered as she wiped her tears with her fingers. "That goes for my unpleasant run-ins with Courtney as well. I'll pray for her and I'll try to think of her as the person she was when Britain first spoke of her. I recall how much respect he had for her and his whole family gave her rave reviews as a worker," Sabrina respectfully explained. "He always spoke polite of her even after Rome broke up with her," Sabrina closed her eyes in thought for a moment. Then she blinked open her eyes with a serious expression. "I'm sure you all know that Courtney had and still have feelings for Britain, and although he doesn't return her feelings, he has always spoke kindly of her." Sabrina pointed to the pitcher of iced water on her bedside table.

Charles stood up from the bed and stepped over to her bedside table and poured water into a white form cup and handed it to her.

"Thanks, Father," she said as she slowly took a sip of water. "Courtney is a complex person and she seemed to have developed such a dislike for me. Nevertheless, I'm so crushed that she shot us and shot herself in the stomach like that." Sabrina took another sip of water. "We all tried to talk her down, but she was too far gone. She wouldn't listen to me and she wouldn't listen to Britain and she wouldn't listen to Kenny. We all desperately tried," Sabrina tearfully explained. "But as Father reminded us, I will not focus on that adverse event. I'm going to try hard to focus on how she was before her breakdown when Britain spoke so kindly of her."

Samantha shifted in her seat with overwhelming memories, but she managed to keep her composure as she spoke. "I can recall when she was dating Rome. She seemed quiet and reserved."

Starlet and Sabrina nodded as they looked toward Samantha waiting to listen to what she had to say. Charles looked toward Samantha as well.

Samantha smiled. "I guess we all remember when Courtney was dating Rome." She held up one finger. "Except you, Father, of course," Samantha quickly relayed. "But needless to say, it was an awkward time at Franklin House during those days."

Samantha noticed as her father slightly raised an eyebrow at what she had said. She nodded toward him. "Father, it was an awkward time visiting Franklin House. But not because of Courtney," Samantha said and paused. "Mrs. Franklin didn't seem to care that much for Courtney," Samantha shared. "Actually, Father, sometime it was downright comical. Mrs. Franklin would go out of her way to avoid conversations with Courtney. Nevertheless, Courtney paid her no attention and would just walk up to her and start a conversation anyway," Samantha slightly laughed and then grabbed her face with both hands. "I don't mean to be rude toward Mrs. Franklin, but honestly I didn't care for her cold shoulder toward Courtney; and even though, Courtney and I were never friends, I was impressed how she stood up to Mrs. Franklin."

"I liked that about her too," Starlet added. "Because you are right, it was extremely awkward how Mrs. Franklin would obviously not converse with Courtney. It made me feel uncomfortable because although Courtney didn't show it, being treated that way surely had to make her feel extremely uncomfortable," Starlet sadly reflected. "It's good we all have some good memories of Courtney to share right now while she's fighting for her life. Father, she wasn't always the foul person she transitioned into," Starlet said.

Samantha nodded. "That reminds me of how happy Rome seemed with her. During the time she was dating Rome, Paris mentioned on several occasions that he had never known his brother to be so completely at ease with a woman before," Samantha shared. "I know she was supposedly in love with Britain while she was dating Rome, but she seemed happy with Rome whenever the two of them were together at Franklin House or other parties that we all attended," Samantha recalled. "I have a concrete image of her in my mind from that time. She seemed nice with good manners."

Starlet nodded. "You're hundred percent correct. That's the same image of her that leaps out at me. That image of her when she just seemed like a down to earth sweet girl," Starlet reflected. "When Sydney told me that his mother didn't approve of Courtney, I was surprised and couldn't figure out why, since she seemed like such a nice young lady."

Samantha nodded. "Paris and I felt the same and couldn't figure out why his mother had such a beef with Courtney. Then after a while, we both just didn't take his mother serious regarding her remarks about Courtney. We felt Mrs. Franklin was just being too hard on Courtney. However, that Christmas Eve at Franklin House proved Mrs. Franklin's point that Courtney wasn't all she seemed and not quite as nice as we thought," Samantha humbly said and discreetly shook her head. "Nevertheless, I can't wrap my head around what happened yesterday. It's not something that any of us will soon forget. It was such a devastating disastrous occurrence. The biggest tragic was how Courtney shot herself and harmed all of you," Samantha sadly uttered.

"Who told you guys what happened?" Sabrina asked.

Samantha exchanged looks with her father and Starlet, and then she spoke in a heartbreaking voice. "Kenny gave a statement to the police and then he was kind enough to stick around and shared everything that happened with us. The ambulance was waiting to wheel him away, but he wouldn't allow them to bulge until he had told us everything."

Sabrina grabbed her mouth and swallowed hard. "Kenny gave the statement and told all of you and the authorities everything that occurred?"

Samantha nodded. "Yes, it was Kenny Ross."

Sabrina wiped tears from her sad eyes. "That's good to hear. I'm just so pleased that he's okay. My life flashed before me and I watched Kenny die a thousand deaths when I thought his sister had killed him," Sabrina sadly mumbled, looking toward Samantha. "I don't know Kenny as well as you and Starlet but after the courageous way he handled himself yesterday." She held her chest with both hands. "I have a newfound respect for that young man."

Samantha nodded with sad eyes. "Yes, Kenny is okay, but needless to say our hearts dropped when we pulled into the driveway and saw you and Courtney lying on the lawn and Britain lying on the porch." Samantha inhaled sharply and trembled at the recollection of yesterday's events. "Then we found Kenny lying on the living room floor," she cried, wiping her tears with a facial tissue. "To see that atrocious vision of the four of you was the worst day of my life and probably all of our lives."

"Father, do anyone know how long we were lying wounded before EMS arrived?" Sabrina sadly asked.

Charles nodded. "Fate was on our side. We pulled into the driveway shortly after Courtney shot herself. We actually saw her fall to the ground as we were parked at the community gate. The gate keeper was in a talkative mood and I exchanged a brief conversation with him. We didn't know the young lady had just shot herself. Sitting in the car at the distant we were, it appeared that she had just dropped or fell to the ground," Charles regretfully explained. "I would have asked Sam to pull right in if it had appeared alarming or suspicious. Foul play or gunshots never occurred in our thinking. Therefore, when she dropped to the lawn, we wondered what was going on, but didn't think much of it. Therefore, I continued to talk to the gatekeeper for a few minutes before we drove up and pulled into the driveway," Charles paused to collect himself. "Then, of course, when we pulled into the driveway and got out of the car, we found all of you clinging on to life. It was a devastating homecoming," Charles sadly said as his words choked up.

"So, it wasn't that long at all before you all found us," Sabrina said. "I was frightened out of my mind. At one point, I felt I didn't know what was real and what wasn't. The fact that no one was home, not even one servant. It didn't feel real. I wanted to wake up from my nightmare but it wasn't a bad dream. It was all happening in real time and no one was home," Sabrina cried. "I wondered where all of you were? I cannot recall a time ever that the entire estate was deserted like that."

"You know where we were. We were at the WJJ Theater to see Starlet sing," Charles quickly reminded her. "Did you forget Starlet was singing at the downtown charity event? I gave the staff time off to attend the event as well. We thought you would make the event, but when you never showed we just figured you had other plans with Britain," Charles humbly explained.

Sabrina shook her head. "I knew about it. But as the day progressed, it completely slipped my mind among all the chaos that consumed me. I was so caught up in pandemonium that the charity event and the fact that Starlet was scheduled to sing, completely faded to the back of my thoughts." She looked toward Starlet with apologetic eyes. "I'm sorry I forgot."

"You know you don't have to apologize. No apology is necessary," Starlet assured her. "I'm sure it was terrifying to realize no one was around to hear or stop Courtney from her violent rampage. Franklin House was empty as well, since all the Franklins did the honors of attending the charity function as well," Starlet explained with a solemn face. "So, please, sweet sister of mine, no apology. Also, I don't want you to feel guilty that you missed the event. If I had been in the middle of all that chaos I would have forgotten the event as well," Starlet assured her.

"But it wasn't just a regular charity event," Sabrina sincerely acknowledged. "It was also your song event," Sabrina importantly stressed. "You performed and I missed it because of the dreadfulness that happened yesterday," Sabrina mumbled as a wave of sadness ripped through her.

For a moment she would be okay, and then suddenly all the events of yesterday would pop right back into her head and overwhelm her with sorrow; and at the moment she was experiencing one of those moments. "Why did that dark tragic have to happen, why?" Sabrina sadly asked.

"No one knows why," Samantha softly answered. "Crazy unexplained things just happen sometimes and there's no making sense of it when it does. Just like when we lost Mother. It made no sense then and it makes no sense now, but yet Mother is gone."

"That's so true," Sabrina agreed. "One day she was with us and the next day Mother was gone and it will never make sense why we had to lose her."

"Exactly," Samantha nodded. "It's just like what happened yesterday will never make sense. We have to keep mindful of what Father said and find a way to move past the devastation of yesterday," Samantha humbly said.

"One big blessing out of yesterday is that Kenny Ross is in good condition," Sabrina strongly relayed. "He was such a hero yesterday and when he gave his statement to the police and told all of you what happened, he probably didn't say how he risked his own life to save me and Britain."

Charles, Samantha and Starlet looked toward Sabrina with curious expressions on their faces. Charles touched her arm. "What did the young man do that constitutes he risked his life for you and Britain?" Charles asked.

"Father, it was beyond frightening. It was dread and terror unlike I have ever known," Sabrina cried. "Every minute and every second. But Kenny threw himself in front of Courtney's gun so that Britain and I could get away," Sabrina tearfully explained. "We were all upstairs in my room and Courtney Ross had us cornered with her gun. She had threatened to shoot me, and Britain wanted to step in front of me. But Kenny threw himself in front of his sister's gun all while he was standing there bleeding from both of his hands that she had sliced with a switchblade," Sabrina sadly explained.

Charles nodded and smiled. "I agree that the young man is a hero. What he did was nothing short of incredible. He's Courtney Ross's brother, is that correct; and his name is Kenny Ross? I would like to meet him and let him know how grateful I am for his gallant heroic efforts to help you and Britain."

Sabrina glanced at Samantha and patted the side of her bed. Samantha stepped over to the bedside and took a seat on the bed. "I know you and Kenny were fairly good friends back in college, and last month you thought you could be friends again. But you basically stop associating with him because of his heavy drinking," Sabrina explained in a low voice for Samantha ears only. "And I also know that he still has a crush on you. But what I'm really trying to say about Kenny is that he's a good guy. I saw what he was made of yesterday. He's really a good guy and I'm so thankful that he's okay."

Samantha looked down at Sabrina and smiled. "Yes, Kenny is doing okay, and I also agree that he's a good guy. I may have shared with you that I had an opportunity of my own to see what he was made of last October when I thought I would lose Paris. Long story short, Kenny took a stand and made sure that didn't happen. He walked into our living room and magically made Paris and I realize our special connection and what we meant to each other. I'll always be grateful to Kenny for saving my relationship with Paris."

"Wow, Kenny Ross did all of that?" Sabrina asked with surprise in her voice. "I recall that Kenny was at the center of why you and Paris were having problems, but I had no idea he was instrumental in the two of you patching things up. If you shared this already I guess I wasn't really listening. I probably didn't want to hear the good about him at the time. However, I hear you loud and clear now, and that's wonderful what he did. I'm glad he was able to help you and Paris realize your special connection and what the two of you means to each other," Sabrina explained to Samantha in a low voice.

"Me too," Samantha said. "He's a real decent person and what he did for you and Britain was remarkable above the call of duty. However, we still cannot lose sight that Kenny is not a saint," Samantha said in a low voice.

"Why would you say that at this time?"

"I'm saying it, because it's true. Just a month ago you didn't think it was a good idea for me and Kenny to reconnect as friends. You were concerned about his drinking problem," Samantha reminded her.

"I know that, but what he did for me and Britain proves he's really a decent person! He was willing to put our happiness above his own," Sabrina softly stressed. "He put his life on the line."

"Yes, I agree that Kenny is a decent guy. But I'm just saying that we both know he's a heavy drinker who sometime allows his alcohol to control him. Therefore, he's also fighting his own demons," Samantha said.

"That may be all true. But in my eyes and in Britain's eyes, Kenny is the hero who saved our lives," Sabrina said with conviction.

Samantha stood from the bed and left Sabrina's bedside as Charles Taylor took the seat on the side of the bed where Samantha left.

Sabrina smiled and touched her father's arm. "Father, I'm so relieved and happy to hear Kenny Ross is doing okay," she said and paused. "Samantha mentioned that Kenny lost his job when his father went to prison."

"Is the young man out of work?" Charles asked.

"I'm not sure. He may have another job by now. But I did hear Samantha mention that he lost his job at the restaurant where his father worked, right after his father was sent to prison." Sabrina stared at her father for a moment in silence before she continued. "Father, I do think Kenny is down on his luck right now; and he might be between jobs. Therefore, it just dawned on me that maybe we can find something for him at the company. If not, I'm sure Britain will find something for him at Franklin Gas."

Charles nodded and waved his hand. "We'll see what's available at the company. Do you know any of his work background?" Charles inquired.

"I'm not that knowledgeable about his work history. But one thing I do know, since college. Samantha mentioned he has mostly worked in restaurants. But she also said he has a degree in business management."

"That's good enough. We'll change Mr. Ross status back to an employee. Frankly, I'm indebted to the young man and I'd be honored to offer a job to the brave young man who saved my daughter's life," Charles said assuredly. "All he needs to do is just let us know when he's ready to come aboard."

Sabrina took her fingers and wiped a tear from her cheek. "Thanks, Father. I'm sure Kenny will be pleased with whatever position you offer him at the company." She swallowed hard and paused a moment as she looked at her father. "You know Father, when you first took a seat at the foot of the bed before I talked to Samantha, you had a solemn look in your eyes," Sabrina softly uttered. "You had just gave me that awful news about Courtney's critical condition; and my heart skipped a beat because I thought you were going to say the same about Kenny," she sadly explained. "I thought you were going to say he was in critical condition or didn't pull through," Sabrina tearfully uttered, and then swallowed hard to collect herself. "Kenny saved all of us and then found the strength to give the authorities and all of you the insight on what had occurred at the mansion."

Charles nodded with a solemn expression. "Yes, Sweetheart, that young man did exactly that," Charles replied with deep sorrow in his eyes as the image of yesterday, discovering them all clinging to life, flashed in and out of his mind and ripped at his heart each time unlike nothing ever had. He hadn't witnessed anything in his life that mirrored more distress and grief than arriving home and finding his daughter, her boyfriend and her friends barely clinging to life. The most distressing devastation was discovering Courtney lying on the lawn in so much blood from a self-inflicted gunshot wound.

"Kenny was so brave. It was almost as if he had no regards for his own life. He wanted to protect me and Britain from his sister, and he used himself as a human shield. He almost lost his life in the process!" Sabrina said with conviction, wiping her tears.

Chapter Eight

Sabrina managed to get ten minutes of sleep before she blinked open her eyes and scooted slightly up on her pillow. She looked toward the open door and smiled as warmth dashed through her when she saw Kenny walking into her hospital room. He looked the picture of health, except there were white bandages on each of his hands.

"Hi Kenny," Sabrina spoke. "You're a sight for sore eyes." She beckoned for him to come to her bedside. "I'm so glad you're okay. You risked your life for me and Britain and I'll be grateful for the rest of my life for the way you tried to protect us."

Kenny nodded and waved toward Samantha and Starlet as he headed toward Sabrina's bed. Charles stood up from his seat on the edge of bed, and stepped across the room to be seated on one of the four comfortable chairs in the room. After Charles took a seat, Sabrina pointed toward her father.

"Kenny, I would like for you to meet my father, Charles Taylor." She smiled toward her father. "Father meet the man of the hour. Kenny Ross. He's the heroic young man who saved me and Britain's life," Sabrina introduced him with a smile.

Kenny stepped across the room to where Charles was seated and nervously reached his hand out and they shook hands. "It's an honor to meet you Mr. Charles," he meekly said.

Charles quickly stood as he shook Kenny's hand and then he took his seat again. "Likewise, young man. The honor is mine. We owe you a debt of gratitude," Charles seriously said as Kenny stood there looking down at him.

Kenny felt oddly uneasy in Charles Taylor's presence. Although, at the moment, he was being crowned as a hero, in the back of his mind he wondered if Charles Taylor was aware of his inappropriate conduct toward Samantha when he grabbed and kissed her in a drunken state.

"How are you, young man? I see you're dressed in your street clothes." Charles observed. "Although I'm sure they haven't released you."

Kenny shook his head. "No sir, I haven't been released yet. My room is just down the hall from here. I managed with my bandage hands and mostly the assistance of a nurse to get into my clothes. I desperately wanted to get to this room and pay Sabrina a visit," Kenny said as he stepped over to Sabrina's bedside and took a seat on the edge of the bed.

Sabrina looked at Kenny with solemn eyes. "I thought..."

Kenny quickly spoke before Sabrina could finish her sentence. "I know what you were about to say. Courtney thought she shot me too," he said sadly as he looked down at his bandaged hands for a moment. When he felt at ease enough to look in her sad eyes, he could barely contain himself as water welled up in his eyes. Yet, he managed not to shed a tear as he spoke. "However, when I charged into her, she fell against the wall and immediately her arm with the pistol pointed upward to brace her fall. The gun went off and I fell to the floor, but not from a gunshot wound. I went in shock from the knife wounds," he explained timidly as if being in the company of Charles, Starlet, Samantha and Sabrina made him overly nervous.

Sabrina stared at Kenny's hands as if she had just noticed them. "Both of your hands are unavailable to you. You won't be able to drive or do anything for yourself. Have you thought about how you're going to cope and manage with doing simple things for yourself like feeding yourself and dressing?" Sabrina placed both hands over her mouth and couldn't stop her tears. "It's not fair what happened to you. It wasn't your fight. You were just trying to look out for us, now you can't even do anything for yourself." Sabrina cried.

Kenny looked down at his hands and frowned. "I know I have a long road ahead of me; and I'm not kidding myself about how I'm going to see myself through this. But right now while they keep me hospitalized I'm managing okay. The nurses and aids are assisting me with whatever assistance I need. Once I'm released, it will be a different story," he said solemnly, wondering how he would manage at home without a nurse. "I'm counting on Trina and Mom to give me a hand."

Sabrina nodded. "That's right. Your Mother and Trina will be around to help you."

Kenny shook his head. "I'm counting on them, but I'm not sure how that's going to work. They both have jobs that they can't afford to lose by staying home to wait on me. Therefore, I'll probably catch holy hell since I can't even hold a fork to feed myself."

Kenny uncertain words caught Charles Taylor's attention as he quickly looked toward Kenny and called his name, "Kenny."

Kenny looked toward Charles with an apprehensive look on his face. Kenny wasn't sure why Charles Taylor was asking for his attention. Therefore his nerves tightened against his already broken heart as his indiscretion with Samantha flashed in his mind.

"Yes, Sir, Mr. Charles," Kenny said respectfully.

"Young man, I just overheard what you were saying to my daughter." Charles held up one hand. "And by no means do I mean to interrupt your conversation, but in this case I felt compel to do so just to give you a peace of mind. I don't want you to fret about anything from this day moving forward," Charles assured him as he nodded at Kenny.

Kenny stared thankfully at Charles, but he wasn't quite sure what he meant.

"I'm sure I haven't made myself clear. Therefore, I will elaborate further by telling you this. Young man, once you are released you'll manage just fine. I'll see to you having a twenty-four hour nurse to assist you until you can start assisting yourself again. This nurse will be well versed and quite proficient in medical care and household care. She will be sent to your home immediately to arrive at your home immediately upon your arrival from the hospital. I will give strict details for the nurse to assist you with a variety of things, including but not limited to: bathing, grooming, dressing and eating. This medical professional will also be instructed to assist you with personal chores that you cannot do such as your laundry and preparing meals. She will also run errands to drop off of pick up dry cleaning or other things if you so need," Charles gratefully informed him.

Kenny looked at Charles attentively feeling great gratitude as he slightly nodded his head. He felt like he was dreaming and couldn't believe Charles Taylor was being so generous to him.

"Kenny, I want you to feel deserving of the services. Is that clear?"

Kenny smiled. "Of course, Mr. Charles. I'm appreciative. I just cannot believe your generosity."

"Well, young man. Believe it. Please do not hold back on anything you need assistance with while the nurse is onsite assisting you. Do you understand what I'm saying?" Charles asked.

Kenny nodded. "Yes, Sir. I understand. You want me to let the nurse do what is needed so my hands can heal properly without me trying to use them unnecessarily," Kenny answered.

Charles nodded and smiled. "That's correct. Your hands need to heal and you need to allow them to heal. Besides, the nurse I send to your home to assist you will not mind whatever is needed of her. She will be paid an obscene amount of money for her time. On top of that, she'll remain at your home around the clock until your hands are healed. I will of course pay your mother room and board while the nurse is onsite at your home. I'll make it clear to the nurse that she may have to sleep on a sofa in your home if you don't have a guest room. But she'll be stationed in your home until you no longer need assistance. The day you call me and tell me that you no longer need the nurse. That's when I'll call the agency and have her duties ceased."

"Mr. Charles, I can't believe you are doing this for me. I'm so grateful. But I don't want to cause you any unnecessary expense."

Charles smiled. "Let me worry about that, young man."

"I just mentioned it because the doctor informed us it could take nearly a month or more before I'll have the use of my hands again."

Charles nodded and smiled. "That sounds logical that it would take that long. But listen, young man. I want you to know, a month, two months or however long it takes for your hands to heal that's how long you'll have your 24 hour nurse." Charles nodded, smiling. "Are we clear?"

Kenny stared at Charles for a moment as if he was lost for words, then he smiled. "Yes, we are clear. Thank you, Mr. Charles. Nothing I can say seems adequate enough for your generosity. But know, I really appreciate your consideration for my condition."

"You don't have to thank me, young man," Charles told him. "I don't know you that well, but the fact that you would risk your life to save another speaks volumes about your character. Throwing yourself in the front of a bullet, risking your life for someone else, is the bravest most selfless act of any human being. Therefore, you earned the twenty-four hour nurse and much more. I'm just pleased to have this opportunity to return the favor and do something for you."

"Thank you, Mr. Charles for your kindness."

"Don't mention it."

"I would just like to say, I know what my sister did was greatly immoral and disturbed," Kenny sadly said. "I would like for you to know how sorry I am about everything that happened. I'm especially sorry about what she did to

Sabrina and Britain and herself," Kenny said as he collected himself and pushed back his tears.

Charles nodded. "Thanks for your apology. But it's not necessary. Of course, you love your sister. But you're not responsible for her actions."

"Thank you, Mr. Charles for your understanding. But I'm sad to say, nobody in my family knew Courtney was that close to the edge. I knew she was struggling with some issues but I didn't know she was sick and at the point where she was," Kenny sadly explained. "I keep going over and over in my head trying to figure out that one thing that could have made a difference to help me to help her."

"Sometimes there's nothing anyone can do to change the course of history no matter how much we regret and wish things could have been different," Charles caringly said. "But I want you to know that we all know your sister is in critical condition, and we're all praying for her. Apparently no one knew she was so ill. But at least after she recovers from her injuries, she'll be able to get the proper care and therapy that she needs."

"Thanks, Mr. Charles. But I do feel that I bear some of the blame," Kenny sadly admitted. "You see, I moved out of the house when I should have known better. I knew we were all having a tough time dealing with the issue of what my father had done; and how he was sent to prison for almost taking my mother's life," Kenny explained looking toward Charles. "It's been tough and a nightmare for us all. But with the absence of my Dad, my sisters and my Mom needed me around even more. Therefore, I keep thinking the same thoughts over and over. If I hadn't moved out of the house when I did, I would have been able to spend more time with Courtney," Kenny said with a choked up voice. "Maybe I would have been able to detect the signs of her heading for a breakdown. But I guess I was too wrapped up in my own life that I didn't think to take the time to notice how hers had crashed down around her."

At that moment Kenny life flashed before his face. His self-absorbedness concerning himself with alcohol that he was oblivious to some things happening around him. In his mind's eye, he could picture his sister drowning in a physical lake of despair as he stood on the bank of the lake with a bottle of vodka in his hand, oblivious to her cry for help. At that moment, a cold chill rushed over him and he knew in that instant that he would never take another drink of alcohol of any kind. The taste of alcohol was dead to him, just as the addiction to alcohol that had driven his sister to do such maddening things.

He shook his head as his mind was drenched with sadness. "Mom and Trina are both devastated over what happened. They are heartbroken beyond words over Courtney's critical condition. They are at her bedside; and when I leave here I'll go to Courtney's bedside. We all want to be there when she opens her eyes. It was such a tragic shock since none of us knew the extent of her problem. She clearly had lost sight of right and wrong and needed to see a doctor. As I mentioned before, I was too absorbed in my own issues to notice my sister's problems. I didn't have an inkling that she needed that kind of help. If I had, I could have done more to have prevented what happened to her and the rest of us."

"Kenny, stop doing this," Sabrina firmly said. "You're blaming yourself. Don't! It's not your fault. You're a good person and a good brother to Courtney. I have noticed how you have always been there for her, picking her up after work when she had car trouble," Sabrina caringly reminded him. "You showed up at Franklin Gas front door time after time just to work on her car when it would break down for whatever reason. You're a good brother to Courtney and you need to acknowledge and remember that," Sabrina softly reminded him.

"Maybe you're right, Sabrina. But hearing it doesn't make me feel any better."

"It should," Samantha added. "You're a good guy and you need to stop trying to pin Courtney's breakdown on your shoulders," Samantha compassionately urged him.

"She's right," Sabrina agreed. "No one had a clue to the extent of Courtney's mental state and just how far gone she was. It's easy for all of us to speculate now and realize just how unwell she was, especially after what has happened. But Kenny, how could you have known? Your sister, Trina, didn't know and your Mom didn't know and nobody else knew," Sabrina strongly stressed. "So please, will you do us all a favor and stop blaming yourself, okay?" Sabrina seriously urged.

Chapter Nine

No one left Sabrina's hospital room. They all sat quietly as Sabrina managed an hour of sleep before she opened her eyes to the nurse giving her a little white pill and a sip of water. Then her eyes followed the kind nurse as she headed across the floor out of the large room. Her eyes lit up and her heart warmed when she noticed Veronica, Catherine and Britain headed inside of her hospital room. They were slightly smiling with a somewhat solemn look on their faces as Veronica wheeled Britain through the door. They had a thick, soft white blanket wrapped around Britain. He was smiling with not a single scratch on his handsome face, but Sabrina could see weakness in his clear eyes.

"Good afternoon everyone," Veronica said as she wheeled Britain's wheelchair over near Sabrina's bedside. She leaned over and kissed Sabrina on the forehead and then lifted Sabrina's right hand and patted it. "Beautiful young lady, you look the picture of health," Veronica said, as she touched her chest with both hands and held them there as she spoke. "Hearing what happened to you kids shattered my heart and broke it in so many places." She glanced at Charles and the two of them exchanged looks. "Just as your Father, I'm so humbly thankful that you kids are doing okay," she said softly looking in Sabrina's eyes.

Veronica reached out and gently touched Sabrina's cheek. "I'm so pleased that your injuries are few and that you're on the mends just like this handsome young man that's seated in this wheelchair," she said with a voice filled with compassion as she placed her hand on Britain's shoulder and smiled. "He would not sit still until I wheeled him in here."

Charles felt a rushing to his heart when it flashed in his mind how blessed they were that his daughter and Britain were both fine after such a heinous ordeal that could have easily taken both of their lives. Therefore, to lighten the mood, he discreetly inhaled sharply and looked toward Veronica. "Smart minds think alike," Charles grinned. "Earlier we convinced this one to stay put in bed. Believe me when I tell you, she wanted to do just what that one convinced you to do. She wanted to make a trip to his room."

Veronica glanced around and her eyes connected with Charles. Her heart filled up every time she saw him. She knew it was love that she felt for him and knew the day was coming when they would completely declare their love to each other. But as she was lost in thought momentarily thinking of a future with Charles, he continued.

"While we were trying to get Sabrina to stay put in bed, you without a doubt were helping this one out of bed," he said lighthearted.

Veronica looked at Charles and smiled. "That's true. But I'll have you know his doctor wasn't for this trip. Nevertheless, we're here anyway. Because I guess nobody really tells Britain Franklin what to do," she said lighthearted. "Besides, nothing short of stuffing him into a straitjacket would have kept him from Sabrina's room," Veronica caringly explained as she left Britain's side and walked over near Charles and took a seat in a chair next to him.

Britain didn't have the strength to lean over and kiss Sabrina, and she didn't have the strength to lean over and kiss him. They held hands and looked at each other smiling.

Seeing Britain and having him by her side made things seem right again in Sabrina's world.

"Everything is going to be fine, Sabrina. We'll both get through this and get on with the rest of our lives," Britain said with sad eyes, lifted her hand and kissed it.

Britain nodded at Kenny who was seated on the opposite side of Sabrina's bed. "It's good to see you're okay. You're looking well." Britain glanced at Kenny's hands. "But your hands have you at a disadvantage. Are you in any discomfort?"

Kenny slightly shook his head as he looked down at his bandaged hands. "No discomfort so far. All the discomfort is in my brain thinking about all the icky, villainous foolish schemes my sister masterminded," Kenny sadly moaned. "All just to destroy someone else's life."

"It's a deeply sad thought. But you need to let it go," Sabrina urged.

"I know you're right. But it won't escape my mind how I had my head in the clouds and didn't know she needed help," Kenny sadly grumbled.

Sabrina reached out and touched Kenny's arm with her left hand. "Britain, he's blaming himself. None of what happened is his fault. He wasn't aware of Courtney's state of mind and had no inkling of what she was up to. So, can you please try to convince this heroic courageous guy that it's not his fault," she said as water filled her eyes.

Britain was silent for a moment caressing Sabrina's right hand as if he was in deep thought, and then he took a deep breath and looked at Kenny. "Kenny, listen to Sabrina and believe me when I say, absolutely nothing that took place yesterday was your fault."

"I just feel so guilty," Kenny sadly admitted.

"Well, you have nothing to feel guilty about," Britain strongly stressed. "However, on the other hand, I do have something to feel guilty about," Britain acknowledged.

Sabrina and Kenny stared at Britain surprised at his statement. Sabrina touched the top of his hand. "You also have nothing to feel guilty about regarding yesterday."

"So what are you getting at?"

Britain looked at Sabrina and nodded. "I'm getting at how I lost my head. I owe Kenny so many apologies until I don't even know where to start."

Kenny looked at him puzzled. "I don't think you owe me any apologies."

"Okay, I'll make myself clear. I need to apologize for punching you in the face, all based on an assumption."

"Thank you," Kenny sadly mumbled. "But there's no need to apologize. My sister had us all wrapped around her finger. We were all assuming what she wanted us to assume."

"You're right, of course," Britain agreed. "But I still feel I need to apologize for assuming you knew what your sister was up to."

Kenny took a deep breath and stared up at the ceiling for a moment and then shook his head. It bothered him that Britain thought he could have been mixed up in his sister's scheme.

"I deeply apologize," Britain told him. "Because for a while I thought you knew what Courtney was up to; and looking back I showed you great disrespect by accusing you of such trickery and defrauding," Britain sincerely explained.

Kenny held up both bandaged hands, shaking his head. "Britain. I understand where you're coming from. I know how it appeared to you. You don't have to say a word further," Kenny assured him.

Britain held up one finger as he continued. "I'm also finished. But I need to say this complete apology to you. So, just bear with me and listen. Because on top of it all, I need to apologize for thinking you were being fresh with Sabrina," Britain sincerely stated in a low voice that only Kenny and Sabrina could hear. "I'm not proud to admit I entertained such thoughts about you that were completely unfounded. My only justification, I felt like I had walked into another dimension yesterday. I'm certain we all felt sort of that way. My concentration was flooded with indistinct thoughts that were jammed in my head. For the brief time I was at your house yesterday, most of my awareness was based under false pretense," Britain softly explained. "Hindsight shows us that nothing was what it seemed or appeared and because of that I was rude to you, Kenny. Therefore, I apologize for even envisioning or contemplating such ill-mannered thoughts about you," Britain sincerely said with his eyes on Kenny. "So, that's it and I hope you'll accept my heartfelt apology.

Kenny nodded. "Okay, I accept your apology. But as I told you before you started, I felt there were no need for your apology to me. But just the same, thank you. I see it like this," Kenny strongly stressed. "We were all reacting to what we thought were the facts. Courtney got me inside under false pretense just as she did you and Sabrina. We were all tricked by her. Therefore, that's why I figured no way did you owe me any apologies. Britain, you are a standup guy and you had every right to punch me if what you thought was true was actually true. Anyway, my sister was the biggest loser! She lost her sanity. Now she's fighting for her life. I pray she makes it so she can get the help she needs. I just still can't believe she went over the edge like that," Kenny sadly uttered.

"Kenny, you are right," Britain agreed. "It was a heartbreaking tragic that happened yesterday," Britain said, and paused as the realization of the incident ripped through him. He kept his composure with glassy eyes.

"We're all so blessed," Sabrina thankfully mumbled.

"That we are," Britain agreed. "But I'm deeply remorseful and contrite that Courtney is lying in a hospital bed in critical condition," Britain sadly stated.

"I pray from the deepest part of my heart that she will completely recover," Sabrina sincerely uttered.

"We all want that," Britain caringly replied. "But Kenny. I want you to know, that no matter how we look at what happened yesterday and try to examine it or piece it together to make sense of it all. Its done and we all have to move on," Britain compassionately said. "The bright side of this darkness is that our eyes are open to Courtney's illness. Therefore, when she recovers and get released from the hospital, she'll be able to get the professional help she needs to be herself again."

Kenny eyes were wet with tears but no tears fell down his face as he kept his eyes glued to Britain's face, listening to his every word.

Then Britain glanced caringly toward Sabrina as his eyes locked lovingly with hers momentarily before he glanced back toward Kenny. "I suppose we all feel somewhat responsible. Deep down I do and I'm sure Sabrina does as well. Nevertheless, we shouldn't feel that way. It's not our fault what happened to Courtney," Britain stated with conviction. "It's not your fault." He pointed to Kenny. "It's not her fault." He pointed to Sabrina; and it's not my fault." He touched his chest.

Britain discreetly shook his head as sorrow overwhelmed him for a moment. He felt agonizing sorrow that Courtney had tried to take her own life and was now fighting for her life. Flashes of Courtney's former self when they first hired her flashed in his mind. Images of the soft spoken, kind and friendly young lady that he remember as a loyal dependable employee dances in his mind. Therefore, it overwhelmed him how she could have changed so dramatically in a dangerous disturbing way in plain sight.

After a brief moment of silence, Britain looked at Kenny with the deepest compassion in his heart. "Therefore, Kenny, you can take my advice or leave it. But the biggest favor you can do for you right now is not blame yourself for the dark devastation that took place at the Taylor's estate yesterday."

Britain swallowed hard as sorrow engulfed him. He took a deep breath; and as he tried to get through to Kenny and comfort him, in the next corner, Veronica smiled as she conversed with Charles, who seemed pleased in her presence. Standing at the end of Sabrina's hospital bed, Catherine appeared disturbed. She felt restless as she paced back and forth at the foot of the hospital bed. She was content that Britain and Sabrina were both fine and would make a full recovery. However, deep down at the core of her being, she felt unglued inside like her whole world was falling down around her. She was overwhelmed by a desperate feeling that weighed on her shoulders. Day after day it was clearer to her that she would not be able to forget Julian as she thought. She missed him extremely and wanted him back in her life. But she also knew he had moved on with someone else that he was happy with.

She paced back and forth at the foot of Sabrina's hospital bed, and no one noticed her anxiousness. She felt out of place and figured a conversation with someone might would calm her nerves. Therefore, she decided to walk over to the window and join Starlet and Samantha. But just as she headed in their direction, she turned around when she overheard them conversing about Courtney and the events of yesterday. Catherine didn't want to join in on such an unbelievable heartbreaking conversation. Therefore, she stepped back over to the foot of Sabrina's hospital bed and continued to pace back and forth.

Britain, Sabrina and Kenny looked toward the end of the bed and Catherine's eyes caught theirs. Catherine wasn't sure if they were looking toward her because they found her pacing the floor to be annoying and distracting. Nevertheless, she glanced toward them and smiled and immediately stop pacing as she took a seat on the foot of the bed. She took a deep breath and held her hands tightly as happy times with Julian saturated her thoughts.

Britain, Kenny nor Sabrina made any comments about Catherine's anxious behavior, they just jumped right back into their conversation.

Kenny nodded. "I hear your words, but they just need to stick in my brain."

"In time they will," Sabrina said sincerely. "None of us could have helped Courtney before this incident. We couldn't see into her mind. She was really in a bad way," Sabrina meekly uttered. "But now since we all know the state of her mind, once she recovers, we can all do what we can to help her heal. But in the meantime, Britain is right. We just all need to get on with our lives and try not to dwell on what we can't change or do anything about. That tragic day is behind us now," Sabrina sadly uttered.

Kenny shifted in his seat on the bed and took a deep breath as he tilted his head back, looking toward the ceiling to hold back his tears. "You're right, Sabrina. It is behind us now and the biggest debt was paid by Courtney. She almost emptied her gun on us. Then turned it on herself. The cops found the pistol in her hand. It had one bullet remaining."

Chapter Ten

    One month after Sabrina, Britain and Courtney's hospitalization, they were all released from the hospital. Britain and Sabrina were still under doctor's out-patient care. Courtney was physically out of the woods. But she was still deeply troubled mentally and were now residing at the extreme psych ward of the Shady Grove Institution, a courtesy of Don Taylor. Kenny hands had healed and he had full use of them. He was now gainfully employed as a middle executive at Taylor Investments, courtesy of Charles Taylor.

    It was less than one week left in June 2014, which found Sabrina and Britain and the entire Taylor and Franklin family greatly disappointed that Sabrina and Britain had cancelled their wedding plans indefinite. But Britain and Sabrina felt too sadden over the disaster with Courtney that almost turned into a fatal tragedy. They needed time to heal and reflect on their parts that led to Courtney's breakdown. They were deeply sadden by her departure from reality. They felt awkward planning their wedding while Courtney was greatly ill. Therefore, Britain and Sabrina's wedding were on hold for the foreseeable future.

    In the meantime, a dark cloud hung over Catherine's head over the mismanagement of her life and messing up her chances with Julian. Therefore, the moment she found out that Julian and Mildred were no longer dating, it gave her hope that maybe she and Julian could try again. She gladly took the opportunity to drive up to the lake house after Veronica informed her that Julian had received permission to spend his vacation at their lake house for two weeks. Julian had stressed to Veronica that he needed to get away and preferred to spend his two weeks vacationing at the Franklin lake house. He had heard many wonderful things about the property and he was honored to secure it for two weeks. Veronica explained that the family never allowed anyone other than family members to inhabit the property. But she made an exception for him in hope that his presence at the lake house would give him and Catherine an opportunity to reconnect with each other. Therefore, the same day that Julian rented the lake house, that Friday, June 24th, Veronica strongly encouraged Catherine to swallow her pride and take a chance by driving up to the lake house to visit him. Julian had picked up the keys and took possession of the cottage at ten o'clock that morning. Veronica informed Catherine at three that afternoon after she arrived home from the library. She also encouraged Catherine to persuade to give a good effort at Julian to commission some of his paintings to Taylor Gowns. Angela Taylor was willing to pay top dollar for his artwork.

    Julian was grateful for the opportunity to vacation at the Franklin lake house and felt no four star hotel or resort could be better. He appreciatively offered to pay Veronica the same amount he had agreed to pay to stay at the Doubletree Hotel. Veronica accepted his check without hesitation. Although, he stressed that his time there would be for relaxation, and spare time to paint. He mainly had chosen to get away to regroup from Mildred's sudden Dear John note. Mildred told him out of the blue that she could no longer date him. He was stunned since he had high hopes for a possible future with her and assumed she felt the same. Therefore, her sudden rejection explaining that she couldn't be totally happy with another man since the death of Antonio Armani completely baffled him. However, she stressed to Julian that she didn't want to mislead him.

    Julian decided to use his time at the lake house painting outdoor sceneries. Painting was his hobby but his artwork was outstanding and professional enough to display in any art gallery. Yet, he was never interested in painting professionally to commission his work. Veronica and Catherine had seen and admired his paintings in his new home and had discussed at length how he could make a fortune from his work. They were both confused and baffled that he wasn't interested in making money from his talent. But what they didn't know was that Julian didn't see his paintings as something he could make a fortune off of. But Catherine hoped she could persuade him to change his mind.

    Catherine thoughts and worries came to mind as she parked her car to the left of the lake house. Then she killed the engine and gathered up her priceless Rebecca Minkoff purse and black leather briefcase from the car seat beside her. She pushed open the door and stepped out of the car. But before she could step up on the porch, Julian opened the door and stepped out on the porch. He was wearing a pair of jeans and a black shirt. Catherine stood there for a moment enjoying the sight of seeing him. She smiled at him.

"Hi Julian, how are you enjoying our lake house?" Catherine asked, trying not to sound too anxious about her visit.

"Hi Catherine." He smiled and glanced at his watch. "I just got off the phone with you not that long ago. You made good time driving this way."

Catherine nodded. "Yes, I did. I was dressed and ready to take off when I called and asked if it was okay for me to drop by," she said laughingly. "I know you haven't been here that long. But how you like it? Are you enjoying the place?" she asked.

"Yes, I'm enjoying the place and I like it just fine." He stood there smiling. "This is one lovely spot. I'm sure you and your family has enjoyed it tremulously," he smiled.

"I have always loved it here from the time I was small. I think what I like the most is all the peace and quietness."

"That's exactly what I'm looking for," he said as he noticed her briefcase. "I see you didn't come empty-handed." He pointed to her briefcase.

"I hope you don't mind that I brought some of my work with me?"

"No, that's fine. But what kind of work is it? Is that library work?"

She nodded, not wanting to tell him that Angela Taylor had dropped off some documents; and that she actually had legal documents inside the briefcase for him to sign in case he agreed to sell some of his paintings to Taylor Gowns.

"So, do I get an answer? What kind of work?" he insisted.

"I'll just say this. I promise what's in this briefcase will not get in the way of our visit."

"Catherine, I'm not worried about that as long as you didn't just drive up here to try to talk me into selling my paintings to Angela Taylor?" he seriously said, rubbing his chin. "I hope your visit is genuine and more about seeing me than getting your hands on my paintings for Angela Taylor."

"It is more about you," Catherine quickly assured him. "I couldn't wait to get up here to see you. However, you are aware of my stance about obtaining your paintings for Taylor Gowns. Afterall, I left you lots of messages about that," Catherine politely reminded.

"Yes, you did. But Catherine, I think I was absolutely clear in my message," he said lightheartedly and grinned.

"Yes, Julian. You were quite clear in saying you're not interested in selling any of your paintings to Taylor Gowns or any other establishment. And even though I do feel quite strongly that you should take Angela Taylor up on her offer; this is a social visit. You said it was okay for me to come, and here I am." Catherine glanced toward the briefcase thinking about the important documents inside. "Not to say, I'm not going to mention your paintings at some point during my visit," she admitted.

Catherine stepped up on the porch and Julian stepped toward her and threw his arms around her in a big hug. The clean, bold scent of his familiar Polo cologne, mingling with the fresh country air, reached her nose with alluring awareness. They stepped inside of the cottage as he kept looking toward her briefcase. It was packed with work papers and documents slightly sticking out.

"Catherine, I know you said this is just a social visit." He narrowed his eyes at her, smiling. "And I said it was okay for you to drive here for a visit," he said with a confusing look on his face. "But I'm wondering if you actually drove out here to try and twist my arm." He rubbed his hand across the back of his neck. "I'm sorry to assume, Catherine. But from the grip you have on that briefcase, something tells me you're here to pitch for Angela Taylor," he said seriously as he discreetly looked her up and down. His eyes smiled with approval of the two piece pale green pantsuit she was wearing by the pricy designer Gentry.

Catherine nodded. "It's not exactly what you think. I drove up here Julian because I jumped at the chance to spend some private time with you," she softly admitted. "However, I won't lie about the rest."

"And what does that mean?" he asked.

"It means, although I didn't drive up here for the sole purpose of trying to convince you to sell some of your paintings to Taylor Gowns, I'm prepared to do some more talking for Angela Taylor," Catherine admitted. "You can't blame me for at least trying, right?" Catherine said laughingly. "There's no need in beating around the bush with you, Julian. From what I have seen of your work. It's clear. You're a brilliant painter and you should sell your work for the whole world to see and enjoy it! Plus, you should make the kind of money your paintings are worth," Catherine strongly stressed. "And in this case, you have that opportunity with Angela Taylor's interest in your work."

Julian pointed to the sofa for Catherine to be seated as he took a seat in the chair opposite the sofa. "I'm curious to know how Angela Taylor found out about my paintings."

"It goes like this. The portrait you gave me depicting a rain forest is now hanging in the foyer at Franklin House. Charles Taylor noticed your name and put two and two together that the painting could be authored by our next door neighbor, Julian Bartlett. After Veronica confirmed his suspicious, he told his brother, Don Taylor, who is co-owner of Taylor Gowns. He told his soon to be divorced wife, who runs Taylor Gowns, about the painting. Then she asked her brother-in-law Charles Taylor to ask Veronica and me to ask you to consider commissioning some of your paintings to her boutique."

Julian smiled. "So, that's how the story goes. I was just wondering how those big wigs found out about my paintings."

"Julian, I know I lost my right to give you advice when I left our relationship hanging. But you would do good to rub shoulders with those big wigs. You could make more money than you could ever imagine if you allow Angela Taylor to sell your paintings in her boutique."

Julian nodded. "I don't doubt that. I probably could."

"There's no probably about it. It's an absolute certain you would," Catherine cheerfully encouraged him. "Have you ever shopped in there?" Catherine asked as she pressed her back against the cushion of the sofa.

Julian shook his head. "I can't say that I have."

"Okay, have you ever shopped at Neiman Marcus?"

"Yes, once and that was enough," Julian said seriously and held up both hands. "Don't get me wrong. I would love to spend a day in Neiman Marcus filling up a shopping basket. However, I don't have money growing on trees like the rest of you."

"Don't put me in the group with the Taylors and Franklins."

"Why shouldn't I? You are a Franklin, are you not?" he asked.

Catherine nodded. "Of course, I'm a Franklin. But I explained to you how I have never had the Franklin fortune. I told you how my birthright was taken from me by my own parents. Veronica and my nephews are as rich as they come. But I don't have a dime of my own money," Catherine softly mumbled.

"I know you told me all about how your parents disinherited you. But, Catherine, I find it hard to believe that you have no money of your own."

"When I say no money of my own, I mean I'm not the owner of any of the Franklins accounts. Veronica and my nephews own all the Franklin wealth inherited from my parents and my brother. Although, I have to admit Veronica gives me the privilege and complete access to the house budget account."

Julian looked at Catherine curious. "What does that mean?"

"It means, I have the authority to use the account as my own."

Julian shook his head and held out both hands. "What are we doing here?"

"What do you mean what are we doing here?"

"I mean just that. You drove here to talk about other people's finances?"

"Julian, why are you getting an attitude? It was brought up and I was just explaining myself. Besides, you asked me a question."

"Well, Catherine, just consider the question unasked. I wasn't sure if I should have accepted your invite to drive up; now I wonder if I made a mistake."

"Listen, Julian. We don't have to discuss this any further. I was just basically trying to explain how Taylor Gowns is on the same scale as Neiman Marcus. But I guess I sort of got off track. But just think of the prestige that would come your way."

He shook his head and drew an attitude as he leaned back against the chair cushion. "Catherine, just let it go," he said with an irritated edge. "I thought I made it clear that I'm not interested in becoming a commercial painter and getting myself involved in all of that red tape." He raised both hands. "My plate is full and I was barely able to squeeze in this much needed time off my job. Besides, if I had wanted that for my paintings, I would have made it happen a long time ago! Long before I ended up in real-estate, buying and selling homes." He frowned. "So art galleries are out, even that upscale Taylor Gowns boutique that belongs to Angela Taylor," he firmly stated in a frustrated voice.

"I know what you said Julian, but surely it can't hurt to think about commissioning some of your paintings to an upscale establishment like Taylor Gowns," Catherine stressed. "Besides, I have nothing to gain. I'm only pushing it because it's such a huge opportunity for your artwork. Plus, Julian, you shared some of your personal finances. You mentioned how you need to watch your budget. So, all I'm asking is that you seriously give it some thought. You either need the extra cash or you don't. For such an important opportunity like this, there's no time to let your pride get in the way," Catherine seriously pointed out.

He didn't respond as he stared in space as she continued to talk.

"Julian, what do you say? It can't hurt just to think about it."

Julian rubbed his hands together. "Catherine, I don't want to sound like a broken record. But you're seriously wasting your time," he mumbled, looking straight ahead as if his mind was somewhere else. "You wouldn't understand my passion for painting and my reasons behind why I paint and why it's not something I'll do for money."

His statement captured Catherine's attention and she looked attentively at him. But she didn't comment.

He looked seriously at Catherine. "I true is, it's not big mystery. But I paint to console myself."

Catherine seriously stared at him. "To console yourself?" she asked.

Julian nodded. "That's correct. I paint to console myself. It's really a long story behind it all."

"Please share it with me," Catherine encouraged him. "If it's something you don't mind sharing."

"It's not something to hide. I don't mind sharing it," Julian assured her. "This unique talent all started because of my mother."

"How wonderful that your mother encouraged you to stick to your painting. I'm sure it was great to have the support and encourage of your folks," Catherine said, reflecting on what she considered a lack of support from her parents.

"That's true. I did have great support and encouragement from my folks. But in this case of painting, my folks never encourage me toward painting because they never knew I was a painter."

Catherine laughed. "You have lost me. I thought you had said you got into painting because of your mother."

"You thought correctly," Julian quickly said. "However, it wasn't because my mother encouraged me. It was because of my mother's death," he said and paused as the room seemed suddenly quiet.

Catherine sat looking at him speechless. She was lost for my words since his statement had stunned her.

Julian nodded. "Yes, it was because of my mother's death. I started painting one week after my mother died. I had never picked up a paint brush before that day."

"Can you recall what made you decide to pick up a paint brush that day?" Catherine curiously asked.

"Yes, I can recall very well; and the best way I can describe it. I had this huge urge to paint my mother's face so I wouldn't forget her."

"I guess you had to go shopping," Catherine said.

"You're right. I went shopping and purchased the paint and supplies I needed," Julian humbly explained. "I never will forget that day. I had a need to paint all kind of images of my mother; and by doing so, it consoled me and made me feel close to my mother."

"Thanks for sharing," Catherine softly said. "That's a beautiful unique story of how you had never painted in your life. But suddenly because of your urge to pain your mother, you became an astonishing extraordinary painter."

Julian nodded. "I guess you're right. My painting abilities have surpassed all my imagination. But the bare truth is, the painting eased my grieving and helped me tremendously to cope with my mother's death. I was thirty-eight at the time. That's been over twenty years ago."

Chapter Eleven

    Catherine and Julian continued to discuss his extraordinary painting ability, when suddenly it hit Catherine like a hard punch in the stomach when it dawned on her that Julian was grieving the loss of his relationship with Mildred. She figured that's why he had decided to spend time at their lake house away from everyone to paint in privacy. Suddenly all her enthusiasm sunk deep inside of her and she wondered why she had even bothered to drive up to the lake house to visit him. Clearly, he was still very much in love with Mildred Ross, she thought to herself as she looked toward the floor. Then she looked toward Julian. "I get it now." She quickly stood up from the sofa and grabbed her briefcase. "I think I'll just leave."
    He firmly stared at her and pointed to her seat. He didn't want her to leave. "Catherine, please be seated and let's talk."
    Catherine shrugged her shoulders. "What is there to talk about?"
    Julian held out both hands. "You bothered to drive all this way just to pitch Angela Taylor's wishes. I'm not interested, so now you're ready to hop in your car and leave?" he seriously asked. "Catherine, give me a break," he snapped. "I tried to explain to you why I'm not interested in selling any of my paintings. My dead mother engrossed me into this hobby that turned into a miracle of sorts. I wouldn't feel right selling any of the paintings. I don't want financial gain from my mother's demise," he firmly explained. "Besides, why are you so hell bent on pushing me toward an artistic career that I have no desire for!"
    Catherine thought better of her hastily decision and took her seat back on the sofa. "I think you do have a desire for it. It's all you do in your spare time," Catherine said. "Besides, actions speak louder than words. All your extra time seem to be consumed with painting."

"Catherine, I don't deny that. But it's just a hobby that takes my mind off of other problems."

"I get that," Catherine firmly exclaimed.

Julian didn't comment to her remark as he continued. "It's solely for relaxation. If I had to do it to earn a living, it would be like work to me and I wouldn't want to do it at all." He shook his head. "I really don't get you, Miss Catherine Franklin. When I was interested in you, I couldn't get you to give me the time of day. Now my head is somewhere else, and you're suddenly my best friend interested in my artistic future. Why is that?" He held out both arms.

"You have an incredible talent and I think you should use it, especially for the kind of money you can obtain from having your paintings sold by Taylor Gowns," Catherine strongly stressed with an irritated undertone. "So tell me Julian. What's the problem?"

"I just told you the problem. It wouldn't feel right making money from something I started doing to get over the loss of my mother."

"Julian, Veronica thinks I'm not put together too tight. But what you just said doesn't make an ounce of sense to me. Think about it. I'm sure if your mother was still alive she would be the first to tell you to make good with your God given talent. Mothers want the best for their children, and I'm sure your mother would want you to succeed with your paintings. But you know your mother better than I. What is your gut telling you? She would say reach for the stars wouldn't she? Don't you think so?"

"My mother was as good as the days are long and you're right. If she could she would say go for it, son?" He nodded with a distant look in his eyes.

"Great! Problem solved if your mother wouldn't mind." Catherine held up both hands. "Now, Mr. Julian Bartlett, there is no problem."

He looked at Catherine with serious eyes and nodded. "You couldn't be more wrong. There still is unquestionably a problem."

"Okay, Julian. What's the problem now?"

"I'll tell you, Miss Catherine Franklin, what the problem is now?" He snapped irritated. "The problem is, this is my business and I would like to keep it that way! If that's not too much to ask?" He stared seriously at her.

Catherine was speechless and not sure what to make of his attitude.

"Listen, Catherine. Don't get me wrong. I'm not trying to be rude and I know I have an attitude. But it's not aimed at you. I'm just not having a good day and on top of a bad day, you're adding on things that I could care less about."

"Well, excuse me for caring."

"Listen, Catherine. In my spare time I do love to paint. But as I told you it's only for the relaxation of it and how it helps me to forget things I don't want to remember. The peace of mind and freedom. Okay? Not financial gain!"

"I'm sorry, Julian, if you think I'm trying to be too pushy, and maybe I am. But I can see your point. I just feel you're being stubborn not giving it a chance."

Julian narrowed his eyes at her as if he could see right through her. "Once and for all, Catherine Franklin, when will you get it through that head of yours that I'm not interested in what Angela Taylor is offering?"

"You haven't even heard what she's offering," Catherine pointed out. "Of all things, we can agree on! I'm sure you like money, don't you Julian?" Catherine asked, and then answered for him. "Well, of course you do. The only thing that would keep you uninterested in trying to make more money is if you were already independently wealthy like my sister-in-law and four nephews. But if you're like me, you're not."

Something about her statement made him a bit more willing to listen. "Okay, Catherine," he said, "What exactly is Angela Taylor offering me?"

"One thing I know for sure is that she's going to offer you a lot of money."

He narrowed his eyes and raised an eyebrow with a slight smile. "When you say a lot of money. What kind of figure are you referring to?" he asked. "Besides, did you hear Angela Taylor say she would offer me a lot of money?"

Catherine didn't immediately answer Julian as she smiled and nodded.

"You are nodding at me but I cannot read your mind. Did Angela Taylor say anything at all to you in terms of the kind of money she's willing to dish out for my paintings?" he seriously asked.

"No, Julian, I didn't actually hear her say anything in terms of what she would pay you for your paintings. But she's extremely interested and want your paintings like crazy. She's filthy rich and I'm sure she's willing to pay you well. She's the one who told me they're worth a fortune."

Julian nodded. "They are worth a fortune. Therefore, anything under $250,000 for each paintings is out of the question," he said.

Catherine looked at him stunned. She figured he had to be kidding and was purposely not taking him serious. She shook her head and waved both hands. "You are impossible, Julian Bartlett!"

"Catherine, you know I'm just kidding around with you about a quarter of a million for each painting." He looked her straight in the eyes. "How could you have taken me serious for a second? You know I'm not about that, but I have to be on the level. I'm not kidding around about not being the least interested in selling my work. So let's drop this conversation this second. Enough is enough!" He leaned his back against the chair. "As I said, I'm having a bad day and it would be good to hear something pleasant for a change." He paused for a second and then blurted out. "I'll be straight with you. Mildred really pulled the rug from under me when she called it quits. I was living an illusion thinking we were building toward something solid. But here I am at your lake house trying to get Mildred Ross out of my system."

"She's a nice lady," Catherine admitted.

"I think I can hear a but coming," Julian said.

"You're right, and but is coming," Catherine admitted.

"Okay, let's hear it. What do you really think of Mildred?"

"You don't want to hear what I really think of that woman."

"Yes, I want to hear. You said, she's a nice lady. But apparently you didn't actually mean that compliment."

Catherine nodded. "Yes, I meant it. I know Mildred is a nice lady. But I'm never going to feel warm toward her and I think you know why."

"Yes, I can assume it has to do with Antonio involvement with her."

"Yes, Julian. You're correct about that; and the fact that Mildred Ross comes with too much baggage. How did you ever get tangled up with her in the first place?" Catherine asked. "Antonio would be alive today if he had stayed clear of her."

"Catherine, you sound a bit jealous. It's not nice to place Antonio's death on Mildred's head. But I guess its all water under the bridge. The lady is no longer interested in a relationship with me and I need to move on. You made yourself clear when you came to my house and said you would like to try again. However, with me being wrapped up into another woman, how is that supposed to work?" He gave her a serious stare. "But who knows, maybe we'll have a fighting chance even if I'm thinking of Mildred."

"Julian, that's not funny. Why would you say something like that?"

"It puts us on equal footing and level the playing field since I'm sure you would be thinking of Antonio Armani if he was still alive," he seriously relayed. "That is the reason why we couldn't make it. You couldn't get over the man. He's dead and buried but he singlehandedly ended our relationship. You may not admit it. But it was quite obvious while we were dating since all you wanted to talk about was Antonio Armani. Therefore, that's why I can assume that you were too preoccupied with thoughts of him to commit to me at the time."

Julian's words stabbed at Catherine and she resented him mentioning Antonio. He knew Antonio was her one sore spot that she didn't want to relive and think of how foolish she had been in the past. She rubbed the back of her neck, screaming inside over what he had just said. She dared him to rub her nose in the past by bringing up Antonio's name? But she couldn't really say anything since she knew he was right.

After a bit of silence, not aware of her building anger, Julian pointed to the pitcher of iced tea, which was sitting on the end table next to his chair. "Why don't we have a glass of iced tea, and then if you really feel you need to, you can finish telling me about Angela Taylor's offer?" He said, softly.

"So, you don't mind listening?"

"I guess you're right. It won't hurt me to just listen." He stood from his seat and poured iced tea into the one glass sitting there and passed it to Catherine.

"But why now?" Catherine asked. "You just said yourself it would be a waste of time, especially if you're still dead set against the idea."

"I know I said that," Julian said as he headed toward the kitchen to fetch another glass. "But I think I have been a bit rude to you. You drove all this way and I shouldn't allow my sour mood to make me so acidity toward you just because my emotions are all over the place," he apologetically said, as he stepped back into the living room with a glass in hand.

He lifted the pitcher and poured iced tea into the glass and then took a seat in his chair. "You think things are going fine and without any indications that they are not, then bam you're out of someone's life!" He lifted the glass to his mouth and took a sip of iced tea.

"Julian, are you still referring to what happened with Mildred Ross? When you make a statement like that. I'm not sure if you're referring to the end of your relationship with Mildred or how things ended with us."

"Does it really matter?" he said calmly. "You both gave me the boot. But enough of that. Regarding the issue at hand. I have had a change of mind about never selling any of my paintings; and now I'll listen and try to be more understanding," he said reassuringly.

"It's good to have an open mind to the possibility. But I must say I'm surprised you have had a change of heart so quickly." Catherine lifted her glass to her mouth and took a sip of iced tea. "I'm not sure if you really know what you want right now," Catherine griped.

"You could be right. But at least I have decided to at least consider it." He turned his glass up to his mouth and finished the iced tea before he lowered the glass. "However, Catherine, put yourself in my spot for a moment.

If someone were pushing you toward something that you were not interested in, how would you react? So just calm down."

"Julian, I was calm until you brought up Antonio's name."

"Okay, I apologize for that," he humbly said. "If you could see things from my prospective you would be able to relate. Antonio Armani is dead but yet he holds your heart along with Mildred's. How do you think I feel? The two women in this town that I tried to date were both stolen from me by a dead man."

Suddenly Catherine had an attitude, upset that he had brought up Antonio's name yet again, she felt just to spite her.

"Don't do me any favors, Julian Bartlett!" Catherine snapped.

"Don't do you any favors? You wanted me to listen. I didn't listen. You got upset. Now I'm saying I'll listen, and you're telling me not to do you any favors. I'm just trying to be polite," he said with a hint of anger in this voice.

"Well don't be polite!" Catherine waved her hand. "Be a jerk the way Antonio was! At least Antonio didn't pretend to be a nice guy. He was who he was," Catherine angrily fussed. "You can't fool me Julian Bartlett."

He frowned, folding his arms. "I don't know what you want, Catherine."

She glanced down toward the floor, shaking her head. Then her head came up with a quick snap and she hopped off the sofa. "I'll tell you what I want!" She shouted. "I want to get away from you! Now!" She angrily snapped. "I apologize for any inconvenience I may have caused you, Mr. Bartlett! I'll just be on my way!" Catherine griped, grabbed her briefcase and purse from the coffee table and was halfway to the door before he hopped out of his chair to stop her.

"Okay, if that's the way you feel, maybe you should just leave," he firmly stated. "Please don't bother coming back!" His words rolled out sharp as nails.

Chapter Twelve

Catherine was very upset but deep down she really didn't want to leave as she headed across the room toward the door. He rushed to her and grabbed her left arm and pulled her just inches from him. She looked up at Julian with burning anger in her eyes and she could see anger in his eyes. But before she could jerk from his grip, suddenly out of the blue his mouth came down on her's in an urgent demanding kiss. Before she could analyze her feelings of whether she wanted to be in his arms or not, he released her lips and jerked away. He turned his back to her and shook his head.

"Julian, what was that all about? You yell at me, then grab me and kiss me. What's going on with you?" Catherine dropping her briefcase to the floor.

"Catherine Franklin, I'll tell you what's up with that?" He turned back around to face her, raised both arms and stared at her accusingly. "You are! It's been a hell of a long time since I have allowed you or anyone else to get under my skin. But in a short time, you put me through some changes when you made me think you wanted a relationship and suddenly you didn't. Now, I'm going through the same hell again."

"Julian, I apologize for my attitude right now; and I cannot apologize enough for my behavior before. It wasn't intentional. I was just stuck in a rut that I couldn't get free of. In the process I destroyed our relationship." Catherine took a step toward him and placed a hand on his arm. "Please, don't be upset and continue to hold animosity against me for how I treated you," Catherine pleaded, and then tiptoed up and pressed her lips to his mouth in a gentle, forgiving kiss. "Please, Julian, is there any way we can start over?"

Julian studied her face looking up at his, the bitterness gradually faded from his features. "I'm not upset with you, Catherine," he mumbled, gently pressing her to his chest, his arms holding her tight. "Not anymore."

Catherine threw her arms around him. She kissed him on the neck. She discovered that the feel of Julian was warm and smooth and it felt comforting to be held by him. She felt right where she wanted to be.

Julian put both hands under her chin and raised her face toward his.

"I am sorry, Catherine, that I said I wanted you to leave and not return. You have to know I didn't mean that." He kissed her tenderly and that kiss seemed no less than incredible in the wake of their recent argument.

Then, as if the recent events were no more than a faded memory of long ago, they surrendered to each other passion and desire to be in each other's arms. Their anger had instantly subsided as if it had never been there. She was thinking how wonderfully soothing his hands felt as he ran them up and down her arms and across her shoulders. He held her and pulled her closer.

What Catherine felt for Julian was passion in the purest form. It was the kind she had never known. Being next to him she had no real control! The fresh intoxicating scent of his cologne somehow heightened her desire as the softness of his face rubbed against hers.

As Julian slowly released Catherine's lips, her mind slowly focused back to earth as her body brushed against his. He was both the cause and reason. It was an endless circle that had no beginning or end. Her mind attempted to think, but she felt consumed with mindless desire that he had created in her. Her legs seemed like a mass of jelly, making her feel like a feather.

Catherine felt starved for love and passion. She had never had real love and real passion in her life. She was aware of Julian's mental attachment to Mildred Ross. But she wanted to be with him if just for one night. Her overwhelming desire for him surprised her. It was like it was unpredictable and could lie dormant just beneath the surface, and then like a flower, bloom into life. Then, too, it could blossom and fade just as quickly. But the essence of desire was spellbinding and mesmerizing when it came in the form of an amazing man like Julian Bartlett. And apparently, Julian felt the same passions stirring in him. Without releasing Catherine from his embrace, he sat down in his chair and held Catherine on his lap. His hands gently caressed her waist and up and down her sides, warming the skin beneath the material of her blouse. Then suddenly Catherine was seated in the chair and Julian was on his knees in front of her.

Catherine's arms found their way around his neck where she held him tight for a while before moving her hands slowly down his back. And as her hands journeyed down his back to his sides, she discovered a sensitive spot that seemed to make him slightly tremble as she gently caressed and stroked him while melting from his touch. He was everything that she felt a man should be. He was like a cool breeze, a breath of fresh air, and the embodiment of a real man. His strength was solid and she felt the desires in her scream out for the desires in him. He breathed excitement into her with his own breath. His mouth left a trail from her mouth to the center of her neck. Each gentle kiss breathtaking beyond Catherine's imagination. She didn't draw back or try to stop him when he started unbuttoning her purple blouse. She held her breath as each button was removed from its socket. Julian smiled as his hands slightly trembled as he slowly unbuttoned her blouse. Then he kissed her skin and made a trail down the side of her neck to her shoulder.

Delighting in his caress as he delighted in caressing her, his fingers inched their way under the elastic band of her white bra, pulling the bra away from her skin as he caressed her.

Catherine asked herself. "Is Julian what I want? Can I settle for a man who is completely hung up on another woman? But the man and the larger than life feelings he aroused in her seemed inseparable.

"Julian?" she softly said. His name brought excitement deep in her.

"I want you, Catherine! I want all of you! Do you feel the same?" He asked in a manly hoarse voice as he continued to caress her.

Catherine realized she had to think clearly no matter the excitement.

"Yes, Julian. I feel the same," she softly said.

The moment came that she had half feared, half prayed for. Julian pulled her closer as he kissed her against the neck. He was gentle with her at first, but he quickly became more demanding as his own excitement grew. Catherine held his shoulders, bracing herself to him as he kissed her.

"Oh! Julian, what are you doing to me?" There was a slight hesitancy in her voice as her hands slipped inside his shirt and touched the firmness of his solid chest. To touch him felt so natural.

"Don't be afraid to feel Catherine," he softly whispered, his hands pushing her blouse off of her shoulders as he kissed her there.

Catherine wondered how she could do anything but feel when his touch thrilled her deeply. She felt Julian was her last chance at love. She felt like she was going insane with desperate desire for him.

Julian wanted her and she couldn't deny wanting him too? It was nothing like the anxious feeling she felt back in high school for Antonio Armani and Jack Coleman. His touch felt right. Her mind and body felt comfortable with him. Something was happening to her that she did not fully understand. But she did understand how special he was to her, and equally special were the emotions he had unleashed in her. She thought how from the moment she met him, he had always been special to her. Now with Antonio never returning, Catherine desperately wanted to win Julian back.

"I'm not afraid, Julian," she said, as her eyes never left his.

He stood to his feet, took both hands and pulled her to hers into a gentle embrace. He tenderly held her in his arms, his embrace felt like a blanket of protection from the outside world. And his kiss felt like a promise of all that still awaited them. A kiss that went far beyond anything she had ever dreamt a kiss could be. His mouth was making love to hers, slowly and deliberately. She knew what might come next. Julian wanted them to make love. It seemed the most natural thing being close to him. But she knew his passion for her was only about sex and not about love.

Julian took a seat in one of the side chairs and pulled Catherine down onto his lap. He kissed her softly. Suddenly they were forced back to reality by the sound of a car engine pulling into the driveway.

"Don't you think we should see who's out there?" Catherine asked as part of her was still lingering in the warmth of the passion that had sizzled between them. It wasn't something to be shaken off easily.

"Why should I?" He said. "I don't want visitors and don't expect any."

"I know, but just the same someone just drove up." Catherine hopped off his lap, testing her legs before letting go of his hand.

Julian stood and their eyes locked with each other, looking at each other for a moment in silence. Their silence meant they were both sorry about the rude behavior they had displayed toward each other. They stood face to face, as Catherine glanced down and realized in her worked up state that the first two buttons on her purple blouse were unbuttoned. Her body still tingled from his touch and his eyes melted into hers as if he longed to reach out and pull her back into his arms to ease the burning passion that she had stirred in him. His desire and his need for her were clearly noticeable as yearning poured from his eyes. Then, as if by some mutual accord, the adrenaline between them was allowed to ease, and the passion to fade.

"Catherine, I should see who just pulled into the driveway."

He didn't want to step outside and deal with who had pulled into the driveway. His eyes told her that he wanted to stay put, to take her in his arms and make them both forget that anything existed outside of the lake house. Nevertheless, reality had a way of intruding as she straighten out her long violet skirt and buttoned up her top, stepping away from him, allowing him to head outside to tend to the visitor.

Chapter Thirteen

Julian walked back through the front door after a short while with his visitor. Catherine had managed to freshen up a bit. She had brushed her hair and reapplied her makeup. She looked refreshed and untouched but the desire for him still glowed in her eyes.

She smiled standing near the fireplace as he closed the door and headed across the room. "Is your visitor gone?" Catherine asked.

Julian nodded. "Yes, he's on his way. He was an insurance agent who recently moved to the area. He got lost off of Algonquin Road and ended up on Country Lane Road. He said he was relieved to see the cottage on the hill and our vehicles parked out front. He had really gotten shaken up. I directed him back to Algonquin Road," Julian explained.

"Good you got him back on the right road. Maybe next time he'll invest in a GPS," Catherine grumbled. "How can he expect to sell insurance if he can't find his way around?" Catherine griped.

"Give the guy a break. He just moved to the area," Julian stressed.

"That's more reason why he should have invested in a GPS if he expect to sell insurance in a new area," she dryly grumbled.

"Okay, that's it. I know you are not upset with that stranger for getting lost," Julian firmly said. "Before I stepped outside everything was good between us. What happened in those few minutes that put you in a tailspin?"

"I guess the fact that things were good between us. But I'm very clear on how you feel and what you want; and I know it's not me!" Catherine sadly said.

"Catherine, where is this coming from? We have crossed this bridge. We are friends." He held up both hands. "Yes, I still have it bad for Mildred but she isn't losing any sleep over me. It will take some time to get her out of my system. But in the meantime, we can be friends. Besides, I do enjoy your company."

Catherine looked at him and smiled. "I enjoy your company to. But it is getting late, Julian. I think I should get my things together and be on my way back to Franklin House. I don't want to get lost and end up on the wrong road like that insurance agent," she said laughingly.

Julian smiled. "Of course that wouldn't happen since your car practically drives itself with a state of the act GPS system built in. So you need to come up with another excuse for trying to take off."

"No really. It is getting late and I think I should head home."

Julian looked as though he was trying to understand the message he read in her eyes. "You're driving back to Franklin House this evening?"

"My plans were to drive back," Catherine said.

"I thought differently," Julian told her.

"What do you mean you thought differently? How could you have thought differently? You have made it clear that we can only be friends. You are thinking of another woman. Therefore, why should I stay over?"

"That's true I would like for us to be friends and I'm still very much emotionally attached to Mildred. But I would still very much like for you to stay over. I have enjoyed your company tremulously. I know I came here to be alone to clear my head and think. But once you leave I'll be more than alone. I will be lonely," he admitted. "So, Catherine, what do you say? I would love your company for the weekend, why not stay here? If you were wondering about the sleeping arrangements. You're welcomed to one of the guestrooms." He smiled.

"Julian, if I spend the weekend here with you. That would be interfering with the relaxation and peace you have planned for yourself. It will defeat your purpose for renting this place and getting away."

"I mean it, Catherine. It would please me very much if you stayed," Julian said in a sincere voice with his eyes focused on hers. "So, go ahead and call up your folks and tell them you'll staying here at the lake house with me?"

While thinking over his offer, Catherine realized if she did stay she wouldn't have to listen to Veronica constantly discussing what a mistake she made by messing things up with Julian. On the flipside, she would be tortured being so close to Julian. Plus, she felt she would be tempted to bring up the subject of the opportunity Angela Taylor has on the table for him. Catherine felt Julian was greatly mistaken if he thought she had given up on the idea of securing him as a client for Angela Taylor.

There was a glow in Julian's eyes when she turned to face him. "You have talked me into it. I gladly accept your invitation," she quickly said. "But I don't think I'll be making that call to Franklin House about staying here."

"Why not? I think you need to call home so they won't be worried."

Catherine nodded. "You are probably right at that. I'll give Veronica a call before we retire for the night."

"You should probably call home now," he strongly suggested.

Catherine shook her head. "I'm not going to call right now. If I call Veronica will want to know the status of our relationship; and assume we are back together if I tell her I'm staying the weekend with you. Therefore, I'll just stay here and let her know tomorrow how I spent my weekend."

He held out both arms. "If you think that's best? But I don't see why you can't just say you're spending the weekend here."

"I just told you, Julian. I don't want to get roped into a long conversation into explaining our relationship to my Veronica."

"Relationship?" He smiled. "We have a relationship?"

"That's what I mean. If it's confusing to you, just imagine how confusing it'll be to Veronica?"

He nodded. "I guess you have a point."

"Of course, I have a point," Catherine agreed. "I just can't casually call her up and say I'm spending the weekend with you. They all know we're no longer dating each other."

"Seems like Veronica and your nephews really looks out for you. You are blessed to be a part of such a devoted family," he acknowledged.

Catherine nodded. "I know I'm blessed and I love my family. But all I wanted in life was the same as most others. I wanted someone to love me that I loved in return. I wanted my own home and a family of my own. But I have scratched all those things from my list. All of my life dreams passed me by."

"I'm a believer of not really scratching things off a list if they mean so much," Julian said. "I believe in fighting for a dream."

"Fighting is good and I have fought all my life. Therefore, I think it's good to know when to stop. But I'm not really complaining. I'm just sharing with you. Besides, I'm not really hurting financially, but I'm living under my sister-in-law's roof, enjoying life off her wealth and the love of her children."

"Catherine, I know you said you're not complaining. But it sort of sounds like you are. From my viewpoint, you're living well."

"Julian, you're right. I am living well. But you don't get what I'm saying."

"If I don't get what you're saying. Explain yourself," he softly suggested.

"I know I have it good and I'm blessed. But I pictured my life differently when I was a young college student."

"How did you picture your life?" Julian asked. "Coming from a powerful rich family. I'm sure your parents set goals that they wanted you to achieve."

Catherine smiled. "You're exactly right. My parents did set impossible goals that I knew I would never meet."

"Do tell."

"They wanted me to be a doctor, and although I finally mastered mathematics, I was never business or career driven. Even my folks knew that when I was still a teenager. But they kept pushing me to attend medical school. They desperately wanted me to make something of my life that they could be proud of. But I had no drive for a career and just simply wanted to be loved," Catherine sincerely explained.

"Well, we all want to be loved; and most desire a career," Julian said.

"I know. But I was always detached from those kinds of determined thoughts about climbing the ladder and having many treasures."

Julian laughed and shook his head. "I guess a determination for having something in life would evade someone like you, Catherine."

"Julian, should I be offended?" Catherine drew an attitude from his statement. "What do you mean by that?"

"I'm just pointing out that a determination for a successful career possibly would evade someone who's already living in the lap of luxury," Julian explained. "But I'm sure there are many rich people who strive for a successful career and strive for more riches," Julian thoughtfully explained.

Catherine nodded. "Just like my family. I didn't strive for success. But my brother, Ryan, was very career driven. But I always just wanted someone to love me and a family of my own," Catherine solemnly reflected. "That wasn't asking for much I thought."

Julian shook his head. "Not asking for much. I think it's the single most thing sought after in this lifetime."

"Well, most people end up with it," Catherine quickly replied. "I don't know what I did in life that children and a family of my own would pass me by. I have basically been alone all my life, chasing love that was always an illusion. Even the love from my parents was an illusion. I couldn't live up to their standards so they quashed their love."

"I'm sure your parents loved you," Julian assured her. "Plus, I know Veronica is dating Charles Taylor at this time. But she was alone for twenty years. Catherine, you're not the only person lonely in the world."

"Veronica was never alone. She always had her sons. Besides that, before Ryan died they were happy and shared enough love to last a lifetime."

Julian nodded with solemn eyes. "I think I get your point."

"Good, now if only you could see my Angela Taylor's point." Catherine smiled. "Just teasing. "But I'm warning you right now, Julian Bartlett, I'm not through with you yet." Catherine shook her finger at him. "I'm sure I can still make you see reason. If I have to, I'll keep you up all night showing you where you are wrong about not pursuing a painting career."

"You might keep me up all night Miss Franklin, but I can guarantee you that my paintings will have nothing to do with it," he said in a sensuous voice.

"We'll see about that." Catherine smiled. "Look, Julian. I'm serious but I'm also somewhat teasing. I realize I came on too strong when I first arrived forcing Angela Taylor's offer on you. I'm sorry about the way I carried on."

"It's okay. We both carried on."

"I know, but I would like to make it up to you."

"Okay, how do you suppose to do that?"

"Dinner is on me." Catherine held out both arms.

"That will work. Your apology and a meal are both accepted," he said, smiling with both arms pointed toward the kitchen. "Help yourself to the kitchen. I have made myself quite familiar with most of the surroundings. Therefore, if you are looking for anything in the kitchen and not sure where to look. Let me know and I'll tell you where to find whatever you're after in the kitchen if you have forgotten where everything is."

"Okay! It's settled." Catherine cheerfully said. "I'm making you dinner."

He quickly cut her off and placed one finger on her lips. "No, I need to correct you in your oversight. You'll make us dinner; as in the both of us."

"Yes, I will make us a wonderful dinner."

"We need to check the refrigerator," Julian quickly said. "I didn't stop for any grocery. I'm not sure what's here in the refrigerator," he told her.

"There's no need to check the refrigerator." Catherine shook her head. "I plan to leave here and go shopping for our meal."

"You plan to drive somewhere and shop for grocery for our dinner?"

"Yes. I want to go shopping and pick up something wonderful and delicious." Catherine headed toward the front door. "Dinner is on me and I plan to make it a meal you won't soon forget," Catherine excitedly told him.

"No, wait a minute, Catherine. I appreciate the thought. But I don't want you to do that."

Catherine smiled. "But I want to do it."

"Please, Catherine. I don't want you to leave and go through the trouble. We can order take-out. Maybe a pizza or something," he strongly suggested.

"Julian, I want to do this. I won't be long," she assured him. "It makes me happy to do this." She glanced at her gold Gucci watch. "We still have a few hours before dark. I'll drive into town, pick up the things I need and be back before you have time to miss me," Catherine said, hopeful he would agree.

He smiled and nodded. "Okay, if that's what you really want to do." He gently grabbed her arm. "But I would prefer you didn't leave. As I mentioned. We could easily order take-out."

Catherine shook her head. "No take-outs for us. This is a meal I plan to cook on my own." She smiled as she hurried toward the front door.

Julian smiled. "Okay, if you insist. But hurry back. My stomach feels like I haven't eaten in days," he said as he watched the door close behind her.

Julian was smiling as he took a seat on the sofa and grabbed his face with both hands just staring out into space. Catherine presence had stirred a lot of old memories in his mind. Most of his memories of his time with her were good. But many of his memories of her were painful and disappointing. Yet, he allowed himself to go deep into thought of the time when he felt strongly for Catherine. He crossed both legs on the coffee table as he relaxed his head back on the cushions of the sofa. Then he placed both hands behind his head as he stared up at the ceiling. He was smiling to himself looking up as he recited in his mind the poem that Catherine had inspired in him during the brief time they had dated. He wasn't a poet and realized the poetry wasn't even a good poem. But during his short courtship to Catherine he had treasured the piece of writing, and had read and recited the poem in his mind numerous times before he gave up hope of a relationship with Catherine.

Catherine the Unreachable Rose

Catherine is that unreachable rose that drifted into my life one day.
Then she swiftly drifted out of my life one night.
I wonder will she ever know what she had come to mean to me.
As I fell hard for someone that at first I couldn't see.
Catherine is that unreachable rose whose eyes were a sight to behold.
I wonder will she ever know she was the one I wanted to hold.
Catherine is that unreachable rose that faded into the night.
I wonder will she ever know how much she brought me light.

Chapter Fourteen

  Catherine rushed across the porch smiling, down the steps and across the yard to her white Mercedes. Once inside her car, she inhaled sharply and then started the engine and headed out of the driveway as her smile felt glued to her face. Her thoughts were centered on the wonderful possibility of another chance with Julian. Deep down she knew she wanted him back as she drove toward Country Lane Road at a steady pace. Her thoughts shifted for a moment when it dawned on her as she admired the tree lined country road that she had no idea where she would stop to pick up their dinner. She had just promised Julian that she would make dinner. But making a home cooked meal from scratch would be out of the question, since it dawned on her that she wasn't a good cook. Therefore, to save herself a lot of embarrassment, she figured it would make more sense to stop and purchase their home cooked meal.

  After a twenty minute drive down Country Lane Road far away from the lake house on the outskirts of Barrington Hills, Catherine noticed the upscale Royalty Seating restaurant that she and Veronica had dined at together a few times. She stopped and ordered them each a New York Strip Steak dinner along with mashed potatoes and fried green beans and two mixed green salads.

  For the first time in a long time, Catherine's thoughts were filled with excitement and she felt happy inside. The dinner plans she had made with Julian meant everything and she wanted everything to be perfect. Soon, she was turning her car in the direction of the lake house and arrived back before dark. She killed her engine and stepped out of the car with the two bags of food. She noticed the bottle of wine that she had brought from Franklin House when she decided to visit Julian. It was still in the car on the front floor passenger's side.

Before she could make her way up the walkway, her eyes lit up as Julian stepped his tall, slender frame out on the porch. He was smiling and the sight of him literally took her breath away for a moment. He had apparently made good use of the time she was away. He was now dressed in a pair of casual black slacks and a red shirt.

"Something smells good. Is this my home cooked dinner?" He teased.

Catherine smiled and pointed toward the car. "There's a fine bottle of wine on the front floor passenger's side," Catherine said with a big smile on her face, hurrying inside past him.

She headed straight for the kitchen; and after placing the two bags on the kitchen counter, she stepped back to the front door. "Julian, could you also grab my overnight case off the back seat?" she kindly asked.

He glanced around smiling as he grabbed the handle of the car door and saluted to her with his left hand. "Your request is my command. One overnight case off the back seat coming right up."

He fetched her overnight case and the bottle of wine as she stepped back into the kitchen. She took the containers of food out of the bags and placed them on the kitchen counter. After doing so, stepped into the living. Julian grabbed her overnight case and showed her down the short hallway of the lake house to one of the three bedrooms. He opened the door and placed the overnight case inside the soft green room. He didn't step into the room; he left her alone to unpack her things.

Momentary Catherine returned to the kitchen and was pleasantly surprised to find that Julian had draped the table with a white tablecloth and set the table with precious rose border China plates, silverware, and a pair of 24kt gold candlesticks with two rose candles.

"Julian, the table looks wonderful." Catherine held out both arms. "What a nice surprise. Are those your candlesticks or do they belong to the lake house?" she asked.

Opening a drawer at the counter, he nodded. "Those expensive gems belong to your family."

"They're elegant and beautiful," Catherine said, lifting one, examining it closer, and noticing the 24kt gold engraving. "Being here with you is almost like being here for the first time. I cannot recall ever seeing these candle sticks before," she said, smiling.

"Thank you," he said, placing the two matching candles in the center of the table. Then he gave her a small smile and pointed toward the fireplace.

"Take that lighter off the fireplace mantel and light the candles, if you like," he suggested.

"I would love to." Catherine stepped toward the fireplace. "Mr. Julian Bartlett. I never knew you were so romantic."

He smiled. "Well, I don't know about all that. I just thought something a little special was in order!" He nodded.

Catherine smiled. "Something a little special?"

"Yes." He smiled. "Since you went through much trouble to get us this nice meal."

"It was no trouble." Catherine held out both hands.

He nodded and smiled. "Be modest if you like, but just the same it was generous of you to put yourself out like this." He paused, looking at her.

"Really, it was no trouble at all. I enjoyed every single minute. I wanted to do it."

"Here you are my guest, and I know we're no longer in a relationship. Nevertheless, I should have treated you and taken you out for dinner. You would have liked that, right?"

"Yes, that would have been nice too."

"Yes, it would have been nice and the gentleman thing to do. But instead I allowed you to jump in your car and drive into town to buy dinner for us." He reached in his pocket and pulled out his wallet and started looking through the money section.

Catherine felt anxious and her instincts told her he was about to hand her money toward the food she had purchased. "What are you doing?" she asked.

He didn't answer, just carefully looked through his wallet and then pulled out a hundred dollar bill and handed it to her. "Here take this."

"Julian, why are you handing me money? I told you dinner was on me, remember?"

Julian nodded and smiled. "I know what you said, Catherine. But take the money."

"But it's my treat and I said I would treat you to dinner."

"Listen, Catherine. I appreciate the gesture. But you are my guest and it actually should be my treat. But before you get any misconceptions about me. I want you to know that I'm not some narrow-minded man who's against women's right and I'm not some chauvinism jerk. And in some other setting if you offered to buy dinner like for my birthday or some other occasion, I would be just fine with it. But at this point, with you as my guest. It doesn't feel right sticking you with the bill. Besides, you drove all the way up here to the lake house to visit me. I just wouldn't feel comfortable allowing you to foot the bill for our dinner. So, please take the money."

"Okay, sure, if you insist."

"Catherine, of course, I insist. Take it and I'll feel more like a gentleman."

"Julian, of course I'll take the money. I get your point as well," she said as she took the hundred dollar bill and placed it in her pocket. "Julian, what part of dinner is on me that you don't get?" Catherine teased.

"I thought you just said you get my point?"

Catherine laughed. "I do get your point. I was just teasing you."

"Okay, but listen. Your offer was a sweet gesture and I appreciate it. It's kind of neat to think of someone else spending money on me for a change. But really, in this case, why should you have to pay for dinner? You are my guest and as I mentioned. You took the trouble of driving up here. Not to mention you are dealing with some issues yourself."

Catherine nodded and smiled. "Thanks again. You're a pretty swell guy. I didn't expect it and it didn't dawn on me that you would pay for dinner anyway."

He cut her off. "It's a lot you don't know about me Catherine. I wasn't born rich and privileged. But I have always been a gentleman. Besides, you don't have an income."

Catherine nodded. "Technically that's true. But I'm also not hurting for cash."

"That may be true. However, I think you mentioned to me once about how Veronica limits your access to the house budget funds," Julian reminded her.

Catherine nodded. "She does but not in the way you think."

"I don't think I follow," he said.

"It's true that she limits my access. But only the amount of funds that I can withdraw within a twenty-four hour period."

"Okay, I see. That make sense. Of course," he said.

"Yes, it does make good smart sense. It wouldn't be practical for Veronica and my nephews to set up my financial access any other way. Being her sister-in-law and their Aunt doesn't make me immune to ripping off the family fortunate."

Julian smiled. "The greed for and the love of money has destroyed a lot of families." He laughed. "I know you are joking around but what you said is very true."

"But just for the record. I would rather fall to my death than to ever do a single thing that would dishonor my dead brother and his sons. Taking a dime more than I'm trusted to take from the house budget funds would be doing just that."

"I noticed that you didn't mention Veronica."

"What do you mean?" Catherine asked.

"Well, you just said you would rather fall to your death before dishonoring your brother and nephews but you didn't mention your sister-in-law."

"I didn't mention her because I don't have the same bond with her as I do with my nephews and as I had with my brother," Catherine explained. "She has been good to me; and before you asked me out or fell for Mildred Ross, I know you were interested in Veronica. But seriously, Julian. As much as I appreciate everything Veronica has done and is still doing for me, I wouldn't call her an honorable person."

Julian looked at her with surprised eyes. "You wouldn't call her an honorable person? I'm surprised to hear you say that about Veronica. She seems honorable to me."

Catherine smiled. "I figured you would think so. And maybe you're right. Maybe she does have some honor. I know one thing about her that I would bet my life on."

"What's that?" Julian asked.

"She wouldn't blink an eye or hesitate to lay down her life for her sons. I have never met anyone more devoted and loving toward their children," Catherine said with conviction. "I guess that alone makes her honorable."

"That makes her very honorable compared to those who have abandoned or even murdered their own off springs," Julian seriously stated.

Catherine nodded. "Besides, I know a little about how it feels to feel unloved by your parents. If just one of my parents had shown me the kind of love and devotion that Veronica shows to her children maybe I wouldn't have turned out as troubled as I am," Catherine sadly uttered. "And maybe I wouldn't have ended up so unlucky in love."

"I think we need to get on a different subject. Don't you?" Julian suggested.

"Not really. Friends are supposed to be able to discuss anything with each other."

"So, you and I are friends?" Julian asked.

"Yes, I think we are," Catherine smiled.

"Catherine, I'm glad to hear you say that. Because that's really all we can be. As I told you before, Mildred is still very much in my thoughts," he stressed seriously.

Catherine knew he was being honest and she appreciated his honesty, but she still didn't like his confession. She swallowed hard as she lit the candles, and then looked at him and smiled. "I will get everything laid out for us. All I need from you at the moment is to show me where there's a serving dish. You said you have looked the kitchen over and know where everything is. All my life growing up and coming here to the lake house, I have never once spent any time in this kitchen. Therefore, I definitely do not know where anything is." She held up one finger. "But after you do that, could you be so kind to wait in the living room until I call you in for dinner?" She suggested, giving him a warm smile. "This is going to be a treat for me to spend time in this kitchen and actually wait on someone, other than someone always waiting on me."

Julian narrowed his eyes at Catherine in a jokingly way and nodded. He stepped over to the cabinet, pulled opened a cabinet door above the sink and removed a serving platter and a serving bowl, placing them on the counter, then headed out of the kitchen. "I'll see you in a few," he said, as he turned and saluted to her on his way out.

The moment he stepped out of the kitchen, Catherine started lying out their dinner. Julian had placed two wine glasses on the counter, and ten minutes later as Catherine was pouring wine into the glasses, Julian reappeared in the doorway. He stood there for a moment with his arms folded and watched her until she glanced around and noticed him standing there. She smiled and nodded. "Good timing," she said.

"You mean I didn't step in here for nothing," he grinned. "I couldn't sit on that sofa and breathe in the smell of that delicious food any longer. I'm starving," he said, smiling at her as she stood at the counter filling the wine glasses. "Besides, I figured your few minutes were up," he said teasingly with his back propped against the doorframe.

Catherine held out both hands to him. "Please do come in. Dinner is served."

They talked and laughed during dinner and not once did they mention Antonio or Mildred's name. Julian seemed more at ease and relaxed than earlier. Catherine was pleased that he seemed to have enjoyed his meal, finishing up everything that she had placed on his plate. He gave her the sense that he was enjoying her company.

"You can relax and I'll do the dishes since you went out and picked up the meal," Julian said to her. "Not to mention, you laid it out without even allowing me to lift a finger," Julian leaned back in his chair, smiling.

"Thank you, Julian. But no thanks. I want you to stay right in your chair," Catherine said getting out of her seat. "The least I can do is clean the kitchen after I allowed you to pay for the dinner that I said would be my treat?" Catherine grinned, placing a restraining hand on his shoulder.

Julian stayed seated at the table finishing up his coffee as Catherine cleared the table and placed the leftovers in the refrigerator. She then filled the sink with warm soapy water, and just as she was getting ready to wash the dishes, he stared at her with a surprised look in his eyes. "Catherine, what are you doing?"

She smiled at him, pointing to the sink of dishes. "What does it look like I'm doing?"

"It looks like you're roping yourself into an unnecessary chore," he said laughingly.

Catherine nodded. "You are 100% correct. But I don't mind being roped at this sink at the moment. I plan to leave this kitchen the way I found it."

He glanced at this watch. "You're being a very helpful houseguest."

Catherine glanced over shoulder and smiled at him. "Thank you, sir. I'm trying."

"Yes, you are. But you're my houseguest and I don't want you using your time doing housework. Besides, why should you?"

"I should because I want to."

"No way, Catherine. You won't convince me that you prefer to stand at that sink and do dishes when we can think of something else that's more fun to do," he seriously stated. "So, please. Can you humor me and put those in the dishwasher?"

Catherine shook her head with her back to him as she continued to hand wash the dishes. "Thanks for your effort to get me out of the kitchen," she said laughingly. "But serious Mr. Bartlett. I don't think so. I want to and will do these dishes by hand."

He smiled shaking his head. "Okay, if you insist."

"Yes, sir. I insist."

"Thank you. That's fine. But it fails me to figure out why you would trouble yourself with work that you don't have to do?"

"I can't explain it. I'm just so excited to be spending this time with you," she confessed. "And somehow, doing these dishes by hand makes me feel useful," she cheerfully admitted.

He smiled. "Okay, be my guest. But since you're insisting on doing those dishes by hand," he said and paused as he stood from his seat. "I can't let you do them by yourself," he said as he stepped over to the sink and stood beside her. "Besides, as I said, you're my guest."

She stopped washing the dish that she held in her hand and placed it back in the dishwater, wiped her hands on her clothes and stared at him smiling.

"Now you're insisting that the two of us stand here and wash the dishes?" Catherine laugh. "I don't think its room enough in this sink for four pair of hands.

Julian nodded. "I agree. But listen up. Here's the deal." He smiled at her. "I'll grab a towel and dry as you wash."

Catherine shook her head. "Julian. Please go into the living room and relax. I would like to do this for you," Catherine strongly insisted.

"Okay, have it your way. I'll wait in the living room," he said grinning as he walked slowly into the living room.

Catherine recent thoughts about being his wife someday had suddenly consumed her. But she knew his heart was set on Mildred Ross and he couldn't seem to shake how Mildred had rudely blew him off just when his heart was set on getting to know her better. Catherine wanted to keep her wits and figured a marriage between she and Julian would most likely never happen. Nevertheless, for this one evening, she wanted to indulge her fantasies about him. She thought as she rinsed a wine glass under warm running water and then placed it in the dish rack.

The kitchen had pale yellow walls with shiny hardwood floors with all white appliances. The kitchen windows were draped with white sheer curtains that allowed the sun to pour in, keeping it bright and sunny on clear days. With beautiful thoughts of Julian with her, it took no time at all to return the lake house kitchen to its original spotless condition."

Chapter Fifteen

Relaxed after dinner, Julian found Catherine in the green room going through her overnight case. She glanced over her shoulder as he stood in the doorway, propped against the doorframe with both arms folded.

"I was just noticing how nice it is out tonight."

Catherine smiled. "Yes, I know. I cracked the window to let some of the fresh night air inside."

"That was a good idea. I should have thought of that," Julian said. "The old house smell a bit stuffy and shut in."

"Yes, it does. But as far back as I can remember, it has always smelled this way. I guess it's the scent of time captured in these walls."

"Maybe, but since it's such a pleasant night. I was wondering would you like to take a walk." Julian asked.

Catherine eyes widened with surprise. "Take a walk in dark?"

"Sure, why not?"

"It's a nice thought. But where would we walk? It's nothing but woods surrounding the lake house," Catherine said.

"I figured that much. But I think it will be relaxing to stroll in the woods on such a nice night." He glanced at her overnight case. "If I can tear you away from that case. Besides, what's in that case?" Julian curiously asked. "You didn't realize you would be staying over. So, how did you happen to bring an overnight case along?"

"It's an overnight case. But it's not filled with clothing. I keep it in my car at all times. It's actually an oversize makeup case," Catherine explained.

Julian nodded. "I see. So, do you want to take that stroll or not?"

Catherine smiled. "Sure, why not? It probably will be relaxing," she said as she quickly closed the lid of the overnight case that sat on the bed.

Julian eyes sparkled with excitement. "It will be relaxing and fun too."

Catherine grabbed her face with both hands, took a deep breath and then looked at him and nodded. "You have convinced me about the relaxation and fun. But have you decided where we'll walk? Do you want to walk in the woods or down the highway?"

"I figured we could take a stroll down by the duck pond I spotted earlier when I first arrived here," he suggested. "I don't think the main highway is a good idea. Therefore, that leaves the lake house grounds and surrounding woods that are vast I'm assuming."

"You are correct," Catherine agreed. "The grounds and surrounding woods are extremely vast."

"Well, are you ready for our night stroll in the woods?" Julian asked.

Catherine nodded. "Sure, I'm ready."

"Good! Let's go." He smiled, turned and headed down the short hallway toward the living room.

Catherine hurried behind him as they stepped outside into the calm, pleasant night. They eagerly headed toward the duck pond behind the lake house; and as they walked along the bank, they could hear what sounded like hundreds of frogs softly croaking, and an occasional splash as a duck landed on the surface of the water. The moon left a sparkling reflection across the clear waves that danced across the clear water pond.

Side by side, they left the banks of the pond and walked a short distance into the wooded area behind the pond. From Catherine's eyes it was a night touched my hope and possibilities. They were spending romantic time together and that's what she had hoped for. Now she would have all weekend to try to make him forget Mildred Ross.

The air was calm with a hint of chill as the soft breeze perfumed the air with fresh wild flowers and stirred into the soft grass at their feet and the trees overhead.

"Let's sit here on the glass for a while," Julian suggested. "It's dry and the moon is so bright overhead. It's really a lovely night," he said and stared into space for a moment trying to fade Mildred out of his head. Then he looked at her and pointed toward the ground. "So would you like to sit on the grass?"

Catherine stared down at the ground. She had grew up at the lake house but hadn't once sit on the grass on the back grounds. She looked at him and smiled. "Sure let's sit on the ground," she said as they both eased down and took a seat on the grass. "It is a lovely night. I'm glad I decided to stay," she told him.

"I'm also glad you decided to stay. Do you ever drive up here for a little relaxation?"

"I wish I could say yes. But I have been so wrapped up into other things until I have allowed this beautiful resort to slip my mind. When I was young and my folks were still alive the four of us came up here often. They loved it here and so did my brother."

"Your brother, Ryan Franklin, was Veronica's husband and the father to your four nephews. I have heard and read a lot about him." Julian nodded. "From what I read, he was one of a kind generous honorable person."

Catherine smiled. "I cannot disagree. Ryan was just that wonderful. He got all the praise because he deserved it. I got none because I was the screw up in the family," she dryly admitted. "But we won't get on that subject. We'll stay on the subject of this little piece of heaven." Catherine looked at Julian. "I will tell you that I spent more time here after Antonio was murdered than I had ever spent here. It was my refuge to get away from everyone and all the reporters. Veronica thought I was volunteering at the library, but I would be here freeing my mind with the relaxation of this little safehaven."

"Someone with a hobby like mine, painting or writing. This is the perfect resort to sneak off to and allow creative artistic flow," Julian said, staring out into the dark space.

He was without exception the kind of man she wanted in her life and couldn't believe she had pushed him away when she had a chance with him. Now she could only hope he would develop feelings for her again. She had low self-esteem and felt her chances were slim and next to none up against Mildred Ross who was one of the most beautiful women she had ever laid eyes on. Mildred was a flawless beauty with a good heart which highlighted her beauty. Catherine was attractive but had no confidence in her looks.

"Does resorts like this inspire your portraits?" Catherine asked.

"What do you mean?" he asked.

"I mean, do you go to resorts and out of way places to be inspired to paint your portraits in an effort to do your best painting?"

"Not really. I have a painting room in my new home in the sun room on the first level. I go there and paint whenever the urge hit me. But I actually haven't been in that room in two weeks. I need to take a walk around the house to make sure dust isn't an inch thick on my furniture," he said. "I'm hoping to hire some staff in the next couple months. I just cannot swing it at the moment."

Catherine didn't comment. She had heard the rumors about the state of his financial affairs. Plus he had shared with her about his financial struggle.

But she felt awkward discussing his financial affairs. But he sensed her tension from the look on her face after mentioning he couldn't afford any staff.

"It's not a secret. Besides, you already know I'm on a tight budget. I informed you all about my finances when we were dating."

Catherine nodded but didn't comment.

"Besides, everybody in the community probably know about my financial struggles by now, since that article in the society section theorized my problems as trying to keep up with the Franklins. Stating in bold print that I bit off more than I could chew when I purchased the Coleman mansion. But I just want you to know, I'm not worried about what's being said and printed. Things will work out for me in time," Julian assured her.

"I'm sure things will work out for you. We love having you next door," Catherine assured him.

"I love being next door. But I still might lose the place?"

Catherine nodded. "Yes, I have heard that. But if you're not worried. I'm not worried. It takes time to piece together a fortune to maintain an estate that elaborate. I say hats off to you for your accomplishment in purchasing the mansion. Therefore, I have a world of confidence in you to make it all work out."

"Thank you, Catherine. That's the nicest thing you could have said to me. I really appreciate your board of confident," he said, slipping an arm around her shoulders, pulling her closer. Slowly, she allowed her head to rest against his chest. One hand encircled her softly, coming to a stop just above her waist.

Catherine's heart was racing, aware of Julian's presence from the top of his head, where the calm wind had blown a couple leaves into his thick hair, down the length of his body, to the hand on her knee. His hand felt strong as she savored his touch, snuggling closer to him. She felt at peace with herself for the first time in a very long time. Perhaps coming to the lake house to experience such a quiet, peaceful existence as Julian had done, all the chaos and non-essentials of life had been filtered out.

Catherine thought her heart would stop when Julian bent his head, traveled his lips across her shoulder. His kisses also felt quiet and peaceful and right. Then with the blink of an eye, his mouth was on hers, kissing her passionate. She had never experienced so much warmth from a man. Antonio and Jack had never shown her warmth and passion. This was her first time. His kiss was warm with the tantalizing awareness of deep desire. She lost herself in his kisses as he gripped her shoulders tenderly. She found the feel of his lips against her far more spellbinding than anything she could imagine.

She melted inside as his hands massaged the sensitive skin at the base of her back in slow, circular motions. His hand felt slightly cool against her skin. She wanted to completely connect with Julian as she felt lost in his embrace. When he pressed her onto the grass, he kissed the side of her neck, and then the bare skin of her shoulder.

Julian hands moved softly over her body as if she was something fragile. Catherine could not remember ever wanting to be touched in the way he was touching her. But the right words failed her when she wanted to tell him how he made her feel, and how she wished to make him feel the same happiness.

Catherine hands softly caressed his chest and he inhaled sharply.

"Catherine, your touch is wonderful!" he softly said. "I want to make love to you tonight," he whispered. "Are you okay with that?"

Catherine didn't hesitate. "Yes, Julian. I want you to," she confessed. He was everything she wanted and needed. The complete motivator of the emotions that consumed her! The complete force of the intense sensations that poured through her! She had a lifetime of desires that his kisses fulfilled. The mild night breeze blew against their faces as Catherine spoke Julian's name.

"Julian, what's happening?" she asked, holding him tight.

"I'm not quite sure," he answered. "But is this what you really want?" he asked.

"Yes, being like this with you is what I want," Catherine softly mumbled.

For as long as Catherine could remember, Antonio had been everything to her. He had been everything she couldn't have. Now, she had replaced all her passion that she carried for Antonio Armani onto Julian. Suddenly, it was like nostalgia of what she had felt for Antonio was stirring inside of her for Julian. In her heart, Julian had become like a solid rock of hope for her, that she would finally find love for once in her life. She was in awe of the fact that he had somehow become her world.

"I'm glad to hear that. So, I'll tell you what's happening," Julian said in a whisper. "We are lying here on the grass enjoying each other. I know I'm deeply enjoying myself," he said assuringly.

"I'm enjoying myself to," Catherine assured him. "But we're supposed to be friends. What we're doing can give a woman hope of more," Catherine seriously said in a whisper.

"Catherine, from the tone of your voice you're sounding serious. Do me a favor and just live in the moment. I don't have any answers for you. I just know it feels damn good to hold you in my arms," he softly whispered. "And I know I want to make love to you, Catherine. Here and now!" He said between kisses as they laid on the grass. "Is this what you want?" He whispered against her neck.

"Yes! Julian, being in your arms is exactly what I want," Catherine softly whispered.

Julian released her and sat up. "I don't want to take advantage of you. This isn't why I asked you to spend the weekend. I want us to be clear on what's happening with us. If we make love it will not mean a commitment or change the status of our relationship," he seriously explained to her. "I also don't want you to feel used. Therefore, if you are hesitant and would prefer not to go any further. I'll understand and respect your choice."

"Julian, I understand and I want this to happen between us," she assured him.

Julian nodded and smiled with a gleam in his eyes. He laid back on the grass beside her and grabbed Catherine in his arms and kissed her. Soon they had shed their clothing and were making love on the grass under the moonlight in the woods behind the lake house. For a while, all the sounds around them had vanished as if the earth had stop spinning. Then suddenly the wind stirred through the trees and grass again; and the sound of the crickets and frogs started singing again.

Still wrapped in his arms, Catherine slowly opened her eyes, knowing at that moment that being with Julian had given her a glimpse of what real love felt like. Julian held her sturdy in his arms as he kissed the side of her neck.

"Catherine, how do you feel?" he asked. "I have to admit. I could hold you and kiss all night." He raised himself up on one elbow and stared down at her.

Staring back at him, she smiled. "I feel fine," she said cheerfully and then shook her head smiling. "No I feel better than fine. I feel happy and content and all those beautiful things that I thought I would never feel."

"I feel the same," he admitted. "Nothing is weighing on me. No sad or worried thoughts, just good ones. You know why?" he asked.

"No, I don't know why, Julian. So tell me why you're feeling so great?" she curiously asked.

"Okay, it's quite simple. I'm feeling so content at this moment. Because tonight here on the grass secluded on the back grounds at your lake house, you are mine, Catherine Franklin, and I am yours," he whispered caringly.

Catherine sat right up as she buttoned her blouse. "Julian, what a special thing to say. Thanks for saying that," she softly uttered as she touched his face.

He sat up and started buttoning his shirt and then he stood and slipped into his slacks. "It felt right to say it. We're here secluded together. It feels like we're secluded in our own private world. I know once we get a good night's sleep and face the light of day, it will probably look different. But right now it feels right to say we belong to each other."

Catherine smiled to herself as she continued to step into and straighten out her clothes. She watched him as he raked dry leaves from his clothing and went into thought thinking to herself, "How perfect my life would be if only Julian and I could be apart of each other's lives every day and every night? But I shouldn't stress myself out with hopeful thinking. I need to stay focused on the present. We had this night. As he said, the light of day may look different. But at least we have tonight," she thought.

Julian glanced at her as he stepped into his shoes. "What are you smiling about?"

"I never knew it could be like this," Catherine said, looking in Julian's eyes. "I want to be truthful with you."

Julian smiled. "The truth is always good."

"I just want you to know how special you are to me," Catherine lovingly whispered to him.

When Catherine slipped into her shoes, Julian caressed the side of her face. "Believe it or not, you're special to me also," he told her.

"Thanks for saying that to me, Julian."

"You don't ever have to thank me for giving you a compliment," he seriously stressed as he touched the side of her face again. "Catherine, I want to tell you something. Something that you don't seem to know."

"What can you tell me that I don't seem to know, Julian?"

"I can tell you how beautiful you are." He paused. "That is something you don't seem to know. Every bit of you," he whispered, leaned in and kissed the side of her face.

"Wow, thank you," Catherine stumbled with her words as her cheeks flushed.

"You shouldn't seem so surprised to hear me say that about you. It's a known fact that you come from beautiful genes. The entire Franklin family is one big picture of beautiful peoples. But the beauty I see in you is more than just physical," Julian lovingly said.

Catherine nodded. "I agree. I do have a beautiful family. But I have never thought of myself as beautiful. I feel I'm attractive but I wouldn't go as far as to say beautiful."

"Well, maybe you wouldn't for yourself. But you are quite beautiful. Besides, beauty is in the eye of the beholder," he softly whispered.

"And you are the beholder?" she asked, teasingly.

He nodded. "Yes, I am. But enough about your beauty and how you cannot see it. I have a better idea. Let's go back to the lake house to a comfortable bed." He pulled Catherine close to him. "I want to make love to you again," he whispered, grabbed her hand and they walked hand-in-hand to the cottage.

When they reached the lake house, standing on the front porch kissing, Catherine slightly pulled away. "I think I'll go inside and hit the shower." She glanced down at her wrinkled, grass-stained skirt and blouse. "Plus, I'll throw these in the washer since I don't have a change of clothing."

"Ok, while you do that I'll be next in line." He glanced down at his clothing. "My clothes are in no better shape. But in the meantime, I'll raid the refrigerator to see what I can find that resembles a dessert for us," he said as he pulled open the front door.

They stepped inside and Catherine headed straight to the bathroom. Walking down the short hallway, she was in a daze thinking of the beautiful time Julian and she had just spent together. Even the warm, refreshing shower did not wash away the wonderful sensations in her stomach, which was a courtesy of being with Julian. She fantasized about Julian as she relaxed under the soothing shower. When she stepped out of the shower, dried off and slipped into a long red nylon nightgown and matching robe that she found in one of the dresser drawers. The new Saint Laurent nightwear belonged to her. She had left it there over a year ago.

After slipping into the nightwear, she went looking for Julian and found him in the kitchen looking through the refrigerator. He glanced around at her as she stood in the doorway smiling. "Did you have any luck finding anything that resemble a dessert?" she asked.

He smiled with his hand on the door handle of the refrigerator. He closed the refrigerator and placed his back against it. "I'm afraid not."

"No ice cream, cookies or fruit. Nothing." Catherine raised both hands and smiled.

He smiled. "We'll think of something." His eyes smiled with delight from the sight of Catherine standing there in the nice red nightwear. Her eyes admired him as well. The sensuous tension in the room grew into a huge flame as their desire for each other blazed out of control once again.

"I know I keep saying this, but you are quite attractive!" Julian whispered, taking a step toward her. Then he stopped and glanced down at his clothes and grinned. "I think I better take my turn in the shower before I come anywhere near you."

Catherine smiled. "I think you're fine just the way you are," she assured him.

Julian felt a great need and desire for Catherine as he stepped away from the refrigerator and flipped off the kitchen light. He slowly stepped across the kitchen floor toward her. He took her hand in his and led her down the short hallway to the master bedroom of the cottage. When they stepped into the room, he lifted her hand and kissed it, then released her hand and headed toward the connecting bathroom.

"Catherine, I won't be long in the shower," he said, pointing toward the bookcase in the corner of the room. "Maybe reading will help the time go quicker."

"I don't think I can concentrate to read," she said.

He grinned. "You can't concentrate to read? I wonder why? Sounds like we're both on the same page." He glanced over his shoulder and smiled. "Your best bet is to be seated and relax. I won't be long," he said as he disappeared into the bathroom.

Catherine was filled with anxiousness as she stood in the center of the large bedroom wondering just how she was supposed to go about trying to relax. It was a large stunning room with the same affluent egg shell white furniture that she remembered as a child. The queen size bed was covered with a vintage bedspread the shade of lemon. The curtains were sheer and in the same shade of lemon. She remembered as a child that her parents always stayed in the master bedroom. It had the same lemon and white wallpaper and antique white carpeting that she remembered as a child. She wondered how something so old could still look so unused and new.

Catherine was still anxiously excited when Julian stepped out of the bathroom. He smiled at her, wearing only a bath size dark green towel hitched about his waist.

"This has always been the most beautiful room in the house," Catherine softly said to him.

"I agree. I looked at the other two bedrooms and they're all nice. But this one is fabulous. So, I decided to camp out in here during my time here."

"Perfect choice. My parents always stayed in this room."

"Now, you and I will share it together," he said as he took several steps toward her, and then Catherine was in his arms, being swept up and onto the bed. The moment they fell over on the bed, he took her hand and pulled her out of the bed and started undressing her. He untied the long red sash and slipped the robe off her shoulders. He didn't remove her nightgown as he stood back and removed his long black bathrobe.

Julian anxiously caressed her back with both hands and soft kisses at the same time. Catherine was in heaven from his passion, never experiencing anything so romantic before. Then they were in bed together once again holding each other tight. She felt she was losing herself in Julian's arms, and she wanted to welcome it with all of her mind, body and soul. Somehow in surrendering to him, she knew she would love him always. Afterward, with their arms wrapped around each other, they both fell into a peaceful sleep.

Chapter Sixteen

Catherine opened her eyes and yawned, then stretched out both arms toward the ceiling. She happily turned to her side to say good morning to Julian, but she discovered he wasn't in bed. She quickly threw the covers off of her and hopped out of bed. She looked at the small gold clock on the bedside table and noticed it was seven o'clock in the morning. She rubbed both eyes and made her way to the shower. After she dressed and headed down the short hallway to the living room, she noticed Julian didn't seem to be in the house. But she didn't bother to look for him as she stepped into the kitchen and helped herself to a cup of coffee that Julian had already brewed. She took the cup and stepped out on the porch and took a seat on the steps. It was a rare treat for her to simply sit there doing nothing, letting her thoughts travel freely. It was a restful change from the hectic pace of everyday life at the mansion.

A short while later, she finally took her empty coffee cup back to the kitchen and placed in the dishwasher. While standing with her back against the kitchen counter thoughts of yesterday came to her. She thought of the time when she first started dating Julian and how desperate he was to get to know her better. But she was wrapped up in thought of Antonio. She couldn't see Julian for the decent man he was. Now she was on the opposite end of the spectrum desperate to get a second chance with him while his heart was wrapped up into someone else.

Catherine stared at the ceiling and let out a deep sigh. Thoughts of the past with Julian only made her feel sorry for herself. Therefore, she pushed the thoughts from her mind and headed out of the kitchen's back door.

Catherine strolled out onto the immaculate back grounds and down by the duck pond. She spotted Julian in a distant near the duck pond down on his knees gathering a handful of white and purple wild flowers that were blossoming all at the edges of the ground. He glanced around at a crackling in the grass, then he stood to his feet with a handful of flowers behind his back as he headed toward Catherine.

"Hello, early bird," Catherine smiled. "What are you doing out here?"

"And a good morning to you, Miss Catherine Franklin," he said. "I'm out here enjoying the early morning freshness of this quite serene place."

"Why didn't you wake me so I could come out and enjoy it with you?"

"It wouldn't have been a surprise." He smiled.

"What wouldn't have been a surprise?" she asked. "Finding your side of the bed empty wasn't a pleasant surprise."

"I almost woke you with a kiss. But you looked so peaceful lying there. Besides, as I said, it wouldn't have been a surprise if I had brought you out here with me."

Catherine smiled. "I guess you'll tell me what you're talking about eventually since I have no clue."

Julian brought his hand from behind his back and handed her the bunch of flowers he had just picked. "These wouldn't have been a surprise."

"Wow, they are beautiful," Catherine excitedly told him. "How thoughtful and sweet of you. Thank you," Catherine said, smiling as she held the flowers with both hands and lifted them to her nose. "You're full of surprises, Mr. Bartlett. You're an early riser with a romantic side. To come outside and pick flowers just for me."

"Well, you're welcome." He smiled, looking at her. "You are my guest and since I'm stationed here for the next two weeks and have decided not to leave site, I figured I would come out here and find you a nice bouquet to sort of take the place of not being able to leave here and take you out to a nice dinner."

"I didn't come visit for you to take me out," Catherine told him.

"I know, but I sort of feel like I would like to show my appreciation for your company. It's kind of neat having you around."

"Well, thanks again for the flowers. How did you ever find them?"

"When I first arrived, I walked the grounds and noticed them all about the edge of the grounds." He pointed toward the edge of the back grounds. "See all those wild flowers growing along the edge of the grounds. Probably at one point you had flower gardens out back here," he figured. "When you were little coming here with your parents. Do you remember there being any flowers gardens?"

"I remember specifically when I was about ten years old, the lake house had lots of flowers all over the place. On the front and back grounds. My parents had a regular gardener taking care of the grounds at that time. His name was Matthew Madden. But now an agency takes care of all the landscaping for us."

"Matthew Madden. I think I have heard of him," Julian said.

"You probably have. He's the caretaker at the Blue Angels Cemetery. So if you have ever been to Blue Angels Cemetery you have probably seen him."

"He must be quite elderly if he used to work for your parents."

Catherine nodded. "Yes, he is quite elderly. But he also used to work for us. He was let go a few years back. But his son still works for us."

"Is his son also a gardener?" Julian asked.

"No, his son is our chauffeur, Fred."

Julian nodded. "Yes, I have noticed him coming and going from the estate quite often. He seems to be a decent guy."

Catherine nodded. "Yes, Fred is okay."

"You say that as if Fred isn't your favorite person," Julian commented.

"No, I didn't mean it like that. I really mean he's okay."

"Somehow, I get the sense there's some animosity toward him," Julian said after detecting coldness in her voice toward Fred. "So, what's the story with your chauffeur that has you harboring animosity toward him?"

Catherine shook her head. "It's not animosity. However, I'm not as fond of Fred as I once was. To make a long story short, he and I went to school together and were fairly good friends when we were younger. Then later in life after he started working for my folks he did something or rather attempted to do something that completely broke my trust in him," Catherine seriously shared.

"Okay, what did your chauffeur do that broke your trust?"

"It's not something I'm at liberty to share. But trust me, it was a huge error in his judgement," Catherine said as she reflected on Fred's failed attempt on Antonio's life.

"Okay, it's clear you're not comfortable sharing your chauffeur misdeed. Besides, it's not something I need to know," Julian said. "But here's something I need to know."

"What's that?" Catherine curiously asked.

"Are you ready to head back to the cottage?" he said teasingly.

Catherine laughed. "I thought you seriously wanted to know something. But you're just teasing."

"I'm teasing. But I still need an answer," Julian said.

"Sure, let's head back," Catherine said as she started walking alongside him toward the lake house.

"I'm glad you like the flowers. I figured the flowers would also brighten up the kitchen table." He rubbed dry pieces of grass from his right pant leg. "I figured I couldn't go wrong with a nice bouquet."

"Julian, you're really a thoughtful guy," Catherine said, smiling.

"Of course, that's me, thoughtful Julian," he said in a teasing way.

Catherine sniffed the flowers with her eyes staring up at him. She felt at peace and contented with Julian.

"Julian, it is so peaceful out here. If my family didn't own the place I would seek to buy it."

He pointed toward the back door of the cottage. "I'm starving right now." He grinned. "What do you say to the two of us whipping up some pancakes and fried eggs?" Julian suggested. "I looked through the cabinets and there's plenty of pancake mix, also fresh eggs. So what do you think of pancakes and fried eggs?"

Catherine nodded her agreement. "Pancakes and fried eggs sound great. I'm starving too."

Chapter Seventeen

     Julian and Catherine had spent most of Sunday afternoon outdoors. They had spent hours walking along the grounds and in the woods, where they sat on the grass for a while to enjoy a picnic at noon. Sitting near a blossoming rosebush covered in white roses, they relaxed upon the grass. Then later in the day, after they had enjoyed their picnic of finger sandwiches, fruit and cheese along with a bottle of red wine, they spent a few more hours walking and exploring outside. They were now relaxing, cuddled together on the living room sofa as the last ray of sunlight poured through the windows of the bright spacious lake house living room. All the blinds were opened allowing the bright day to spill through all the windows dispensing throughout the room. Julian was glancing through the newspaper, reading some sections of it and throwing some sections aside. Catherine was fascinated and overwhelmed by her time with him. She found her eyes glued to his face. Suddenly he was the most attractive, loving man in the world to her. She watched him as he seemed deep in concentration reading the paper. She wanted to reach into the past and erase all the unpleasant memories and replace them with all the good times that they had just shared. She discreetly watched him read over the paper, occasionally, his hands came up to rub an unconscious path down his thick hair, a gesture that made her long to run her hands through his hair.
     Sitting there looking at Julian, Catherine's heart was full of love for him. She thought about the saying that a person never miss their water until the well runs dry. In Catherine's mind, she hadn't missed Julian, and hadn't realized the magnitude of her lost until he was out of her life. Now in the past few months, more than ever, he had held an endless fascination for her, both as a person and as an artist. It was a fascination that she couldn't see months

ago when she allowed Antonio Armani to come between them. Her new fascination over Julian seemed endless. He seemed to her like a shiny star at the top of a shelf that was just out of her reach.

She kept reflecting on his lovemaking, realizing she thought of Julian as a real boyfriend. She knew it was true love and not just some thought of love. Her strong feelings for him were glued inside of her heart just like her own blood. She was truly in love with him. But it seems she had realized it too late! As her thoughts overwhelmed her, she felt her eyes getting heavy with water.

"Why had my love for him never occurred to me before when he was crazy about me?" she thought to herself. "Why hadn't it occurred to me when I was chasing after Antonio? Why hadn't it occurred to me when he and I were really together? Why hadn't it occurred to me when he loved me back and sincerely wanted to be with me? When he bent over backward to be with me? Why now when I was just someone he liked and considered as a friend, but not someone he loved? Why here as I look at him over the edge of a Newspaper?"

For a moment or two, her vision blurred in and out, Julian was out of focus because of the tears that had filled her eyes, rolling down her face. Quickly wiping the tears away, she took a deep breath to try to fade out the pain of the hurtful thoughts of how she had messed up what they once had. But as she sat there in thought and he seemed so at ease looking over the paper, her anger and frustration and confusion at herself seemed to rip at her and it took all the willpower she could muster to keep from allowing Julian to see her cry over the past. Regardless of her own lack of control over sad memories, there was little she could do about what had happened. Yet, she sat there trying to will the sad thoughts away, she knew that actions could be controlled, but feelings were a whole different matter.

Julian glanced up from the paper and looked at her and smiled with silence praise, as if he was saying: "I'm glad you're here." He reached toward the coffee table and lifted his cup of coffee. He took a sip and then placed the cup back on the coffee table and continued looking through the newspaper.

Catherine continued to sit there in deep thought:

"Why am I so upset?" She thought to herself.

"What's so wrong with being in love with Julian?" she thought to herself and paused up at the ceiling for a moment.

"Maybe I'm just afraid to be in love at all?" she thought.

Julian seemed so at ease as he seemed engrossed in the paper he was reading. But Catherine was having a discussion in her mind with herself.

"Julian is a wonderful person and an all-around gentleman," Catherine thought to herself as she kept discreetly glancing back and forth at him. But my head wasn't on straight before and I messed things up for the two of us. At the time, I didn't know I was allowing the man I truly wanted to be with to slip right between my fingers. He has an air of real maturity and honor about himself. And with all my heart, I know he would never disrespect and hurt me as Antonio hurt me in the past.

Julian glanced up from the paper and smiled at her. "What are you smiling about? You seem to be housing some good thoughts," he said, smiling.

Catherine nodded and smiled. "You are correct, I am; and they are all about how much I have enjoyed myself here at the lake house with you."

"I'm glad. I have enjoyed you as well," Julian said as he became engrossed in the paper again.

Catherine mind went back into thought about Julian and how he stirred such wonderful feelings in her. She thought to herself.

"Julian stir my feelings and make me feel special when I'm around him, like no other man ever has. But I know exactly what troubling me," she thought and took a pause from her thought for a moment as she took a deep breath.

"What's troubling me is, I wonder if Julian Bartlett really love me? And if he does by chance love me, is it stronger than what he feels for Mildred Ross?" Catherine thought to herself as she discreetly glanced at Julian.

"Can he forgive me for rejecting him and making a fool of myself for Antonio Armani? He has never said he loves me. I'm sure he likes me a lot and he seems to desire me; and still has a physical attraction for me. But does it mean he loves me. What future can a love like mine possibly have if my heart is in love alone? On top of my concern of not being sure if he can forget Mildred Ross and fall in love with me, I wonder if he can trust me again."

Now, sitting across from him, on the twin sofa facing him, which was divided by the coffee table and a round throw rug beneath the table, Catherine had both feet beneath her as she sat there in silence, looking at Julian and sipping her coffee. Her visit was ending quicker than she wanted it to and she daydreamed about the two of them remaining together at the lake house. But she knew she had to leave on Monday morning. She felt it was the only way to get away from him and keep her dignity intact. It was a way to leave without pouring her heart out to him. Her exit would prevent her from making him feel awkward and uncomfortable about her being in love with him when she knew he wasn't in love with her. Survival was said to be the most basic human instinct. Getting away from him was clearly a matter of Catherine's own survival! Because if he couldn't let her know his feelings and love her the way she wanted and needed to be loved, being with him would only cause her pain.

    That night in bed, as Catherine slept next to Julian, she felt blaring pain in the pit of her stomach that feared she would never be with him in that way again. He seemed somewhat indifference. But she sensed his emotions ran deep. But when he reached for her he didn't say a word, as if he knew words would be useless in erasing the sad look in her eyes. But during their lovemaking, it relaxed Catherine and for a while faded out all the fear and stress in her mind. They snuggled in each other's his arms most of the night.

Chapter Eighteen

    The sunrise came too soon over the lake house for Catherine after a glorious night of lying next to Julian. Catherine noticed that his side of the bed was empty as she took both hands and rubbed the sleep from her eyes. He had gotten out of bed. Just as well, she thought, now sitting there on the side of the bed holding her face. She couldn't stop the fullness from coming to her heart and the water from coming to her eyes. Her heart was breaking because she had to find a willingness to leave the lake house and Julian. She wasn't motivated to get out of bed and gather her belongings and say good-bye to a man she had fallen deeply in love with. It didn't seem fair that she had to lose his love before she could wise up to the fact that she couldn't live without him. She had to walk away from him, not knowing if she would ever be close with him again. She had to hold her love for him inside without letting him know her feelings. She had to find the courage to walk away from a decent man she felt true love for. It wasn't a desperate kind of love as she felt for Antonio. It was a quiet kind of love that felt right. Nevertheless, she couldn't tell him. Quickly, she stretched her arms over her head and collected herself; and before her courage failed her, she hopped off the bed and headed straight to the bathroom to shower and dress.
    Seated at the kitchen table, Julian looked up from his cup of coffee when Catherine walked into the lake house kitchen. She couldn't read the expression on his face. He was just sitting there looking calm as if her departure didn't faze him. She was hoping to see a glimmer of sadness in his eyes, but if he was sad about her leaving it was well hidden from his face. Although, she stood there in the doorway with an obvious sad look in her eyes. Without a word, she sat her overnight case and briefcase by the door. The silence grew between them as Julian flashed her a smile and kept sipping his coffee. The

deep serious look in his eyes began to make Catherine anxious and she was hoping she wouldn't lose the nerve she had mustered to help her say goodbye.

"I have to leave, Julian," Catherine softly uttered as overflowing agony and misery were ripping through her stomach.

"I knew you were leaving today," he said. "But I was sort of wondering if you might stay a bit longer? Do you think you could?"

Catherine thought about what he had just asked her as she stepped over to the counter where he had a teacup and saucer waiting for her near the pot of fresh brewed Folger's Coffee. She lifted the coffee pot and her hand slightly trembled as she poured coffee into the cup. With her back to him at the kitchen counter, trying to collect her thoughts and what she would say to him, she had hoped he wouldn't make it more difficult for her by asking her to stay longer. He had just asked her to stay longer; and now, just like that, she didn't know if she would have the courage to actually leave the lake house and head back to Franklin House. Yet, she knew she had to leave. The longer she stayed, knowing she loved him, the harder it would be to walk away. If it had to be done, it was better now that she had found the will to leave.

"Veronica is expecting me and I'm on the schedule for the library this afternoon," Catherine muttered in a low voice, pouring more coffee into her cup to simply give her hands something to do.

Julian nodded. "I figured you were probably expected home," he replied indifferently. "I forgot about your volunteer schedule at the library."

After filling her coffee cup to the rim, Catherine purposely chose to drink it while standing at the kitchen counter with her back propped against the counter. She didn't want to be seated at the kitchen table facing Julian across from her seat as she had done so often in the past few days. She knew her limitations and there were some things she wasn't ready to handle. Being unnecessarily too close to him was one. That could wait until the last minute, when she could say goodbye and quickly get in her car and drive away.

"I'm going to miss you, Miss Catherine Franklin," Julian softly said, wrapping his hands around the coffee cup on the table in front of him.

It was so quiet in the kitchen until Catherine could hear them both breathe. A burning pain felt glued in her chest like a raging fire. "I'm going to miss you, too, Mr. Julian Bartlett," Catherine uttered with a blank face, not wanting to reveal her true emotions of how she was aching inside. The pain was all from having to walk away from him, and what could have and should have been. She already knew how desperately she was going to miss him.

Her face heated, as the muscles in her stomach tightened. "You probably mentioned how long you rented the lake house for?" Catherine asked.

"I rented it for two weeks," he said, sipping his coffee with his eyes glued to hers. "But I wish I was renting it for the entire summer," he said, smiling.

For a moment Catherine was frozen in his eyes. She felt awkward and didn't know what to say. "That would be great if you could," she said, holding her coffee cup up to her lips with both hands.

"Yes, it would be great, but two weeks is all I can spare for my vacation. I'm not independently wealthy as the Franklins," Julian said, tapping his fingers on the table, looking down in his coffee cup.

"Julian, why would you say that to me? I'm also not independently wealthy like the Franklins neither. I have told you a hundred times how I was cut out of the will," Catherine reminded him.

Julian nodded. "Yes, I know all of that. But regardless to what you say Catherine, my instincts tell me Veronica and your nephews would surely grant you your heart's desire," he seriously stated. "I keep telling you how blessed you are to have such a loving family. Deep down I think you realize that."

"Julian, I know I have a loving family, and you're probably right about them granting me my heart's desire. They have always been there for me. But let's change the subject. Before I leave. I need to apologize to you again."

"What do you need to apologize for?"

"For all the rudeness I threw your way when we were dating."

"We have hatched that out. Just let it go," he seriously suggested.

"I know. But I just need to remind you how my mind was in a different place. So much anguish was going on with me. But it still didn't give me a license to be rude, never answering or returning your calls," she said and held her breath for a moment for his response.

He seemed as if he was in deep thought, but didn't reply as he sat there at the kitchen table staring down in his coffee cup.

"Julian, we had such a wonderful weekend together and I probably should not have brought up our past. But somehow the words were coming out of my mouth before I realized it. But I just want to say how I wish things could be the way they were before I messed up and pushed you out of my life."

Julian glanced at Catherine and held her stare with something warm in his eyes. "I feel the same, Catherine. I wish things could be the way they were before you stop taking my calls," he said as if he was in deep thought about her past rude behavior toward him. "But it is what it is. Life has a way of molding itself," he said looking toward her.

"Well, I guess I better get going. I have a long drive ahead of me," Catherine smiled, rinsed her coffee cup and placed it in the dishwasher.

"I'll take that to the car for you." He pointed toward her overnight case as he stood from the kitchen table and headed toward the overnight case and briefcase that sat on the bench near the kitchen doorway.

"Okay, but it's really not heavy at all," she said, trying to keep her sadness hid as she watched him step over to the bench near the kitchen doorway. He grabbed her overnight case and briefcase from the bench.

Standing right behind Julian, Catherine picked up her purse from the bench and followed him out the front door. Silent anguish stirred in her as they walked across the front yard to her white Mercedes. It was parked side by side his black Mercedes. Catherine fumbled in her purse for her car keys, hoping not to locate them. Finally she grabbed them from the bottom of her purse and unlocked the trunk. She sadly watched as Julian placed her overnight bag and briefcase inside the trunk, then stood to the side.

He didn't say a word as Catherine reached into the trunk and zipped her briefcase to make sure all her papers would be secure. Then Catherine closed the trunk as he continued to stand back not saying anything. He had asked her to stay longer, but he had not talked about starting their relationship over. She felt he no longer wanted a relationship with her. In her heart, she felt she had been reduced to someone that he only wanted to sleep with.

Then the moment finally arrived that Catherine had dreaded. How would she make a gracious exit without breaking down with emotions in front of Julian? She stood before him smiling. Then threw her arms around him as he gripped her tightly in his arms. They held each other for a minute, and then she quickly kissed him on the side of his face and turned slowly, pulled open her car door and slid inside. She quickly started the engine, punched a button and lowered the driver's side window.

"I enjoyed your company, Miss Catherine Franklin," Julian honestly said.

"Thank you, I enjoyed your company too," Catherine said, raised her hand and waved goodbye as she slowly drove out of the driveway. Her eyes were glued to the road in front of her as she fought the urge to look back.

"I love you, Julian Bartlett," Catherine said to herself as she drove away.

That had been one of the happiest weekends of Catherine's life and as she drove away, she had no idea if Julian would call or ever spend time with her again. Then she reflected on what Veronica had told her that she would lose Julian if she didn't put forth an effort to show him that she wanted to be in his life. Now it seemed as if it was too little too late. Only time would tell if Julian would ever give her a second chance.

Chapter Nineteen

    One year after Catherine visited Julian at the lake house, Veronica was standing at Julian's front door. The year had swept through so quickly; and on this warm breezy Friday, June 5, 2015, at one o'clock in the afternoon, Veronica noticed Julian's car parked in the driveway and rushed over to catch him at home. She knocked softly on the front door and then it dawned on her that he had no servants. She wasn't sure if he was in the shower or tucked away somewhere in the large house that hindered him from hearing the knock. Therefore, she decided to ring the doorbell and after a couple minutes of standing at his front door wondering if he would answer the door, Julian stretched the door open and smiled at Veronica with surprise in his eyes.
    "Hello," he said awkwardly, not sure what to make of her visit.
    "Hello, Julian, I'm sorry to just drop in on you like this. But I was hoping to get an opportunity to speak with you for a moment," Veronica said, noticing that he was professionally dressed and was apparently on his way to work.
    He glanced at his watch. "Sure, I have a little time before my next appointment. Please, do come in." He held the door as she stepped inside.
    "Please be seated where you like," Julian said as he flipped the lock on the door and then walked across the room and took a seat in his favorite chair near the fireplace as Veronica took a seat on the long sofa facing him.
    "Can I get you something to drink?" He looked toward his bar on the left wall. "I think we have a few bottles of decent wine that I could offer you."
    Veronica shook her head and smiled. "Thanks, Julian. But this isn't really a social visit. You mentioned you have to get to work soon and I don't want to take up much of your time. I'm actually here on Catherine's behalf."

Julian leaned forward in his chair and stared surprisingly at Veronica. "You're here on Catherine's behalf? I don't mean to be rude, but what does that mean?" he asked.

"I'll admit I'm sticking my nose in where it doesn't belong but I'm tired of listening to Catherine go on and on about you being on the fence with her. Therefore, Julian, you need to decide whether you want to be with Catherine or Mildred. You need to make your decision soon!" Veronica stressed. "If you allow this to linger much longer I'm afraid Catherine will not be around."

"Why is that?" he asked.

"She's very distraught and has decided to take a cruise around the world," Veronica announced.

"Well, that might be the thing to help her feel better," Julian commented.

"Listen, Julian. She doesn't really want to leave town and we especially doesn't want her to leave the states in the condition she's in."

"What condition is that? Antonio been dead for a year and a half now so I know she can't still be grieving the guy," Julian grunted.

"Of course, she's not still grieving Antonio Armani. But she's desperately unhappy since she feels you are stringing her along in the hope that Mildred Ross will change her mind and come back to you. Seriously, Julian. I read Mildred write up in the paper. She made it clear in that article last month that she intends to remain single for the rest of her life. Those were her words when asked how she felt about the pending release of her ex-husband due to be released on good behavior in 2017. She said I'm divorced from the man and I plan to stay divorced with no future plans to ever remarry my ex-husband or anyone else. That's what Mildred Ross said. Therefore, she made it crystal clear that she's done with relationships," Veronica bluntly said.

Julian sat there lost for words and surprised at Veronica's tone.

"I'm sorry to be so blunt but we're both adults and there's no time to beat around the bush. My boys and I love Catherine and she has experienced one letdown after the next where men are concerned. That's why I'm here to say, if you don't see a place in your life for her, just tell her and set her free," Veronica strongly suggested. "Otherwise, if you do want Catherine, please let her know. The only way she won't take off is if the two of you reunite."

"Is that what she told you?" Julian asked.

"Yes, Julian. She and I had an in-depth discussion about her cruise, which she isn't that excited about. Yet, she feels it will help get you out of her system if the two of you are not going to get back together. For the past year of spending limited time with you and moving toward no commitment, she is very discouraged. She feels everybody life is going forward except her own."

"I think our relationship is fine. We see each other and spend time together and get along fine," Julian said. "Besides, what is she basing this on?"

"Basing what on?" Veronica asked.

"The fact that everyone's life is moving forward except hers. I would like to know why she came up with that notion," he grumbled.

"It's not a notion," Veronica quickly relayed. "She's probably looking at her own family. I'm engaged to Charles, my sons are engaged and she's the only one at the mansion that seem to have no future to look forward to. And if I might add, I also read about your son's engagement. So, there you have it, Julian. With all this bliss around Catherine, she's a complete mess. But I can tell you without a doubt that she wants to be with you." Veronica seriously stated. "But the million dollar question is, what are your feelings for her? Should she just forget you? One way or another, she needs to know where she stands with you," Veronica firmly said. "I know this discussion about your personal affairs is highly irregular. And it may not be my place to be over here pushing it down your throat. But, I have never been the one to conform to the proper channels where my love ones are involved."

Julian felt on the spot. But kept his composure. "I feel I have been quite open and honest with Catherine. I think she knows where I stand. I told her in so many words that my heart isn't in a wholehearted relationship with her."

"If you don't mind me asking? Why is that, Julian?" Veronica asked. "Is it true what's being printed in the Community Page?"

"I can't answer that since I don't read that paper," Julian told her.

"Well, I'm the first to tell anyone that the paper is printed of mostly rumors. Yet, I make a habit of reading that paper every Monday when it's published and delivered to my door. I want to be the first to know if they ever decide to print rumors about me or anyone in my family," Veronica definitely stated. "However, with that said, you still haven't answered my question."

"I haven't answered because I'm not sure what you're asking."

"I'm referring to the rumors that are being printed in the Community Page that you are still carrying a torch for Mildred Ross after all this time?"

Julian held up both hands. "If that's the rumor you're referring to. It's not a rumor. It's true. I'm definitely still hung up on Mildred."

"But you read the article. Mildred isn't interested in a relationship with you or any other man."

Julian nodded. "Yes, I heard about the article. But my heart feels what it feels. Nevertheless, I'm not a blatant fool to believe she'll come running back into my arms. I'm not holding out hope for that. My heart still cares deeply for her and I can't help if I'm still hung up on the lady."

"I understand that. But you're a smart man and realize life goes on. You did spend that time with Catherine at the lake house last summer. She told me all about it." Veronica held up one finger. "Please forgive my bluntness, but the things she told me didn't sound like a man that only wanted one woman. So, excuse me if I don't believe you're still that hung up on Mildred Ross."

"Well, did Catherine also tell you that although, we spent that time at the lake house, I told her right at the start how I was still hung up on Mildred? Yet she still chose to stay and spend that time with me. I was very open with Catherine about my feelings for Mildred."

"I get that Julian. But I'm also aware that Mildred Ross broke up with you over a year ago and made it crystal clear you two were done for good."

"Who told you we were done for good?"

Veronica smiled. "Do you need to ask? I'm sure you know who told me."

"I do need to ask because it doesn't sound like Catherine informed you. Therefore, it sounds like you have spoken to Mildred. And I was under the impression that you and Mildred were not social with each other," Julian inquired. "It's not like you invites her over for tea," Julian rudely assumed, not pleased that Veronica was pressing him about his feelings for Catherine.

"Julian, I apologize if I interrupted your day or if I have offended you. Surely that wasn't my intentions. However, what I came to say needed to be said. Now, it's left up to you to examine your feelings for Catherine." Veronica stood from his sofa. "I strongly stress upon you for my sister-in-law's and your own sake to examine your feelings to either get with her or let her go. The point I'm trying to make, anything will beat the misery she's in now," Veronica headed across his large living room toward the front door.

Julian didn't reply as he rushed across the room to open the door for her. She stepped through the door and slowly headed across the porch toward the steps, Julian spoke. "Your visit caught me a little off guard. But I did hear every word you said, and I will do as you have asked. I'll seriously search my heart and reflect on where I see myself with Catherine."

Veronica leaned her back against one of the six pillars on his porch. "Please do. Because if you see yourself nowhere with her, have the necessary conversation to allow Catherine to move on," Veronica softly suggested, and then turned on her Bloomingdale's low taupe flats and headed off the porch, across the front yard and toward the driveway to her car.

Julian nodded as he glanced at his watch, then pulled the door closed behind him. He coded in the house security system, then headed off the porch to his 1:30 appointment that he would still be on time for.

Chapter Twenty

Later in the evening, nearly an hour after dinner had been served at Franklin House, Natalie answered the front door and showed Julian into the living room; and he sat there on one of the sofas anxiously waiting for Catherine to appear in the room. He was just shutting off his phone when Catherine stepped into the room. She walked quickly across the floor toward him and took a seat on the sofa next to him. She smiled with surprise eyes.

"This is an unexpected nice surprise, which I must say is unlike you," Catherine cheerfully said. "I'm not complaining, but in the past you always called first. You never showed up unannounced."

Julian nodded and smiled. "You are correct. But if I can recall correctly, that consideration always found me at the outside looking in," he quickly said lightheartedly, as he continued with both hands held out. "You always found a reason why I couldn't drop by, remember?" he reminded her.

Catherine smiled. "You are absolutely correct. But that was ancient history, a year and a half ago. Over the past year and a half I haven't given you any excuses to keep you from dropping by. I just thought you didn't want to."

Julian nodded. "You're right, it was my choice to stay away as much as I did," he admitted.

Catherine smiled. "I'm glad you're admitting that fact. Because I know I was on the level and shared with you how much I wanted the two of us to get back on track. I pretty much did and said all I could to no real avail on your part. So, after so many attempts and trying to convince you to give us another chance, I backed off some and that's why you haven't heard from me as much," Catherine sincerely explained. "You seemed content with seeing me every once in a while and I figured that's all I was going to get."

"I guess you get a taste of your own medicine and know how I felt when I was all in and you pushed me aside," Julian reminded her.

"Julian, why are you bringing up ancient history? Besides, during the time you're referring to, you know I didn't have my head on straight and my thinking was impaired."

Julian nodded. "Okay, that's your excuse and you're sticking to it."

"What do you mean? You know the confusion and the torment I was going through at that time."

"You're right. I know now what a bad time you had of it. But at the time I was in the dark since you didn't give me the courtesy of a phone call or a text to let me know what was going on with you. Therefore, that's a sore memory for me. I was deeply hurt by your brush off when I thought we were getting closer."

"I know. But as I said, it's ancient history and fortunate for us both. I have seen the errors of my ways for a long time now," Catherine sincerely uttered. "But, I know you didn't drop by to discuss how you're still ticked at me about our missed opportunity to be together a year and a half ago. I hope your visit here this evening is because you missed me."

"You're right, Catherine. My visit this evening is because I have missed you. I have actually missed you a lot," he said assuredly.

Catherine smiled. "That's good to hear. It's actually wonderful news because I have missed you more than I can say."

Catherine noticed what she was wearing and silently wished he had called and informed her of his visit so she could have looked her best. She felt slightly uneasy wearing chance clothing with her hair pulled back in a ponytail un-styled.

Julian glanced about the large room noticing they were alone, then he grabbed both of her hands, looking in her eyes. "I know I told you I dropped by because I have missed you," he said and paused, smiling at her. "That's true, Catherine. But it's not the whole reason why I have paid you an unplanned visit," he said with a serious look on his face. "But you might be able to guess."

"You look serious, but you're smiling. Therefore, it must be good whatever the reason." Catherine paused and thought for a moment. "Let me see, it's not my birthday. So, I have no idea why you have dropped by unplanned. So, just tell me."

Julian nodded with serious eyes. He felt excited and assured in what he was going to tell her. "Well, here's the real reason I dropped by. I'm here because I've made up my mind about my future plans and moving on."

Catherine swallowed hard as she stared at him. Suddenly her heart raced with anxiety. "So, I guess you dropped by to inform me that you're moving on without me?" She sadly grunted. "I dreaded this day would come. After an entire year of casual dating here and there with no mention of a commitment, I figured you would eventually get to the point where you didn't want the relationship at all."

Julian smiled at her. "Catherine, are you finished?"

Catherine shook her head as disappointment ripped through her. She had drew an attitude of her assumption. "No, I'm not finished. I have just one question for you."

"Okay, what's your question?" he asked.

"Please be honest with me," Catherine stressed. "I think I deserve that much from you."

"Catherine, I plan to be nothing else but honest with you," Julian assured her. "So, what's your question?"

"I just want to know are you moving on with Mildred Ross."

Julian looked at Catherine and slowly shook his head, and then smiled at her overactive imagination trying to assume his thoughts. "Just give me a moment and I'll explain my decision."

Just then Natalie stepped into the room with a serving tray of hot tea. She placed the tray of tea for two on the coffee table and as she turned to leave the room, Catherine softly and politely said.

"Natalie, wait just a second."

Natalie stepped in front of Catherine where she was seated on the sofa with Julian. "Yes, Miss Catherine."

"Natalie, I just want to thank you for the tea. But I didn't request it."

"I know, Miss Catherine," Natalie answered.

"It's considerate of you to bring it in to us," Catherine said gratefully. "But in the future, please wait for my request."

Natalie didn't comment as she stood there staring at Catherine in confusion. After Natalie didn't reply, Catherine cautiously continued, hoping she hadn't offended Natalie.

"Natalie, I would like for you to wait for my request, only in case tea isn't the beverage of choice and I prefer you serve something different," Catherine politely said. "I'm sure you understand."

It dawned on Natalie that Catherine thought she had taken it upon herself to serve them tea. She wondered if she should clear up the misunderstanding or just say okay and walk away. But Natalie decided she didn't want Catherine to think she had brought in the tea of her own decision.

"Miss Catherine, I do understand. And of course, in the future I'll wait for your request. But I do need to tell you something that I feel a little awkward saying."

Catherine looked at Natalie curiously wondering what Natalie could possibly have to say to her after a direct directive about when and when not to serve tea to her guests. "It's fine Natalie. Say what you feel you need to say," Catherine encouraged her.

"I just wanted to tell you, I didn't bring in the tea at my own discretion. I was given instructions to bring it in to you and Mr. Julian," Natalie politely explained.

Catherine swallowed the lump in her throat. "I beg your pardon, I'm sure I didn't give you instructions to bring in the tea. I wasn't even aware of Julian's visit until he arrived. There's no way I could have given you those instructions."

"No you didn't give me the instructions. Someone else in the household gave me the instructions to bring tea in to you and Mr. Julian."

"But no one knew he was here except you and me."

"Before Miss Veronica left the premises, she instructed me to serve the two of you hot tea. I received the request from Miss Veronica."

Catherine swallowed hard as her blood boiled. But she kept her composure. "Thanks, Natalie. That clears up the misunderstanding," Catherine softly said. "So, that will be all."

After Natalie stepped out of the living room, Catherine down casted her eyes at Julian. "I'm assuming Veronica knew of your visit?"

Julian nodded with a straight face. "Yes, she knew."

"May I ask, why did you feel compel to keep Veronica abreast of your visit to me?"

"Catherine, I can see you're getting a little heated. But don't get your feathers all ruffled. It's a long story."

"Okay, so it's a long story," Catherine said. "I have the time to hear it, since I especially would like to know how Veronica knew you were paying me a visit before I knew."

"It's no big deal. She and I had talked earlier."

"Earlier when?"

"Earlier during the day when she dropped over and paid me a surprise visit. I wasn't expecting her," Julian reluctantly shared.

Catherine frowned, shaking her head in irritation. "I cannot believe the gall of her. She paid you a visit?"

"Yes, and if you'll let me explain, I will."

Catherine instantly drew an attitude and held up both hands. "The floor is yours. Please explain."

Julian shook his head. "I might as well tell you. Veronica has been a champion of our relationship from the start. She paid me a visit not to butt in your personal life as you're assuming, it seems."

"It's not about thinking she's butting in. It's about she had no right to butt her nose in our affair."

"I can tell you're ticked and I was not pleased during her initial visit. But after I reflected. It made me realize she showed up at my door because she cares a great deal about you, Catherine," Julian firmly stated.

"Of course, she cares," Catherine agreed. "Her control efforts are always about how much she cares. I just would prefer if she stayed out of my affairs."

"Lighten up. Her mission was to light a fire under me."

"Well, did she succeed?" Catherine heatedly asked.

"My answer leans toward yes, since she proceeded to tell me of your plans to travel around the world."

"So, she told you about my possible cruise?"

"Yes, she did and much more," Julian said. "Bottomline, she made it crystal clear that if I don't share my feelings with you, I could lose the chance," Julian explained.

"I'm not sure I'm following you, Julian. But either way, Veronica should have stayed out of it," Catherine agitatedly grumbled.

"Well, as I stated, I felt the same way when she first showed up at my front door unannounced catching me off guard the way she did. But as I said, it came to me that she wasn't trying to meddle or be intrusive into our personal affairs."

"But all the same she was," Catherine griped.

"Listen, Catherine. She was looking out for you. But I must say, she was rather bold in pushing me to take a stand and share my feelings with you."

Catherine eyes widened as she stared at Julian. "So, what are you saying? Do you have feelings for me?"

Julian nodded. "Of course, I have feelings for you, Catherine."

"Oh, of course, you do; and of course I should know that, considering how clear you made it last year up at the lake house how you were totally hung up on Mildred Ross," Catherine grumbled sarcastically.

"Yes, I was honest with you. I wanted a relationship with Mildred greatly at that time. But the truth is quite clear. Mildred doesn't want a relationship with me. I think better than a year is long enough to make her point."

"So, after a whole year of carrying a torch for another woman, you have decided to settle for me?" Catherine dryly asked.

"Julian shook his head. "Catherine, it's not like that. I'm not settling for you. I have feelings for you. The same feelings I had before I met Mildred. The truth is, I wanted to bury these feelings and never revisit them after you totally and completely disappointed me when you ignored me as if I didn't exist!" Julian admitted. "I know you have explained yourself and I have had time to process it all and I accepted your explanation that you didn't mean to be intentionally rude. In a nutshell, your behavior toward me was due to the fallout of what you were going through at that time," he inhaled deeply. "Nevertheless, the way you ignored me was a cold slap in the face."

Catherine looked eagerly at Julian as her heart raced. It sounded more and more as if he was on the brink of starting over with her in a real manner instead of just being friends with no commitment.

Catherine pointed toward the coffee table at the tray of tea and Julian nodded yes. Then she strung from her seat and slowly poured them both a cup of tea. She added sugar and cream to each of their cups then handed Julian his cup as she slowly took her seat back on the sofa beside him with her cup in hand.

Julian took a sip of tea and smiled at Catherine. "I'll get right to the point of my visit. I have thought long and hard and I think there's a chance for us after all. If you still want to give the relationship a chance."

Catherine smiled and nodded. "Of course, I would love to give it a chance." Catherine leaned forward, placing her cup of tea on the coffee table, then held up both hands. "I have waited what? A year and a half to hear those words from your mouth," she cheerfully said to him.

Julian smiled. "That sounds good and here's what I propose. How would you like to move into the Coleman mansion with me and Oliver?"

Catherine stood from the sofa and slowly walked over by the fireplace. She placed both hands on the mantle with her back to Julian. His request was unexpected and caught her off guard. She turned and looked at him with her mouth open. She was speechless for a few seconds before she spoke. "I must say you don't waste any time. You had me hanging on wondering if you could forgive me and give us another chance instead of just hang out buddies. Now in the same breath, you want to try again and live together!" She held up both hands.

"That's correct, Catherine. I don't want to waste anymore time. I want to be with you in every sense of the word."

Catherine held out both arms. "Except marriage, I assume."

"Maybe it could be a possibility down the road. But clearly we don't know each other well enough to consider marriage," he seriously uttered. "And honestly, I have never really been a fan of marriage, which I'll share with you one day," he said and paused momentary, as he grabbed his face with both hands and looked toward the floor. The thought of marriage made a painful old memory push against his chest.

Catherine noticed that he seemed a bit disturbed. "Julian, are you okay?"

He nodded and smiled as he looked at her. "Sure, I'm fine. "But I'm still dealing with some disturbing memories in regards to marriage."

"But you have never been married, is that right?" she asked.

"That is absolutely correct. However, what I never shared is how much I wanted to marry Oliver's mother; and we were engaged to be married until she skipped town never to be seen or heard from again," Julian solemnly shared. "She left infant Oliver with my mother and supposedly she was going to run an errand. But she never resurfaced."

"Julian, I can only imagine how devastating that must have been for you?"

"Yes, it was. But let's get off that subject and back on to our happier discussion about living together," he said. "But seriously, now that you have a little insight about my past in regards to marriage. Maybe you can understand why I feel my suggestion of living together would be perfect." He rubbed both hands together. "We could live under the same roof and get to know everything about each other."

"I think I'm getting excited. But first I need to pinch myself," Catherine cheerfully exclaimed. "I thought I had messed up our connection forever. And besides that, I thought you would never get over your feelings for Mildred Ross. Will wonders ever cease? Now we are discussing possibly living together," Catherine excitedly said, as she sat back down beside him.

"I know you haven't given me your answer yet. But I want you to know I talked to Oliver and he's pleased and in favor of our possible living arrangement. He said it would lively the big house up to have a woman under the roof."

Catherine leaned in and kissed Julian on the side of the face. "I won't keep you in suspect any longer. My answer is yes. I would love to move in. But, not right away. I think we need to go through the normal process of dating; and when it feels right I'll call the movers and have my belongings moved from Franklin House to the Coleman mansion. Besides, Veronica and the boys will be really pleased. Besides, since it's not an immediately move, it will give them time to get use to the idea of me leaving the mansion," Catherine excitedly explained.

"So, you're okay with my suggestion?" Julian asked. "Do you think you would be happy co-existing with me? That is, when you decide you're ready to move out of here?"

Catherine nodded. "Of course, I'm sure I'll be happy co-existing with you. You make me happy, Julian. I can breathe around you. It's like night and day from my memories of Antonio. Loving him when he was alive kept me in a constant state of dread." She leaned in and kissed the side of his face again.

Chapter Twenty-One

Larry and Courtney were seated at the lunch table together in the upscale cafeteria of Shady Grove. Four other patients were also seated at their table. The lunchroom had the look and ambiance of an elegant upscale eatery. It gave the patients a sense that they were dining in a fine restaurant instead of the reality of being confined in a mental institution. The large elegant cafeteria was decorated in cotton white and sea green. The walls were painted in sea green with white baseboards and white window casing. At each window hung long sheer sea green curtains. Each of the twenty-Five round tables that seated six were draped in white table cloths. On each table sat a green and white bouquet of silk carnations. The floor of the cafeteria and the entire facility was laid in white marble.

Larry had been at the facility for two weeks but this Monday was the first day he had noticed Courtney. He had an eye for attractive females and found Courtney quite appealing from the moment he spotted her seated at the table. He chose to sit at the table where she was seated, right next to her because he wanted to introduce himself and become acquainted with her.

The moment he was comfortable in his seat, he looked at her and smiled. "My name is Larry Westwood. I'm on the second floor."

Courtney didn't look toward him or respond to his introduction.

He continued to smile, looking toward her, hoping she would respond. "I'm leaving here on Friday," he cheerfully told her and paused. "And if you don't mind, I would like to know your name?"

Courtney glanced at Larry and quietly snapped. "Please don't talk to me. I could care less about your itinerary. Besides, I don't talk to nit wits," she said, and then raised her hand for an attendant.

A short redheaded attendant rushed across the cafeteria to their table. It was Helen Madden. She had been hired as a lunchroom attendant a year ago, two months after Courtney was admitted. She gave up her position at Taylor Gowns to avoid seeing Oliver in and out of the dress shop visiting Trina.

"Yes, Miss Ross. What can I get you?"

Courtney pointed to Larry. "You can find this man another table away from this one. He's bothering the hell out of me," she rudely grumbled.

"How is Mr. Westwood bothering you?"

"He's trying to talk to me and I don't talk to people like him."

Helen immediately drew an attitude at Courtney's words. She wasn't sure if Courtney was being obnoxious or bias. "Miss Ross, I need you to clarify your statement."

"Clarify what statement?"

"When you referred to people like him, what did you mean by that?" Helen firmly asked. "Of course, you know Shady Grove has a zero bias tolerance on the books," Helen reminded her.

"I know about that policy, but it's for the workers and not the patients," Courtney rudely snapped. "How can you hold a bias statement against someone who doesn't know what they're talking about?" Courtney laughed.

"You are correct in regards to the workers. However, it also apply to the patients that are of sound mind."

"Thank you, if you're saying I'm of sound mind. That's the point I was trying to make." Courtney pointed around the room. "Isn't it obvious that everyone in this room is a little nuts like Mr. Westwood? That's why I don't belong here among all these fruitcakes," Courtney strongly fussed.

"Miss Ross, please calm down or I'll be forced to call your doctor and you'll be confined to your room again."

"Please, Miss Madden. Don't call my doctor. I hate that short fat man and how he talks to me like I'm a child. He wouldn't hesitate to stick me in my room; and I hate that! I hate being among all these screwballs. But I hate being stuck in my room even more!" Courtney inhaled sharply. "Miss Madden, when is this nightmare going to end for me?"

Helen stared at Courtney and counted to five. "Well, Miss Ross. I'm not a doctor as you know. I'm just a lunchroom attendant. But I think I can answer your question or give it a good shot," Helen seriously replied.

Courtney stared curiously at Helen. "Please do, Miss Madden. Just tell me what you can. I have a life that's passing me by every day that I'm confined here in this facility of oblivious fools," Courtney whispered up to Helen in a low voice.

Larry and the other four patients seated at the table were busy eating their lunch and didn't seem distracted by Courtney and Helen's conversation; and didn't seem aroused by Courtney's disrespectful language in regards to the other patients at Shady Grove.

Helen glanced about the cafeteria to see if any other workers were within earshot of her conversation with Courtney. When she didn't notice anyone nearby, just two other attendants at the other end of the cafeteria, she looked at Courtney and nodded.

"Miss Ross, here's what I think. You have been here a year, around the same length of time I started. Maybe just a couple months before I was hired. However, what I have observed is remarkable. In the beginning you would sit at the table during your meals and wouldn't talk or make eye contact with anyone. You barely would eat all your food. You walked slow and appeared distraught. When someone spoke to you, you wouldn't always respond and acknowledge that they had spoken to you. You were a very sick young lady. However, at this stage, you're interacting with others," Helen encouragingly told her. "Nevertheless, your attitude and disrespectful language need to be toned down. But other than that, I think you're on your way out of here real soon," Helen assured her.

"How soon is real soon? This place stinks of insanity!" Courtney griped. "Being here messes with my head. It makes me think I should be here when I know I shouldn't."

Helen held up one finger as she glanced toward the cafeteria front entrance. She heard her name being paged. "Excuse me," she said without looking back toward Courtney as she stepped away from Courtney's table.

After Helen stepped away, Larry gently touched Courtney's arm to get her attention. "I'm really sorry if I bothered you. It wasn't my intention. I just wanted to meet you. I won't bother you again," Larry assured her as he lifted his glass of cherry Kool-Aid and took a swallow.

Courtney shook her head as she glanced at Larry's glass in his hand. "What is that you're drinking? I know it's not what I think it is. Not here in this supposedly catering to the rich facility."

Larry looked at her and smiled at the thought of her talking to him. "I don't know what you think it is." Larry held the glass out and looked at it. "It's just a glass of cherry kool-Aid."

"How did you manage that?" she griped.

"How did I manage what?" he asked, nervously.

Courtney humped up her shoulders and shook her head. "It's not important. I was just wondering how you managed to get your hands on Kool-Aid in this highbrow madhouse." Courtney asked. "It's not on the beverage list."

"I know it's not on their beverage list," Larry confirmed. "This is a fancy place and my Mama and Daddy told me they wouldn't have Kool-Aid on their drink list. But since I only drink Kool-Aid. When they decided to check me in for an evaluation my boss told me and my Mama that he would request Kool-Aid to be served with my meals for lunch and dinner during my entire stay here," Larry explained.

"Your boss?" Courtney shook her head. "You have a job? Who hired you?" Courtney rudely asked and then waved her hand. "Nevermind, don't answer that. Apparently you work for some filthy rich person if they saw fit to pay through the nose to have you admitted here."

Larry nodded. "Yes, you're right. Mr. Charles is very rich. He's also a good boss to make that special request for me."

Courtney swallowed hard and almost got choked off of air when Larry said the name Mr. Charles. Courtney sat there with her heart racing, wondering if he could be referring to Charles Taylor. She was about to ask him when Helen strutted back over to their table.

"Mr. Westwood," Helen said as Larry looked at her with his full attention.

Helen smiled at him. "Everything is fine. I just want you to know a message just came through for you from Starlet Taylor. She asked me to relay to you to pack and be ready to leave the facility on Wednesday instead of Friday," Helen said and then glanced at her watch.

Courtney grabbed her stomach with both hands as her mouth fell open. It had just dawned on her that Larry was connected to the Taylor family. One of the families she had been obsessed with. But knew she had blown her chance of ever being close to anyone in the Taylor or Franklin family ever again. Now, she was sitting side by side with someone who worked for the Taylors and that made her feel privileged. If she couldn't be friends with a Taylor or a Franklin, she was pleased to be associated with one of their workers.

Chapter Twenty-Two

Courtney seemed engrossed in her daydream about discovering Larry's connection to the Taylor's. She didn't immediately notice when Helen tapped the table in front of her to get her attention. But Courtney was looking down, tapping her fork lightly on her plate. She was still in deep concentration about how pleased she was to know Larry was connected to the Taylors.

"Miss Ross, did you hear me?" Helen softly asked.

Courtney glanced up at Helen and smiled. "I'm sorry, Miss Madden. What did you say?"

"Can I be of further assistance before my shift ends?" Helen said. "I think you wanted Mr. Westwood to move to another table. I'm sure he wouldn't mind moving to the next table if that will please you."

Larry immediately stood up from the lunch table and grabbed his meal tray. "Sure, I don't mind moving to the next table not one bit. I'll just move to the table to the left," he said heading to the next table.

"Where are you going?" Courtney anxiously asked.

Larry looked around at Courtney. "I'm taking the next table so I won't bother you."

"Don't be silly," Courtney laughed. "I was just kidding around with you when I said that. You don't have to leave the table." Courtney stood, stepped over and grabbed Larry's arm and ushered him back to his seat.

"Please be seated and forgive my big mouth. I didn't mean what I said about you leaving the table," she insisted.

Larry placed his tray on the table and then took his seat. He was puzzled by her actions of insisting he not leave the table since she had made a fuss to Helen about wanting him to leave her present.

When Courtney took her seat back at the lunch table next to Larry, Helen stood there with her mouth open. "I don't know what just happened here. But Miss Ross. I'm impressed and glad you were kidding around. However, I guess Mr. Westwood and myself took you at your word. You appeared quite adamant when you first called for my attention," Helen reminded her. "Nevertheless, I'm glad the issue has been resolved and you two can co-exist at the same table."

Courtney smiled at Helen. "I'm glad to."

Helen nodded. "That's good. So, once again I'm quite impressed with your manners. It goes back to what I was telling you earlier. I believe you'll be released soon. Displaying consideration and apologizing for being rude takes courage."

Helen walked away smiling. She was pleased Courtney had apologized to Larry. She found Larry attractive with an innocent, kind nature. She had been attentive to him since his stay at the facility.

Courtney sat there looking at Larry as he eat his lunch. She pushed her tray aside, no longer hungry for the egg salad sandwich, chicken soup and sliced peaches on a bed of lettuce with cottage cheese. Her hunger had turned into curiosity and possibilities as she discreetly watched Larry eat his lunch. Knowing he was connected to the Taylors instantly made him important to her as she silently thought of what she would say to warm up to him.

"My name is Courtney. What's yours?"

"I'm Larry," he mumbled, not looking toward her.

"So, you work for the Taylors?" Courtney casually asked, in a friendly cheerful manner. She was on her best behavior.

Larry nodded, surprised she had introduced herself and was now asking him a question. He didn't want to appear too excited or overbearing toward her. Therefore, he didn't look her way as he continued to eat this food. But just as he figured she wouldn't say anything else to him, she asked him another question. "Do you know all the Taylors?"

This time Larry didn't answer as he took the last bite from his sandwich. After he chewed the food in his mouth, Courtney thought he would answer her. But he took his napkin and wiped his hands. And it was clear to her that he was preparing to leave the lunch table. Therefore, desperate to talk to him, she tapped his arm.

"Larry, did you hear what I asked you?"

Larry looked at her and nodded. But didn't speak.

"Well, why didn't you answer me?" she asked.

"I didn't answer because I don't want to bother you. You asked me not to talk to you, Miss Ross, and I'm trying to respect what you asked of me. I don't want to get in trouble. You could be trying to get me in trouble."

Courtney drew an attitude at what he said, but pulled it right in and smiled. "Why would you think that of me?"

Larry shrugged his shoulders. "Well, I'm new here and you said you didn't want me to talk to you. But now you're talking to me. I thought if I talked back, it's a trick to tell Miss Madden I'm bothering you."

"It's not a trick." Courtney smiled. "I told you I was just kidding around about those things I said earlier. "So, please, stay seated."

Larry eyes widened. He was pleasantly surprised. "You want me to stay in my seat here at the table so we can talk?"

Courtney nodded with a big smile. "That's exactly what I want. I don't know many people here. It would be nice to have someone to talk to."

"But I thought you didn't want to talk to any of us at this facility. You said all the patients here are fruitcakes," Larry reminded her.

Courtney laughed. "Larry you're funny." She held up both hands. "I know I said that. But I was just blowing off steam."

Larry shook his head. "You seemed serious and also upset."

"But I wasn't," Courtney softly said. "Besides, what I said, I meant in a nice way. Please don't take me so serious. I was just vending with Miss Madden because I want to get out of this place. I'm sure you can understand. You want to get out of here too. Don't you?"

"Yes, I want to leave and understand you wanting to leave this place. But I thought you said those things because you feel you don't belong here."

Courtney smiled. "You're right. That's exactly how I feel."

"Do you feel that way because you feel you're smarter than the other patients?" Larry asked looking in her eyes, thinking how pretty she was.

Courtney shrugged her shoulders. "It's not that. I just know I don't belong here. At least not anymore," Courtney said. "It has nothing to do with thinking I'm smarter than the other patients. I promise. I don't think that."

"Well, I think you're smarter than the other patients and also prettier."

Courtney smiled at his unexpected compliment. "You think I'm pretty?"

"I think you're very pretty. Too pretty to be in a place like this. This is a place for someone like me. But not you. I'm here because I have a condition." Larry glanced about the cafeteria. "Everyone here seem to have a condition. But you seem different than the rest. You don't seem to have a condition."

Courtney stared into space for a moment. Larry words made her think deep about herself and why she had been committed to Shady Grove. She looked at Larry with serious eyes. "I know I look like I don't have a condition. But that's because the condition I had is gone." She grabbed both cheeks and stared down at the lunch table."

Larry didn't comment as she seemed sad. After a bit of silence, she looked at him seriously. "In the beginning I had a very serious condition."

"Okay, if you had such a serious condition, what happened to the serious condition that you had?" Did your doctor make you better?" Larry curiously asked. "If your doctor made you better that's good news. My doctor can't make me better. My condition won't go away," Larry explained.

"Larry, my condition left because my doctor was able to heal me. They told me it was a temporary condition. It was temporary insanity."

"I guess my condition is permanent insanity. I'll always be crazy."

"Larry, don't say that," Courtney firmly said. "Why would you call yourself that?"

Larry smiled as he relaxed in his chair. "You sound like my Mama. She doesn't like for me to call myself crazy. But it just comes easy for me to say it."

"But why should it come easy for you to call yourself crazy?" she asked.

"Maybe because my grandma called me crazy. She always said I was!"

Courtney grabbed her water bottle and took a sip of water. She had gotten choked up on what Larry had just told her. She was smart enough to know that those words from his own grandmother were mental cruelty. She tapped Larry's arm to get his full attention. "Excuse my manners. But your grandmother sounds awful." Courtney shook her head. "A grandmother who would call her own grandson crazy must be nuts herself," Courtney suggested.

Larry laughed. "I agree with you about Grandma Lulu. It was something wrong with her. But she didn't think so. She always said it was me."

"You're speaking in the past tense, I guess she's no longer with us."

"No, she's dead."

"I'm sorry to hear about your loss. But she was wrong about you."

"Thank you, Miss Ross."

"Don't call me that. Call me Courtney. I consider you a new friend."

"Okay, I'll call you, Courtney. But I'm confused about something," Larry said and paused, sharing in her eyes.

"What are you confused about?"

"I'm confused that a very pretty girl like you would want to be friends with me. Most pretty girls won't even talk to me," Larry humbly confessed.

"Larry, I'm not like most girls. I have been through the ringer and back and I just want to be happy and spend time with someone who really wants to be with me. I did something really bad in the past. I made a huge mistake."

"We all make mistakes," Larry said.

"That's true. We do all make mistakes. But what I did was worse than a regular mistake," Courtney glumly shared with him.

"How bad of a mistake was it?" he asked. "I'm sure it wasn't as bad as you think. I'm sure you didn't kill anyone," Larry sort of joked.

Courtney eyes widened at the word he used. It made her feel uneasy since her breakdown almost made her a killer. "Larry, don't joke about something like that."

"I'm sorry I used the word kill. I'm just trying to tell you that your mistake probably isn't as bad as you think."

"Thank you, Larry for saying that. But my mistake was so bad that it made me an outcast. That's why I don't have any friends. The people who used to be my friends are no longer my friends. They don't want to be around me or anywhere near me." Courtney held up both hands. "I'm really not complaining about my outcast treatment because I brought it on myself. I don't blame any of them for not wanting to be around me. What I did was very bad and saying I'm sorry, which I am, would never be enough to make it right. So, I might be cute with all my marbles back in place. But I don't have any friends because nobody wants to be my friend," Courtney sadly shared.

"You sound sort of like me. But I have gone through solitude and seclusion all my life. Being lonely and loneliness is something I have gotten used to. But meeting you makes me feel less lonely since you know what I mean about loneliness," Larry said, smiling.

"Yes, I do know what you mean. The both of us understands loneliness. But it also means something else," Courtney smiled.

"Something like what?" Larry asked.

"It means we have something in common," Courtney cheerfully said.

Larry nodded, looking at Courtney. "You're right. We do have that in common. I didn't think we had anything in common. But I was wrong since we both know how it feels to be all alone wishing for a friend to talk to," Larry excitedly spoke, feeling more comfortable with Courtney. "I want a friend and you want a friend. Now we can be friends to each other."

Larry and Courtney were so enthralled with conversing with each other until an hour passed and they hadn't notice the lunchroom had emptied out. Everyone had left and all the tables had been cleared and wiped clean.

"Larry, I can't tell you how wonderful it feels to have a guy look at me with warmth in his eyes and not pity or contempt." Courtney smiled. "Plus, you have really nice eyes."

Larry blushed. "You think I have nice eyes?"

Courtney smiled and nodded. "Yes, I do. I think your dark brown eyes are nice and friendly to look at."

"Thank you. I really like looking at you too. You're one of the prettiest girls I have ever seen other than the Taylor girls. They are all very pretty. But my Daddy and Mama told me in the beginning when I first moved in with them that I couldn't ask those girls out or be too friendly with them," Larry shared, tapping his fingers on the table looking down. "You, see, when I first moved on the Taylor estate, I was taken with Sabrina until my folks fussed and pounded into my head that it wouldn't work."

A sharp pain rushed through Courtney's stomach at the mention that he had be drawn to Sabrina. It made her momentarily relive a flicker of the agony that had pushed her over the edge. That thought that she wasn't as desirable to Britain as Sabrina.

"But I'll tell you right now, Courtney. I would pick you over Sabrina."

Courtney smiled as a feeling of acceptance rushed through her. "Why would you pick me over Sabrina Taylor? Do you think I'm prettier than her?"

Larry shook his head. "It's not that. You're pretty and she's pretty. But I would pick you because you want to be my friend just as I want to be yours."

"That's true. But I'm sure Sabrina wanted to be your friend as well. I know her well enough to know how friendly and compassionate she is."

Larry nodded. "You're right. She wanted to be my friend. But that was all. She's in love with Mr. Britain. They plan to get married this year sometime. They set a date for last year for July fourth. But they didn't get married on that date. Something happened and they cancelled the wedding. But Miss Sabrina told me a few weeks ago that they plan to set another date as soon as a sick friend is well again. Then my Mama told me that she didn't know or understand why Miss Sabrina and Mr. Britain were waiting for a sick friend to recover. Because the sick friend did something not good to Miss Sabrina and Mr. Britain." Larry shook his head with disgust in his eyes at the thought of someone being unkind to Sabrina and Britain. "Miss Sabrina and Mr. Britain are two good people. They treat me good and everybody good. I don't understand why someone chose to do something bad to them."

Courtney was staring into space feeling guilty as Larry spoke. She knew she was cured. Otherwise, hearing him speak of Sabrina and Britain being unfairly hurt wouldn't have bothered her. She also knew she was healed when the thought of them putting their future on hold for her also made her feel guilty.

Chapter Twenty-Three

    Larry sat there at the table with his stomach in knots wondering why Courtney was suddenly quiet. She was looking down at the table as if she was sad about something. He swallowed hard building up his nerve to say something. He wondered if he had offended her or if she no longer wanted his company. He just wanted her to speak and make him aware of what was on her mind. A few minutes later, after it appeared they were just going to sit there in silence, he gathered his nerves and tapped her on the arm. "What's the matter?" he asked. "Is it something I said?"

    "No, it's nothing you said," she said assuredly. But it was something he had said. He had brought it to her attention that he wasn't pleased that someone would hurt Sabrina and Britain. Courtney felt sad being the person that had hurt them. But knew she couldn't breathe a word of the truth to him.

    "Are you sure? We were discussing who would want to hurt Miss Sabrina and Mr. Britain and then you just stop talking," he reminded her.

    Courtney smiled at him. "I know. But it's not anything you said."

    "I hope not. But you don't seem in a good mood right now. So, maybe you just don't want to talk anymore."

    Courtney kept smiling at him. "I'm enjoying our time together."

    "You say that. But you still seem sad about something," he said.

    "No, I'm not sad; and I apologize for my silence. I was in deep thought."

    "Deep in thought. That sounds important or trouble," he said.

    "It's not either. I was just thinking about something that's not important. So, I apologize again for my rudeness and being preoccupied."

    Larry wasn't convinced that she really wanted to continue in his company. "I'll understand if you're tired of talking. I can leave and we can talk again some other time. I don't want to annoy you and push you away. You make me feel like Christmas is here," Larry cheerfully said.

Courtney liked Larry nice teeth with above average looks. She also liked his clean-shaven fair complexion and short curly black hair. However, based on his talk, she could tell he was somewhat mentally challenged. But it didn't bother her. She was excited he wanted to talk to her. His connection to the Taylors and the Franklins made her desperate for his acceptance. She grabbed her mouth in a loud cough at the thought, wondering would he still want her as a friend if he knew about her crime against Sabrina and Britain.

"Larry, I'm not tired of talking to you. Not even a little. I'm having more fun talking to you than I have had in a long time," she cheerfully admitted.

Larry laughed. "I'm glad you said that. Because I have never had this much fun. Now I hate to think of Wednesday."

"Why do you hate to think of Wednesday?"

"I leave here on Wednesday."

Courtney grabbed both cheeks as her mouth fell open. "That's right. That message you received from Starlet."

Larry nodded as he kept smiling. "That's okay. We'll talk again before I leave. Maybe we'll share a table at dinner this evening, and tomorrow morning for breakfast," Larry eagerly suggested, hoping she would be in favor.

Courtney smiled and nodded. "That sounds great. Also, if you would like, you can come see me after you check out on Wednesday," Courtney blurted out, hoping he wouldn't think she was being too forward.

"You want me to come back here to visit you?" Larry asked.

"Yes, you can come see me after you leave. Do you drive?"

"I don't drive, but the Taylor's chauffeur will drop me off," he told her.

"Do you mind taking public transportation if the chauffeur doesn't bring you? Somehow, I doubt if their chauffeur will bring you here to visit me."

"Don't worry. I know the chauffeur will do me a favor."

"How can you be so sure?" Courtney asked.

"It's my Daddy."

"Your father is the Taylor's chauffeur?"

Larry smiled. "Yes, it's my Daddy. I won't have a problem coming here to visit you. But I want to ask you something."

"Okay, ask me."

"I heard Miss Madden, you'll be released soon. You also told me the condition that brought you here is gone and you're well. So, what I'll ask is can I come to your home to see you? You might not be here much longer."

Courtney smiled. "That's a splendid idea. I was hoping you would ask me could you come see me. Larry that would make me very happy."

Larry smiled. "That's great. Now I want to ask you another question."

"Okay, sure. Ask me anything you like."

"Do you have a boyfriend?"

Courtney quickly replied. "No, I don't have anyone in my life right now."

Suddenly Larry got nervous and lost his nerves to ask her to be his girlfriend. Courtney noticed he wasn't silent looking down toward the table. She tapped his arm. "You seem sad all of a sudden. Do you have a girlfriend?"

Larry looked at her and smiled. "No, I don't. I have always wanted a girlfriend. But I haven't been lucky to have one."

"Why not, Larry?" She searched his face. "You're a nice-looking man."

"My Mama says that all the time that I'm a nice-looking man. She told me I look like that actor Richard Gere when he was in this 30's like me."

Courtney nodded. "I can see that. You do have a strong resembling to Richard Gere. But of course, as your mother said, when Richard Gere were much younger before his dark hair turned completely all gray."

"Thank you for saying I resembles Richard Gere. But I don't think I'm handsome like he is. Even with his gray hair, he still looks better than I do."

Courtney smiled. "You might disagree, but I think you resembles him."

"It doesn't matter since I'll never be like that man. He's probably not afraid to approach women. I don't have a girlfriend because I haven't tried to approach anyone to acquaint myself with." Larry lifted his glass of Kool-Aid and took a sip. "Besides, I don't know what to say to a girl and the thought of rejection is scary. It's a bad feeling that makes me feel I'm not good enough. The same bad feeling I have felt about myself over the years growing up."

Courtney shook her head with sad eyes as she listened to Larry.

"I'm sorry to tell you. But it wasn't good. I didn't have one single person around to talk to except Grandma Lulu."

"Why not? I don't understand."

"It's the way Grandma Lula wanted it. And when the mail carrier started coming around to see me, Grandma Lulu pulled a shotgun on the lady."

"Why did your grandmother do that?"

"She said that mail lady was too old for me. But I didn't stop talking to her. We met in privacy in the woods three times before Grandma Lulu tracked us down and ran her away at gunpoint.

"Sounds like your grandma was out of her mind," Courtney told him.

Larry nodded. "I agree with you. I think Grandma Lulu was out of her mind. It wasn't good for her to stay home not talking to other people and she didn't want me talking to anyone."

"Was your grandmother a church-going person?"

"Yes, she went to church and drug me with her. But at church she only talked to the preacher and one other old lady." Larry held up both hands. "But you don't have to worry about Grandma Lulu. She's dead. I told you she died."

"I know you told me your grandmother passed away. I wasn't thinking she would be an issue. I'm mostly thinking about our current issue."

"We have an issued?" Larry asked.

Courtney nodded. "Yes, our social life. You don't have a girlfriend and I don't have a boyfriend. So, what should we do about our single status?"

"I plan to change my status. I'm tired of being single," he told her.

Courtney heart raced and she became anxious at his announcement. "Who are you changing your status with?" Courtney hoped he would say her.

"I don't know who I'm going to change it with. I just know it will be soon." He looked at Courtney with warm eyes. "I hate going to the movies alone; and I won't ask my Mama ever again. I mean, I don't mind taking her to the movies. But my Daddy gets mad when I ask her. He said I don't need my Mama tagging along when I'm out socializing. But I was taking Mama to keep from being out alone. He told me I should try asking a girl out."

"That was good advice from your father."

"It was good advice but I haven't used it," Larry solemnly admitted.

"Why haven't you?"

"I want to. But it's hard to get up my courage to ask someone out."

"It's not hard for you to sit here and talk to me," Courtney said.

"I know it's not hard to talk to you. But it's a reason for that."

"What reason is that?" Courtney curiously asked.

"You don't mind talking to me," he seriously replied, and then laughed. "But you see, this may sound funny, but most girls don't mind talking to me until they start talking to me," he sadly admitted. "That's what I have experienced and my Mama said they can't tell I have a condition until they start a conversation with me. So, I figured I just shouldn't say anything to a girl or ask her out. Because I can't be with her and not talk. But Mama says that's how they know I have a condition when I talk."

"Well, they are stupid. Talking to you made me want to talk to you." Larry nodded, looking down at the table. He felt a pull toward Courtney and he had a strong sense that she liked him. But his fear of rejection was stronger than his will to ask her out.

Chapter Twenty-Four

    The time was ticking along as Courtney and Larry were still seated in the Shady Grove cafeteria. She had a strong feeling that he wanted to ask her out, but she sensed he was too nervous to do so. She knew they couldn't spend much more time in the cafeteria and her patience was wearing thin as she discreetly kept glancing at the big wall clock. She wanted to be his girlfriend, but she didn't want to push it by suggesting it herself. She didn't want to seem too anxious. Therefore, she glanced at her watch. "Maybe we should head to our rooms. It's going to be time for my 3:00 o'clock medicine soon," Courtney told him with no pep to her voice.
    "Sure, we can head to our rooms if you are ready to leave. But it's only 2:30." Larry looked at the big white clock on the cafeteria wall. "We can stay here and talk a while longer. But only if I'm not bothering you."
    "Larry, I have made it clear to you that you're not a bother. You're a breath of fresh air to me. Talking to you is all I want to do. I dread going back to my room and looking at those four walls."
    "Well, why did you suggest we leave?"
    "I thought maybe you wanted to leave."
    "Why did you think that, Courtney? Please believe me when I tell you. Spending time talking to you is all I want to do for the rest of the day, tomorrow and all the days after tomorrow," he excitedly admitted.
    "That sounds like you plan to spend a lot of time talking to me." Courtney smiled, as her face warmed and her heart raced at his enthusiasm of spending time with her.
    "I guess it does; and I hope I can if you'll let me."
    "Of course, Larry. I'll let you."

"Okay, in that case, will you think about letting me be your boyfriend?" Larry held up both hands before she could answer. "You don't have to decide right now. Just give it some thought and think about if you would want me for your boyfriend."

Larry unexpected request was what Courtney had waited for. She accidently showed too much excitement when she jumped up from her seat and slapped her hands excitedly. "Thanks for asking." Then she thought better of her anxious behavior and calmed her tone as she continued to stand there looking down in his dark brown eyes. "Larry, I don't need to think about it. I already know my answer is yes." She leaned down and kissed him on the side of the face and then took her seat.

Larry looked warmly at her. "I can't believe you just said yes. Just like that without thinking about it. I also, can't believe you just kissed me on the side of the face," Larry seriously said to her. "I must be dreaming. Stuff like this don't usually happen to me. I get a yes and a kiss in the same day from the same girl."

Courtney nodded with a smile. "Yes, you do. It's official. You're my boyfriend," Courtney raved, smiling. "I'll introduce you to my family when you come visit me at home. I'll give you my number and you can call and text me as much as you like. Plus, you'll visit me here until they send me home."

Larry felt more excitement than he could ever remember. "I want to meet your family and let you meet Mama and Daddy. I also want to introduce you to the Taylors. They'll be happy to know I have a girlfriend. They'll all be happy for me. They know how much I wanted a girlfriend."

"Larry, you have made me so happy. I feel I have something to look forward to now. Having you in my life. I know you won't judge me. I can be myself and you'll still like me," Courtney said, feeling good cheer for the first time in months. "I know I don't really deserve someone like you. But I'm so thankful you came into my life."

Larry looked at her with serious eyes. "I think you deserve someone better than me. You need someone who doesn't have a condition. I'm not doing you a favor. You're doing me a favor by being my girlfriend. I hope you're not doing it because you feel sorry for me."

"Oh, no, Larry. I don't feel sorry for you. I respect your honesty and candor. You are a genuine person. Why would you think I would feel sorry for you? I should be wondering if you feel sorry for me. Afterall, I am an outcast now. None of my old friends want to be around me," Courtney reminded him.

"Well, I'm wondering if you just feel sorry for me."

"Why would you assume that?" she asked.

"It comes to mind since you didn't seem to like me when we first met. You didn't even want to be at the same table with me," Larry reminded her. "I know you said you were kidding around. But I'm a good judge of the truth. I might not have all my marbles. But I can tell when someone is not being truthful."

Courtney jaw dropped. "Larry, what are you trying to say to me?"

"I'm just telling you that I know you were not kidding at first and I want to know why you changed your mind about me." He held up both hands. "Believe me, I'm glad you changed your mind and I'm glad you have decided to be my girlfriend. But I know you didn't like me very much at first," Larry firmly pointed out.

Courtney dropped her head. He had caught her off guard. She didn't expect him to call her out on her own words that she claimed to be her just kidding around. He had backed her into a corner and she didn't want to tell him the truth. However, she realized if she lied, he would most likely tell her she was telling another tale. She didn't want to risk losing his trust.

"Courtney, if we're going to be together we need to trust each other. You can trust me. Just tell me why you changed your mind about me. I won't get upset."

Courtney looked at Larry and noticed how sincere and friendly his dark brown eyes looked from the chandelier light overhead. "Okay, Larry. You're right. If I have learned anything I have learned how lies don't pay off. So, I will tell you the hard truth and trust you'll still want me as your girlfriend after I do." Courtney held her face and paused up at the glittering chandelier for a moment before she looked at Larry with serious eyes. "You're right. At the start of lunch when I noticed you sitting next to me, I was upset with you and didn't want you to talk to me or be near me. I wanted you away from my table."

Larry was silent as he digested her confession. Then he looked at her with hurt eyes. "Why did you hate me?" he asked. "Is it because of my condition?"

"No, Larry, I didn't know about your condition when you first sat here. I just knew you were a man and I didn't want you near me. It wasn't personal."

"It sounds personal," he sadly mumbled.

"I can tell your feelings are hurt. But I promise you, Larry. It wasn't personal. Any man committed at this facility could have taken your seat and I would have given them the same cold shoulder. I just didn't want any of the male patients that's committed here to talk to me or be near me," she honestly explained. "For some misguided reason I felt I was better than Shady Grove men patients."

Larry nodded and was silent for a moment. Then he looked at her with curious eyes. "Okay, I guess that explains why you hated me in the start," he said to her. "And I do believe the explanation you just gave me. "But what I'm most curious about is why you changed your mind and felt a Shady Grove man was okay to talk to afterall?"

Courtney was nervous and felt silly. She looked at him with a nervous smile. "It was two reasons. You told me your boss was Charles Taylor. Then I heard Miss Madden give you a message from Starlet Taylor. After I discovered you were a part of the Taylor family I was honored to know you and wanted to know you better."

Larry jaw dropped and his eyes widened. But he continued to listen.

"At that point, I really looked at you and realized how decent looking you were. You're fairly tall and slender. You're dressed well in neat blue jeans and a white shirt. You're clean shaven and you have nice curly black hair cut low to your head. You're a real catch as far as I'm concerned and I was surprised to hear you're single," Courtney humbly and nervously confessed. "Therefore, I was blown away and ecstatic when you told me you wanted me to be your girlfriend."

"You need to slow down a little," Larry suggested. "I need to be clear on what changed your mind about me. Therefore, if I heard you correctly, you think I'm nice-looking and you like me because I work for the Taylors? Are those your reasons for changing your mind about not talking to me, which now have led to me asking you to be my girlfriend?" Larry seriously inquired.

Courtney nodded. "I have to admit, I was impressed to hear you were connected to the Taylors. That was my initial attraction and the reason I didn't want you to leave the table. However, after we started talking and I observed your honesty, I felt honored to be in your company; and even more honored that you wanted me in your life," Courtney said with conviction.

Larry nodded. "Okay, thank you for being honest and trusting me enough to be honest. I can tell you're telling me the truth. But tell me why my connection to the Taylors initially attracted you? I know they're rich. But that's not it, is it?"

Courtney shook her head, looking down tapping her right fingers on the table. "You're right. They are very rich people. But that's not why I wanted to be with someone connected to them. The truth is, I used to be friends with Sabrina Taylor," Courtney reluctantly shared with him.

Larry smiled. "That's great. Sabrina is a good person. She'll do anything to help anyone. She's a good friend to have. I'm glad she's my friend."

Courtney was silent for a moment, looking down toward the table. Larry glanced at her but didn't say anything to break her concentration. Then she looked at Larry with sad eyes. "I know Sabrina is a good person. But when we were friends. I was sick back then."

"You were sick with your condition?" Larry compassionately asked.

Courtney nodded nervously as she looked Larry in the face. "That's exactly correct," she said and paused. "And because I was so sick and not myself. I destroyed our friendship. She'll never be friends with me again," Courtney sadly admitted. "But I figured by dating you, it will keep me close to her family and maybe by some miracle one day I'll be able to show her how sorry I am."

"Thanks for sharing that with me." Larry gently patted the top of her hand.

"Now that I have told you, do you still want me to be your girlfriend?" Courtney anxiously asked.

Larry nodded as he looked at her. "Yes, I still do. It didn't matter why you changed your mind. I just wanted to know why. But now that you know I have a six sense about lies, do you still want to be my girlfriend? Because if I think it's not the truth, it usually isn't the truth; and I'll insist on the truth," Larry warned her.

Courtney laughed. "Larry, I need to be with a man like you that can tell when I'm lying and call me on it. If I had been more truthful and a better person I'm sure my life would have turned out a lot different than it has. I wouldn't have so many things in my past to be ashamed of. I'm twenty-five years old and I feel twice my age because of the stuff I have been through," Courtney sadly admitted, grabbed her face and shared into space for a moment before she turned and looked at Larry. "But this place has helped me a lot to put things in perspective."

"In what way do you think it has helped you the most?" Larry asked.

"Mostly it made me face myself. I can't blame anyone but myself. I had really good people in my life who cared about me, but I was selfish and didn't care about anyone."

"You don't seem like that kind of person," Larry complimented.

"I know because that person wasn't me. Somewhere along the way, I lost myself and became someone I didn't recognize. I had suffered a mental break and didn't realize it as I continued to try to live a normal life with my abnormal thoughts and behavior. Then one day my mind completely separated itself from reality and I went completely off the rails and almost destroyed myself and many others," Courtney sadly confessed. "That's how I messed up my friendship with Sabrina."

"Listen, Courtney," Larry said as he softly touched the top of her hand. "I can tell it makes you sad. But don't worry about what happened to mess up your friendship with Miss Sabrina. She's very understanding. If I talk to her on your behalf I'm sure she'll forgive you and the two of you can be friends again."

Courtney shook her head and stared at Larry with desperation on her face and in her eyes. "Thanks for caring. But please don't say anything to Sabrina about me. Don't mention my name; and please don't mention that we're friends." She grabbed his right hand between both of her hands and gripped his hand tightly. "Please, please! A hundred times please! You have to promise not to mention my name to Sabrina," she pleaded. Then glanced down at the grip she had on his hand. She immediately released his hand. "I'm sorry I grabbed your hand. I just need you to promise not to mention me to Sabrina."

Larry was puzzled and confused by her desperate behavior of pleading with him not to mention her name to Sabrina. His eyes widened with confusion.

"Courtney. I'm sorry. But I don't understand. Why wouldn't you want me to tell her? She's a good person and would be happy for us."

"If you tell Sabrina, I'm afraid the Taylors might keep you from dating me. I'm serious Larry. They want nothing to do with me and I don't blame them."

"The Taylors are not like that. I know them well. They would never treat you that way. Why do you think they would?" he seriously asked.

Courtney looked at him but didn't comment. She wanted to share the incident with Larry but the fear of losing him wouldn't let her.

"Maybe you should tell me what happened between you and Sabrina that's so bad?" Larry seriously suggested. "She's nice and you're nice. So I can't imagine that it would be something too bad."

Courtney shook her head with sad eyes as she looked at Larry. "But Larry, I wasn't a nice person a year ago. I was a very sick person and while I was sick I did something to Sabrina that's unforgivable," Courtney sadly told him.

Larry shook his head. "Nothing is unforgiveable. It's just up to the person to find it in their hearts to forgive."

"You're right, Larry."

"So, what did you do to Miss Sabrina that you feel is unforgiveable?"

"Larry, I would rather not mention what it was. But there is something I can tell you," Courtney humbly uttered.

"Okay, just tell me what you can tell me," Larry urged her.

"Well, what I can tell you and I want you to believe me from the bottom of my heart. I was very sick back then when I made those mistakes. But I'm no longer sick and I wholeheartedly promise you, I'll never allow myself to go down a path of self-destruction like that again to hurt Miss Sabrina or anyone else ever. I have learned my lesson."

"I'm glad to hear that. But Miss Sabrina is a good person. I know you were sick. But why not mess with a bad person during your sickness. Why did you mess with a good person like Miss Sabrina?" Larry asked.

"I did it because I hated her," Courtney honestly admitted.

Larry was stunned at her confession. "You hated Miss Sabrina? Why?"

"I cannot give you a logical answer. Because I had no logical reason to hate her. I was just sick out of my mind; and my hatred for her is what helped toward my mental break."

"That is so sad. You were sick with hatred without a reason," Larry said with compassion.

Courtney sadly nodded. "That's true. But there's something else that I should tell you."

"What's that?" he asked.

"Although, I had no logical reason to hate her. My sick mind had manufactured a reason to hate her."

Larry eyes widened with anticipation of what Courtney would say. "And what reason did your mind manufacture for you?"

Courtney shook her head in shame. "I really wish I didn't have to tell you how far gone from reality I was. But I will share it with you. It's about Britain Franklin."

"Okay, what about him?" Larry asked.

"My mind manufactured the belief that Sabrina had taken my boyfriend," Courtney regretfully shared. "I was in love with Britain Franklin. But he wasn't in love with me. And because of my sickness, I blamed Sabrina for things that I know now were not her fault."

Larry nodded. "It was because you hated Miss Sabrina for being with Mr. Britain, who you felt was your boyfriend. You felt that way because you were sick. Mr. Britain wasn't your boyfriend. But your mind thought he was."

"That's right. I was sick to think that way. Britain was never my boyfriend. He was only a passing acquaintance who talked to me about work related business."

"Okay, now can you tell me the bad thing that you did to Miss Sabrina that broke your friendship with her forever?"

Courtney swallowed hard at the thought of revealing her crime to Larry. She wondered would she be able to say out of her mouth the despicable crime that her sick mind was guilty of. But before she could comment in anyway, they looked up at Helen Madden coming across the cafeteria floor toward their table. Helen was wearing a sage green jacket with her purse hanging on her shoulders.

Larry and Courtney looked toward Helen and smiled as she quickly approached their table. "I told your nurse I would find you here in the cafeteria talking with Mr. Westwood," Helen said, smiling as she stepped up to the table and handed Courtney a bottle of water along with a small white cup that contained one white pill. "She asked me to bring your medicine down since she wasn't sure when you would be returning to your room."

"Thanks, Miss Madden. I didn't forget about my 3:00 o'clock medication. I thought of it thirty minutes ago. Then it slipped my mind as we were engaging in conversation."

"That's fine, Miss Ross. You have it now and its 3:00 o'clock on the head. All is well," Helen said as she turned and stepped away from the table and headed toward the cafeteria front exit. Helen had just ended her shift and was leaving work. Halfway across the cafeteria toward the exit, Helen glanced over her shoulder and smiled toward Courtney and Larry. "Have a good evening."

Larry stood from his seat. "I think we should head to our rooms. I'll see you back at this table or another one at 6:00 o'clock for dinner," Larry said, smiling as he watched Courtney gather her purse, notebook and bottle of water from the table as she stood from her seat.

Courtney and Larry held hands as they walked out of the cafeteria into the hallway. Courtney's room was 1033 on the first floor and Larry's room was 2034 on the second floor. He walked Courtney to her room and she was anxiously hoping he wouldn't ask her the question of what she had done to Sabrina. She felt she had been saved by the bell when Helen walked up. She was sure she would have had to confess if Helen Madden hadn't stepped into the lunchroom with her medication. She knew she couldn't continue to prolong the information from Larry. She knew she had to find the courage to tell him at some point.

Chapter Twenty-Five

It was five o'clock on the nose when Carrie showed Britain into the family room at the Taylor mansion that Monday evening. Sabrina was in the family room busy looking through old photo albums of her grand and great-grandparents. She had been busy looking through photo books for the past fifteen minutes after dressing for her dinner date. It had slipped her mind to inform Carrie of her whereabouts in the house in order to escort Britain to her upon his arrival.

Sabrina had no idea she would be so fascinated by the gowns worn by her grandmothers. She had decided to have her wedding gown tailored from the wedding gown worn by her great grandmother on her father's side to honor her great grandmother. But she was especially pleased with the style and layout of the gown. It was beyond elegant and her great grandmother looked like a fairy tale princess in the gown. Therefore, with much consideration and painstaking reflection, she had donated the other wedding dress and the bridesmaid's dresses that had been purchased a year ago to the American Red Cross. She deeply adored the wedding dress and the bridesmaid's dresses that she had chosen for the original wedding date, but chose not to use any of the attire that had been purchased for the original date. She had also changed the wedding colors to white and soft pink. The bridesmaid's dresses would be designed slightly different from the original dresses. They would be made from white satin and lace material highlighted with a soft pink sash around the waist. The groomsmen's tuxedos would be made of white satin and cotton material highlighted by soft pink shirts underneath. The bridal party as well as the bride would carry bouquets of white roses mixed with small pink roses, tied with pink ribbons.

Sabrina had decided on a simpler traditional wedding instead of the royal gala planned before. They had a new date slated for Saturday, August

27, 2016. She and Britain mutually decided not to hold the ceremony in France. After a year of reflection through physical and mental healing from the disaster caused by Courtney, Sabrina especially wanted less publicity and hype surrounding their wedding.

Sabrina glanced up from the stack of ten photo books that were scattered about the large cherry wood square table. The table seated eight and they used it for family board games and playing cards. Sabrina smiled when she saw Britain heading across the room toward her. He was dressed in black slacks and a silk black shirt along with shiny burgundy shoes and a chic burgundy dinner jacket. She closed the photo book in her hand and stood from the table.

"Hi, I'm glad Carrie let you in." She glanced at her watch. "I completely lost track of the time." Sabrina smiled. "I got so caught up in looking through all those old photo books. But, however, as you can see," she said, as she held both arms out and turned around in a complete circle. "I'm ready."

Britain smiled. "Yes, I can see you're ready. You look absolutely beautiful as usual. I'm not sure there's a dress on the market that you wouldn't make look good just by being in it," he said, as he admired the calf length mauve dress she was wearing with a fashionable mauve jacket and chic mauve shoes. He walked up to her and they embraced, looking lovingly at each other.

"That's a mighty tall compliment, Mr. Franklin."

He nodded. "That's right and it was quite genuine. Your beauty overshadows anything you could ever wear?"

Sabrina laughed. "I'll hold you to that thought until our wedding day. When you see me walking down the aisle in my radiant new gown, yet to be designed and made, maybe you'll think twice about your statement," she playfully said.

"I'm sure I will not think twice about my statement. However, one thing I am sure of. On our big day, you'll be a sight to behold," he assured her. "No wedding gown between here and the moon could ever overshadow you in my eyes."

Just as Britain was about to lean in and bring his face down to kiss her, Carrie stepped into the room. "Excuse me, Miss Sabrina. I'm double-checking with you about dinner," Carrie politely and quietly said. "I have listed you as out for dinner. You won't be joining the family for dinner, is that correct?"

Sabrina nodded and smiled. "That is correct, Carrie. Britain is here to take me out to eat. We have dinner plans at the Crystal Café."

Carrie smiled. "That is one elegant place. I ate there once on Sam's and my 40th wedding anniversary. I remember it like yesterday. Sam had to work an entire month to pay off the credit card he used for our dinner that evening," Carrie shared with them in a serious tone.

Britain and Sabrina looked at each other and smiled. "For a Monday night, maybe the Crystal Café isn't the best choice for this evening," Sabrina commented.

Britain held up both hands. "It's up to you. We did just dine there on Friday. But, I should point out. We do have reservations that were booked far in advance."

Carrie frowned. "I hear they glare at cancellations," Carrie quickly added.

Britain nodded toward Carrie. "That's true, Carrie. But we're members of the VIP list. Cancellations don't get us in that much hot water," he said, and then looked toward Sabrina. "Therefore, Sweetheart. We can call and cancel if you would prefer to dine somewhere else this evening instead."

Carrie shook her head and smiled. "Listen, you two. Don't go and change your dinner plans because of my comment. Don't pay me any mind about how expensive the place is."

"But you do have a point," Britain agreed. "It is quite pricey."

Carrie laughed in a discreet manner. "Yes, it is. But I also know, any establishment the two of you frequent would seem too costly to me and Sam. I was just talking about the experience Sam and I had on a tight budget. I didn't mean to make the place sound unappealing. The Crystal Café is a beautiful elegant restaurant. Besides, why shouldn't you two go? You definitely don't have to count pennies like me and Sam." Carrie laughed, but quickly caught herself and raised one finger. "I was just kidding about counting pennies. But I think you know the point I'm trying to make. So, go and enjoy and if it wasn't so inappropriate I would tag along and bring Sam with me. Of course, I would make Mr. Britain foot the bill," Carrie said jokingly, and then held up both hands. "I hope you two know I'm just kidding around about me and Sam tagging along," Carrie assured them.

"You definitely are welcomed to come along with us," Britain said, and nodded toward Sabrina. He looked at Carrie and smiled. We know you're just kidding with us. But if you're ever not kidding. Please come along. You and Sam are welcomed to be our guest," Britain offered.

Carrie looked at Sabrina and Britain for a moment with a serious stare and then smiled. "You two are too generous. But thanks for the invitation," Carrie said and held up one finger. "Reflecting back, dining at the Crystal Café was such an enjoyable evening for me and Sam. Then they handed us the bill and spoiled the moment. However, I think I'll keep your invitation in mind," Carrie said heading out of the room.

Chapter Twenty-Six

Thirty minutes after Sabrina and Britain left the Taylor mansion, they were seated at a cozy table in the refined exclusive Crystal Café restaurant. They had finished their meal, now having coffee and dessert, when Sabrina smiled across the small round table at Britain as she forked a piece of chocolate cake into her mouth. "I'm so pleased to hear the latest report on Courtney's mental well-being. She's finally healthy again."

Britain nodded as he brought his coffee cup up to his mouth and took a sip. "It's splendid. I know. I got the same report from Mother. Apparently your father is keeping Mother abreast and then she's relaying to us about Courtney's condition."

"It's been a long time coming but apparently she is almost ready to be released," Sabrina cheerfully said. "That's such wonderful news. I have prayed so hard for her recovery. Because as long as she was sick I just didn't feel comfortable going ahead with our plans."

Britain nodded as he poured a drop of cream into his coffee. "I do understand how you're feeling relieved. I feel the same," he said. "This is the best news. It really lifts a lot of worries about the prognoses of her health off of our shoulders. Based on the report, it seems she's nearly back to the young lady we first hired."

Sabrina smiled excitedly as she continued to enjoy her slice of chocolate cake. "I never thought I would be so excited and happy to hear any news about Courtney Ross. But I'm so extremely happy and grateful that the doctors at Shady Grove were able to help her; and she's going to be fine."

"One thing I'll never forget about Courtney from that time. She was a good solid worker," Britain recalled.

"I have heard you say that," Sabrina smiled.

"I'm sure you have. My brothers and I used to constantly praise her loyalty and dependability. Besides, being such a devoted employee back then. She was also very polite and friendly. I know you didn't know her that well at that time. But you got a glimpses of her behavior when she was dating Rome. She was as different as day and night from the person she transition into during her illness," Britain recalled.

"You're right," Sabrina agreed. "I didn't know her that well during that time. But she was always polite and friendly when I would see her at Franklin House with Rome."

"She was vastly different then," Britain recalled.

"Do Sydney plan to rehire her?"

"The family and I had a meeting regarding Courtney's status at the company and we all agreed, with the exception of Mother, that it wouldn't be fair or proper to dismiss her because of the tragedy she spearheaded resulting from her mental breakdown."

Sabrina swallowed hard. "So, I guess Sydney will rehire her?" she asked.

Britain nodded. "That was the plan. We had decided she deserved her job back since she wasn't responsible for her actions during her breakdown. Therefore, we met with her mother and informed Mrs. Ross that Courtney's job would be waiting upon her release from Shady Grove."

Sabrina listened intensively as she looked across the table at Britain.

Britain held up one finger. "However, we explained to her mother that it would be a position offsite; and needless to say, during the meeting Mrs. Ross was quite grateful and pleased to know that once her daughter was well again her job would be waiting."

"Based on your explanation, it sounds like your plans to rehire Courtney fell through," Sabrina softly uttered.

Britain smiled. "Yes, you're right. Several weeks after our meeting with Courtney's mother, while we were preparing and putting in place an offsite position for Courtney, we received a letter from Mrs. Ross."

"A letter?" Sabrina asked.

Britain nodded. "Yes, a personal letter addressed to the four of us to inform us that Courtney had been offered a teaching position upon her release and she had accepted the position at Barrington High."

Sabrina grabbed her face with both hands and held her cheeks in good cheer. "Britain, that's incredible news."

Britain stared seriously and caringly at Sabrina. "Yes, its wonderful news and I'm happy for Courtney as well. But Sweetheart, you act as if your happiness depends on Courtney's happiness," Britain said dryly.

Sabrina smile faded as she glanced down at the table for a moment and then looked at Britain and didn't comment.

"Sabrina, it bothers me how you're taking what happened to Courtney on your shoulders. You have been this way ever since we were released from the hospital while Courtney was still hospitalized. You know you're not the blame. But you still feel guilty that you somehow drove her to insanity as if you could have controlled it."

"I know it's obvious in my behavior and reactions and you're right, I know it's not my fault. But yet, I do feel somewhat responsible," she softly admitted. "It's a feeling I can't seem to shake," she said and looked Britain in the eyes. "You know, it might make me happier if you wouldn't constantly remind me of how obvious I am."

Britain shook his head. "I won't keep that promise. You definitely need to stop arranging and pacing your life according to Courtney's wellness. Afterall, we both know that Courtney brought all that happened to her on herself. And of course, we wish her well. However, we can't build our lives around her wellbeing."

"Of course, you are right. But I'm extremely pleased to hear she's going to obtain a teaching position. That's what she went to school for. Plus, I recall you telling me how desperately she wanted to be a school teacher when she was first hired at Franklin Gas. The position you placed her in was supposed to be temporary until she landed a teaching position," Sabrina reminded him.

"That's true and she always reminded everyone," Britain recalled. "Then she took ill and lost sight of reality and all she was interested in was figuring out some way to hurt the both of us," he regretfully admitted.

"The good news is," Sabrina cheerfully said. "We won't have to wait much longer before we walk down the aisle. Our big day is just one year in front of us."

"I agree its good news," Britain smiled. "But I would consider it better news if you and I were already married. You know, I was never in favor of waiting and putting off the wedding," Britain told her.

"We decided together, remember? You agreed to postpone the date when I suggested it."

"Of course, I agreed darling. We had no other choice but to postpone the original date. We were both recovering and still under our doctor's care by the time July 4th rolled around," Britain softly pointed out. "I guess what I'm getting at, I didn't expect you to set the date for two years after the disaster that occurred."

Sabrina nodded. "I didn't want to push it that far in advance. But I went with August 27, 2016 to give us enough time to be completely out of our doctor's care."

"Yes, we need to heal and get healthy," Britain agreed.

Sabrina lifted her coffee cup and took a sip. Holding the cup with both hands she lowered the cup to the table and silently stared down in the cup.

Britain noticed her sudden silence and asked. "Is something the matter?"

She looked across the table at him and smiled. "Everything is wonderful now after that encouraging report about Courtney. I was just thinking about Courtney and what we all went through when she was sick."

Britain slightly shook his head. "I'm glad she's going to be herself again. But I try not to think about the ordeal of that day."

"Actually, I try not to think of it either. Somehow it just popped in my mind. Probably because I was thinking about my other reason for pushing our wedding date two years off from our original date. The reason is Courtney's health. I desperately wanted Courtney to be up on her feet when we walked down the aisle. I know I was pushing the date out far, but figured two years would be enough time for Courtney to heal. And it's looking hopeful since in one year the doctors are very encouraged and reports she's almost back to normal," Sabrina explained.

Britain looked at her nodding his head, but he wasn't pleased with waiting yet another year before they walked down the aisle. "I know how you feel and I respect your feelings and accepted your decision and the new date. However, just for the record, I'm not pleased about waiting," Britain told her.

"I know you're not pleased and I respect that because I'm also not pleased that I'm making us wait. We have shared many conversations about how it wasn't our fault that Courtney ended up institutionalized. And deep down I know it's not our fault. Yet, a part of me still feels like it is and I wouldn't be completely happy moving on with our happiness knowing Courtney Ross is still ill and institutionalized, knowing she lost sight of reality because of me and her belief that I had somehow taken you from her. In her mind during her illness, she felt I had stolen you from her. She told me on a few occasions that if I hadn't moved to town, you and she would have gotten together," Sabrina said.

"That's absolutely not true. Even if you hadn't moved to town, Courtney were never on my radar as a possible romantic interest. I always thought of her as a girl who liked my brother. She and I were just friends and I did like Courtney a lot at that time. But once again, not romantically. Basically, she was friendly and kind and just a good person back then. Plus, she was one of our best workers and the customers loved her," Britain shared. "Besides, I have shared this before; and regardless, Courtney was very ill and it wasn't our fault what she did to us and her brother." Britain paused in Sabrina eyes. "Yet, I get why you have chosen to wait and pushed our wedding date out so far. You're doing what your conscience is guiding you to do. I respect you for that. And although, I didn't want to wait, I know it's the bride's day and I want my bride to be happy. Two years doesn't seem that long considering what we went through and how blessed we are for the opportunity to share our lives with each other," Britain caringly said.

Sabrina nodded. "You are right. We are so bless. We didn't end up with any permanent damage or scarring from our wounds; and Kenny hands are perfect as if he never wore bandages for a month. What we went through was horrific. But over the past year I think it made us closer if that's possible. However, I do regret that we disappointed all our family and friends when we cancelled the wedding and changed the date to over two years in the future," Sabrina softly uttered.

Britain nodded. "For the most part I believe they understood. However, Mother was fit to be tied. She didn't understand why we were pushing the date so far out. I dared to mention you felt guilty about celebrating our happiness while Courtney Ross, who tried to hurt us both, were institutionalized in an insane alyssum. If I had shared that with Mother, she would have hit the ceiling."

Sabrina smiled. "I'm glad you didn't share that with your mother. Because you're absolutely correct. Miss Veronica would have hit the ceiling. We know Courtney was ill when she did all her damage to our families. Yet, even before Courtney fell ill, Miss Veronica never seemed that warm toward her."

Britain nodded. "That would be correct."

"I recall her visits to Franklin House while dating Rome. Your mother didn't seem to socialize with Courtney that much," Sabrina recalled. "But let's change the subject now," Sabrina suggested.

"Okay, sure. Name the subject," Britain suggested.

"Okay, I love the new name you gave your company."

Britain smiled with pride. "Thanks. We're all pleased with the new name."

"I'm curious how did the four of you decide on the name Franklin Enterprises?" Sabrina asked.

"Frankly, it was simple with no effort on our part. We were going through some of Father's old papers and found a file labeled future projects. We looked through the file and spotted the document suggesting the name change, and decided to implement it. But it was our decision to enclose the two gas pumps in brick pillars as souvenirs of the old Franklin Gas Company that was started by my great grandfather."

Chapter Twenty-Seven

Five minutes before Larry were due downstairs for dinner, Courtney rung his room phone. He lifted the receiver on the second ring as he took a seat in the comfortable gray chair near his bedside table. "Hello. This is Larry Westwood."

"Hi Larry. It's me, Courtney."

"Hi," Larry laughed excitedly. "I'll see you in a few minutes. I put on my best blue shirt just for you." He kept smiling, pleased to talk to her. "I hope you like it."

"I'm sure the shirt looks nice. But I'm calling to tell you I won't be able to sit at your table for dinner this evening."

Larry smile immediately faded as he didn't comment.

"I'm sorry to cancel out on our plans of having dinner together at the same table. But it's my Mom. She's on her way here to have dinner with me. I would have mentioned it earlier but she just called to remind me that she's on her way. Her visit for dinner had completely slipped my mind," Courtney said apologetically. "I hope you're not too disappointed.

"I'm disappointed. But it's okay. I understand. You can't disappoint your Mom. It's good she's coming to have dinner with you. My Mama came and had lunch with me one day. I was glad to see her and I know you'll be glad to see your Mom."

"Yes, I will. But maybe we can see each other later in the evening. We can meet in the game room," Courtney suggested.

"Okay, we can play cards. I like playing cards and I'm sort of good at it."

"That sounds good," Courtney said as she heard a knock on her room door. "I'll see you later. My Mom is here," she said and ended the call.

Courtney hung up the phone and hurried to open the door. She stretched the door open to Mildred's smiling face. They hugged and Mildred kissed Courtney on the cheek and then closed the door.

"You look mighty happy and cheerful this evening," Mildred noticed as she took a seat on one of the twin yellow chairs in Courtney's room.

Courtney kept smiling as she took a seat on the side of her bed. "Mom, you are right. I am cheerful. I feel like my life is coming back together. Wally has promised me a teaching position, which gives me something to look forward to when I'm released from here. Although, it hinges on the condition of me receiving a complete clean bill of mental health."

Mildred nodded. "I'm sure you'll receive that clean bill of mental health upon your release," Mildred assured her. "Otherwise, they won't release you without it."

"You're right, Mom." Courtney cheerfully agreed. "I'm counting my blessings. I know how blessed I am that Wally care enough to do that for me, considering how awful I treated him when I was sick." Courtney held up one finger when she heard the knock on the door. "That's our dinner. Just a second," Courtney said, as she hopped off the bed and stepped across the room to the door and opened it. The dinner attendant handed her one tray of food and a bottle of water; and followed her into the room carrying the second tray of food and bottle of water. He placed the food tray and water on the table, nodded toward Mildred and quickly headed out of the room. He closed the door behind him and then rolled the serving cart away from the door.

"Mom, I hope you like veal steak. If not, the mashed potatoes and California vegetables looks tasty," Courtney said as removed the plastic covering from the food trays.

"Sure I like veal steak," Mildred said as she took a seat at the table. "Besides, I'm quite hungry and anything will do at the moment."

"Did you come here straight from your job?" Courtney asked as she took a seat at the small round table.

Mildred nodded. "Yes, I came straight here and didn't get an opportunity to have myself any lunch earlier. I meant to but someone called in sick and I did her workload. Therefore, I worked up until it was time to leave. Needless to say, I worked up quite an appetite," Mildred said as she forked mashed potatoes into her mouth. Then she looked across the small table at her smiling daughter and Courtney appeared to really be enjoying her meal."

Mildred hadn't seen a glowing smile on Courtney's face since long before her breakdown. "So cheerful one, do you plan to tell me what has happened to bring such a glowing smile to your face?" She stared at Courtney with a curious smile, and then raised one finger. "However, before you share your possibly happy news, I should probably share something with you that isn't the best news."

Courtney smile faded as she grabbed both cheeks and shook her head. "Oh, no. Mom. I hope it's not bad news. What is it?"

Mildred looked at her daughter in silence for a moment. But she knew she couldn't keep the disappointing news from Courtney. "I'm sorry to be the bearer of bad news. But there's no way around telling you this," Mildred reluctantly said.

Courtney kept shaking her head as great concern ripped through her stomach and showed on her face. "Mom, is it regarding Shady Grove?" Courtney placed her fork on the table beside her plate.

Mildred nodded as she lifted the water bottle and twisted off the cap. "Yes, it's regarding your stay here at Shady Grove."

"I guess its bad news about my release date from this place."

"Yes, dear. I'm afraid that's correct. We all jumped the gun a bit in our thinking, feeling it was going to be quite soon after the doctor's last report."

"Mom, what are you saying? I guess the last report was incorrect?"

Mildred shook her head with disappointed eyes. "It wasn't incorrect."

"The report said I'm no longer a threat to myself or anyone else. It also stated there's no signs of insanity," Courtney reminded her mother.

"I'm aware of what the report said. We just read too much into the report. We assumed they would release you soon. But the likely release date that came along with the report that arrived in my email today is no time soon," Mildred told her.

"Mom, what is the possible release date. If I'm back to myself one hundred percent, they can't continue to keep me here. You can tell your boss. He's paying out a lot of money to this place for my care. The longer they keep me here the more money they gain," Courtney disappointedly stated. "So, will you ask Mr. Don Taylor to check into why they are still holding me here when I'm better?"

Mildred lifted her water bottle and took a sip. "I agree you are better. But maybe you're not one hundred percent better the way they know you should be. Just give these professionals the time they need to do their job. It's in your favor."

"Mom, I know it's in my favor. But I'm feeling fine and I don't have any wild crazy thoughts running through my head like before."

"That's good," Mildred nodded.

"I know it's good," Courtney agreed. "So, could you please ask your boss to check into why they're still holding me here?"

Mildred shook her head and stared seriously at Courtney. "No, I will not ask Don Taylor to question the staff here about your care or release date. Besides, they wouldn't give him any information anyway. He's not family."

"He's not family, but he's filthy rich," Courtney grumbled.

"Being rich doesn't award a person the right to another person's private medical files or personal records," Mildred seriously stated.

"Maybe not, but I'm so upset now." Courtney stood out of her seat. "I'm better and I'm still being punished. I don't think that's fair." She shook her head, looking down at her plate of food and bottle of water.

"Don't think like that, Sweetie. Please be seated and have your dinner. You have barely touched your meal. At least open your water and take a sip. You need something in your stomach. Being hungry and weak is not going to allow you to function at your best. You need to be your best to get released."

Courtney threw up both arms. "What good is that to be my best? I am my best and they're still keeping me here. I just want to go home."

"We all want you back at home. We miss you like crazy," Mildred assured her as she stared sympathetically in Courtney's eyes for a moment. "But listen, sweetheart. It's for the best. We know you're getting the best care possible in here."

"But Mom, I'm well. I know I'm better."

Mildred nodded. "Of course, you are better and you probably are well, but not all the way." Mildred paused. "Let me see if I can explain this to you. It reminds me of baking a cake. It can look done but not completely done. Then you take it out of the stove before time and it falls in the middle. That is what would happen to you if they released you too soon. You could have a relapse. That's my best guess. Because the reports I received today explained that you're much better. But it also indicates you won't be released for at least another year," Mildred sadly told her.

"How will I survive another year in this madhouse, Mom?"

"It's not a madhouse," Mildred quickly protested. "Please, don't think and speak negative of this facility."

"The doctor informed me of the same thing, not to think and speak negative of the facility. But I hate being locked up in this place," Courtney strongly stressed as she wiped a tear from her left eye. "And it's not just being locked up here. It's the idea that I'm locked up and not free to live my life."

"It's rotten news, I know," Mildred sympathetically said. "But we have to assume that those in charge know what they're doing."

Courtney sadly folded her lips, staring across the room in space. She didn't comment as the thought of staying longer at the facility crushed her spirits and put a damper on her mood.

"Sweetheart, try to focus on the positive," Mildred suggested.

Courtney shook her head. "If I could think of something positive I would focus on that. But my positive thoughts have been crushed with the news that I'm not leaving this place any time soon."

"I know that's unexpected very depressing news. But yet, you have to be strong and try to look on the bright side. Try to think of the positive of where you are. If you had to be in a facility like this. You ended up in the best facility of this kind in this country. This is a state of the arts facility. I heard the food is wonderful; and enjoying this delicious prepared meal proves that's true." Mildred glanced about Courtney's room. "And look at this beautiful room."

"Mom, I don't care about any of that. I just want to leave here and go home. It doesn't matter how beautiful it is or how great the cooks are. This is still a mental institution," Courtney sadly grumbled. "The prettiest rooms and the best food in the world can't change the facts that it's an asylum," Courtney sadly fussed. "Besides, I want my life back so I can start my new teaching job. Being stuck in here. I could end up losing that job now." She held up both hands.

"Don't go borrowing negative thoughts," Mildred firmly stated. "Besides, why would you say that, Courtney? We both know, Wally is not in the habit of making empty promises. And he specifically told you that when you're released with a clean bill of mental health, he'll hire you at his high school," Mildred quickly reminded her. "And you know Wally is a man of his word. I cannot see that young man reneging on his offer."

"Mom, I know Wally better than you; and I can definitely see him reneging. Because when he offered me the job, he was under the impression that I would be released from here soon."

"I know. I was here when he visited and offered you the job. But sweetie, during his visit, we were all under the impression that you would be released from here soon. Frankly, that's how the first report demonstrated and characterized itself," Mildred disappointedly explained. "Now we know differently and all you can do is call Wally."

"I can't call him, Mom. I'm afraid of what he might say," Courtney admitted.

"I'm sure he'll understand. But if you would prefer, I can give him a call for you. I'll explain the misunderstanding and give him the status of your release."

"Wally wants to help me. But he's a business man with a school to run. He'll probably scratch me off the list," Courtney sadly mumbled.

"I don't think so. I'm sure he'll understand how we all misunderstood."

"Mom, seriously. I know you're trying to keep my hopes up." Courtney shook her head. "But I doubt Wally will hold a job for me after you explain to him that I'll be stuck behind these golden walls for another year."

Mildred nodded. "Of course, he'll probably be disappointed. But on the other hand, when he promised you a teaching job. It wasn't like he was holding a job for you. I'm sure he isn't holding a particular position for you. He'll likely give you what's available when you're released," Mildred strongly pointed out.

Courtney frown wrinkles smoothed from her face as she nodded, looking at her mother. "That makes sense. Maybe the extra year won't hinder him from hiring me when I'm finally released."

"I'm sure it won't. So, listen Sweetie. Please don't worry. The extra year won't lose you the job. Also, it would help to just bear in mind exactly what he said to you when he dropped by here to visit."

"Mom, I can't remember his exact words."

"Well, I can," Mildred quickly replied. "The bottomline is that he knows you couldn't give him a specific release date. That's why I keep reminding you of what he said. His exact words were: Once you receive a clean bill of mental health from here, he would give you a teaching position at his high school."

Courtney nodded. "That is what he said. No particular release date were ever mentioned. But we gave him the impression it would be sooner than another year."

"That may be true. But I say, don't worry about it. Just count your blessings young lady. Look how far God has brought you. You were a very sick young lady. I mean very sick both mentally and physically ill with the self-inflicted gunshot wound to your stomach!" Mildred inhaled sharply and shook her head. "I know how thankful I am to have my daughter in one piece and on the road to complete wellness; and I also thank God every morning and night during my prayers for the huge blessing of sparing you a criminal record." Mildred grabbed her face and paused for a moment as she reflected on how thankful and blessed their family were.

Courtney sat quietly listening to her mother.

Mildred looked at Courtney with thankful eyes. "We are so blessed you didn't end up behind bars. Even with your illness, that could have happened."

"Mom. That depresses me. Why would you bring that up?" Courtney shook her head. "You know I was very sick at that time. I would never normally do something like that and I hate it happened."

"I know you hate it happened. But keep in mind, if the Taylors and Franklins were not such incredible people, they wouldn't have cared about you and how sick you were."

"You're right, Mom. Those people have compassionate beyond the call of duty. Kind as the days are long."

Mildred nodded. "Yes, that is true."

Courtney shook her head in disappointment. "Mom, I remember how I trashed them during my illness," Courtney wiped a tear with the back of her left hand. "I would have rather died than to have been the person that I had become. My reality was so backward that I hated those people based on fabricated lies in my head that I had manufactured against them. Yet, with all the pandemonium I caused, they still didn't hold any of it against me," Courtney sadly recalled as she dried her tears with her dinner napkin.

Mildred smiled. "Yes, the Taylors and the Franklins are as good as it gets. I know I owe them a huge debt of gratitude. Anyone else most likely would have thrown the book at you. But the Franklins and the Taylors had compassion for you even during their own pain and agony of that horrific act you committed in the name of insanity," Mildred strongly stressed.

"I'll never be able to repay any of them," Courtney sadly mumbled.

"That's true. But they are not looking for a repayment from you. What they have done for you, it comes from the goodness of their character; and also it probably helped in your favor that they knew the other side of you before your breakdown."

Courtney dropped down in her seat at the table as if she had a hundred pounds in her lap. Suddenly she looked drained as she stared at her mother attentively.

"Yes, young lady, you have a lot to be thankful for. Starting with no criminal record due to the kindness and consideration of the Taylors and Franklins. Therefore, please do not worry about getting out of here. Try not to let it consume your thoughts."

Courtney nodded with sad eyes. "I'll try. But it's so hard being away from home and my work and the routine of a daily life."

"I'm sure it hard. But your release will come when its time. Just follow the rules and stay positive," Mildred urged. "You were very sick; and as I said before, I'm definitely the brilliant doctors here know what they are doing. Look how far you have come? While you were hospitalized you stayed in the woods for a while before we could catch our breath. Then when you turned the corner and your body healed, we had another obstacle to get through with your mental health. After you were first released from the hospital and admitted here, I cried nearly every night on my knees praying for you to come back to us," Mildred said with watery grateful eyes.

"I don't recall much about my hospital stay and my first few months in here," Courtney admitted.

"Well, Sweetie, I can tell you, your sister, your brother and I were at our wits end praying and hoping for a miracle for you to return to us. Visiting you were very painful and gloomy for us; and I'm sure you know, especially Kenny. How he took your tragedy inward and blamed himself a lot. I constantly tried to talk some sense into his head to make him see it was nobody's fault. Bad things happen to good people all the time," Mildred strongly stressed.

"I often wonder why my world had to come crashing down around me," Courtney sadly mumbled.

"As I said, horrific things often happen in life and sometime it's nobody's fault."

"Mom, do Kenny still blame himself?"

Mildred smiled at Courtney and then shook her head. "I'm pleased to let you know that your brother finally let go of the guilt he was carrying around," Mildred caringly said.

"That's good to hear, Mom. I'm glad. Because he never had anything to feel guilty about."

Chapter Twenty-Eight

Mildred suddenly felt like she was having dinner alone. It had been several minutes since Courtney had said a word. Mildred sat across the table from Courtney eating her meal. But she wondered why Courtney suddenly seemed suddenly distraught.

"Sweetheart, why are you suddenly so quiet?"

Courtney glanced over at her mother with sad eyes. "I'm not quiet."

"You are quiet. You haven't said a word in several minutes."

"It's nothing, Mom."

"It seems like something with that look on your face."

"What look?"

"Suddenly you seem troubled or disturbed."

"Mom, I'm just thinking about a few things."

"Well, whatever you're thinking about seem to be affecting you in a negative way," Mildred casually pointed out.

Courtney nodded. "You're right. It's not a happy thought."

"Just push those negative thoughts out of your head," Mildred suggested.

"That's what the doctor said, and that's what I often do. But sometimes it's not easy to push them away so quickly."

"What put you in this suddenly glum mood if you don't mind me asking?"

Courtney looked at her mother but didn't respond, sadly staring into space.

"If I have to guess, it must be about your brother," Mildred quickly said.

Courtney eyes widened in a glance at her. Mildred was right in her assumption.

"Mom, why do you think it's about Kenny?"

"Well, I'm assuming of course. But it must be. You shut down right afterward. We were discussing how he had let go of the guilt of what happened with you."

"Mom, I'm glad Kenny pushed that guilt off of his shoulders."

"I'm sure you're pleased he's not carrying that guilt around any longer since he was not to blame for any of that devastation that took place," Mildred caringly said.

Courtney sadly nodded. "I'm very pleased Kenny stop blaming himself."

"That's good and I'm sure you're happy for your brother."

"Yes, I'm very happy for Kenny."

"That's good. But you still haven't answered," Mildred said.

"Answer you about what?"

"I asked if you were suddenly down because of your brother's news. I know you're happy for him. But hearing it still affected you," Mildred pointed out. "But if it's not about your brother's news, please share with me what has you so down right now?"

"Mom you're right in your assumption. It's about Kenny's news. You mentioning Kenny letting go of the guilt."

"So, you're sad about that?" Mildred asked.

"Yes, Mom. But not in the way you may think. I'm sad because he has nothing to be guilty about. That is what made me sad," Courtney admitted.

Mildred shook her head. "I'm not sure if I follow you."

"Mom, I'm happy Kenny let go of the guilt. But I'm sad that I never will."

"In time you will, and you have to believe that," Mildred said.

"I want to believe it. That's what get me through each day – believing I'll one day let go of all the guilt that I feel so heavy on my shoulders," Courtney said mumbled.

"In time you will completely heal and put it all in perspective. I'm sure the doctor has told you this as well."

"Yes, Mom. However, as hopeful as I am of being able to let the guilt go. I just wonder if I ever will, since it's really all my fault. I'm the blame for that devastation. It all falls on my shoulders. Although I know I was sick. I can't seem to detach my actions from my regular reality. Especially, since I hurt so many people. During my illness I was far outside of the realm of reality," Courtney humbly confessed. "It was the saddest time of my life."

"Yes, it was a sad time for all of us," Mildred sadly recalled. "I know it affected you in such a crushing way."

Courtney nodded. "Mom words fail me to explain my sad reality of that time. I remember most of it. But it was so horrible until bits and pieces have completely vanished from my mind," Courtney sadly relayed.

"Sweetheart, I remember in the beginning how we just wanted your life to be spared even if your mind wasn't. We just wanted you back. But you were somewhere else. In a place that felt safe. I say that because while being hospitalized as well as your first few months in here, whenever we visited you, you would sat and stared as if we were not even there. You knew who we were but you didn't want any of us around. You wouldn't interact with others for nearly five months. Then slowly I saw signs of you returning to us and I knew God had answered our prayers. We were on pins and needles and faced much heartache hoping and wondering if you would ever come back to us." Mildred held up both hands. "Now look at beautiful you. I think these doctors here are miracle workers to bring you back from the brink of no return. That's why I have complete faith in their ability. But listen. I know you are tired of being here at Shady Grove. But please think about what I have said and how blessed you are and our entire family. Besides, I'm convinced you have turned the corner for the better and doing so well because of this state of the art facility. Normally, average working class people like us don't get the benefit of an institution like this. Only the very rich can afford to pay such lavish prices. But by the grace of God and the goodness and compassion of my boss, you have and will continue to receive the best possible care. I mean, what are the odds that the uncle of the young lady you attacked would foot your hospital bill and also your mental health bill?"

Courtney grabbed her face and inhaled deeply as all the things her mother said ripped through her and overwhelmed her with warmth as she thought of all the blessings her mother had reminded her of. She picked up her fork and started eating her dinner. "You are right, Mom. I have a lot to be thankful for. Because as much as I hate being here, the opportunity to be here to get the top of the line help that I need is a huge blessing."

Mildred let out a sigh of relief. She was glad to see Courtney smile again. "There's that smile that you had on your face when I first walked in the room. Maybe you can share with me what had you so excited with that happy smile when I walked in the door." Mildred took her white cloth napkin from her lap and wiped her mouth and hands.

"It's good news but I'm not sure if I should share it right now. When I thought I was leaving here soon I was more excited about sharing it. But now knowing I'll be stuck here another year, he might not wait for me," Courtney said, as she took her last bite of steak.

Mildred smiled. "Have you meet someone? That is wonderful news if you have." Mildred smilingly shook her finger across the table at Courtney's nose. "You see I was right in all the talks we had where you cried thinking there would be no one out there that would want to be with you because of your breakdown and what happened. But if you have met someone, apparently he knows you're in here and why. But he likes you anyway."

Courtney nodded. "You're right. He knows I'm here but he doesn't know why I ended up here. I shared most of it with him but I didn't share the whole story. I just confessed that I did something really bad. But I didn't tell him what. But I plan to tell him. He made it clear that he wants me to be completely honest with him about things."

Mildred kept smiling, anxious to hear about Courtney's new friend. "So, who is this young man and how did you meet him?" Mildred nodded. "How quickly we forget. It had slipped my mind some of the new ways of meeting people. Therefore, you most likely met him online on one of those dating sites. Is that correct?"

Courtney smiled and shook her head. "No, I met him the traditional way. The old fashion way."

"What are you saying, dear? How is that possible? You're confined in here in this facility," Mildred reminded her.

Courtney nodded. "Yes, I'm confined here but I'm not isolated," Courtney stressed. "Mom, this place is crowded with family members, medical professionals and staff executives coming and going all the time."

"Okay, I get it. You met your new friend here."

"That's right. We met here at this facility during the lunch hour, just today," she said excitedly.

Mildred looked at her daughter indifferently. "That's great, Sweetie. Good for you. I'm happy you met someone. You seem quite happy about this young man."

"Mom, I can't believe how excited I am about this new man in my life."

Mildred smiled. "I can see the light in your eyes. So, I'm assuming the young man was here visiting a family member or a friend?"

Courtney stared at her mother and didn't readily answer. Then she shook her head. "No, he wasn't here visiting a family member or a friend."

Mildred waited as a smiling Courtney just stared at her without continuing.

"If he wasn't visiting a friend or a family member I guess he must be on staff here," Mildred assumed. "Is he one of the nurses or doctors?" she curiously asked.

Courtney smiled, shaking her head. "How I wish he was on the medical staff."

"That's fine, Sweetie. Everyone can't be on the medical team. But I'm sure any position here pays well. So, does he work in the administration offices?"

Courtney smile faded to a serious stare. She could see it was obvious that Mildred thought he was a worker at the facility. She was now reluctant to say he wasn't. "Mom, he doesn't work in the administration offices."

Mildred sensed a shift in Courtney's happy mood to anxious. "Listen, Sweetie. It doesn't matter what he does here. He can work in the laundry room or maintenance; and even if he sweeps the floors, that's fine too. I was just curious about his work here."

"Well, Mom. You don't have to be curious about his work here," Courtney mumbled.

Mildred raised both hands. "Let's drop the subject of the young man's work. I guess you feel I'm prying and being too inquisitive. But you seem so happy and I just wanted to find out about your new friend. But if you don't feel comfortable discussing him right now. Listen, we can change the subject."

"Mom, you misunderstood. I don't mind discussing my friend."

"It didn't sound that way when you said I didn't have to be curious about his work."

"Mom, I said that because he doesn't work here. He's a patient."

"Oh, you met one of the patients?" Mildred asked with surprise in her eyes. "I didn't expect to hear that." Mildred stared silently at Courtney for a moment, and then smiled. "That's fine. I'm just happy you're happy."

"Mom, you were convinced he was a worker here. Are you sure you're okay that's he's one of the patients?"

"Of course, I'm okay. It just didn't dawn on me that you were referring to another patient. But I guess that makes more sense than one of the workers asking out one of the patients. So, come on Sweetie, and tell me about the young man. When was he committed and how long he's here for, if you know?" Mildred casually asked.

"He hasn't been here long. He was just committed a week and a half ago and he's actually leaving the facility this coming Wednesday."

Mildred smiled with surprise in her eyes. "Just a two week stay. It sounds like your new friend didn't have much of a condition."

"He told me he just came here for an evaluation. But apparently his condition is permanent and can't be fixed," Courtney casually shared. "That's what he told me."

Mildred drew somewhat alarmed, not knowing the condition of the new man in Courtney's life. Courtney had come a longs way in working toward getting her life back on track. Mildred didn't want any more relationship drama to be connected with her daughter's fragile mental health. "Did he by chance mention his condition?" Mildred asked with concerned eyes.

"Not really, other than unkind things that his grandmother said to him. He told me how his grandmother used to constantly call him crazy."

Mildred frowned and shook her head. "I'm sure his grandmother didn't mean those unkind statements toward him. It was just name calling, which I might add was crude and didn't make it right. Nevertheless, mentally cruel as it was, I'm sure she didn't mean those unkind words toward her grandson,"

Chapter Twenty-Nine

Mildred turned and looked toward the door when someone knocked. "Someone is at the door," Mildred said.

"I'm sure it's just the cafeteria attendant to pick up the empty food trays," Courtney said as she quickly stood and gathered up the two trays, along with the dirty plates, silverware and dirty napkins and rushed across the room toward the door. She opened the door and passed the two trays to the attendant. Then she stood at the door and waited as the attendant placed the empty trays on the cart, and after the attendant pushed the serving cart away from her door, Courtney closed and locked the door. She stepped back across the room and dropped on the bed and fell over on her back with both hands under her head.

"Mom, I'm so excited and disappointed at the same time."

Mildred smiled, still seated at the small round table. "I know why you're excited. But why are you disappointed?"

"Mom, you know why. I'm of course, excited about meeting someone. But very disappointed I won't be released from this place to start living my life again. Besides, my new friend may not be too eager to wait around for me."

"Why do you feel he may not wait for you? You didn't give him the impression that you were about to be released, did you?"

"In a way I did. That's what I thought, Mom. Remember, you made it seem I would be released soon."

Mildred slightly frowned with sympathetic eyes. "I know based on that good report. And although it was a good report, I regret getting your hopes up when I was so far off track with my assumptions; and my assumptions, needless to say, has put you in somewhat of a pickle with Wally and your new friend. Nevertheless, I think Wally will understand. And if this new friend is worth his salt and really interested in starting a serious relationship with you, waiting for you to be released out of here won't pose a problem. He'll come here to visit you up until the time of your release."

"Mom, I hope so."

"I'm sure you do, Courtney," Mildred said, noticing the sparkle in Courtney's eyes. "However, young lady. I can see how taken you seem to be with your new friend."

"You're right, Mom. I haven't been this excited about anything in a very long time."

"I can see it in your eyes. But please be realistic about this young man," Mildred firmly suggested.

"Mom, what do you mean?"

"I mean just what I said. I'm not trying to be a downer. But we both know how you can allow yourself to fall to quickly and too hard for someone," Mildred reminded her.

"Mom, I know you're referring to how I fell for the Franklin brothers and ended up in here." Courtney wiped a teardrop. "Mom, I'm so far beyond thinking that way. Because it really wasn't about the Franklin brothers. It was about how I felt about guys with their status. I was determined to be with a rich man if the was the last thing I accomplished. It really didn't matter who he was, as long as he was a millionaire," Courtney solemnly confessed.

"Oh, my goodness, young lady. I had no idea you felt that way."

"Mom, it's how I just to think."

Mildred smiled. "Well, I'm glad it's past tense."

"Yes, Mom. It's past tense. I don't feel that way anymore. But if I'm honest, even before the breakdown I felt that way," Courtney admitted. "I had a false sense of worth about myself, thinking I deserved to be with a wealthy man. That's why I turned Wally down and wouldn't date him when he wanted to be with me. I felt he wasn't good enough for me since he was poor at the time," Courtney sadly admitted.

"Sweetheart, I'm glad you can be honest about all of this now."

"Mom, which has been part of my healing process while committed in here. The doctors tell us that we have to be completely honest with ourselves and about ourselves before we can completely heal."

"I'm glad you can be completely honest about your past thinking. But I would like to know, if you know what gave you that frame of mind. I know I have never instilled those kinds of thoughts into you and Trina," Mildred said. "Especially to feel you're entitled to be with someone rich, and to think a poor man wasn't good enough for you."

"Mom, you're right. You have never pushed us in that way of thinking."

"Well, do did?" Mildred asked.

"It was Grandma Emma."

"Your Grandma Emma instilled those thoughts in your head?"

Courtney nodded. "Yes, Mom. It was Grandma Emma. She preached constantly to me and Trina about marrying a rich man. When we were in high school she had many conversations with me and Trina about holding out for a rich guy. She made it seem as if, if we didn't hold out for a rich husband, we would be throwing our lives away with a poor one," Courtney told Mildred.

Mildred shook her head. "Grandma Emma didn't do you and Trina any favors by filling your heads with that non sense."

"I know she didn't do me any favors because my doctor told me that her strong encouragement toward rich men played into my breakdown," Courtney sadly admitted.

"Your doctor told you that?" Mildred asked alarmed.

Courtney nodded. "Yes, and it makes sense. Because when the Franklin brothers dumped me, it devastated me on a profound level since I felt they were my only and last chance to marry a rich man."

"Well, I guess you're right. But please don't tell your grandmother that she's indirectly the blame for your breakdown."

"I won't tell Grandma Emma. But I'm glad I told you. Because I have completely changed from my former self. I don't need a rich man in my life to make me happy. I just need someone who wants to be with me for me. His bank account doesn't matter."

"I'm so proud of you that you have your priorities in order," Mildred complimented her. "And I'm glad you have met someone that makes you happy. But now, I think your main concern should be coming clean."

Courtney eyes widened as she stared at her mother. "Coming clean?"

"Yes, you need to come clean with the young man about why you're here at this facility."

Courtney nodded. "Yes, I know."

"Be completely honest and let him know how you landed in here. The whole story and nothing but," Mildred strongly suggested.

"I'm not looking forward to sharing my awful dreadful news that landed me in here. But I know I need to tell him, and I plan to tell him tomorrow. We're supposed to see each other later and play cards in the game room. But I'm not sure I'll tell him then. But tomorrow for sure since he leaves on Wednesday."

Mildred glanced at her watch. "It's almost 7:30. I should head home so you and your friend can meet up and play cards." Mildred stood from the table. "It just dawned on me. You didn't share your young man's name."

"Oh, that?" Courtney mumbled.

Mildred downcasted her eyes and gave Courtney a serious stare. "What do you mean, oh, that? Is there some reason you don't want to share his name?"

"Mom, of course not. His name is Larry Westwood. He's very special."

"Of course, he's very special. Any friend of yours is special to me."

"I'm serious, Mom. Larry is very important. He's employed for a very exclusive estate in the area. He's an assistant grounds person for the estate."

That peaked Mildred's interest. "So, he works for an exclusive estate?"

"Yes, he does."

"I'm curious. I know most of the exclusive estates in the area. Which one does he work for?" Mildred curiously asked, as she grabbed her jacket from the coat rack near the door.

When Courtney didn't answer Mildred looked around as she slipped into her jacket. "Did you hear me, dear? Did Larry share which estate he keeps grounds for?"

Courtney didn't answer Mildred. "He's not the fulltime grounds person. He's just an assistant. His father also works there and he also assist his father with other duties," Courtney said.

"Is there a reason why you have chosen not to answer my question and reveal the estate where he works?" Mildred asked, then stared at Courtney and shook her head. "Don't tell me he works for the Franklins." Mildred eyes widened with curiosity. "He doesn't work for the Franklins does he?" Mildred suspiciously asked.

"No, he doesn't work for the Franklins," Courtney quickly replied. "But you might as well know. He does work for the Taylors."

Mildred had just threw her purse on her shoulder and pulled the door opened. But closed it right back and fell against it as if she was exhausted. Courtney news shaken her.

"Out of all the men in this town, you have to meet someone who's working at the property of the young lady you unintentionally terrorized? It's not a good idea! And normally I never really butt into any of you children's social lives. But in this case, I think I should," Mildred said, frantic by Courtney's news. "You had a breakdown and almost lost your life because of your misplaced hatred for Sabrina Taylor. I don't think you should date someone who works for that young lady. By doing so, it keeps you in her world. Your health is very important and close proximity to Miss Taylor is not a good or healthy idea! Besides, with what the young lady has been through, I'm sure this news would be quite stressful to her," Mildred strongly stressed.

Courtney grabbed her face with both hands and held it. "Mom, I hear you. But you need to hear me. I'm lucky Larry wants to date me. Before him no one was asking; and I doubt anyone else will."

"You're being pessimistic."

"I'm not being pessimistic. I'm being realistic. Think about it Mom. Would you want your son to date some female that spent over a year in a mental institution?"

Mildred paused before she answered. "I know it won't be easy. But once you're released and back home. I'm sure you're meet some nice young man," Mildred encouraged.

Courtney shook her head. "I'm not so sure I will meet anyone once I'm released; and I'm not so sure about Larry pursing me once I tell him what landed me in here. Mom, he may decide against dating me once I share that horrific chapter of my life. Then I'll probably end up alone for the rest of my life," Courtney cried.

"Don't talk like that. You're a smart beautiful young woman. Don't you forget that? Also, you need to remember how you once had the attention of one of the richest, most respected young men in this state? You're destined to meet a fine man once you're released from this institution," Mildred encouraged her.

"Mom, meeting a fine young man is over for me. Nobody of real status and stature is going to want to date someone who was once considered nuts."

"Don't talk like that. Besides, what's important is a decent young man. He doesn't have to be rich. You need to drop those kind of thoughts. That's what caused your sickness in the beginning, putting your hopes in the richest guy on the block. Just be thankful and hopeful to meet a decent kind young man who cares about you."

Courtney nodded. "Mom that is how I'm thinking now."

"Well, that's good. Because I have faith that some lucky young man is going to be proud to grab you up and have you in his life."

"But I have already met that person. Mom, I'm so blessed to know Larry. At first I thought he was kind of weird," Courtney sincerely admitted. "But I pushed for his attention because he was connected to the rich Taylors." Courtney shamefully confessed. "I'll admit that's what drove me to get him to talk to me. And although, he seemed sort of slow from the way he talked, I was still determined to get him interested in me because of the Taylors. But

Mom, the surprise is on me. He completely fascinated and captivated me. It's hard to explain and you'll have to meet him for yourself. But my point is, the more Larry and I talked the more I wanted to talk to him and the more I liked him. He makes me feel important and special. When he looks at me I know he's only thinking of me. I really like him and hope things can work out for us."

Mildred shook her head. "Darling dear, I can't think of any way that can make it work for you and this young man. I want you to be happy."

"But you don't want me with Larry," Courtney sadly mumbled.

"That's not exactly true. I do want you with Larry if he's who you want."

Courtney nodded with a big smile on her face, staring straight in her mother's eyes. "I can't explain it. But I feel special and accepted in his company."

"Okay, here's a thought. If he sticks with you after you share with him the fallout from your illness and the incident that landed you in here, that will tell the tale if he's still willing to build a relationship with you; and if he is, then you can approach the subject of him leaving the Taylor estate."

Courtney jaw dropped as she grabbed both cheeks with surprised eyes. "Approach the subject of him leaving his job at the Taylor estate?"

Mildred nodded. "Well, if he doesn't work for them that roots out the conflict of you and Sabrina. Wouldn't you agree?"

Courtney smiled. "Mom, that's a good idea. Maybe I'll approach the subject after I share my living nightmare with him." Courtney stood near the closed door with Mildred. "Mom, before you leave, promise me you won't mention Larry to anyone. I don't want the word to get out that we're dating before I tell him about what I did when I was sick."

"I won't say anything to anyone Courtney, Sweetie. But if I'm honest, I wish you were seeing anyone other than this young man. But I won't rain on your parade and tell you there's no hope for you and this young man, that you want to be with so desperately," Mildred said, as she left Courtney's room.

Chapter Thirty

On Saturday March 19, 2016, Courtney was released from Shady Grove Institution. Larry kept his word and visited her twice a week for a whole year by the courtesy of being driven there by his father's limousine. Larry had shared with his parents that he had met someone at Shady Grove when he was a patient there. But he hadn't shared her name with Sam and Carrie since Courtney had asked him not to, to prevent the news from spreading to the Taylors. Nevertheless, during the course of a year of seeing each other, Courtney still hadn't shared with Larry her near fatal crime against Sabrina, Britain and her own brother. And with no knowledge of Courtney's identity, Sam and Carrie were very pleased that Larry had met someone that seemed genuinely interested in him. He shared with them that he wasn't sharing her name because he was waiting to introduce her personally. They thought nothing of the fact that he kept his new girlfriend's name a secret.

The Saturday of Courtney's release, Larry invited to dinner. Sam and Carrie were anxious to meet Larry's new friend. He had kept her identity a secret for the entire year of their courtship per Courtney's request. Sam and Carrie had discussed among themselves that they hoped his new friend wasn't deeply mentally impaired. They were aware Larry had met her at Shady Grove and assumed she was along the same mental level as Larry.

Carrie told Larry to have his guest arrive for dinner at 8:00 o'clock. The three of them were dressed for dinner in their Sunday clothing. Carrie had set the table with their best dishes and silverware. They were all anxiously and restlessly waiting in the living room for Courtney to arrive. The dinner table looked better than Carrie could ever remember. It was draped with a white table cloth with two candles lit in the center. Carrie was dressed in a dark blue knit two piece suit and Sam was dressed in his Sunday black two piece suit with a white shirt and a black tie. Larry was dressed in a pair of fashionable gray pants with a white shirt, gray tie and dark gray dinner jacket. He sat quietly and anxiously on the sofa next to his mother as his father sat in the side chair. It was 8:10 and Larry was concerned Courtney wouldn't show.

"Maybe she changed her mind about me. If she did I'm not surprised. She's too pretty to be with someone like me anyway."

Carrie playfully slapped his knee. "Don't talk negatively about yourself. I think this young lady realize what a nice guy you are. Sam and I can't wait to meet her," Carrie said just as someone rang the doorbell and then knocked.

Sam looked toward Larry and beckoned him with both hands toward the door. Larry quickly hopped up from the sofa and rushed to the door. He pulled it opened to Courtney's smiling face.

"Hi, Courtney. It's good to see you. Please come in and meet my folks," he said as she slowly stepped into their living room.

Larry quickly closed the door, and then stood beside Courtney as Carrie and Sam both stood from the sofa to step near Courtney and shake her hand.

"Mama and Daddy, meet Courtney Ross. She's my new girlfriend," he said and smiled at Courtney. "Meet Carrie and Sam Westwood, my folks."

Sam smiled. He was surprised to see such a nice looking young lady interested in Larry. He wasn't aware Courtney was who had terrorized Sabrina. But Carrie inhaled hard to keep her composure as she held out her arms toward the dinner table. "Let's have a seat at the table. Dinner is ready."

They all took a seat with Courtney sitting next to Larry.

"I hope you like spaghetti and meatball," Larry cheerfully said to Courtney. "I asked Mama to make it. It's my favorite food." He pointed to the iced tea pitcher. "But I also asked Mama to make iced tea. I told her you didn't like kool-Aid. But when I first moved here from Tippo, Mississippi a few years ago, Mama told me Kool-Aid was mostly a kid's drink. But I grew up on it and Grandma Lulu didn't make anything else to drink except hot coffee. I just love Kool-Aid," Larry said, talking a lot because he was nervous.

Courtney was his first formal girlfriend and first girl he had brought home to introduce to his parents.

"Help yourself, Courtney," Carrie friendly said, with a forced smile, trying not to make eye contact with Courtney.

Sam was grinning and pleased to see Larry with what seemed like a decent young lady. Plus, he felt although she looked smart, that she was probably on Larry's mental level since she was once a patient at Shady Grove. "So, Larry, tells us that the two of you met last year while he was a patient at Shady Grove," Sam commented to make conversation.

Courtney nodded as she lifted the bowl of Spaghetti and meatballs and placed two meatballs on her plate, but no spaghetti. "Yes, Mr. Westwood. The day I met Larry really turned my life around for the better. He's a wonderful man. This past year spending time with him twice a week when he came to Shady Grove to visit me was like a lifeline." She emotionally held up both hands. "It's been peaceful and reassuring to know someone like Larry."

Sam smiled, looking across the table at Courtney. "A pretty girl like you, I'm sure you have had many boys chasing you." Sam looked at Larry. "I hope my son realize how lucky he is to have a nice girl like you interested in him."

Larry nodded and smiled as he bit into a breadstick. "I know how lucky I am. Courtney is pretty and she's smart too." He excitedly looked from Carrie to Sam. "She's a school teacher. I never thought a school teach would want to be with me." He held up both hands. "So I know how lucky I am. I mean, I know I can't drive and she'll have to drive us everywhere in her car." Larry looked toward Courtney. "But I'll pay for the gas. I'll even buy her a new car if the one she has isn't that reliable," Larry seriously stated.

Courtney shook her head. "I don't need a new car, Larry. My car is reliable and I don't mind driving."

Carrie swallowed hard when Larry mentioned buying Courtney a new car. It dawned on her that Courtney was probably with her son because he had told her about the inheritance his Grandma Lulu left him. She was aware of Courtney's breakdown and that Courtney had supposedly done many awful things in the name of her mental illness. Nevertheless, Carrie wondered if Courtney was up to her old tricks. She didn't believe Courtney was with Larry out of genuinely care, she felt it was Larry's money or the opportunity to get close to Sabrina and Britain again. She wasn't sure but she would find out. "Tell me, Courtney," Carrie said. "Where do you teach and what subject?"

Courtney smiled as she looked across the table at Carrie. But Carrie didn't look toward her. Carrie kept her head down toward her dinner plate as she wrapped her fork in spaghetti.

Courtney was pleased to answer. "I was hired at Barrington High and I start work there on Monday," she eagerly shared.

Sam picked up a bread stick and broke it in half and rubbed the half stick into the spaghetti sauce on his plate. "What subject you'll be teaching?"

"Oh, that's right, Mrs. Westwood asked me that question. I'll be teaching mathematics. I may not be able to remember what I ate for breakfast yesterday. But I don't forget numbers," Courtney said with confident.

Carrie didn't look toward Courtney, still looking down in her plate cutting a meatball into four pieces. "Being a school teach is a status position," Carrie said as she placed a piece of meatball in her mouth.

"I guess so, Mrs. Westwood. I've never thought of teaching as a status job. My Mom taught school and my father's mother, Grandma Emma did to. I can't say they ever mention teaching as a status position," Courtney said.

Sam grinned toward Courtney. "Well, when we were your age, a teaching position was a pretty fancy job to have."

"That's true." Carrie nodded, as she poured more iced tea into her glass. "So, tell us Courtney. How do you feel about Larry's work? I don't think he'll ever have a status position or even an office job to compete with you."

"That's fine." Courtney looked at Larry. "He's a good man and I have been through some major heartbreak chasing after men with status positions. I feel blessed to have found Larry."

Carrie wasn't convinced. But Courtney was sincere. She had fallen in love with Larry for who he was. She felt whole and loved by him. She looked beyond his mental short comings straight into his heart of gold.

"Larry tells us you were at Shady Grove for a couple years," Sam commented as he ate the last bite of food on his plate. "Do you mind if we ask why they kept you there so long?" Sam laughed. "Frankly, I can't believe you were ever a patient there. Although, Larry did share with us that you told him how sick you were when you were first committed. He mentioned that something happened in your life that pushed you over the edge. You had a temporary insanity condition that the facility cured you of," Sam stated.

"If you don't mind Mr. Westwood, I would prefer not to share what put me in Shady Grove right now." Courtney looked at Larry. "I haven't shared it with Larry yet. I think he should hear it first. I do plan to tell him soon."

Sam nodded. "I understand. It's your private business." Sam took his green cloth napkin from his lap and wiped his hands and mouth.

"We have chocolate cake if you would like dessert," Carrie offered.

"No, thanks, Mrs. Westwood. I need to get home." Courtney stood from her seat and grabbed her purse that hung on the back of her chair.

They all got from their seats and followed Courtney from the kitchen table to the front door. Larry quickly kissed her on the mouth and then they all said good night and Courtney left.

Carrie watched as Larry headed to his room and a spirited Sam stepped into their bedroom and closed the door. She was boiling mad as she gathered her purse and car keys from the end table, and grabbed her coat from the coat rack. She slipped on her black wool coat and quietly rushed out the front door.

Chapter Thirty-One

Courtney pulled into the driveway feeling uplifted about her dinner at Larry's house. But when she killed the motor and looked through her rearview mirror she noticed a pair headlights pulling in right behind her. She thought it was her mother or Kenny. Therefore, she grabbed her purse and slowly stepped out of her car. But her jaw dropped when she spotted Carrie exiting the car behind her. Courtney curiously waited for Carrie to walk over near her. Courtney heart started beating fast with anxiety to see that Carrie had followed her home. She knew an immediate visit from Larry's mother most likely wasn't good news.

"Hi, Mrs. Westwood. Did I leave something behind at your house?"

Carrie nodded. "Yes, you did."

"What did I leave?"

"You left my lovesick son," Carrie snapped.

Courtney eyes glowed in the moonlight with confusion. "I'm sorry. What did you say? I don't think I heard you correctly."

Carrie was boiling with anger. "You heard me correctly. But I'll repeat it. I said, you left my lovesick son behind."

"I still don't understand," Courtney humbly said.

"I'm sure you don't understand. But you will by the time I'm finish."

"Mrs. Westwood, what are you trying to say? By the time you're finished with what?"

"By the time I'm finished chewing you out!"

Courtney swallowed the lump in her throat and by now she was shaking with nerves. She wasn't sure what had gotten Carrie so heated with her.

Carrie took a deep breath and calmed herself. Then she looked at Courtney with solemn eyes. "I'm glad I caught you; and now that I have calmed my nerves, I'll explain my sudden visit," Carrie said calmly as she inhaled deeply. "Sam and Larry doesn't know I followed you. But I had to. I need some answers from you, Miss Courtney Ross."

Courtney nodded. "Sure, Mrs. Westwood. I'll answer any question you ask me. I have nothing to hide."

"Okay, let's start with why have you filled my son's head with false hope that you want to be with him? You know you don't really want my son! What games are you playing this time?" Carrie shook her head. "If I had used my head years ago, I would have turned you away when you came seeking out Sabrina." Carrie held up both hands. "But that's water under the bridge. What I need to know is what game you're playing with my son?"

Courtney looked down at the ground, and then lifted her head to look Carrie in the eyes. "Mrs. Westwood. I understand why you're suspicious. I'm the first one to admit, I did some awful things in the past. So awful that I cannot bring myself to relive any of those dark memories in my mind. But in my defense, I was very sick back then. I would never do something like that in my right mind. I'm sorry about how much I hurt Sabrina, Britain and my own brother," Courtney strongly stressed.

"I know you spent two years at Shady Grove and you supposedly is well now. But jumping into a relationship with a young man that's connected to the Taylors would make anyone wonder if you're playing games again, especially since my son is not your type," Carrie firmly fussed.

"I agree hundred percent. You're right."

Carrie eyes widened with surprise. "What do you think I'm right about; and what do you agree with hundred percent?" Carrie curiously asked.

"I was referring to what you said about Larry not being my type."

"So, you admit he's not your type?"

Courtney nodded. "Yes, I do agree he's not my type. But I should make something crystal clear. In the past I wouldn't have considered Larry my type. But I'm sure you know how my type is what messed me up in the head," Courtney candidly said. "I promise I'm done with chasing after the Franklin men. I'm done with blaming Sabrina because Britain Franklin rejected my advances and wasn't interested in me. Shady Grove cured me of those ill feelings. I just want to be with Larry," she sincerely explained.

Carrie had a big frown on her face, shaking her head. "Okay, if it's not the Taylors or Franklins you're after, it must be my son's money. That's got to be it. Please be honest with me." Carrie placed both hands on her chest. "Are you listening to me? Please don't mess up my son's life the way you went and messed up the Taylors and Franklins. I can see it in your eyes, and you appear to be sorry for the crimes you committed while you were ill. Nevertheless, it still happened. You could have killed all four of you."

"I know Mrs. Westwood and I'm deeply sorry. I have served my time in a mental institution," Courtney firmly, but politely stated. "The doctor said I can't blame or punish myself for what happened. I'm supposed to move forward knowing I won't allow myself to fall into such a rut again," Courtney strongly explained. "The doctor also told me that I deserve to be happy in a normal relationship. And what I have with your son is so unique, considering at first, I was thinking nobody would want me."

"I agree, of course, you deserve to be happy in a normal relationship with someone who loves you. However, I'm suggesting you find someone else other than my son. Frankly, I'm not convinced that you would be interested in him if it wasn't for his money."

"Mrs. Westwood. I have no idea what you're talking about. Why are you saying I'm after your son's money? He works as an assistant ground person. He can't make much more than a teacher's salary. He may not make as much," Courtney seriously stated.

"Don't try to play me young lady. I know you know about Larry's money. He told you at the dinner table that he would buy you a car if you needed a new one."

"I heard him say that but I wasn't paying him much attention about the new car. Besides, I told him my car is fine."

"Play it off if you like," Carrie heatedly fussed. "And maybe you will end up with my son. But nobody will convince me it's not because of the quarter of a million in the bank that his Grandma Lulu left him."

Courtney jaw dropped. She had no idea Larry had money. She just figured she would coexist with a decent man that loved her and they would be happy just getting by. Now she learns Larry has money, which left her speechless and from the look on her face, Carrie immediately knew that Courtney had not been enlightened about Larry's money.

Courtney grabbed her face and stared at Carrie. Larry told me about his Grandmother Lulu. But she didn't sound like someone who had money to leave him. The way he described her, she sounded quite poor," Courtney seriously stated.

Carrie nodded. "His Grandma Lulu lived in a very poor manner. Sam and I didn't know she had the money until after her death."

"Maybe it's none of my business but if she was living in such a poor manner, and made Larry live that way as well, how did she accumulate and end up with all that money to leave him?"

"Maybe it is none of your business," Carrie said. "Just do me and my husband a favor and break off whatever you have started with our son. Please!" Carrie pleaded and paused. "But maybe I won't have to worry about you breaking off with him."

"Why is that?" Courtney asked.

"Once you tell him what you did to Sabrina he'll end it."

"I must admit, I'm afraid of the same. But I know I have no other option but to be honest with him and tell him about that dark incident in my past."

"It's been a year since the two of you been seeing each other," Carrie reminded her. "Why haven't you told him already?"

Courtney eyes watered. "For the same reason you just mentioned. I'm afraid he'll break up with me."

"You should be afraid he'll break up with you. Because that is hundred percent likely after you share with him about your crime. Besides, Larry is protective and crazy about the Taylor girls. When he hear what you did, he won't stay in a relationship with you, Miss Courtney Ross!"

Courtney heart raced at the thought of Carrie telling Larry before she could. "Please, Mrs. Westwood. You won't tell him, will you?"

"No, I won't tell him. But I expect for you to tell him real soon. Because once you do, that will be the end of whatever you got going on with my son!" Carrie strongly warned, and then turned on her heels and walked to her car and drove away.

Chapter Thirty-Two

Carrie arrived back on the Taylor estate to their two bedroom quarters with a crushed feeling inside of her. She felt anxious and deeply concerned about Courtney's involvement with her son. She was terrified history could repeat itself with the tragedy Courtney had caused with Britain, Sabrina and her own brother back in 2014. Quite shaken she stood outside of their front door and dried her eyes with the back of her palm. She couldn't stop the tears from falling from her eyes as she gently and carefully placed the key in the front door and unlocked it.

She had turned off the living room lights when she left home. But to her surprise she slowly walked into the living room to find it brightly lit up. She swallowed the lump in her throat when she glanced to her left and spotted Sam seated on the sofa with a huffy look on his face. She shook her head at him as she slowly closed the door. Nevertheless, she didn't say anything to Sam as she anxiously headed straight toward the kitchen. He immediately flew off the sofa in a heat and rushed into the kitchen behind her.

"What's the heck going on, Carrie? I thought you were in the kitchen cleaning up. I step in the kitchen for a bottle of water probably no more than a couple minutes after you left. The living room was dark and you were nowhere to be found," he fussed. "So, tell me, Carrie. What in the world was so important that you had to sneak out and leave home without mentioning it? You haven't done that before! Not in all the years we have been married."

Slipping out of her coat, Carrie was drained with despair as she shook her head at Sam. She hung her coat and purse on the back of a kitchen chair as if it took a lot of effort. Then she turned her back to him to wipe her eyes dry; and then without much energy grabbed her white apron from the back of a kitchen chair and slowly tied it around her waist. Sam continued to stand there waiting for her explanation.

"I don't know where to start," she finally sadly mumbled, as she propped against the kitchen counter with her arms folded.

"Just start from the beginning, Carrie," Sam angrily grumbled. He was frustrated and aggravated and just wanted to know what was going on. "So, are you going to tell me why you sneaked out of the house? Dammit, Carrie. You had me worried. You haven't left the estate like that before without letting me know."

Carrie stared at Sam with sad eyes. "We have a huge problem on our hands," she regretfully said as she started gathering the dirty dishes from the kitchen table.

Sam stepped up behind her and tapped her arm. "Okay, we have a huge problem. But what the hell is it?" he firmly asked. "Whatever it is, from the looks of you and the sound of your voice, I don't think now is the time to clean the kitchen. I think we need to talk," he strongly suggested. "So, please, just put those dirty dishes back on the table and come into the living room and talk to me."

Carrie nodded. "Maybe you're right at that. This is something we definitely need to talk about," she said as she placed the stack of dirty dishes back on the table. She stood at the table for a moment staring down shaking her head at the depressing thought of Larry being tangled up with a young woman that had a breakdown two years ago and almost murdered her boss's daughter. The thought made her sick to the stomach and she dreaded telling Sam.

He stood there watching her as she stood there with both of her hands on the table looking down. But after she continued to stand there staring down, Sam lost his patience and snapped.

"What are you doing standing there like that?" he grumbled.

"I'm trying to think."

"What are you trying to think about?"

Carrie waved her hand. "Let me be. I'll be there in a moment," she said as she was trying to figure out how she would give him the news.

"Carrie, come on in the living room and let's talk."

When Carrie made no effort to head into the living room, Sam walked up to Carrie and grabbed her arm and led her into the living room where she took a seat on the sofa.

Moments after Carrie took a seat on the sofa, she hopped up and stepped back into the kitchen and grabbed her coat and purse. Sam hopped up and followed her. He was losing his patience.

"Carrie Westwood, what are you doing?"

"I'm just getting my coat and purse."

"I can see that. But why? Just let it be. We need to talk about this problem you just mentioned. It seems you're doing everything to avoid doing so," he fussed.

Carrie nodded. "This will just take a moment," she mumbled, as she stepped over to the coat rack to hang her coat and purse.

Sam threw up both arms in the air. "I give up. If you don't want to discuss it. Then don't. I'm heading back to bed," Sam fussed.

"Oh, please, calm down," Carrie said. "I agree with you," she said to Sam, as she headed away from the coat rack.

Sam stood there shaking his head. "Okay, but what do you agree with?"

"I agree that we need to discuss the problem. But not here in the living room or the kitchen. Let's head into our bedroom. Its more privacy in there," Carrie glumly suggested.

"Okay, sure," Sam said, heading toward their bedroom.

In their bedroom, Sam took a seat on the bed and watched for several minutes as Carrie paced back and forth in front of the dresser.

"Well, out with it," Sam demanded. "I'm on pins and needles wondering what's going on."

"It's about that young lady Larry just had over for dinner tonight," Carrie told him.

"What about her? I guess you went snooping and found out something about the young lady that's not good?" Sam disappointedly fussed. "That's a darn shame!" Sam snapped. "Why did you have to go and do that?" He pointed toward Larry's bedroom door. "Larry really likes that girl."

"I know he really likes her. But don't go and accuse me of snooping," Carrie snapped. "That's not what I did. Sam, you need to calm down and listen."

"I'm calm. I'm just pissed as hell that you sneaked out to meddle in Larry's social affair."

Carrie shook her head as she stared at Sam. "Will you please listen to me?"

"I have been listening for the last fifteen minutes since you walked through that door." Sam raised both arms. "My goodness, Carrie. You haven't told me a damn thing. All I know is that you sneaked out of the house right after the young lady left, and now you are back saying we have a problem regarding the girl," Sam fussed.

"Well, if you'll stop fussing and listen. I'll tell you what the problem is."

Sam held up both hands. "My goodness, what kind of a problem can it be? The young lady is damn good looking and got her head on straighter than anyone I thought our son would end up with."

"Yes, Sam Westwood. She's mighty pretty and she's no dummy! But I followed her home and told her to stay away from Larry."

Sam jaw dropped as his eyes widened with confusion. "Carrie, why did you butt in and do something so imprudent like that? I don't care what you heard about the young lady if Larry is happy with her and she's happy with him. It's not our place to butt in. He's long past twenty-one, you know. Last time I checked our son was a thirty-three year old man. We have no right to butt into his lovelife," Sam sharply insisted.

"Well, when he first moved in with us, you butted in when he showed interest in Sabrina Taylor," Carrie snappy reminded him.

"Of course, I stuck my nose in his personal life at that time! It wasn't a good idea for him to develop a crush on his boss. Only because we work for the Taylors. Otherwise, I wouldn't have butted in," Sam firmly stated. "Besides, you were with me on that decision. We both knew it wasn't a good idea for him to get tangled up with Sabrina Taylor."

Carrie nodded. "I agree. But, that's why I butted in and told Courtney Ross to stay away from Larry. I urged her to break off what have developed between them. He works for the Taylors and Courtney is the young woman who went off her rocker two years ago and shot Miss Sabrina, Mr. Britain and her own brother," Carrie sadly shared.

Sam jaw dropped, then he grabbed his face with both hands and hopped off the edge of the bed. "Hot damn! That's the worst news ever!" He stared at Carrie. "Are you absolutely indisputable sure she's the girl who caused all that mayhem?"

Carrie glumly nodded. "Yes, I'm positive."

"I'm questioning it because nothing appeared in the paper accusing anyone in particular. All we know is that Miss Sabrina and Mr. Britain were both hospitalized due to a shooting incident on the Taylor's estate caused by one of Sabrina's friends. They never mentioned the name of the friend," Sam recalled.

"Her name wasn't in the press or on the news because the Taylors and Franklins were able to keep her name out of the news. But Miss Sabrina confirmed to me that it was Courtney Ross."

Sam grabbed his head with both hands and shook it. "Therefore, when she walked through the door tonight you knew exactly who she was?" Sam asked.

"Yes, I knew who she was. But what are we going to do?" Carrie asked.

Sam shook his head. His good mood and encouragement for Larry and Courtney were broken as he dropped back down on the edge of the bed. "Let's think about this thing for a moment." He looked at Carrie. "The young lady is well now and about to be a teacher at Barrington High. No way could she get hired working with children if she wasn't completely well. So that's a good thing. Besides, she got the best care from that upscale Shady Grove. Therefore, her family must be financially stable to roll out that kind of dough for 24 months," Sam assumed.

Carrie shook her head as she stared at Sam with her back propped against the dresser. "Her family is as poor as we are."

Sam stared with surprised eyes. "Are you sure about that? Shady Grove only cater to the rich and famous or those with rich and famous bankbooks."

"I'm telling you, Courtney's family didn't pay for her medical bills for Shady Grove," Carrie said, but stopped herself.

Sam held up both hands. "What are you waiting for? Who paid her mental health doctor bills for her care at Shady Grove for the past two years? If you're hesitating to tell me because it was our son, I guess he's broke now!" Sam shouted.

"You're right, Larry would be broke. As much as it cost to stay in Shady Grove for one day, and time it by 730 days." Carrie took a deep breath, glad it wasn't her son's inheritance that footed Courtney's bill. "But it wasn't Larry's money. It was Mr. Charles's brother, Mr. Don. He paid for that young lady's medical care at Shady Grove."

"What are you telling me? You mean Mr. Don paid for the medical care of the young lady who almost killed his niece?" Sam confusedly asked.

"Yes, Mr. Don paid for her medical care so she could get the best possible care." Carrie held up both hands, shaking her head. "Don't ask me why he did it."

"I'm not going to ask you why. But who told you? This is my first time hearing about it."

"Courtney's mother works for Mr. Don at Taylor Investments. Apparently he paid Courtney's medical bills as a favor to Courtney's mother," Carrie told him. "And I know this because Sabrina confided in me."

"That's a tall favor to do for one of your employees. He was surely out of millions." Sam waved a hand. "But that's what the Taylor's do. They love helping others," Sam nodded.

"That's true. But the point I'm trying to make is how that girl is just as poor as we are. We are probably much better off than her family."

"Carrie, why were you even making that point? What difference does it make? So, she's poor. That's not a crime," Sam said, not thinking of their real issue.

"Sam, I don't think you have thought about what this really means. How will it look to Miss Sabrina? We cannot expect her to accept or be happy for Larry involvement with the young lady who shot and could have killed her. Do you understand now why Larry needs to break off with this young lady?" Carrie sharply asked.

Sam glumly nodded. "I agree. It's a sticky situation. But the young lady is well now and won't be hurting anyone again. Larry needs a good woman in his life. It's not like there's a girl waiting in line for him. He was damn lucky this girl fell for him considering his limitations." Sam raised both arms. "I would hate to be the one to keep him and this young woman apart."

"Me too, but it would be disloyal dating Courtney Ross. The girl who caused so much heartache and mayhem for Miss Sabrina," Carrie pointed out.

Sam shook his head. "Maybe we should leave it alone."

"I wish we could. But Sam, you know we can't leave this alone."

"Why can't we? Apparently Larry must be okay with it. He still wants to date the girl. It's just one big mess. Our son has always wanted someone in his life. Then he finally meets someone that's interested. Now they may have to go their separate ways." Sam took a seat in a side chair and slipped out of his shoes as he glanced toward Carrie. "You didn't answer me. I asked you, do you know how Larry feels about what she did to Miss Sabrina?"

Carrie turned back the covers on the bed. "I have no idea what he thinks and he doesn't know what he thinks. Since he doesn't know what Courtney did."

"What do you mean, he doesn't know?"

"Courtney told me tonight that she hasn't told Larry yet."

"They been seeing each other for a whole year, but he doesn't know what landed her in that loony bind?" Sam asked.

"Sam, don't call it that. Shady Grove is a beautiful place."

"It might be beautiful. But people are not going there for the scenery. It's a mental institution. And if you end up there, it's because all your marbles are not in place. If they are in place, they are not working properly," Sam firmly stated.

"That may be so but the issue at hand is our son. He's asleep in his room and happy with a girl for the first time in his life." Carrie pointed toward the left wall toward his room on the other side of the wall. "Now, he'll either have to give up that girl or seem disloyal to the people he works for. Therefore, the best way to make this all go away is for him to cut ties with Courtney Ross."

Stepping into his PJs, Sam shook his head. "I don't think Larry will do it. He's in love with that girl. I could see it in his eyes and the way he looked at her. Plus dropping him off at Shady Grove twice a week over the past year, he always talked about how much he enjoyed spending time with her. So we need to stay out of it and let them figure it out," Sam strongly suggested. "However, there is something we need to do immediately," Sam said buttoning his PJ's top as he drop back in the bedside chair.

"What should we do immediately?" Carrie curiously asked.

"We need to knock on Larry's door."

"He might be asleep," Carrie said.

"Well, if he's asleep, we need to wake him."

"Sam, I know you're right. But maybe we should wait and tell him all of this tomorrow morning," Carrie suggested. "Besides, it's going to be a big shock to him and we don't know how he's going to take it."

"I know how he's going to take it. He's going to take it the same way we have. He'll be extremely disappointed and upset. But he'll get over it."

"Sam before we go knocking on Larry's door. Let think about this for a moment."

"Carrie, what are you talking about? There's nothing to think about. Larry needs to know what his new girlfriend did to Miss Sabrina," Sam strongly insisted as he held up one finger. "And let's not forget what she also did to Mr. Britain and also her own brother," Sam firmly reminded Carrie.

"Sam, you don't have to convince me how desperately Larry needs to know. I know he needs to know." Carrie had just slipped into her nightgown, standing in the closet pulling a robe from a hanger.

"If that's the case, why are you so hesitate? Why wait until tomorrow when we can get it over with and tell him now?"

Carrie glanced toward the floor and then looked at Sam. "This will spoil his evening. He won't be able to sleep afterward. This is one big mess."

"I agree its one big mess that our son is right in the middle of and he needs to know." Sam shook his head. "Looks are deceiving. The young lady didn't strike me as someone who could attempt such awful acts."

"I want her far away from my son. But in Courtney's defense, anyone can have a breakdown," Carrie caringly stated.

"I guess you're right. But let's not get off track," Sam said. "Are you coming with me to talk to Larry or not?"

Carrie nodded. "Yes, I'm coming. But I feel just awful."

"I feel awful to. But we need to get it over with."

"I mean I feel awful that I made Courtney that promise."

"What promise?"

"I promised her I wouldn't tell Larry."

"Why would you promise her something like that?" Sam asked, not pleased.

"She said she wants to tell him herself."

"That would be ideal." Sam nodded. "But that's what I have a problem with. She may want to tell him, but I think she's afraid of his reaction and she keeps putting it off."

"Sam, she said she would tell him; and if he heard it from her, maybe it won't crush him as much as hearing it from us."

Sam shook his head. "Carrie no. We're not putting this off and leaving it in the hands of that young lady. Think about it. My goodness! It's been a whole year since they started seeing each other. She hasn't told him and I don't think she'll tell him now."

Carrie stomach was tied in knots over telling Larry about Courtney's breakdown actions. She looked at Sam and frowned. "Maybe you're right and we should just tell him. I just don't like giving my word and not keeping it."

"Listen, Carrie. You need to get a grip of the urgency of this matter. Besides, you may have promised the young woman you wouldn't tell him. But I didn't promise her," Sam fussed. "You told me, and now I'm going to tell our son. Therefore, in a way, you're not breaking your word."

Carrie frowned at Sam's attempt of dressing up a broken promise. "Well, I don't see it that way. I see it as breaking a promise."

"Whatever, Carrie. Your loyalty lies with your son. Larry needs to know so he can make up his mind whether to stay in that relationship or not," Sam quickly hopped out of the chair and headed toward their bedroom door. He grabbed the doorknob but stood inside the room waiting for Carrie as she buttoned her robe.

"We have stood around discussing this matter long enough. Let's go tell him," Sam said, as he pulled the bedroom door opened.

Chapter Thirty-Three

Carrie nerves tightened as she slowly took a seat on the living room sofa. Sam grabbed a bottle of water from the refrigerator. He twisted off the cap and finished a fourth before he lowered the bottle. Then Carrie watched as Sam strutted from the kitchen over to Larry's bedroom door and knocked twice. Larry opened the door almost immediately. He was fully dressed.

"What's the matter?" Larry asked, noticing the stress on his father's face.

"I'm glad to see you're still awake, son. Carrie and I need you to step into the living room for a while. We need to discuss something."

Larry eyes widened with concern. "Discuss something?" he asked.

Sam nodded. "Yes. Your mother and I have something we need to talk to you about." Sam turned his back to Larry, and stepped over to the sofa.

Larry slowly walked across the room to the sofa and took a seat next to Sam. Carrie took a seat on the other side of Larry as she took his hand in hers. "I didn't expect you to still be awake," she said rubbing the top of his hand, dreading what they were about to tell him.

"I'm not sleepy. I'm still excited about Courtney's visit. I just got off the phone with her. She called me soon as she got home. We have been on the phone talking ever since until Daddy knocked on my door."

Sam patted Larry on the back and looked seriously at him. "I'm not going to beat around the bush with what Carrie and I need to tell you. It's about Courtney and its not good news," Sam warned him.

"If it's not good news about her, don't tell me." Larry attempted to stand, but Carrie held on to his arm. "Please stay seated and hear us out."

Larry frowned toward Carrie with upset eyes. "But I don't want to hear any bad news about her. I love her and if she did something bad before we met. I don't want to hear about it. Maybe she's sorry about it. I don't need to know that stuff. All I need to know is that she loves me and she told me over the phone tonight that she loves me," Larry firmly stated.

"Normally, I would respect your wishes and do as you request, Son," Sam told him. "But in this case, you need to hear what we know. Then if it still doesn't matter, at least we'll know your feelings on the matter."

Deep distress showed in Larry's eyes as he looked at Carrie. "If I say I don't want to hear it. Why are you and Daddy going to tell me anyway? If you told me not to tell you something, I would do as you asked."

Carrie nodded with sad eyes. "I know and we're not trying to be disrespectful of your wishes. But this is something we must tell you."

Larry held up both hands. "Okay, what is the bad news? It won't matter to me. But tell me since it's something you must tell me," Larry sadly insisted.

"Courtney did something bad to Miss Sabrina," Sam told him.

"I know she did something bad and that's why Miss Sabrina won't be friends with her anymore," Larry quickly told them.

The room was completely quiet for a moment after Larry spoke. Sam and Carrie exchanged surprise looks and then stared at Larry.

Carrie eyes widened. "Courtney told you what she did to Miss Sabrina?"

Larry shook his head. "She didn't tell me what she did to Miss Sabrina. She didn't give me any details. She just said she did something bad to her."

Sam and Carrie nodded and exchanged looks. Larry had just confirmed he wasn't aware of Courtney's crime that landed her into Shady Grove.

"I can see that look on your faces and now you think Courtney isn't a good person because of what she did to Miss Sabrina. But I told her, we all make mistakes," Larry stressed with love pouring out of his voice for Courtney. But I could tell from her voice and how anxious she was explaining it, that it was probably really bad. But I also could tell how sorry she was."

Sam and Carrie didn't interrupt Larry. They allowed him to explain as long as he felt the need to. They could tell he had strong feelings Courtney.

He looked from Carrie to Sam. "You two need to give Courtney a chance. I know what she did was probably bad. But she's sorry about it and deserves a second chance. Her friends that won't talk to her must not be nice people. A real friend will forgive your mistakes," Larry kept talking. "Isn't that true?"

Sam patted Larry on the back. "Yes, in some cases. But this case is different," Sam told him.

"It might be different. But she still deserves a second chance to fix her mistake," Larry strongly stated.

"Listen, Son," Carrie glumly said. "Some mistakes cannot be fixed."

Sam nodded. "That's true. But Larry figured right."

"I figured right about what?" Larry asked.

"You figured right when you said what she had done was probably bad."

"Okay, so what?" Larry asked.

"We can confirm it is really bad." Sam caringly touched Larry's arm. "But listen, Son. The fact that she told you that much is notable," Sam said, as he exchanged looks with Carrie. "Sounds like she's trying to open up to you."

"That's what I think also, Daddy. I just know she's trying to be open and honest. She's a good person, and she loves me." Larry looked at Carrie and smiled. "Mama, somebody loves me. Grandma Lulu had told me no girl would ever love me. And I thought Grandma Lulu was right."

"Listen, Son. I know you loved your grandma. But keep in mind. Your Grandma Lulu wasn't right about that or anything else she possibly told you!" Sam firmly said. "She was my mother, God rest her soul. But Mom was a sick bitter old lady from the time you were born. The biggest mistake your mother and I ever made were leaving you in those woods with my loony mother!"

"Grandma Lulu had a condition and I didn't understand her at all. But I still loved her. And I miss her sometime," Larry admitted.

"I'm sure you do miss her sometime. We do as well. But let's get back to the issue at hand. Can you recall a couple back when Miss Sabrina was hospitalized?" Sam asked. "She was sick for a whole month and wasn't able to work or even walk without crutches? You remember that, don't you?"

Larry nodded. "Yes, I can remember."

"Well, she was in the hospital because of Courtney," Sam sorrowfully said, and then paused looking Larry in the eyes.

Larry eyes widened with curiosity. "I don't understand."

"Well, you will when I'm finished," Sam said assuredly.

Larry was shaken by the uncertainty of his father's words to come. He looked down, and then at Sam and nodded. "Okay, go on and finish."

Sam placed his hand on Larry's shoulder. "Brace yourself Son, for what I'm about to say is going to shock you," Sam announced and then paused.

Carrie quickly said. "Just tell him, Sam."

Sam looked toward the ceiling and then let out a sigh. "Okay. Here goes. Your new girlfriend pulled out a gun and shot Miss Sabrina," Sam sadly said. "She also shot Mr. Britain and her own brother."

Larry jaw dropped as he sat speechless staring at his father. After a bit of silence, Larry jumped to Courtney's defense. "If she did something like that she wasn't herself. She told me she would never do something like that again."

"I thought she didn't tell you what she did?" Sam inquired.

"She didn't tell me what it was she had done. She just said she would never do something like that again," Larry sadly explained. "She also told me how sick she was then. She told me Shady Grove made her well again."

"How do you think Miss Sabrina will feel about you dating the young lady that hurt her like that?" Sam asked. "Do you foresee a problem with Miss Sabrina and the Taylors if you stay in your relationship with Courtney?"

"No, I don't foresee a problem with Miss Sabrina and the Taylors. They don't care about who I date. Miss Sabrina may be mad at Courtney for what she did to her. But Miss Sabrina would never want me to give up the girl I love because of something Courtney did when she was very sick. I think Miss Sabrina will be pleased I have someone in my life."

"She may be pleased about the idea of you having someone in your life. But she won't be pleased to hear its Courtney Ross," Carrie sadly said. "No matter whether it was an accident or intentional due to temporary insanity, the victim of the crime feel safer far away from the person who hurt them."

"That's right, Son. Miss Sabrina is a kind hearted person and I'm sure she wishes Courtney well. But I'm sure she doesn't want Courtney connected to her family and in her mix anymore. After all the suffering she endured by the hands of your new girlfriend, no one can blame her," Sam sadly explained.

Larry held up both hands as his patience continued to wear short. He wasn't pleased listening to his parents discourage toward Courtney. "Okay, I have listened. But I'm not going to break up with Courtney just because she did something bad when she was sick. She's well now. She loves me and I love her." Larry stood up from the sofa. "I know something needs to be done."

"You do?" Carrie asked.

Larry nodded. "I know exactly what needs to be done. I don't want Miss Sabrina to be mad at me."

"Son, what do you plan to do?" Sam curiously asked.

"Well, tomorrow early, I'll call Miss Sabrina."

Sam exchanged looks with Carrie and then shook her head at Larry. "Son, that doesn't sound like a good idea. Don't bother Miss Sabrina with this."

Carrie nodded. "Sam is right. Hearing about Courtney will likely distress Miss Sabrina. I assume you plan to call to tell her about you and Courtney."

"That's right. I plan to call Miss Sabrina and request a meeting to talk with her and Mr. Britain."

Chapter Thirty-Four

Sabrina and Britain were seated at a rear table in Starbucks that Tuesday evening after dinner. Starbucks was located on the outskirts of Barrington Hills where Larry had asked to meet them. Larry had suggested nine o'clock as a meeting time. Sabrina and Britain had arrived a few minutes before nine and were seated when they spotted Larry walking through the coffee shop door. It was a few minutes passed nine. Larry was smiling as he walked toward the rear where he spotted Britain and Sabrina seated. He was pleased they had accepted his invite and felt assured they were inside when he had noticed Britain's car when Sam drove him into the Starbuck's parking lot. Sam dropped him off and Larry told his father not to wait. He would call when he was done.

"I always like to be on time but my Daddy had too many red lights," Larry said as he took a seat at the small green wooden table.

"We just arrived as well," Britain said. "Besides, you're right on time." Britain held up one finger for a waiter.

Larry looked at Britain and smiled. "Mr. Britain, they don't come to your table in here. We have to stand in line for what we want," Larry quickly informed him. When I told Mama where we were meeting, she said it was possible that you and Sabrina have hadn't inside of a Starbucks before. So I really appreciate you meeting me here," Larry said thankfully.

"We were glad to do it," Britain said as he stood from his chair. "I'll stand in line for the three of us. What can I get you? We are having honey spice Cappuccinos with cream," Britain said to Larry.

Larry nodded. "I'll take what you're having."

When Britain stepped back over to the table with a paper tray of three Cappuccinos, Larry had a sad look on his face and seemed anxious.

"So, Larry, tell us what do we owe the honor of meeting you here for coffee?" Britain asked as he took his seat.

Larry looked at Britain and smiled. "You are a nice man Mr. Britain. You have always been nice to me." Larry lifted the foam cup of cappuccino and took a sip. "You and Miss Sabrina are good people."

"Thank you, Larry. We think you're pretty swell also," Sabrina lifted her foam cup, removed the plastic lid and took a small sip of her cappuccino. "Actually, Larry, you're as nice as they come."

Larry eyes widened with a big smile as he stared at Sabrina. "You think that about me?" He touched his chest.

She nodded. "Of course. I thought you knew how swell I think of you."

"Well, that's a big compliment. Thank you, Miss Sabrina. I think you and Mr. Britain are as good as they come," Larry said. "I also want to thank Mr. Britain for paying for my drink. But I mentioned on the phone that it was my treat," Larry reminded them. "So, if you don't mind," Larry seriously suggested to Britain. "I would like to pay you back."

Britain shook his head and smiled, waving both hands at Larry. "Thank you. But it's fine. I took care of you."

Larry stood from his seat. "I know you don't mind because you are always doing good things for people. But I keep my word," Larry insisted as he reached in his back jean pocket and removed his wallet. He sit back down in his chair and looked through his wallet and removed a ten dollar bill and handed it to Britain. "Is this enough?" Larry asked.

Britain looked at Larry and didn't immediately take the ten dollars. But he could see Larry was insistent. Therefore, he smiled and nodded as he reluctantly reached for the money. "Sure, it's fine," Britain said as he took the money and placed it in his shirt pocket.

"Thank you, Mr. Britain. I feel a lot better. Now I can tell you and Miss Sabrina why I invited you here."

Sabrina and Britain were both curious to hear why Larry had asked for a meeting with them.

Larry smiled at Britain and Sabrina. "I don't know where to start."

"Well, whatever it is, start from the beginning," Sabrina politely suggested.

"Okay, that's a good idea. So, I guess I'll start by saying, I met someone. I'm in a relationship now. The kind of relationship that you two have with each other," Larry excitedly shared as he smiled happily.

"That's wonderful news, Larry," Sabrina cheerfully said. "I'm so happy for you. I know you wanted someone in your life."

Larry nodded. "Yes, I met a girl and she loves me. I love her too."

Britain reached over and patted Larry's shoulder. "That's fantastic, Larry."

Larry cheerfully grinned. 'Thank you, Mr. Britain. I know I'm a lucky man right now. But I need to be honest about something."

"What do you mean?" Britain casually asked.

"You see, she didn't like me in the beginning. She didn't even want to talk to me the day we met." Larry nodded and grinned. "But it all worked out. She quickly changed her mind and started talking to me when she found out I worked for your family." Larry looked at Sabrina. "Yes, she was impressed that I worked for the Taylors." Larry held up both hands. "But don't misunderstand me. That's not why she fell in love with me. She fell in love with me because she found out I was a good person who really loved her. That's what she told me."

"When did you meet her?" Sabrina casually asked.

"We met a year ago."

"That's great, Larry. You have been in a relationship for an entire year? Why didn't you mention it? I think it's fabulous."

"I couldn't tell anyone because she asked me not to. That's why I'm meeting with you and Mr. Britain tonight. She's afraid you and Mr. Britain hates her and I'm meeting with you to find out if that's true."

Sabrina and Britain were both alarmed at what Larry had said. "Larry, with all due respect to your new girlfriend. Why would she think we hate her?" Britain asked. "Better yet, why would we hate someone you're dating?"

"That's not who we are, and you know that, Larry," Sabrina seriously, yet politely said. She grabbed her face and held it as she stared at Larry. "I guess we're a bit thrown and confused by your statement."

Larry held up one finger. "Well, she used to be your friend, Miss Sabrina. Her name is Courtney Ross," Larry announced.

"Did you say Courtney Ross?" Sabrina asked to be sure.

Larry nodded. "Yes, my new girlfriend name is Courtney Ross. She told me how she did something very bad to you. She feels bad about it and doesn't think you'll forgive her."

Sabrina and Britain exchanged surprised looks; and it was a bit of silence before Sabrina looked at Larry and shook her head. "Larry, that's not true. Britain and I have both forgiven Courtney. It's not good for the body or the spirit to hold on to ill feelings about someone," Sabrina admitted and took a sip of her cappuccino. "But I'll admit I was quite unhappy with Courtney for a very long time. It's been two years since that incident. It's behind us now.

Courtney spent two years of her life getting better and Britain and I are so pleased she has been released from Shady Grove and can go on with her life," Sabrina softly said.

"But my Mama said you wouldn't want me to date her because she hurt you and Mr. Britain. My Mama asked me to break up with Courtney so you and Mr. Britain won't be mad at me," Larry glumly shared.

Britain tapped his fingers on the small round table. He wasn't pleased to hear Courtney was Larry's new girlfriend. He didn't want Courtney in Sabrina's vicinity. "Larry, here's the issue. No disrespect intended. But Sabrina and I would very much prefer to keep Courtney as far away from the both of us as possible," Britain seriously stated. "It just makes sense to stay away from fire if it has burned you once. We have no ill feelings toward Courtney and we wish her well." Britain exchanged looks with Sabrina and they both nodded at each other. "We have both forgiven Courtney and as I said, we wish her well," Britain said assuredly. "And if she needs help in anyway, we are both willing to help her. But we would prefer not to socialize with Courtney due to our past tragic history with her."

"But do I have to stop dating her since I work for you, Miss Sabrina?"

"Larry, you're a grown man in charge of your own life and decisions. No one can dictate who you should or shouldn't date. Your job is secure no matter who you choose to date. Courtney is your girlfriend and you'll be interacting with her. She won't be in our way," Sabrina assured him.

Larry excitedly smiled. "Thank you, Miss Sabrina. May I shake your hand?" He reached for her hand and she allowed him to shake her hand as he continued to talk. "My Mama and Daddy were both wrong about you. You're glad I'm dating Courtney, aren't you?" he asked as he released her hand.

Sabrina touched the table in front of Larry. "Larry, I want to make something clear. You have the wrong notion from me. I never said I was happy that you are dating Courtney. The truth is, I'm not happy that you're dating her."

Larry jaw dropped in confusion as he stared at Sabrina. "But you said you're happy for me and you're glad I have someone. You also said I can date who I want to, that it's nobody business and I won't lose my job."

Sabrina folded her lips and paused for a moment before she replied to Larry. She wanted him to understand her feelings but she didn't want to make him feel too bad. "Larry, all of that is true, and I'm very glad you found someone and that you're dating. Nevertheless, I wish it was anyone else other than Courtney." She reached across the table and touched the top of his hand. "I mean that in the kindest way with no ill feelings toward Courtney. I know she's well. But I still cannot forget what happened in the past; although I feel assured she'll stay well and the two of you will be fine," Sabrina sincerely explained.

"I really thought you weren't mad at Courtney anymore, Miss Sabrina. It sounds like to me that you're still mad at her," Larry sadly said, looking down.

"Larry, I'm sorry if you think that. But I'm not mad at Courtney."

"But you don't want me with her. I thought you did after you said my job was secure and I can date who I choose." He lifted his cappuccino with a trembling hand.

"Larry, that's true. Your job is secure and you can date who you choose. However, I'm being honest when I say I wish you had met someone other than Courtney," Sabrina told him as she exchanged compassionate looks with Britain.

"Miss Sabrina, I hear you but I still think you're mad at Courtney."

"Larry, if you hear me, you should know I would never lie to you. You have my word that I'm no longer upset with Courtney. Britain and I both know the magnitude of how ill she was back then. We witnessed it with our own eyes. But that's behind us. We're moving forward with our wedding plans. We thought Courtney would be a part of our past. Now, you sort of blindsided us with your news that she's your new girlfriend. We'll have to get use to the idea. Because with Courtney in your life, she'll still be indirectly apart of ours," Sabrina said.

Britain nodded with a serious expression on his face. "That's right, Larry. But please don't worry about how we will cope. We will cope and all will work out. We have read all the medical reports, courtesy of Sabrina's Uncle Don. We know Courtney turned the corner and is back to the decent person she was a few years ago before her breakdown."

"Thank you, Mr. Britain for saying that; and thank you, Miss Sabrina." Larry looked from Britain to Sabrina. "You both are saying all the right words. But you still wish I had met someone other than Courtney. That's because you wish her well but prefer not to socialize with her again."

Britain and Sabrina nodded. "That's it Larry. But be happy and if Courtney Ross makes you happy that's great for you," Britain encouraged him. "You deserve all the happiness that can come your way. You're a good man, Larry."

Larry lifted his cappuccino and took a small sip. "I'm glad we had this meeting. My Mama and Daddy will be glad to know I won't lose my job for dating Courtney. They said dating Courtney was disloyal to the Taylors. They scared me for a moment because they told me they were afraid I would lose my job."

Sabrina exchanged looks with Britain as Larry's statement ripped through her stomach to think his parents had considered that possibility of Larry being fired for dating Courtney. "Larry, I'm sure Carrie and Sam were concerned. But surely Carrie and Sam didn't actually think me and my family would dismiss you based on who you chose to date," Sabrina said to him. "Honestly, Larry. Think for a moment. Do you think my family would do something like that, which is so against a person's civil and human rights?" she said with conviction. "I think you know me and my family better than to even consider such a thought."

Larry thought for a moment as he stared down at the table. Then he looked across the table at Sabrina with a solemn expression.

"I'm sorry for thinking that way. Your family and you are good people. You wouldn't do something like that to me or anyone else. Besides, I didn't believe Mama and Daddy. That's why I wanted to meet with the both of you.

Britain glanced at his watch. "We need to get going. I have a meeting early tomorrow that I still need to prep for," he said, looking toward Sabrina.

"We do need to leave," Sabrina agreed as she looked toward Larry and smiled. "Have you shared with us all that you wanted to discuss?" she asked.

Larry nodded. "Yes, Miss Sabrina. That's everything and I'm happy I told you both about my new girlfriend. She thinks I'm pretty and nicest man she ever met. I think she's pretty and the nicest girl I ever met." Larry stood from his seat.

Britain and Sabrina stood from their seats. "That's great you two think that way about each other," Britain said as he patted his jacket pockets for his keys as the three of them stood there at the little green table.

Larry suddenly laughed. "I shouldn't have used the word pretty for me. She used a different word that means pretty but I can't think of what it was," Larry continued to talk as they walked on ahead of him.

Britain and Sabrina waited right outside the door of Starbucks for Larry, who made a stop at the men's room before he stepped out of the coffee shop. "Come with us, Larry. I'll drop you off," Britain told him.

Larry shook his head. "No, thanks. I'll call my Daddy and wait for him. I told him I would call when we were done with our meeting."

"Okay, Larry. But we live in the same house," Sabrina urged him.

"But I don't want to intrude. I want to be independent."

Britain and Sabrina slowly walked away from Larry, leaving him standing outside of the Starbucks entrance. After they were seated in Britain's car and headed away from Starbucks, they were both a tad quiet before Britain commented. "This is really unexpected news," Britain said as he looked straight ahead through the windshield as he drove at a legal speed limit down the street. "When you called and said Larry wanted to meet with us it never dawned on me that he would announce to us that he's dating Courtney. She's his new girlfriend," Britain seriously said. "That's some news to take in. Will wonders ever cease?"

"I know," Sabrina agreed. "I guess I'm still in somewhat shock over his news. He has wanted someone in this life but never believed it would happen."

"What's the odds of that person being Courtney?" Britain said.

"Probably a million to one. He just happen to be admitted to Shady Grove for a few weeks and met her during lunch," Sabrina said. "Those are incredible odds. But I'm just stunned and lost for words and what to think or say about the news we were just given by Larry."

"I agree its stunning information to learn your worker is now dating the young lady who almost destroyed us both. But she is healthy now and Larry can take care of himself," Britain assured her.

"You're right. Larry can take care of himself. He has a good eye and ear for people. He knows who's real and who's not. He'll be able to decipher if Courtney isn't right for him."

"That's good to hear," Britain said. "I'm sure you know Larry quite well."

Sabrina nodded. "That's true. I do know him quite well. Probably better than Starlet and Samantha. You see, Larry and I became quite close when my second mother passed away. It was easy to talk to him."

"I'm glad you had him to talk to. At that time you were not talking to me, remember? That was during our short breakup," Britain reminded her.

"Yes, I remember how silly I was to break up with you. I'm so glad I came to my senses. But back to our issue at hand. Larry is a good decent guy and Courtney was never really interested in his type before her illness," Sabrina said. "And the fact that she is now, is a compliment to her."

Britain nodded. "I agree. She couldn't have chosen anyone any nicer than Larry."

"That's true," Sabrina agreed. "But I must admit how this whole situation is depressing. I was pleased to hear about Courtney's release. It freed up my conscience and I was glad she could finally go on with her life. But, I never wanted the two of us to be interconnected again. Now, on top of everything of finally feeling relaxed and getting the final arrangements together for the wedding, Larry tells us Courtney is back in the center of our lives," Sabrina miserably mumbled.

    Britain glanced at his watch. It was ten o'clock. "I know it's getting late. But we need to round up everybody and have them meet us at your house. This is vitally important news that needs to be shared with the family now," Britain strongly suggested. "I wouldn't want Starlet or Samantha to catch a glimpse of Courtney on your property visiting Larry without first being aware that Larry and Courtney are dating."

Chapter Thirty-Five

    Britain and Sabrina had called their families and asked them to meet the two of them at the Taylor mansion. And in the twenty minutes it took Britain to drive from Starbucks to the Taylor home, Veronica, Catherine, Paris, Sydney, Rome, Amber and the twins had all arrived at Sabrina's home. They were all gathered in the living room in wonder of why Sabrina and Britain had summoned them all together. They figured it had something to do with their wedding plans. But when Sabrina and Britain walked into the living room with disheartened expressions on their faces, suddenly the room became completely quiet. Sabrina and Britain held hands as they took a seat next to each other on one of the two loveseats in the room as everyone else were seated about on the sofas and side chairs. Samantha and Paris were seated on one of the sofas and Sydney and Starlet were seated on the same sofa. Charles and Veronica were seated on the facing sofa, as well as Amber and Rome who each held one of their twins in their laps. Catherine was seated in a side chair preoccupied sending and answering text messages from Julian. She was excited about settling on a date to move into the Coleman mansion with him.

    Britain leaned forward with a serious expression on his face. "Okay, we'll get right to the point," Britain said as he exchanged looks with all who were gathered. "Sabrina and I just left a private personal meeting with Larry."

    Charles eyes widened with surprise as he held up one finger. "Are you referring to our Larry?"

    Britain nodded as he exchanged looks with Sabrina as Charles continued. "The two of you look quite glum. I can't imagine what you could have met with Larry about. He does his work well and sort of keeps to himself," Charles casually shared.

Sabrina looked at her father with serious eyes. "Father, Larry called me earlier in the day and asked if Britain and I could meet him tonight at Starbucks. We met up at nine," Sabrina explained. "I'll admit we were surprised to get his invitation to meet with him. But we were glad to meet with him. Anyway, he wanted to meet with us to tell us he had a girlfriend."

Samantha and Starlet smiled and softly clapped their hands. "That's wonderful news," Starlet said as she exchanged looks with her father. "He was always talking about how much he wanted someone in his life. But he wasn't too encouraged and we would encourage him that someone would come along," Starlet said, smiling. "It's just like sweet Larry to want to meet and tell you two he had a girlfriend."

Sabrina and Britain exchanged looks because they could see how happy Samantha and Starlet were. They knew the whole story would be a big letdown to them.

"Yes, someone came along for Larry," Britain slowly hesitantly relayed.

"That is just incredible news," Starlet cheered.

"It is incredible news," Britain agreed. "However, Larry didn't ask to meet with us to tell us he had a girlfriend."

They all stared at Britain curiously as he and Sabrina exchanged looks. Starlet was very curious. "Well, why did he ask to meet with you two?"

Britain looked at Sabrina and nodded. "I'll tell them."

By now Starlet was very excited wondering if Larry had shared engagement news or something along that line. She excitedly anticipated what Britain would share with them about Larry.

"Larry met with us for our approval and blessings of his new girlfriend."

They all had confusion on their faces especially Starlet. But she was speechless at Britain's announcement as Veronica held up one finger.

"I don't know your worker, Larry that well," Veronica quickly responded. "But why would the young man seek someone's approval for who he dates?" Veronica asked.

Samantha quickly spoke. "Larry is just special that way. You need to hold a conversation with Larry to really get to know him. He's a wonderful man."

Britain nodded toward his mother. "Yes, Mother, Larry is a good person."

"Well, if he's such a good person why have you two gathered us all here to tell us what he told you?" Veronica curiously asked. "Is there something special about him meeting a young lady?"

The room fell quiet for a moment and then Charles touched the top of Veronica's hand. "Larry is one of the best men I know. But due to his upbringing he appears more childlike and vulnerable at time," Charles compassionately shared.

Veronica held up both hands, looking toward Britain and Sabrina. "I thought the meeting was about settling up your new wedding plans. Therefore, I guess I'm not following why we all needed to meet here to hear about one of Charles's worker's lovelife."

Just then Starlet caught a look on Sabrina's face and figured it out. Starlet hopped off the sofa and covered her mouth with both hands. "Oh, no! It's not about Larry," Starlet said with panic in her voice. "It's about the girl!" Starlet stared humbly at Sabrina. "It's Courtney Ross, isn't it?"

Britain and Sabrina nodded. "Yes, that's why Larry met with us to let us know that Courtney is his new girlfriend," Britain told them.

Starlet took her seat back on the sofa next to Sydney. She sat there trembling, shaking her head in anguish of the news she had just discovered. "Father, what can we do?" Starlet asked. "This is an outrage and Courtney Ross presence is the last thing we need in this family," Starlet sadly stressed. "Courtney is going to hurt Larry. He doesn't deserve the anguish she's going to put him through." Starlet wiped a tear from her left eye.

"It sounds glum and none of us are happy to hear she's Larry's new girlfriend," Charles said. "But the good news is, she was just released from the world class Shady Grove with an excellent mental health report. Courtney Ross is well now. She's no longer mentally ill. Therefore, we all need to keep in mind that she was a very sick young woman when she had her breakdown two years ago and caused that unspeakable disaster on this property. Besides, my hands are tied." Charles looked toward Starlet. "Dear, you know as well as I do, whether I'm pleased about Larry's new girlfriend or not, I have no say so over who he should or shouldn't date."

Sydney patted Starlet on the back as she continued to softly cry. "I don't want Courtney Ross anywhere near my family ever again. She almost took my sister's life. But I do I apologize for my behavior. I just cannot seem to keep my composure and stay rational when it comes to Courtney Ross. I know she's well but I'll never trust her. It hurts me to admit this, but I honestly feel she's deceitful and erratic at nature," Starlet candidly said. "It doesn't matter whether she's sick or well; and I also believe she's with Larry because he's connected to this family. I believe deep down she still wants to be near Sabrina and Britain so she can end up causing pandemonium and chaos in their lives again," Starlet said determinedly. "I think if Larry needs to be with someone as dangerous as Courtney Ross, he needs to move off of our property. Dating Courtney is putting us all in danger," Starlet firmly stated, as she wiped tears from her eyes.

Charles stood up from his seat, not pleased by Starlet's uncontrollable emotions. "Starlet, dear. We're all a little unhinged by this news. But let's try to stay calm and keep cool heads and conjure up some compassion for the young woman who just spent the last two years of her life locked away in a mental institution due to mental illness," Charles compassionately reminded his daughter. "We're all on pins and needles; and what she did to Sabrina and Britain and her own brother was unspeakable. But as I said. We have to keep in mind that she wasn't in her right mind. The young lady was extremely ill, and my own brother showed enough compassion to pay a small fortune for her well-being. Besides, we're not in the business of kicking people off of this property," Charles said and paused for a moment, and then exchanged looks with Starlet.

"I'm sorry, Father, for my thoughtless rude outburst. I know it wouldn't be right to make Larry leave the estate. Besides, we would never treat him or anyone that way."

Charles nodded as the stress wrinkles across his forehead smoothed out. "That's hundred percent correct. Therefore, we need to find a way to accept what is and hope for the best outcome," Charles firmly suggested. "I think we can all agree that we're not happy with the situation of Larry dating Courtney Ross." Charles held out both arms. "And nobody can blame us for that. Nevertheless, he's happy with the young lady and she's mentally healthy now. Therefore, as I mentioned before, we need to find a way to deal with it and wish him well."

Starlet looked toward her father. "I guess my biggest disappointment is, of all the people in this town, why did our families have to pay for Courtney's medical bill?"

"Well, your Uncle Don decided to do it to help Courtney's mother. I think you know Mildred Ross is one of Don's workers at Taylor Investments. She started working at the company a couple years ago."

"Father, I apologize if I'm being inconsiderate. But I feel just because Courtney's mother is employed at Taylor Investments is not a good reason for Uncle Don to pay all that money for her daughter's medical care," Starlet objected.

Charles was lost for answers because he had never had to justify being charitable to any of his daughters. They were all charitable as well. In this case, he also understood why Starlet didn't want the family to be charitable to

Courtney. But he still felt oblige to be. "Sweetheart, I understand your frustration toward Courtney Ross. However, the young woman was in desperate need of physical and mental health attention. Her family didn't have any health coverage; and the coverage at Franklin Enterprises, then Franklin Gas, only extended to her physical healthcare. Therefore, to put it in a neat package, Don just offered to cover it all," Charles explained. "Besides, Sweetheart, it's what we do. You know this better than anyone. We always try to help those less fortunate that cannot help themselves," Charles stated with conviction and paused. Then he looked toward his distraught daughter. "Understandable for most. But Starlet, considering your generous forgiving heart. I'm surprised that you're not onboard with the families pitching in to help this young woman."

"Father, I know my attitude makes me appear unkind toward Courtney. But I'm sure everyone in this room feel the same as I do. We don't want her in our mix. But we all wish her well. I'm just angry too death with her and don't feel warm about our families helping someone who hurt us so badly even if she was sick at the time," Starlet admitted. "However, I'm honored to be apart and involved in such a generous caring family. But shouldn't we draw the line when someone is out to harm us?" Starlet exchanged looks with them all. "It's clear Courtney Ross was out to harm Sabrina and Britain. Besides, who can guarantee she won't go off her rocker and try to harm them again?"

Veronica reached for Charles's hand and squeezed it as Charles spoke. "Of course, we draw the line if our family is in clear danger. However, in this incident, no matter how you argue against the young woman, it's a scientific fact that her mind wasn't working normally. She didn't harm the families out of malice. She was insane and clearly wouldn't commit such horrific acts now that she's mentally stable," Charles pointed out.

Starlet nodded. "I know she was insane when she committed the crimes. But I still don't feel our families should have paid or should continue to pay for her medical bills. How does it sound in the press that the families she committed horrible crimes against are paying her medical bills none stop?" Starlet asked, upset with her Uncle Don and the Franklin brothers for pitching in toward Courtney medical bills.

Charles wanted to reassure his daughter. But he couldn't say the one thing that she wanted to hear; and that one thing was, nobody in the Franklin or Taylor family will continue to make payments toward Courtney's medical bills. "We cannot worry about the press," Charles firmly stated. "We have to concern ourselves with doing the right thing. And although, you're not pleased with Courtney Ross, and she most likely will not get invited to dinner.

It was still the right thing to pay her medical bills to guarantee her the best possible medical care for the mental condition that had driven her over the edge."

Chapter Thirty-Six

Veronica looked across the room at Britain. She wanted to know how he and Sabrina felt about everything.

"Son, you and Sabrina met with Larry tonight; and you two are the ones who endured the wrath of that girl's mental illness. Therefore, tell us how the two of you feel about the meeting you had with Larry; and also how you two feel about the connection he has with Courtney Ross?" Veronica seriously asked.

Britain squeezed Sabrina's hand as Sabrina looked toward Veronica. "I thought the meeting was comfortable and quite respectable on Larry's part to want to make us aware of his new relationship with Courtney," Sabrina softly said, as she glanced at Britain and then looked back toward his mother. "But in terms of how I feel about Larry's connection to Courtney. I basically feel just like what Father just said. Britain and I shared our feelings with Larry. We explained to him that we're glad he has someone in his life. But we made it clear that we wished it was someone other than Courtney. However, after we shared that. At first, he thought we were mad at her from our statements. But we explained that we had forgiven her and were not upset with her. And although, we were not angry with her, we still didn't want her in our vicinity. Therefore, at the end of our meeting he appeared to be clear on how we felt and why," Sabrina softly explained.

Samantha shook her head as she patted the top of Paris's hand. "I know Courtney Ross is a very beautiful girl, but knowing the heartbreak she put our families through, especially Sabrina and Britain, I'm surprised Larry decided to date her," Samantha said. "Therefore, I agree with Starlet. I think Courtney sought him out because he's connected to this family. I know Larry is a good man. But he was never the type of guy Courtney dated in the past. It's more logical that she probably saw him here at the estate when she used to visit and decided to get close to him in an effort to stay connected to Sabrina and Britain."

Sabrina spoke up. "I'm not sure if Courtney spotted him on the grounds when she used to visit."

"It's possible she saw him here," Samantha quickly uttered.

"You're right. It is possible. However, Larry told us tonight that he met Courtney at Shady Grove when he was a patient there a year ago. They have apparently dated for a year in secret," Sabrina shared.

"This keeps getting worse and worse," Starlet complained. "He didn't just start dating her. They have dated for an entire year."

Sydney grabbed Starlet's hand and held it tight. "It's not hopeless as it seems. Everything will work out. We'll do everything in our power to make sure Courtney Ross stays mentally healthy. Your Uncle Don took care of her in-patient care. Now we want to make sure she can continue all her out-patient care," he said considerately. "Her follow up visits to Shady Grove are quite important," Sydney thoughtfully explained.

Starlet grabbed her face. "It doesn't matter what kind of outpatient care she receives, I just want Courtney Ross to stay away from both of our families. Is that so unreasonable?" she looked at Sydney and firmly asked.

Sydney looked at her with sympathetic eyes. "It's not unreasonable. Of course, you feel that way even if you have to be strong to stand up against those feelings."

Starlet wiped a tear with her fingers. "But I guess I'm not that strong. If that sounds uncaring, I can't help it. I thought I would never stop drowning in my sorrow every time I thought about that horrible day when we found Sabrina on the front lawn clinging to life from a bullet Courtney had put in her."

"I know how you feel and we probably all feel the same," Sydney caringly said, as he caressed and held her hand. "But it doesn't do anyone any good for us to rehash what happened." He looked toward Sabrina and Britain. "Sabrina and Britain managed to find a way to forgive Courtney. They are coping with the past devastation and found a way to deal with her presence. They went through the anguish. Therefore, those of us who didn't, should follow their lead," Sydney caringly suggested.

Samantha nodded. "Well, if Larry met Courtney at Shady Grove, that destroys my theory that she sought him out at the estate and knew he worked for us," Samantha glumly mumbled, exchanging looks with Starlet. "So maybe their relationship is a coincident."

Sabrina held up one finger and shook her head. "Courtney didn't seek him out at the estate. That part is true," Sabrina said and paused, exchanging looks with Britain. "But I do need to tell all of you what Larry confided in us."

"What he confided in you?" Starlet curiously asked.

Sabrina nodded. "Yes, he confided in us that Courtney wasn't interested in him when they first met," Sabrina announced.

The room fell quiet with all eyes on Sabrina as everyone seemed surprised by her announcement. She solemnly nodded, changing looks with everyone in the room. "Those were his words."

Starlet grabbed her face with both hands and stared at Sabrina. "What are you saying?"

"Larry told us she only seemed interested in him after she found out he worked for us," Sabrina told them.

Starlet exchanged looks with Samantha. "That proves she's up to her old tricks if he admitted that to you and Britain. But why would he admit something like that?"

"I think the point Larry was trying to make is that Courtney originally started talking to him during lunch one day at Shady Grove because of his connection to us," Sabrina softly explained. "But because he's such a great guy she ended up falling for him. Yet, I'm not convinced her feelings are genuine for Larry. And although, she has been given a report of a sound mind with a clean bill of mental health and a new teaching position, I'll probably always have a flicker of doubt toward her," Sabrina humbly admitted.

Veronica looked at Rome and Amber and noticed their year and a half old twins were both asleep in their arms. Rome was holding little Ryan Rome Franklin and Amber was holding little Angela Bailey Franklin. "We haven't heard anything from you and Amber. What do you think of this situation?" Veronica casually asked them.

"It is what is," Rome quickly replied. "Courtney had a breakdown two years ago and caused a lot of pandemonium in both of our families. But she was just released from Shady Grove with a clean bill of mental health; and I think we just need to wish Larry and Courtney well." Rome exchanged looks with everyone gathered. "We need to try to push the past out of our minds and allow Larry and Courtney to go their separate ways with their lives without it causing so much tension for ours," Rome strongly advised. "Her medical reports, from my understanding are excellent. Plus, a new teaching position was offered to her. Therefore, I think we're looking for trouble where there is none. We can't allow her horrific past to cloud our judgement toward her future," Rome firmly stated.

Amber looked at Rome with serious eyes and shook her head. "Sweetheart, you are being very considerate as usual. However, in this case, the girl was prone to unusual behavior before her breakdown. Therefore, I'm just as concerned as Starlet and Samantha about her possible motives. Granted, maybe there are none," Amber softly and politely said. "However, I do think it's only natural at this point that everyone is apprehensive and hesitant to accept her at face value. I know in my case, the memories are too horrific to think about and I push them to the far corner of my mind every time I have a flicker of thought of the agony I felt seeing Sabrina and Britain lying in those hospital beds at the hands of Courtney Ross," Amber calmly said, as her words somewhat choked her up. "And although, Courtney is no longer ill, I personally believe she's dating Larry Westwood for a reason that she feels will benefit her. I don't claim to know what that reason is, but I strongly believe that's what she's doing." Amber nodded toward Starlet.

Starlet nodded toward Amber. "I'm incline to agree with you. I believe she has an ulterior motive."

Rome stared curiously at his wife. "Honey, that's not a nice thing to say. Plus, it's conjecture and hypothesis. None of us really know how Courtney really feels about Larry, and hopefully she has changed during the course of the past two years of being institutionalized from a major breakdown. Therefore, I believe you are confusing the past with the present to assume she's dating Larry for an ulterior motive."

Amber looked at Rome and nodded. "Darling, I'm sorry. You could be right at that. It's just hard to separate the past from the present. When I think of Courtney Ross it's hard to think of her as being in her right mind and sane again. Hearing her name reminds me of all the chaos and trouble that was lined up in a path behind her. The unspeakable pain she caused is always there at the forefront of my thoughts."

Rome nodded. "Yes, Sweetheart. It's at the forefront of all of our thoughts for sure."

"I know but it still feels so fresh to me," Amber admitted.

"Probably since Sabrina is your best friend," Rome said.

"Maybe you're right because no matter how hard I try to push those memories out of my head, they are still there," Amber said.

"Yes, those sad memories are there in the back of all of our minds. They will probably never cease to exist in the corner of our minds. Something that devastating never really fades completely from one's thoughts. Nevertheless, we all have to rise above it and try to get past it and push it to the back of our minds," Rome strongly suggested as he exchanged looks with everyone in the room.

Amber nodded. "That's a beautiful sentiment to strive for."

"It's beautiful only when it's accomplished," Rome caringly stated. "Seriously, we need to see Courtney for the sane individual that she is now."

Amber touched Rome's arm and caringly said. "I know I will try and I wish her well." Amber glanced toward the floor momentarily and then looked at Rome. "But I have to be honest. It's not easy. I wish I didn't feel so negative toward her," Amber glumly mumbled. "I'm aware how she was under the influence of mental illness when she committed those crimes, and I keep praying to forget. Every single day I pray to forget. Nevertheless, two years later, I feel the same as Starlet and Samantha." Amber glanced about at everyone in the room. "I wish her well and good health. But, there's never going to be a close feeling inside of me for her. Deep inside I just have this feeling that Courtney Ross cannot be trusted," Amber solemnly admitted as she turned to Rome and touched his hand. "That's not conjecture, Sweetheart. That's just my instincts about her. Besides, Courtney Ross is probably untrustworthy to every one of us in this room. Trust has to be earned and maybe she'll earn people's trust again. But right now, all we have is her deeds of the past as a reference," Amber seriously stated.

Rome nodded. "Maybe she cannot be trusted. But it does none of us any good to lose any sleep over the fact that Larry is dating Courtney," Rome seriously stressed. "All we can do is hope for the best for Courtney and Larry. Her mother is very grateful for the continued financial help from the family for Courtney's healthcare. She has promised to keep us abreast of Courtney's wellbeing." Rome looked down at little Ryan Rome in his arms and then looked down at little Angela Bailey in Amber's arms. "We need to get home and get these two in bed."

Britain and Sabrina exchanged looks and nodded toward them all. "Thanks for dropping everything and meeting us here on such a short notice," Sabrina caringly said. "We wanted all of you to know right away about Courtney's connection to our families," Sabrina softly told them. "And as we said before, Britain and I are not thrilled that Larry is dating her. But we do wish Larry and Courtney well. And I'll say this. Larry is a genuine person and he's quite sharp. So, if Courtney isn't being on the level with him, he'll find out and probably won't keep seeing her."

Samantha nodded. "Larry is sharp and has a good ear for the truth. I hope she has changed. But if she's playing games, Larry will see her real colors and probably break up with her."

Sabrina held up one finger. "I agree he probably will break up with her if she's not on the level. However, on the other hand, if by some chance, she does love Larry," Sabrina said and paused. "It's completely possible she really does love him. He's a very likeable man that would mean a world of good for Courtney. She could finally be happy with someone she loves that loves her in return."

Chapter Thirty-Seven

It was nearly eleven-thirty when Veronica and her family left the Taylor's premises. Charles, Sabrina and Samantha lingered in the living room just briefly before they headed upstairs to their rooms. Then only the vague sound of the old antique grandfather clock could be heard. Suddenly the large bright elegant room was quiet and still as Sydney sat on one end of the sofa and Starlet sat at the other end of the sofa. Sydney was looking toward her as she looked down toward the carpet. He had his legs crossed, stretched out in front of him as both arms rested across the top of the sofa. Although, it was getting quite late, he decided to stay at the Taylor mansion for a while longer in hopes of calming Starlet's nerves over her disapproval of the help he and his family was giving toward Courtney's medical bills.

He was almost lost for words since Starlet new unsympathetic attitude toward Courtney was uncharacteristic of her. Yet he understood her unwilling to forget the horrific act of Courtney's due to the magnitude of the crime. Therefore, he braced himself as he tried to think of what he would say to calm her, since he had witnessed her relentless confrontation with her father. He was aware of how much she was on edge about Larry's new connection with Courtney Ross. He was also aware of the depth of her distress and distraught over the fact that the Taylors and Franklins were being responsible for Courtney's medical bills.

"Hi, down there," Sydney said from the opposite end of the sofa.

Starlet looked toward Sydney and smiled, and then looked back toward the carpet. "Hi, it's getting late, don't you think?" Starlet said, not wanting to listen to what she figured Sydney was going to discuss with her.

Sydney nodded and glanced at his watch. "Yes, you're right and I don't plan to stay long. But I hope you don't mind that I stayed behind for a while. I couldn't leave with you in such a disturbed state."

Starlet didn't look toward Sydney as she mumbled. "I'll be okay."

"I'm sure you will. But I just wanted you to know how sorry I am that you're so distraught over the news about Larry and Courtney's courtship," Sydney caringly said. "It's very stressful I'm sure. But you really need to find a way to let it go. Stress is not good for the body," he humbly said as he watched her stare down at the carpet.

She looked toward Sydney with sad eyes. "I know you're right; and I feel I'm trying. It's just hard. I thought Courtney Ross was out of our lives for good and now she's right back in the middle." Starlet held up both hands. "She can now show up on our property anytime day or night." Starlet shook her head in disbelief.

"I'm sure that's not a pleasing thought to you," Sydney cautiously said.

"It's a terrifying thought." Starlet grabbed her face and held it, shaking her head. "I probably feel so strongly about this because of my encounter with Courtney on the day of that horrifying event."

Sydney nodded. "That's right, you had mentioned an encounter with her that morning."

Starlet stared seriously at Sydney. "It was eerie. I had an opportunity to observe her irrational behavior up close and personal right before her breakdown." Starlet held up both hands. "That's why I just don't want her near my family again."

Sydney nodded, looking starlet in the eyes. "No one is blaming you for that, sweetheart."

"I know no one is blaming me. But it's making me appear uncompassionated."

"Well, we both know you're not uncompassionated," Sydney said assuredly. "No one thinks that about you. My goodness, young lady. You're one of the most compassionated individuals I know."

"I don't feel compassionate right now."

"But you know you are."

Starlet shook her head. "But I'm not compassionated toward Courtney Ross." Starlet glanced down toward the floor.

"Maybe not. But no one can blame you for that," Sydney caringly stated.

"But the rest of my family is showing her compassion. Even Sabrina who she almost killed is showing more compassionate toward Courtney than I am. Therefore, maybe I'm not the most compassionate person you know," Starlet sadly mumbled in disappointment of herself.

"Listen, nobody is perfect and we all try hard to be above board in these kinds of situations. But sometimes we just can't. Nobody blames you for your hostility and animosity toward Courtney Ross." Sydney touched his chest. "We all have our feelings toward her and I don't think anybody in either family is willing to sit and break bread with the young woman. However, we did recognize how she needed medical care that her family couldn't afford. We reached out and helped in that way."

Starlet scooped down the sofa closer to Sydney. "You Franklin guys are just unlike anyone I know," she politely said. "Your heart is so big it's overwhelming. I wish I could be more forgiving."

"Well, it's how you look at things and this incident in particular," Sydney caringly said, as he reached and held her hand. "It's really how you allow it to affect you. I think as far as myself and my brothers are concerned, we have hostility about things just like the next person. Yet, it's how we allow it to affect us. We try to live above it. An example is how I preferred to show compassion to Jack Coleman instead of wrath. I struggled against wishing him an ill fate, and chose not to inspite of his anguish and distress he threw on my family," Sydney reflected on the past and continued. "Another example is how Rome dealt with Courtney deceit when the two of them were dating. He treated her like a princess but after he discovered she was secretly in love with Britain, he break up with her and he didn't linger in sadness. He accepted it for what it was and went right on and connected with someone who truly loved him. Now he and Amber are blissfully happy with two beautiful children."

Starlet looked at Sydney with a solid look on her face. "I believe you can separate yourself from the horror Courtney inflicted on our families, since she isn't really in the middle of yours. She'll have access to our family and property whenever she likes at the courtesy of Larry."

Sydney eyes slightly widened as he felt somewhat thrown by Starlet statement. "Okay, listen a moment. I wouldn't put it that way," he politely said as he glanced at his watch. "Being in the middle of your family and involved with your worker pretty much puts her in the middle of both of our families. However, as I said before, I choose not to allow the devastation that she caused two years ago to affect my sensibility to hinder me from giving her the benefit of the doubt." He caressed Starlet's upper arm as he spoke. "It may seem impossible to you at the moment since you are so rooted in hostility against her. But I believe you can do the same," Sydney softly touched her cheek with the back of his palm. "First of all, you need to try harder not to allow Courtney Ross to be the focus of your thoughts and conversations," Sydney strongly suggested. "If you have to focus on her at all, focus on the fact of how greatly ill she was when she committed her crimes."

Starlet felt a pain in her stomach and discomfort at the fact that Sydney was giving Courtney the benefit of the doubt. She was deeply unhappy about Courtney reconnection with their families. She shook her head. "I know she was greatly ill," Starlet slightly stated. "But what I'm trying to tell you and everyone else who won't listen to me is that I believe Courtney is naturally dishonest!"

"That's a rather strong statement for you to make against Courtney Ross. You don't know her well enough to make such an assumption, especially if you're basing it on her actions and behavior that's connected to her breakdown," Sydney seriously stated and raised one finger. "I believe I'm a better judge of Courtney's character than you are," he warmly and politely suggested. "She worked for us a long while, and was one of the nicest young women on staff. She was also a reliable good worker," Sydney vouched for Courtney as he continued. "Therefore, I believe all the horrific things she did were due to her illness and I don't think it's fair to label her dishonest and a bad person based on those crimes that were committed under the influence of insanity," Sydney firmly stressed.

The Taylor's living room was quiet for an intensively few minutes after Sydney's statement. Then Starlet hopped off the sofa in a huff and stepped across the room and stood in front of the fireplace with her back to Sydney for a moment. Then she turned and looked across the room at Sydney. "I'm sorry I'm so on edge. But you and I have different opinions regarding Courtney Ross." Starlet held up both hands. "I'm not basing Courtney's character on the horrific crimes she committed while ill. I'm basing her character on how she behaved in my home that morning before her breakdown while I was holding a conversation with her. I'm also basing it on how awful she treated my sister, lying on Sabrina when she was pretending to be Sabrina's friend!" Starlet sadly shared.

Sydney stared surprised. "Pretending friendship? When was this?"

"It was not long before her breakdown," Starlet glumly mumbled.

Sydney nodded. "It adds up and I figured as much. Courtney was still ill during all that time."

Starlet covered her face with a deep sigh. "It rips at me for you to keep coming to Courtney's rescue the way you're doing. You're making excuses for her behavior every time I say something," Starlet exasperatedly uttered.

"Listen, I'm sorry you feel that way. I'm just trying to be objective and on the level and give Courtney credit where it's due," Sydney calmly explained. "Therefore, if you would. Think back to the time when Courtney was dating Rome. It was during the time she was visiting Franklin House quite often with Rome," Sydney suggested. "At that time, I'm positive Courtney was completely sane. She was quite pleasant to be around. I'm sure you recall her calm, polite manners when we would all gather at Franklin House. She was always nice and friendly even in the face of my mother rudeness toward her."

Starlet nodded. "I do remember how different she was. And I'll admit, I felt bad for her since your mother wasn't that warm toward her. Nevertheless, knowing what I know about Courtney. I'm not convinced she wasn't just pretending to be nice at that time."

Sydney grabbed the back of his neck with both hands and held them there for a moment as he stared up at the ceiling for a moment. Then he looked at Starlet. "Starlet, I'm listening to you, and you don't sound like yourself. I know you have issues with Courtney Ross but she's well now. Can you at least try to give her the benefit of the doubt until she gives you a reason not to trust her?" Sydney humbly asked. "You have always been selfless and forgiving and that's why I'm thrown by your deep resentment against this young woman."

"I don't like feeling this way about Courtney. I know she was sick but it's hard for me to separate her sickness from who she really is. That's because I have zero trust in her," Starlet admitted. "I'm not ashamed to admit that." Starlet held up both hands. "I just don't want Courtney near our families. Can you blame me?"

"Listen, you don't have to ask me that question. You know I can see your point of not wanting her near our families. Sick or well, we all recall the tragedy at her hands to Sabrina and Britain. Therefore, your statement of not wanting her near our families make sense," Sydney told her.

"But on the other hand, saying unkind things about her and calling her dishonest doesn't make sense?" Starlet asked.

Sydney swallowed hard and shifted in his seat as he kept his composure. "I didn't say that. Please do not put words in my mouth."

"I'm sorry. I'm just on edge about everything. It's been two years since that nightmare and getting over it! And just when I thought Courtney was out of our lives for good, she's right back on center stage to be the star attraction!" Starlet disappointedly complained.

"I know it's going to be hard," Sydney said. "But you need to try as hard as you can to take control of your emotions about Courtney Ross."

"I keep trying very hard. I promise I'm trying and I'm praying about it to. But I just cannot seem to let go of my animosity toward Courtney and what she did to our families," Starlet sadly admitted.

"Just take a deep breath and just let it roll off your back. We'll get through this and I'm sure Courtney will not be a problem for anyone," Sydney predicted.

"How can you be so sure?" Starlet asked, as she stepped back over to the sofa and took her seat back on the sofa next to Sydney.

"I can say it because my instincts tell me Courtney will not commit those kinds of crimes again. I wholeheartedly believe she's completely healthy and will stay that way," Sydney assuredly stated. "Since she'll continue to get the best medical care for her outpatient treatments."

Starlet grabbed her face with both hands and looked at Sydney and didn't speak for a moment. Then she asked. "Your family will be paying for her continued medical care?"

Sydney nodded. "Yes, we will."

"When you say we, who are you referring to?" Starlet curiously asked.

"I'm referring to Franklin House charitable funds account."

"Whose money is that?" Starlet asked.

Sydney lifted an eyebrow and smiled at her. "What kind of question is that, Sweetheart? It's my family money. We all contribute to the fund. It doesn't come from our individual accounts," Sydney told her. "Why are you curious?"

Starlet glanced down. "I'm curious about it because I would like for you to do me a favor if you can."

"Sure, anything. What favor do you need?" he asked.

"I'm sick deep in my stomach about Courtney Ross and I would appreciate if my boyfriend wouldn't be one of the individuals paying her medical bills. Just let Uncle Don continue to do it. Besides, Father said Uncle Don is willing to continue the payments. But your family insisted on footing the outpatient portion," Starlet said to him.

"That's because Courtney Ross should have had the full medical coverage from Franklin Gas. She was only listed with the medical hospitalization coverage and not the mental health coverage. That's why we decided to cover her outpatient care."

"I would feel better if you declined the medical payments," Starlet admitted.

Sydney looked soberly at Starlet. "You can forget that notion. We have already signed on the dotted line. But honestly, I must say, I'm blown away by your request."

"Why are you blown away?" Starlet dryly asked. "I'm not a saint and I don't think it's so far-fetched that I would have animosity toward a woman who tried to kill my sister."

Sydney glanced at his watch and shook his head. "I might as well leave and try to get some sleep before my alarm goes off for work." He soberly stared at Starlet.

Starlet nodded. "Okay."

"Well, I think that's best since you and I are going around in circles right now. You keep stating the same things about Courtney; and I keep trying to vouch for her against those things. We are not getting anywhere right now."

"I'm sure I'm repeating myself, but I don't feel so warm and cozy that my boyfriend is paying the medical bills of a woman I greatly dislike," Starlet sadly mumbled.

"But you don't mind your Uncle Don paying her medical bills?"

"I can accept Uncle Don paying her medical bills more than the thought of you. At least Uncle Don is Courtney's mother boss; and it makes sense that he would want to help his employee's daughter in a time of need."

Sydney nodded. "I agree that it makes sense that Don Taylor would want to help out Courtney because Courtney's mother's is his employee."

"But do you also agree that it doesn't make sense to me that you and your family would want to help Courtney Ross in such a major way?" Starlet asked.

"I agree that you're entitled to your opinion on the matter," Sydney softly said. "If it doesn't make sense to you, it's your right and privilege to say it doesn't make sense."

"I'll tell you why it doesn't make sense to me."

Sydney nodded toward Starlet. "Okay, I'm listening."

Starlet looked at Sydney and paused after she realize she was getting quite emotional over the discussion of Courtney. She held up one finger toward Sydney and took a deep breath before she spoke. "It doesn't make sense that the family of the man she hospitalized would be in line to pay her medical bills," Starlet firmly stated. "I believe in helping the less fortunate. But I believe your family is pushing it too far in this case."

Sydney raised one finger. "Listen, Starlet. We need to be clear on something."

"What do you mean?" Starlet asked.

"You referred to helping the less fortunate. But our help to Courtney is not charity," he said assuredly.

"You're paying something for her that she otherwise wouldn't be able to pay. It sounds like charity to me."

"But it's not a mercy deed from my family."

"I'm sorry. But it sounds like that to me," Starlet told him.

"Starlet, we don't seem to be communicating well about this issue. Because I thought I had made it all quite clear regarding Courtney. That we're paying her medical bills for follow up outpatient treatments because the health coverage should have been automatically included with her benefits. It's offered to all the employees now," Sydney firmly relayed.

"Therefore, when Courtney was hired, it wasn't being offered?"

Sydney nodded. "That's correct. But it should have been. That's why we are footing the bill. Therefore, reach in the depth of yourself and answer me one question?" Sydney asked. "Would you deny Courtney Ross medical care?"

Starlet shook her head. "Of course, I wouldn't deny anyone medical care. Why would you ask me that?"

"Based on this discussion, you're giving me the impression that you would deny Courtney Ross medical coverage. Therefore, I'm glad I had the wrong impression," Sydney told her.

"Yes, you had the wrong impression. I want her to have medical coverage and I don't mind someone paying her medical bills. I just don't want you to do it."

Chapter Thirty-Eight

During breakfast the next morning at Carrie and Sam's kitchen table, they were quite surprised when they noticed the same happy smile on Larry's face as the night before. He hadn't said anything to them the night before after Sam picked him up from his meeting at Starbucks with Britain and Sabrina. But now while they were gathered around the breakfast table enjoying cheese toast and fried eggs, they observed his good mood and felt comfortable bringing up his meeting. Carrie especially wanted to ask him some questions and find out how his meeting went before she finished breakfast to head upstairs at 7:30 to start breakfast for the Taylors.

"I see you're smiling," Carrie casually commented. "I'm assuming your meeting at the coffee house with Mr. Britain and Miss Sabrina went well."

Larry looked across the table at his mother with a big smile and nodded. "Yes, Mama, the meeting went very well. But I do need to say this. You and Daddy were wrong," he said, as he lifted his coffee cup and took a sip.

Carrie and Sam discreetly exchanged looks. They had no idea what he was referring to as he busied himself with his breakfast with no further explanation.

"Well, do you plan to tell us what we were wrong about?" Sam asked as he forked a piece of egg in his mouth, looking toward Larry.

Larry glanced at his father and nodded. "Well, you both were wrong about Miss Sabrina and Mr. Britain."

"Wrong about what?" Carrie asked.

Larry stared seriously at his mother. "You know what, Mama. I'm talking about all that stuff you and Daddy was telling me they might do. But they didn't get mad at me and they didn't take my job."

Looking toward Carrie, Sam nodded. "Well, that's good, Son."

Carrie nodded and smiled as well. "That is good to know."

Sam lifted his coffee cup and slowly took a sip of coffee, and then exchanged looks with Carrie before he spoke. "So, Larry, tell us. How did Mr. Britain and Miss Sabrina take the news about Courtney Ross as your new girlfriend?" Sam curiously asked. "You haven't mentioned their reaction. But considering, I'm sure they couldn't have been too pleased."

Carrie bit a piece of cheese toast. "Yes, you might as well tell us. We won't be surprised to hear they were not pleased."

Larry looked toward his mother. "Mama you're right." Then he looked toward his father. "Daddy, you're both right. Miss Sabrina and Mr. Britain were not pleased about Courtney."

"If they weren't pleased, how do you figure the meeting went well?" Sam asked.

"They both wanted me to say my new girlfriend was anyone else but Courtney. They don't want to socialize with Courtney anymore. But they said they won't have to," Larry anxiously explained. "Miss Sabrina said they have forgiven Courtney for the bad things she did to them two years ago. They're glad Courtney is well again."

"Of course, they're glad she's well. They are good people. You can't blame them for not being happy about your announcement," Carrie seriously stressed.

"I don't blame them. They did say they're happy I have a girlfriend. But they're not happy that person is Courtney. Then they told me, it doesn't matter whether they're pleased or not; I'm a grown man to pick who I want to be with."

Carrie looked across the table at Larry and nodded. "That's true. You're a grown man in charge of your own affairs."

"Thanks Mama for saying that. Miss Sabrina feels the same. She told me her family would never interfere with my personal lovelife. They won't fire me and kick me off their property because I'm with Courtney," Larry anxiously told them, as he kept talking. "Miss Sabrina wasn't pleased that I thought that. I had to apologize and told them that's what you two thought would happen."

Sam exchanged looks with Carrie as he hit his flat palm on the table hard. "You should have left our names out of it," Sam angrily shouted. "You say you're a grown man, yet you need to put me and Carrie in the middle of your business."

"That's right, son," Carrie agreed. "We don't think it's a good idea for you to date some girl that went off the rails and put a bullet in your boss's daughter." Carrie held up both hands. "But it's your life and in your defense, the young lady was ill. But I'm in agreement with your father. Just leave us out of it."

Larry looked from his mother to his father. "I told you, Miss Sabrina said it's my civil and human right to live my life with the girl of my choice. But you and Daddy acts as if they have a real problem with me. I'm sorry I mention what you and Daddy said. She was mad that I even thought that way. Then I felt bad that I had told her what you and Daddy said."

"Of course she was upset that you would think her decent family would dismiss you for who you chose to date," Carrie said. "But believe us, the Taylors are not happy."

Sam shook his head. "They will deal with it because of their decency. But they shouldn't have to deal with seeing a young woman face who could have taken Miss Sabrina and Mr. Britain's life. It was your place to be big enough not to have put them through that stress," Sam angrily griped. "A couple hours from now when the Taylors and Franklins are gathered around their breakfast table, we don't have to guess their topic of conversation."

"Your father is right. I'm sure your new girlfriend will be the topic of conversation. Miss Sabrina and Mr. Britain were both laid up in the hospital for weeks and off of work for a whole month. They don't need that young woman around to be a constant reminder of the agony they endured from her madness," Carrie strongly suggested.

"Maybe you and Daddy are both right. I don't want Miss Sabrina or Mr. Britain to feel bad and stressed because of me," Larry told them.

Carrie curiously smiled as a glimmer of hope rushed through her stomach from Larry's words. "What are you saying? Have you decided it's best to break off things with Courtney Ross?"

Larry stood up from his seat with a determined look on his face. "I'm going to my room to call Courtney now."

"You're doing the right thing, Son." Sam nodded as he took his napkin and wiped his mouth and hands. "She's a very pretty girl. But you'll meet someone else who won't bring so much tension and sadness to so many around you."

Larry shook his head and held up both hands. "You both think I'm planning to break up with her. But I'm not calling Courtney to say goodbye."

Carrie eyes widened as she glanced up at Larry who stood next to his kitchen chair. "We thought that's what you meant." Carrie was about to take a sip of coffee, but placed the cup back on the table without taking a swallow. She stared disappointedly at Larry. "You said you don't want to cause stress for the Taylors or Franklins," Carrie reminded him.

Larry walked away from the breakfast table, heading into the living room when he blurted out. "I don't want to cause them any stress. That's why I'm going to call Courtney and ask her to marry me."

It was quiet for a moment as Carrie and Sam caught their breath and their bearings. Then they both called out to Larry at the same time. "Please come back to the table and tell us in our face what you just said."

Larry turned around and stepped back to the kitchen table and took his seat. "I said I plan to marry Courtney."

After a moment of silence Larry continued. "That is, if she'll marry me. I plan to ask her today."

"When did you decide this?" Sam filled with frustration, asked.

"I just decided it now. I probably wouldn't have decided to ask her today. I know it's sudden. But I figured, we could get married and leave the Taylor estate. Then the Taylors and the Franklins won't be stressed and reminded of bad memories since they won't see Courtney. We'll move into our own house."

"Is that what you really want?" Carrie glumly asked. She was stunned at his decision.

Larry nodded. "I have thought about it a lot."

"But are you absolutely sure?" Carrie asked.

"Yes, I'm absolutely sure. I know I want to marry Courtney," Larry said and paused, looking at his mother.

"But, I hear a but coming," Carrie said.

Larry nodded. "Yes, you hear a but coming because although I really want to marry Courtney, I'm just not sure if it's what I really want at this particular time. I had planned to ask her later down the road. But I have decided now is a good time, because I think it'll make everyone feel more comfortable," Larry explained in an upbeat tone.

Carrie nodded with sad eyes. "Well, if you insist on being with the young woman, moving away from the Taylor estate would solve the problem of Courtney being a constant reminder to those folks of when she flipped and almost killed those kids."

Sam held up both hands. He was boiling upset. "You barely know this young woman. She could just be after your money," Sam angrily theorized.

Carrie shook her head as she looked with sad eyes and a troubled heart toward her husband. "I thought the same thing at first."

"But now you think that pretty girl love Larry for his personality?" Sam sarcastically asked.

"Why not?" Carrie snapped.

Sam shook his head in frustration. "I can think of a few reasons."

"I can think of plenty good reasons," Carrie quickly replied. "Our Son is a beautiful person," Carrie quickly reminded him.

"Of course, we think so, Carrie," Sam fussed. "But everyone doesn't share our views," Sam angrily grumbled. "Besides that, what changed your mind that Courtney Ross isn't interested in his money?"

"I just know she's not after Larry's money. Seeing the surprise look on her face when I accused her of being after his money. I'm absolutely sure, she wasn't aware of the money Grandma Lulu had left behind for him."

"Maybe not, but I'm still not comfortable with him jumping up to wed this girl just so he can keep her off of the Taylor's estate," Sam firmly stressed.

Larry sat with both elbows on the kitchen table holding up his face listening to them.

"Son, if you want to leave the Taylor estate, you have plenty of money to do so," Sam calmly said. "I don't mean to blow up like this. But your announcement is so unexpected. Besides, your mother and I can help you find a nice apartment. You don't have to marry that girl just because you want to get away from the estate," Sam said assuredly.

Carrie nodded with sad eyes. "I agree with your father. If you move into your own apartment in town, you'll be away from the Taylor estate and you and Courtney can date without her being a constant reminder to the Taylors."

"But I don't want to date her. I want to marry her," Larry stressed.

"I realize that," Carrie said. "However, as you said. This is sudden and we don't want you to leave like this. We feel you should get to know Courtney a little better before you make plans to marry her," Carrie strongly stressed. "Besides, your father and I would like to get to know her a little better as well," Carrie strongly suggested.

"You and Daddy don't know her well. But I know her well. I spent two days a week with her every week for a whole year. She's a good person. She's not bad anymore." Larry lifted the orange juice pitcher and poured more juice in his glass. "I want to marry her because I love her and I know she loves me too."

"Larry, we understand that," Sam dryly grumbled. "But what's wrong with our suggestion of you getting your own apartment and dating the young lady awhile longer?"

Larry adamantly shook his head. "My mind is made up. I want to marry Courtney as soon as she'll marry me. We'll be happy. I have enough money to give us a good life."

Carrie and Sam exchanged looks and then looked at Larry and nodded. "Well, since your mind is made up. At least prepare yourself for the possibility of a letdown. The young lady may not be ready for marriage so quickly," Sam brought to his attention. "She's settling in at home, fresh out of Shady Grove after being confined for the past two years. She's just getting her life back and bonding with her family after being locked away from them for so long. Only being able to spend short periods of time with them during visitor's hours at that institution," Sam explained, hoping to get through to Larry and change his mind about rushing into a marriage in case Courtney accepted his proposal.

"That's true," Carrie agreed with Sam. "Courtney might want to get her bearings and get back into a regular living and working routine before leaping into a huge step like taking a husband."

Larry laughed. "If she says no to me this morning, I'll just keep asking every day until she says yes."

Chapter Twenty-Nine

Larry went to his room and sat in a chair staring at the phone. But he decided not to call Courtney at such an early hour. He told his father, he was taking the morning off and would start work at one o'clock. He was still hungry with just one piece of cheese toast and two glasses of orange juice in his stomach. But he was filled up with different emotions which gave him the illusion that he wasn't hungry. He had a desperate need to see Courtney and confess his love and ask her for her hand in marriage. He felt they could be happy together. Now he prayed Courtney would accept his marriage proposal. Therefore, he stayed tucked in his room trying to decide what he would say to Courtney and how he would ask her to marry him. Once he didn't hear anymore movement in their quarters, he opened his bedroom door and slowly made his way to the kitchen. He pulled out a chair and took a seat at the kitchen table. He sat there and finished two cups of coffee as he thought with great reflection on what his parents had said. They had shared Courtney's bad deed with him and they had given him doubts that Courtney may not accept his proposal. It bothered him that Courtney had committed such a hurtful crime against Sabrina and Britain, but he knew it took place while Courtney was sick and not herself. Therefore, he wasn't pleased that she hadn't shared with him the details of her bad deed upon Sabrina and Britain. He reflected with a pleasing thought that Courtney had at least shared with him the fact of committing a bad deed against Sabrina. Nevertheless, he loved her no matter what and wanted to spend his life with her.

Finally, he stood up from the kitchen table and stepped a short few steps into the living room. He grabbed his cell phone from the coffee table and plopped down on the sofa and anxiously dialed Courtney house phone.

"This is Larry Westwood. May I speak to Courtney?" he tensely asked.

Mildred smiled. "Hi Larry, how are you? I have heard great things about you. I can't wait to meet you," she friendly greeted him. "This is Mildred Ross, Courtney's mother," Mildred warmly greeted him.

"Hello, Mrs. Ross. Thank you," Larry said. Mildred noticed that he didn't sound friendly or happy. "I need to speak to Courtney, if you don't mind," he dryly requested. He felt uncomfortable talking to Courtney's mother.

Mildred smile faded and she became serious. "Larry, I'm sorry but she's in the shower right now. Can I give her a message?"

"How long do you think she'll be in the shower?" Larry asked.

"Maybe for another ten or fifteen minutes," Mildred guessed. "It's 9:30 now. Why don't you call her back around ten? I'm sure she'll be out of the shower by then," Mildred warmly suggested.

"No, I won't call back. Just tell her I know about the bad thing she did and I'll be over at 10:30 to talk to her," Larry said and then hung up the phone.

Mildred hung up the phone and dropped down on the living room sofa with her mouth open. That was her first conversation with Larry and she didn't know what to make of it. He said he knew about the bad thing Courtney had done; and Mildred was aware that Courtney hadn't shared her crime against Sabrina and Britain to Larry yet. Therefore, she knew relaying that message would worry Courtney. But before she could gather her thoughts of how she would mention Larry's message, Courtney stepped into the living room and noticed her mother's disturbed behavior. Mildred was holding her face with both hands looking toward Courtney with surprise eyes as Courtney stepped into the living room. Courtney was fully dressed in a pair of blue jeans and a pink pullover top. She was smiling with her hair pulled back in one long ponytail. Then her smile faded as she noticed her mother's disturbed expression. "Mom, what's the matter?" Courtney asked. "Why are you sitting there with that disturbed look on your face?"

Mildred waved her hand. "I'm okay, dear," she said. She didn't want to alarm her daughter as she tried to think of a smooth way to mention the message Larry had left her.

"Excuse me, Mom. But you don't look okay," Courtney observed as she stood staring at her mother. "Besides, after breakfast when I headed upstairs for the shower I thought you were leaving for work."

"I meant to tell you I'm off today. I took some time off for your homecoming. I'll go back to work on Monday."

"That's good. But you were not off work the other days."

Mildred stood from the sofa and headed toward the kitchen. "I was but I took care of some errands. That's why you didn't see me around the house."

"I see," Courtney softly mumbled, as she took a seat on the sofa and grabbed the house phone in her lap.

Mildred glanced across the room at Courtney and swallowed hard when Courtney took a seat and grabbed the phone. "Who are you calling, dear?"

Courtney smiled toward her mother. "I'm calling my new honey. I know he's at work but I like calling him early. It helps to brighten the rest of my day," she cheerfully said. "Mom, it's a great feeling knowing someone as genuine as Larry Westwood loves me."

"Don't call Larry," Mildred quickly blurted out.

"Why shouldn't I call him?" Courtney stared curiously at her mother.

"You didn't give me a chance to mention. But he just called a few minutes ago while you were in the shower. He's coming here this morning to visit you," Mildred told her. "He said to tell you he would see you at 10:30."

Courtney smiled. "He can be so silly sometime. Why would he call and invite himself over here this early in the morning without letting me know ahead of time? Besides, I told him I would invite him over for dinner one evening and introduce him to the family," Courtney cheerfully mumbled. "But I guess it's okay if he wants to just drop over at 10:30 in the morning. We can have coffee or something." Courtney glanced at her watch. "So, he'll be here in the next hour and you'll finally get to meet beautiful Larry Westwood."

Mildred heart sunk into her chest with sadness that she had to relay such news to Courtney. She could tell how happy Larry made her daughter. "Dear, you truly care about Larry. I can see it in your eyes and behavior."

"Yes, Mom. I truly care about him. I love the man and he loves me. I'm finally happy. Truly happy for the first time in my life. Larry makes me happy. He's not the typical male type that I used to go for with the best cars and clothes. But I know now I don't need those things in my life to make me happy. I just need someone like Larry who loves me and thinks I'm the most special woman he knows," Courtney said thankfully, as she hopped off the sofa and placed the phone back on the end table. "I think I'll head to the kitchen and put on a fresh pot of coffee before Larry arrives."

Standing in the doorway of the kitchen, propped against the doorframe, Mildred looked at Courtney with sad eyes. "Sweetheart, don't go in and make the coffee yet. I need to tell you something."

"Tell me what?" Courtney asked. "Is something the matter? You look sad suddenly. Did you get some bad news about Dad? Did something happen to my father in that prison?" Courtney asked with great concern.

Mildred held up both hands. "Just hold on and listen. It's not your father. Raymond is fine as far as I know."

"Okay, but what's the matter? That look on your face tells me whatever it is, it's not good news."

Mildred nodded. "You're right. It's not good news. It's about Larry."

Courtney eyes widened with surprised. "What about him?"

"I just need to alert you that I don't think the visit he's making here this morning is a social one," Mildred solemnly said.

"If it's not social, is he just dropping by to say hi and leave? Is he dropping something off to me, like a bouquet of flowers?" Courtney wondered, staring at her mother with confusion in her eyes. "I'm confused, Mom. If he's not dropping anything off and the visit isn't social. Why is he dropping by?"

"I don't know, Sweetheart."

"But he is coming over, is he not? You just said he called and said he's coming over at 10:30."

Mildred nodded with a worried look in her eyes. "That's true. He did call and he's coming over at 10:30." Mildred held up one finger.

"Okay, he's coming over. But why do you think it's not a social visit?"

"It's a vibe I picked up from him over the phone," Mildred admitted.

"But Mom. If you're basing your feelings on a vibe, you could be wrong," Courtney said with a bit of relief in her voice.

"You're right. If I was basing it on a vibe, I could be absolutely incorrect. But I'm also basing it on what he said to me," Mildred told her.

Courtney eyes widened with anxiousness and dread. "Okay, Mom. What did Larry exactly say to you over the phone?"

"The young man, specifically told me to tell you that he knew about the bad thing you did and he's coming over to talk about it."

Courtney jaw dropped as she grabbed her face with both hands. "If that's what he told you to tell me. I know why he's coming over. That's it, Mom." Tears started falling from Courtney's eyes. "My happiness is over already. Someone got to him and told him about my crime before I could," she sadly cried.

"Well, maybe it's for the best," Mildred caringly suggested. "You had already planned to tell the young man. Now he knows the whole story and the two of you can move forward with your relationship without any secrets that need to be revealed."

Courtney sadly shook her head. "No, we won't move forward. He's coming to break up with me for sure. How did he sound over the phone?"

"Well, he did sound abrupt," Mildred reluctantly admitted.

"That's because he's done with me," Courtney cried and ran upstairs to her room.

Chapter Forty

Larry felt like a ton of bricks had fallen on him as he sat in the taxi at the edge of Courtney's driveway. Fifteen minutes had slowly ticked by since Larry arrived at the Ross's front door. Courtney had silently pleaded with her mother to tell Larry she wasn't available to visit with him. She tearfully handed Mildred a letter to give Larry. Then Courtney ran upstairs to her room in tears. Mildred discreetly shook her head and took a deep breath to calm herself. She was quite upset with Courtney for refusing to greet Larry based on an assumption that he had shown up to break up with her. Mildred didn't appreciate being thrown in the middle of Courtney's affair. She felt uneasy to face Larry and hand him Courtney's letter. She didn't like the idea of being untruthful to him about Courtney's whereabouts:

March 23, 2016: Wednesday.
Dear Larry,

I'm sorry I didn't' tell you about my crime. I was too ashamed and I didn't want to see that special look fade into disappointment. But I have only myself to blame. I should have told you in the beginning. But I didn't trust enough. I was given a second chance at happiness and I messed it up. I'm so sorry. When my mother gave me your message I knew it meant you were coming to break up with me. I didn't' have the courage to face you. It was foolish of me to think I could start over in life and be happy. You made me happy. But it wasn't meant to be. I hope you'll find someone who will be worthy of your kindness and goodness.

Take care, Courtney.

Larry was beside himself with disappointment and frustration until it didn't seem to matter that the taxi meter was continuously running as he sat on the back seat of the taxi and read the letter that Courtney had given Mildred to hand him. His heart raced with anxiety and his confusion mounted after reading the letter. Suddenly he felt numb and couldn't think as he sat there in silence as he sadly pushed his back against the car seat cushion. He folded his arms across his chest and forced tears not to fall from his eyes.

The taxi driver was waiting for Larry to tell him where to take him next. But Larry didn't say anything to the driver as he stayed silent for a few more minutes to collect his thoughts. Then several more minutes of silence as the taxi driver waited and wondered what the issue was, Larry asked the cab driver did he have a note pad and a pen. The cab driver opened his glove compartment, pulled out a note pad with an attached ballpoint pen and passed the note pad and pen to Larry. Then Larry sat anxiously in the cab and drafted a quick loving letter to Courtney. After he was done, he slowly exited the taxi and quickly strutted up to Courtney's front door and knocked again. Mildred answered the door and he asked her to give the letter to Courtney:

Wednesday, March 23, 2016:
Dear Courtney,

I read your letter and I know you think I'm upset and I know you expected me to breakup with you. But that's not what I want. Therefore, after you read this letter please give me a call. I can't wait to hear what your answer is. I have given it a great deal of thought and I want you for my wife. I truly think we'll be happy together. I came over this morning for two reasons. One reason was to tell you that I found out about your crime against Miss Sabrina and Mr. Britain that happened while you were sick. And I wanted to tell you that I don't hold it against you. You were not in your right mind when that happened. Therefore, it wasn't the Courtney I know and love that committed those crimes. And my second reason for coming over this morning was to ask you to marry me. I know it's sudden and I probably shouldn't have asked you such an important question in a letter. But when I knocked on your door and your mother told me you were not available. I was crushed and very disappointed. I couldn't leave without you knowing why I had shown up. Please call me later.

Love Always, Larry

South Asia Economic and Policy Studies

Series editors

Sachin Chaturvedi, RIS for Developing Countries, New Delhi, India
Mustafizur Rahman, Centre for Policy Dialogue (CPD), Dhaka, Bangladesh
Abid Suleri, Sustainable Development Policy Institute, Islamabad, Pakistan
Saman Kelegama (1959–2017), Institute of Policy Studies of Sri Lanka (IPS), Colombo, Sri Lanka

The Series aims to address evolving and new challenges and policy actions that may be needed in the South Asian Region in the 21st century. It ventures niche and makes critical assessment to evolve a coherent understanding of the nature of challenges and allow/facilitate dialogue among scholars and policymakers from the region working with the common purpose of exploring and strengthening new ways to implement regional cooperation. The series is multidisciplinary in its orientation and invites contributions from academicians, policy makers, practitioners, consultants working in the broad fields of regional cooperation; trade and investment; finance; economic growth and development; industry and technology; agriculture; services; environment, resources and climate change; demography and migration; disaster management, globalization and institutions among others.

More information about this series at http://www.springer.com/series/15400

K. Locana Gunaratna

Towards Equitable Progress

Essays from a South Asian Perspective

Springer

K. Locana Gunaratna
National Academy of Sciences
  of Sri Lanka
Colombo
Sri Lanka

ISSN 2522-5502 ISSN 2522-5510 (electronic)
South Asia Economic and Policy Studies
ISBN 978-981-10-8922-0   ISBN 978-981-10-8923-7 (eBook)
https://doi.org/10.1007/978-981-10-8923-7

Library of Congress Control Number: 2018935857

© Springer Nature Singapore Pte Ltd. 2018
This work is subject to copyright. All rights are reserved by the Publisher, whether the whole or part of the material is concerned, specifically the rights of translation, reprinting, reuse of illustrations, recitation, broadcasting, reproduction on microfilms or in any other physical way, and transmission or information storage and retrieval, electronic adaptation, computer software, or by similar or dissimilar methodology now known or hereafter developed.
The use of general descriptive names, registered names, trademarks, service marks, etc. in this publication does not imply, even in the absence of a specific statement, that such names are exempt from the relevant protective laws and regulations and therefore free for general use.
The publisher, the authors and the editors are safe to assume that the advice and information in this book are believed to be true and accurate at the date of publication. Neither the publisher nor the authors or the editors give a warranty, express or implied, with respect to the material contained herein or for any errors or omissions that may have been made. The publisher remains neutral with regard to jurisdictional claims in published maps and institutional affiliations.

Printed on acid-free paper

This Springer imprint is published by the registered company Springer Nature Singapore Pte Ltd. part of Springer Nature
The registered company address is: 152 Beach Road, #21-01/04 Gateway East, Singapore 189721, Singapore

To my parents

Acknowledgements

A book by Charles Abrams (1964) made a deep impression on me at the early stage of my career. My more thorough exposure to Urban Planning and Spatial Economics happened later through academic interactions mainly with Profs. Otto Koenigsberger, Lisa Peattie, Bill Doebele, Laurence Mann, Michael Woldenberg, Kusuma Gunawardena, Percy Silva, and John Turner. I mention them here with much respect and appreciation.

A few have encouraged me to deliver lectures at specific institutions. An earlier version of Chap. 2 was an address delivered in 1996 to the *Sri Lanka Association for the Advancement of Science* (SLAAS). On that occasion, I was particularly encouraged by the generous words of three eminent scientists: Dr. Wijesekera and Profs. Dahanayake and Indraratna. Subsequently, Prof. Basnayake invited me to deliver an oration in 2002—an event in a series of annual orations established to honor the memory of a much respected teacher of medicine who had an abiding concern for ethics in science. It gave me an opportunity to research the material which resulted later in my writing of Chap. 5. The material in Chap. 7 too was initially presented as a lecture. It was delivered in 2004 on the invitation of the Sri Lanka Economic Association.

Chapter 10 is based on an invited guest lecture delivered in 2010 to a group of Research Fellows in the *Special Program for Urban and Regional Studies of Developing Areas of the Massachusetts Institute of Technology*. I acknowledge the efforts to get me there by Profs. Ralph Gakenheimer and Bishwapriya Sanyal, both from MIT. The subject matter of that lecture summarized the work over many years to prepare a national spatial policy by a government department of Sri Lanka under supervision by a statutory Technical Advisory Committee which I had the privilege of chairing—a position which I still hold. The cooperation extended to me to gather the visual presentation material for that lecture by a few individuals in two organizations needs also to be acknowledged here. They were: Gemunu Silva, Lakshman Jayasekera, Prasanna Silva, and Indu Weeraoori. Dr. C. R. Panabokke allowed me to use a map of ancient reservoirs which he had prepared and published.

Dr. Palitha Kohona, who was Sri Lanka's Permanent Representative to the UN in 2010, was kind enough to give me a personal briefing in his office in New York on the status of the island's ongoing claim to increase its Extended Oceanic Economic Zone. Tannar Whitney helped me to prepare the graphics for that lecture. Chapter 10 is a written version of that lecture which includes here many of its supporting illustrations.

This book would not be a reality if not for the encouragement given to me by the publisher, Springer, their reviewers and editors. I also have to acknowledge my debt to two extraordinary women—Shanta, my wife, and Sarita, my daughter. They, each in their own and very special ways, gave me a great deal of direct help and encouragement to stay on course and complete the task of writing this book.

Contents

1	**Introduction**	1
	Reference	7

Part I Basic Concerns

2	**Development: The Concept**	11
	Preamble	11
	Main Concepts and Theories	14
	Early Revisions	15
	"Growth"	15
	"Development"	16
	Underdevelopment	17
	Resource Allocation	18
	Recent Revisions	19
	References	20
3	**Sustainable Development: Some Philosophic and Ethical Concerns**	23
	Preamble	23
	Some Philosophic Concerns	24
	References	28
4	**Climate Change: The Scientific Consensus**	31
	Preamble	31
	The Scientists' Views	32
	A Report Commissioned by the World Bank	34
	References	37
5	**Science, Ethics, and Development**	39
	Preamble	39
	Some Views from South Asia	41

	Science in the West	43
	Ethics in Science	45
	Ethical Crises in Science	46
	References	48

Part II Spatial Concerns

6 Managing Climate Change in South Asia 53
  Preamble 53
  Climate Change and South Asian Countries 55
    Sri Lanka 55
    Maldives 56
    Bangladesh 56
    India 57
    Pakistan 58
    Bhutan 60
    Nepal 61
    General Observations 62
  Climate and Culture 62
    Unpredictable Events 65
    Response to Disasters: Two Examples 65
  Needed Responses to Climate Change 67
  References 69

7 Managing Urbanization 71
  Preamble 72
  Discussion 72
  The Context 75
  Utopian Visions 77
  Theories from Spatial Economics 80
    Growth Center Theories 80
    The Theory of Duality 83
    Small and Mid-Sized Towns 84
  References 87

8 Urban Primacy 91
  Preamble 91
  The Case Studies 93
    Vietnam 93
    Myanmar 94
    Sri Lanka 96
    Mozambique 98
    Senegal 100
    Ghana 102

	Chile	103
	Peru	105
	Discussion	106
	References	107
9	**Conserving Cultural Heritage Sites: A Case Study**	109
	Preamble	109
	Conservation Work	112
	Discussion	112
	Some Serious Threats	118
	Conservation Principles	119
	Conclusion	120
	References	120
10	**Concerns in Preparing a National Spatial Policy: A Case Study**	123
	Preamble	123
	The Components of a National Spatial Policy	133
	Environmental Concerns	135
	Protected Areas	135
	Protected Areas Category 1	135
	Protected Areas Category 2	135
	Fragile Areas	137
	Other Concerns	137
	Land-Based Economic Activities	140
	Infrastructure	140
	Road and Rail Networks	145
	Sites of Cultural and Aesthetic Importance	148
	A Composite Plan	148
	References	153

Part III Conclusions

11	**A Summary and Conclusions**	157
	Part I	157
	Part II	161
	Part III	163

Appendix A: South Asian Seminar on Small and Medium Sized Towns in Regional Development. Organized in Kathmandu, Nepal by the Quaker International Affairs Programme in South Asia, New Delhi. 9th–16th April 1978 165

Appendix B: The Key Events That Led to Transforming the Town and Country Planning Department of Sri Lanka into the National Physical Planning Department 167

About the Author

Dr. K. Locana Gunaratna is a Fellow and a former president of the National Academy of Sciences of Sri Lanka and a Vice President of the Sri Lanka Economic Association. He is an architect trained at the AA School in London, and received his Master's in City Planning from Harvard University and his Ph.D. from the University of Colombo. He has led many professional associations including the National Academy of Sciences of Sri Lanka, the Institute of Town Planners Sri Lanka, and the Sri Lanka Institute of Architects. Presently, he is a partner at Gunaratna Associates, Chartered Architects, Engineers and Planning Consultants, Colombo, where he uses his extensive experience working with the government in areas such as the Ministry of Urban Development and Mahaweli Development Board. His research focuses on urban spaces and development in Sri Lanka, a topic on which he has written extensively. His publications include the books *Spatial Concerns in Development: A Sri Lankan Perspective* and *Shelter in Sri Lanka: 1978–1991*.

Chapter 1
Introduction

The countries collectively known as the "Developing World" and also alternatively as the "Third World" display a wide variation in the sizes of their populations and land extents. They also differ considerably in their respective geographies, natural resource endowments and in their histories, cultures, ethnicities, and languages. They together contain a broad range of conditions and a very heterogeneous mix of peoples. They are therefore not a subject for easy generalizations. However, despite these many differences, they, both large and small, do share two important common features. They are geographically located mostly in the tropical region of the globe. Historically, almost all of them have been subjugated territories of one or other European colonial power at some time in the not too distant past. This book will refer to them collectively as the "low- and middle-income countries" (LMICs). In their quest for progress, these countries encounter many hurdles. The more formidable of these constitute the subject matter in several chapters of this book.

A broad concern treated with considerable importance here in this book is about the process known generally as "development"—a process, originally conceived and refined in the West no doubt with the best of intentions to engender economic growth in the LMICs. It was seen then as the main and perhaps the only path to national progress. Some critical attention is devoted here to that process. A significant observation is that while the process even with proper application may indeed create economic prosperity among some, it also tends frequently to encourage social and economic inequalities among others. Such inequalities invariably are spatially discernible within most LMICs.

It may be best to clarify at the outset that the words "equitable progress" in the title of this book. It contains some special meanings. One is that they refer to both economic and social advancement that will benefit all strata of the population of an LMIC. Another meaning refers to the fact that there cannot be such progress without that advancement being generally innocuous toward the biophysical environment and is therefore sustainable. Thus, "equitable progress" refers here to a process of national advancement that is economically beneficial, socially just and environmentally sustainable.

Considering that "equity" refers to another important concept of concern here, it may also be useful to clarify the stand being taken on that concept. This subject has been so thoroughly examined by Sen (1995) that it is unnecessary to delve deeply into it here. What needs to be recognized as Sen has done from the standpoint of the subject of economics is that human beings are very diverse in their capabilities and that such capabilities include those that result from inheritances, congenital mental and physical endowments and also those that are enhanced through education and specialized training. Contrary to the rhetoric, as Sen has observed, people are by no means equal. The aspect of equity which is being emphasized here in this book is that of social justice. The need here is to recognize that equality of access to opportunities is what is particularly important because those opportunities provide people with the freedom to strive for what they wish to achieve. That is a key consideration here in respect of equity.

While the majority populations in the LMICs are poor and most of them live in rural areas, these countries also have small population of affluent elites who often but not always live in the cities. The rural share of their populations is generally around 70% with many of these countries now experiencing high rates of rural–urban migration. Another common feature is that many of these LMICs inherited from their colonial past small extents of relatively modern social infrastructure. These limited facilities relating mainly to basic education and health are invariably found in the principal urban areas which are relatively inaccessible to the rural majority. Some of the larger of these countries as, for example, Brazil, India, China, and South Africa, despite their own internal inequalities, appear to be well on their way toward material progress from the standpoint of industry-led economic growth. The smaller of these countries, while not sharing all of these features with their larger counterparts, do share among each other some special common characteristics. One is that they almost all have agrarian economies many shaped more by the requirements of former colonial imperatives than their own needs. Another, which is important but has rarely been recognized in the past, is the existence of "urban primacy"—a characteristic which is a colonial legacy and is more recently beginning to be seen as such.

Primacy as a condition in the smaller LMICs had received some academic attention in the field of Spatial Economics during the mid-1960s and early 1970s. However, it has rarely entered the urban planning discourse within economic development and at stages of project implementation. It was not sufficiently understood that a predominant primate city not only strongly attracts the bulk of the migrations from the hinterland population but also most of the country's developmental resources, and that in doing so, the purpose of plans with equity and spatial distributive objectives of the respective governments is often negated. That primacy is a condition to be given adequate consideration and countered where necessary in the development thrust has still to be generally recognized.

The last quarter of the twentieth century saw prominence being given increasingly to four important globally observed realities. The first was about the severity and worsening state of the earth's biophysical environment. The second relates to global warming and climate change. The third concerns a process which is now generally referred to as "globalization". The fourth reality has to do with the rapidity of urbanization currently taking place with particular intensity in many LMICs. Thus, it has come about that current and future development work in these countries needs to take serious cognizance of these realities. The LMICs have little control over the first three realities although some appropriate measures for mitigating the adversities need to be put in place. Dealing effectively with the fourth, urbanization, requires the recognition that it has been primarily instrumental in the creation of several massive cities with populations of 10 million or more in some of the LMICs and that these "megacities" now present some severe and seemingly unmanageable problems.

Well over half a century has already lapsed since concerted efforts began in the interest of development in the LMICs. There has also been the expenditure of extraordinary sums of money in this cause in the form of direct monetary aid as well as consultancy. While some progress is evident, large segments of the populations in many of these countries of concern have remained illiterate, with the substantial bulk still entrenched in extreme poverty. One of the motivations here was the hope of finding an explanation as to why, after such an expensive, concerted, and prolonged effort, the ongoing drive for "development" in the LMICs has not lead to the complete eradication of hunger, debilitating diseases, and poverty.

This book has been written from the analytical perspective of a South Asian Architect and Urban Planner with a professional career based in a South Asian country spanning over five decades. The entailed professional work involvements have ranged in scale from the design of individual buildings in urban settings to the planning of rural settlements and small towns; to the preparation of research papers on urban issues and cultural monuments at the behest of scientific bodies; and to advising over a number of years on the preparation of a national spatial planning policy predicated upon environmental sustainability. Distillates of these experiences, expressed through a series of essays based on recent presentations made to various audiences, form the contents of eight of the eleven chapters of this book.

It is recognized here in this book that there clearly are inadequacies in current theories and in the current development approaches to dealing with such serious problems resulting from climate change and rapid urbanization in South Asia. Consequently, an effort has been made to identify an alternative set of theories which incidentally are also mostly of Western origin. The good practices that could result with their application in the South Asian context could indeed underpin a more relevant and scientific approach to the problem—an approach which may perhaps be extendable to many other LMICs. Thus, it may be seen that this book is particularly concerned with spatial planning policies that could counter the iniquities and inequalities that often result from the implementation of projects and policies based on conventional development theory in the LMICs.

The book is presented in three parts. Part I titled "Basic Concerns" contains four chapters, i.e., Chaps. 2–5. These chapters provide a base and background material to facilitate the understanding of the technicalities that follow in Part II. Chapter 2 focuses on the concept of "development" itself. It probes the relevant literature in the social sciences to find those seminal ideas and theories, mostly from the West, that have become the established canons underpinning much of contemporary thought in this field—thought which has been disseminated over many decades to the LMICs to generate policies, plans, aid packages, and expert advice. This particular chapter sets out to examine those seminal ideas and the underlying theories for their scientific merit and contextual relevance. Despite the generation of economic growth in some countries at the expense of environmental degradation, the benefits of that growth have become distributed with such disparity as to have clearly not benefited the bulk among the targeted populations.

The facts are now well established but recognized mainly by the scientifically literate public of most countries rich and poor that the entire world has been for several decades and still is in the midst of multiple man-made environmental crises. These crises if not checked are more than likely to generate consequences that could threaten not only the people in the poorer countries but all life on earth. Chapter 3 addresses these environmental challenges that confront the LMICs. It analyzes the philosophical concerns that arise within the more recently promoted paradigm of "sustainable development". Chapter 4 examines the discernable facts established by scientific investigations about climate change as a phenomenon that has arisen in consequence of global environmental degradation.

It is recognized in this book that strong ethical convictions are necessary to drive the sought economic growth to be both inclusive and environmentally sustainable. The success and viability of such efforts directed toward inclusive and sustained progress within an LMIC will depend, on the one hand, on the extent of demand for consumption of goods and services and, on the other hand, on the types of technology and energy utilized for their production and distribution. Controlling and regulating any aspect of these factors are responsibilities of the respective national governments—functions that are neither easy nor always popular. Unfortunately, most political leaders cannot be relied upon to always act with the needed foresight or fortitude. Thus, the fifth chapter explores the role of science, technology, and professional ethics as important factors for viable and sustainable progress in the LMICs. It is argued therein that scientists and professionals governed by ethical codes of conduct need to take upon themselves the leadership in educating the public and establishing the foundation for a collective ethical consciousness that will promote and facilitate good governance and national progress consonant with equity, social justice, and environmental sustainability.

It is generally understood that a strong commitment to science and technology is essential for the LMICs to progress. By progress is usually meant, rightly or wrongly, the generation of economic growth. Foreign direct investment in economic activities of the LMICs and also investment through globalizing industries, especially when they result in technology transfers, are believed to be specifically beneficial for the development effort in the LMICs. But the introduction of new technologies often requires from the local context both skilled and unskilled labor. This need could be satisfied by the availability of a literate and disciplined work force, with some training for the skilled categories in the relevant economic and industrial activities. However, if the whole development effort is not to lead to a new form of dependence and the sought form of development is to be sustainable, the creation of a local human resource pool that is capable of managing, innovating, and indigenizing the technology transfers is most important. This requires not only the training of skilled workers and technicians. That particular segment of the work force should only be the base of the needed human resource pyramid. The rest should include scientists, professionals, and efficient managers at the middle and upper levels, all of whom should have innovative capability. Furthermore, it is best that the needed human resource pool be drawn from the entire population and not merely from the urban areas. This is recommended not only for reasons of equity but for the achievement of better overall results.

Science education is basic to this whole exercise. This may often require changes in education policy in some countries. Exciting the child's curiosity about science is therefore of vital importance. Satisfying that curiosity with good basic science literacy programs within both the rural and urban areas is an essential part of the answer. The training of teachers for such programs is clearly most important. These programs will, in due course, create a demand for more formal science education, not only for its own sake but also as it would eventually lead to better livelihoods for intelligent children. Thereafter, the political process may be relied upon to ensure that the inevitable demand for better secondary schools for both sexes with good science teaching facilities will follow including in the underprivileged geographic areas of the LMICs.

Part II of the book is titled "Spatial Concerns" and consists of Chaps. 6–10.

The broad impact of climate change on South Asia is discussed in the sixth chapter. This discussion involves a brief examination, country by country, on this impact in its social and economic aspects as they require solutions that translate invariably into spatial dimensions.

The scale and pace of urbanization in many of the LMICs today are recognized as being unprecedented in human history. A matter of very special concern presented in this book relates to the phenomena of rapid urbanization as prevalent in the LMICs today. This phenomenon could indeed be seen as a boon for the LMICs but only provided its adversities can be adequately addressed. Chapter 7 deals with urbanization in South Asia. It reviews some of the literature and also identifies some writings and theories which could lead to its better management. The review reveals that the main approaches to the subject involve the discipline of spatial planning. Most of the approaches in current use in South Asia are utopian in essence having originated in the industrialized West in the nineteenth and early twentieth centuries and have since been introduced to these countries. They have been adopted at various times with intention to deal with the problems of urbanization in South Asia. Despite considerable and prolonged efforts to confront the adversities of urbanization, the LMICs in South Asia have seen no breakthroughs. Many influential Western scholars appear in this context to have viewed urbanization as an inevitable, if not desirable process leading to development. Thus, all the usual recommended efforts made hitherto generally converge on dealing with the resultant problems of urbanization in the affected cities themselves, rather than on managing and mitigating its causative factors. These efforts invariably rely on those particular utopian intra-urban interventions.

Chapter 7 also identifies another set of theories also of Western origin but lesser known in South Asia. The contention here is that some of these which are part of the discipline of Spatial Economics could indeed underlie a more relevant approach to dealing with urbanization in South Asia and perhaps also in other LMICs.

In Chap. 8, an attempt is made to revalidate through the presentation of a few new case studies, a theory of fundamental relevance to the desired new spatial planning approach to deal with the multifarious problems arising from rapid urbanization in the LMICs. The theory, also of Western origin, has to do with the phenomena of "urban primacy" and its observable presence to a lesser or greater degree in many of the smaller LMICs.

Many of the LMICs including those in South Asia and also quite extensively elsewhere in Asia have an abundance of sites within them that are of special historical and cultural interest and importance. The identification, study, and conservation of these heritage sites inevitably become not only matters of national prestige within their respective countries but are also often pursued as social and political necessities. Quite apart from their intrinsic value to the local population, some of these sites are also of great interest to other countries and often the world at large. They become destinations for tourists both local and foreign which in turn result in economic benefits and sometimes, inadvertently, adverse consequences.

Chapter 9 considers the case of a particular archaeological site known as "Lumbini", the birthplace of the Buddha. It is located in Nepal near its present southern border with India. The place is of great cultural importance nationally and internationally and has been, quite appropriately, declared by UNESCO as a World Heritage Site. This chapter uses the example of Lumbini to discuss some of the real challenges associated with spatial planning in relation to conservation work and also the protection of such sites from risks that can emerge. It highlights the absolute necessity of steadfast commitment to utilize not only the science of archaeology but also long-sighted spatial planning tools for the conservation of valuable and threatened heritage sites. It is intended that the lessons to be learnt from examining the Lumbini experience will also benefit other ongoing and future projects on conserving the many other sites of cultural importance in South Asia and elsewhere in the LMICs.

The penultimate tenth chapter ends Part II of this book. The main intention of this chapter is to help translate theory to practice. It focuses upon a case study taken from one South Asian country, namely Sri Lanka. It provides the background to the efforts taken and presents with visual illustrations an environmentally predicated national spatial policy. In this presentation, most of the recommended spatial planning theories discussed earlier in this book are implicitly embedded. The underlying national spatial policy elements that emerged, after many years of effort by dedicated professionals, was finally overseen by a far-sighted Cabinet Minister incumbent at the time. Through his efforts, it was approved as national policy in 2007—a rare example of such a policy in an LMIC. It has, unfortunately, not been implemented—a typical problem in many LMICs where implementing long-term national policy has inevitably to compete with shortsighted politics and ever-shifting political agendas. Had at least a few of the recommendations been implemented, some of the damage to lives and property caused by environmental disasters that have intervened in the interim could well have been averted.

Part III consists of the eleventh and last chapter which presents a summary of conclusions drawn from all the foregoing writings.

The texts that form seven of the eleven chapters conceived originally as they were for presentation to various different audiences, contained among them a few unavoidable overlaps in content. These texts have since been revised for the purposes of this book in an effort to minimize such overlaps. Thus, the chapters as they appear now may be read sequentially, or if the reader prefers, separately as discrete essays on their respective subject areas.

Reference

Sen A (1995) Inequality reexamined. Harvard University Press, Cambridge, MA

Part I
Basic Concerns

Chapter 2
Development: The Concept

Abstract The word "development" as a synonym for societal progress acquired a special meaning through its metaphoric association with the Darwinian theory of evolution. This concept of development began in the social science literature with economic growth theories of the 1930s and 1940s as refined in the 1950s. Societies, in this concept, regardless of their separate historic, geographic, and cultural contexts are expected to pass through a pre-ordained sequence of recognizable stages. This "stages" hypothesis, implicit in some of the earlier development literature, was made very explicit around 1971. The forced assumption is that all social systems of the LMICs must replicate the historical processes through which the industrialized societies have already passed. Starting in the 1960s and gathering momentum through the following decades, an important revision in the concept of development has come about at least among some concerned intellectuals. Its advocacy as unbridled economic growth through industrialization has been questioned. The need for environmental sustainability in any path to genuine societal progress has now come to be widely recognized. Furthermore, it is concluded here that development as a concept, based as it is on an ahistoric stance, particularly where it presupposes a progressive process through which all cultures must pass, is clearly unacceptable. There is thus no justification to substantiate a claim that such a concept of development as widely understood and promoted has any basis in science or relevance to the LMICs and to the context of special concern here, namely that of South Asia.

Preamble

Following the end of the Second World War, many of the colonized territories worldwide began to gain independence, a process which took a few decades. The national boundaries of some of these "new" countries and their sub-national regions

---

A revised version of a keynote address delivered by the Author in his capacity then as President, Social Science Section of the "Sri Lanka Association for the Advancement of Science" at their Annual Sessions (December 1996).

© Springer Nature Singapore Pte Ltd. 2018
K. L. Gunaratna, *Towards Equitable Progress*, South Asia Economic and Policy Studies, https://doi.org/10.1007/978-981-10-8923-7_2

had been delineated and defined geographically by their former colonial rulers. During this period starting in the late 1940s, leadership in the industrialized world saw an interest and foresaw a role in helping these emerging countries to achieve progress. To support this process, some international institutions were established. A body of Western scholarship arose concerned with what came to be referred to as "development". Internalized within that body of scholarship were notions, theories, cultural values, and ethical norms as to what national progress should mean and how it may be achieved. Through schemes of monetary support, loans, technical assistance, and higher education programs, the contents of this new scholarship came to be strongly promoted among professionals, institutions, and governments rich and poor. Accordingly, those countries that had experienced colonial subjugation at some period of their history came to be classified as "underdeveloped", "less developed", or "developing" countries. Later, they came to be collectively referred to as the "Third World", the "Developing World", and more recently by a few as the "Global South". This book will refer to these countries collectively as the "low- and middle-income countries" (LMICs).

Several agencies are dedicated to promoting "development" in these LMICs. Some are substantial and operate at the international level such as the United Nations Organization and the World Bank. A few, like the Asian Development Bank, operate at the regional level, while a few more are based in some of the richer countries. Also, there are agencies in the poorer countries backed by their respective governments, which seek and receive external assistance to encourage activities that are expected to foster development.

"Development" is a Western concept. It has been received and acted upon in many of the LMICs with fervor akin to blind faith. More than half a century has already lapsed since concerted efforts began in the interest of development in the LMICs. There has also been the expenditure of extraordinary sums of money in this cause as direct monetary aid as well as for consultancy. Meanwhile, the debt burden resulting from borrowings for development from the richer countries, directly and indirectly, has at times grown to become an international problem. While some progress in the LMICs is evident, large segments of the populations in many of these countries of concern have remained illiterate, with the substantial bulk still entrenched in extreme poverty, disease, and malnutrition (Gunaratna 1996). This situation has also been observed by Mehmet (1999). The very adverse impact upon the earth's environment of past "development" efforts by and for the richer industrialized countries themselves have over many recent decades gained recognition worldwide as a serious problem of magnitude. The study of Ecology has become far more important and a process called "sustainable development" has come into vogue.

This chapter is about the concept of development. It is based on an excursion into the relevant Western literature in the Social Sciences which dates mainly from the early 1950s. It seeks to examine the ideas and assumptions that underlie the concept and also its relationship to other associated concepts such as "growth", "progress", and also "sustainability". An attempt is made to see if the concept has, in reality, a sound basis in science and relevance to the LMICs in general and to South Asia in particular.

The striving for societal progress has followed theories on the nature of society and social change. These latter originated in the early nineteenth-century preoccupations with social and economic disparities found at the onset of industrialization in Europe. Two divergent schools of thought began there: the "revolutionary" and "evolutionary" schools with the latter taking firmer root in the West. Some of the adherents of this classical school used one of two biological metaphors to explain the nature of society. Sometimes, society was likened to an organism subjected to change by volitional forces. At other times, the parallel drawn was with a species of organisms subjected to evolutionary change. This reliance on an evolutionary metaphor is discussed quite thoroughly elsewhere (Nelson 1995).

The concept underlying development and its popularity in the planning literature on social change seems to have been very closely related to the evolutionary metaphor. Darwinian influence is clear. Within this paradigm, Western theorists looking for social change in European history have been much concerned with the changes that took place in the early Italian city-states during the medieval period— the social transformations that did take place at the onset of the "age of reason". This age, the "renaissance", generally constituted for them inspiration for "modernization" and economic growth as processes of change for the better (Black 1966). However, Western theories on the needed social change for progress in the LMICs were generally neither based upon nor even vaguely related to their respective histories.

Thoughts on how progress can be effectively planned for in the LMICs are recent and date from the 1950s. Immediately after World War II, a matter of prime concern in the West was the uplifting of war-ravaged Europe. The accumulated theories of economic growth from the 1930s and early 1940s were brought out and examined. The works of Schumpeter (1934), Keynes (1936), Kuznets (1941), and Rosenstein Rodan (1943) became very influential. The World Bank and the United Nations Organization were set up. Later, with the rebuilding of Europe underway, Western attention then focused on the LMICs. Weaver conveys that a panel of economists invited in 1951 by the newly formed United Nations synthesized the above ideas (Weaver 1981). They thought that if the poorer countries are to achieve the high consumption levels of the West, they must replicate the economic processes undergone by the industrialized nations. They were the first to refer to the rich and poor countries as being "developed" and "underdeveloped". Thus, a substantial body of theoretical literature arose in the West for assisting the LMICs to progress. There were some differences and minor contradictions within that body, but by and large, the various theories were mutually reinforcing (Weiner, 1966). The whole became a formidable collection of theoretical writings which went unchallenged for nearly three decades, except perhaps on polemical grounds.

Main Concepts and Theories

One central concept underlying development was that of a structured and pre-ordained sequence of stages through which all nations and cultures must progress. Perhaps the most articulate proponent of this "stages" hypothesis was W. W. Rostow. He categorized five stages of economic growth in his well-known work with "take-off" as the final stage (Rostow 1971). Progress was seen as synonymous with economic growth, and thus growth in per capita GNP became the main, and for the most part the only index of progress. The industrialized nations of the West with high growth rates were the ones to be emulated. They were to be the ultimate models for the LMICs.

At that time, theories of "disguised unemployment" had gained appeal where the general hypothesis was that more people are employed in agriculture than are needed to produce the current agricultural output and that "surplus" labor constitutes "hidden" or "disguised" unemployment. The most widely accepted version of this hypothesis was that of "structural unemployment". In this, unemployment was attributed to the co-existence of a subsistence agricultural sector with an urban capitalist industrial sector, i.e., a "dualism" in the economy. As Wellisz (1968) explained, all such theories which suggest that the marginal productivity of labor in agriculture is zero justify the transfer of labor from agriculture to industry and that consequently the emphasis was placed on industrialization to generate economic growth. This clearly implied a marked preference for urban as opposed to rural development for national progress. This position was reinforced by the school of social scientists which upheld a theory of modernization based on the concept of "dualism", which has been traced back to Boeke (1953), a Dutch Economist. This school saw the economy of an LMIC as being a duality wherein there exists on the one hand a backward, tradition-bound agricultural sector, where capitalism is not indigenous and is consequently retarded; and, on the other hand, a small, urban industrial sector where capitalism has been imported full-blown from the West. The latter was considered "modern". Development was seen by them as being the process by which the latter progresses rapidly to overtake and dominate the former. Central to this process was the spread of Western knowledge and techniques, i.e., modernization, starting with the urban and moving to the rural areas.

Furthermore, the same theories had it that the entire process of modernization and development can be facilitated and hastened by maintaining an "open economy" within the country and in relation to the outside world. These measures would then strengthen the small "modern" urban sector and help it surpass the backward traditional rural sector. The "open economy" concept is considered relevant not only for modernizing backward countries, but is, in fact, an idea central to classical Western economic theory. The latter suggests that the market mechanism unhampered by governmental interference becomes a "hidden hand" that establishes prices and allocates resources in the most productive manner.

Early Revisions

Starting in the mid-1960s, there has been a gradually mounting body of criticism of the basic concepts of "growth" and "development" in that they contained not only a reliance on biological metaphors but also an ahistoricism embedded in the theory. All the questions that arose were not merely from that quarter which had polemical objections to the particular theories. Respected Western scholars from a variety of fields have raised many of the doubts. While the early criticisms were made at the conceptual level, the doubts that arose later starting in the mid-1970s were often based on empirical evidence from the application of the theories to real-world situations.

"Growth"

It is generally agreed today that the application of growth strategies has resulted in growth of per capita gross national product (GNP) in the LMICs taken as a whole. A UN publication conveys the opinion of many researchers that, while this growth has occurred in overall statistical terms, there has been an unprecedented increase in unemployment, famines, malnutrition, hunger, and poverty (ESCAP 1979a, b). It would seem that "growth" has taken place at the expense of the poor. Thus, the question asked by many is whether economic growth as experienced recently in the LMICs indicates genuine progress. The widely accepted view today is that growth has been very unevenly distributed across these countries and that serious poverty and underdevelopment remain. Lee finds that absolute poverty has increased, not only in contexts of slow growth but also in many of the fast-growing countries (Lee 1981).

This situation has been seen in two ways: first, from the macroeconomic standpoint, where the need to alter the global economic system has been identified. This resulted in the call by many LMICs and some concerned international agencies for a "New International Economic Order", e.g., by the United Nations Conference on Trade and Development (UNCTAD). The second was the search for alternative strategies to those encouraged by economic growth theory. Some of the commonly cited responses to that search are the *employment-oriented* strategy of the ILO and "the re-distribution-with-growth strategy" of the World Bank. According to Lee, the reappraisal of growth strategy has been forced mainly by the statistics of the increasing incidence in destitution as evidenced by widespread malnutrition, debilitating diseases, gross inadequacies in shelter and access to clean water, sanitation, healthcare, and education, i.e., the basic needs of the majority in the LMICs (Lee 1981). A United Nations study states that the UN agencies and a number of donor countries have since begun to advocate a distribution strategy referred to as the *"basic needs approach"* which seeks to satisfy within one generation, the basic needs of income, and services of the poorest segments of the population in the Asian LMICs (ESCAP 1979a).

It would seem that economic growth has often been paralleled at least in the Asian LMICs with a sharp increase in disparities between the rich and the poor. In this regard, it has been responsibly noted in a research study done at Harvard University that:

> Developing Asia's rapid growth in recent decades has...also been accompanied by rising inequality in many countries. Income inequality has increased in 12 out of the 30 countries with comparable data, the 12 accounting for 82% of the total population. In many countries, income inequality coexists with non-income inequality in the form of unequal access to education, health, and basic services among different population groups classified by gender, location, and income. (Kanabur et al. 2014)

There has indeed been some growing general disillusionment about the whole process of development as well in the manner it has been applied in the LMICs. A relevant criticism reads as follows:

> After almost half a century of Western-guided economic development what is the end result? ... in many parts of the Third World, in particular in Africa, South Asia and in Central and Latin America, real incomes have declined sharply and there is more poverty today than in 1970 in an increasingly unsustainable world... According to World Bank statistics, 23 countries had negative per capita GNP growth between 1965 and 1990; between 1980 and 1991 the number of countries in this category had risen to 43. As at 1995, according to the United Nations High Commissioner for Refugees (UNHCR), there were a total of 27.4 million refugees, internally displaced persons and other persons of concern as a result of conflict and strife in the Third World, often caused by poverty and underdevelopment (UN High Commissioner for Refugees 1995:247) ... We lack clear and convincing theories and explanations for persistent underdevelopment and mass poverty in the Third World ...This study aims at putting much of the blame for persistent Third World underdevelopment where it surely belongs—not on the patient but on the doctor and his prescriptions. This means the source of the blame for failed postwar development lies in the faulty prescriptions derived from Western mainstream (i.e. positive) economic theorizing itself. (Mehmet 1999)

"Development"

As already discussed, the development concept as it was espoused was an ahistoric stance which also created a conflict of two biological images. Rhodes, having reviewed the relevant writings of Condorcet, Herbert Spencer, and Max Weber in regard to social change, says that the contemporary view of development is the evolutionary one. He adds that

> One does not have to be Marxist to accept the view that European development cannot be adequately described in evolutionary terms.... (Rhodes 1968)

Nelson, discussing the work of Alfred Marshall, one of the pioneers in this area of the evolutionary metaphor, says that

> ...while he was attracted to "biological conceptions," it is apparent that Marshall never had in mind simply applying biological theory to economics. Indeed, the fact that he felt himself

forced to fall back on "mechanical analogies" tells us that he found it very difficult to develop a formal theory, based on "biological conceptions" that he thought adequate for economic analysis. (Nelson 1995)

Discussing models of society at an earlier time, Dahrendorf (1968) too appears to call for a Galilean–Newtonian reformulation. He seems to feel that a satisfactory model of society must have the capacity to include two types of societies, which are seen here as being equivalent to the "static" and "dynamic" postulates of Classical Mechanics. Reliance on these postulates has also been observed more recently by others (e.g., Nelson 1995). It may also be observed that in these postulates, the stable model may correspond less to current circumstances but more to isolated social groups with closed economies such as traditional or tribal communities. The model of instability and change could represent the other more common generality.

Furthermore, there is considerable doubt as to whether progression through a structured sequence of predetermined stages is in fact a correct interpretation even of Darwinian theory. Skinner, a behavioral scientist, clarifies this point. In discussing social change, Skinner disagrees with the ascribing of values to development, seeing directed change as "growth" and all change as development. He also clarifies what he sees as a common terminological misunderstanding when he says:

>...We call some cultures underdeveloped or immature in contrast with others we call "advanced", but it is a form of jingoism to imply that any government, religion, or economic system is mature.... (Skinner 1971)

It may also be noted that the renowned American Anthropogeographer, Sauer, is very clear in his mind when he writes:

> There is no general law that all mankind follows; there are no general successions of learning, no stages of culture all people tend to pass. (Sauer 1969)

Underdevelopment

Frank was one of the first to hypothesize a relationship between colonialism and underdevelopment (Frank 1969). A world map of the so-called underdeveloped regions coincides almost exactly with the map of the former dependencies of the eighteenth- and nineteenth-century colonial powers. This hypothesis, which suggests a causal link, may be favored at the expense of the "stages" hypothesis by the fact that most of the present developed countries were never underdeveloped. Such views are no longer considered heretical. As Peattie says:

>...Rostow's idea of the processes involved in the take-off (and indeed the very idea of a take-off) have been criticized as excessively simplistic, and the whole discussion is very much abstracted from the real political-economic-social process in society...the underdevelopment of certain nations can be seen as the reverse side of the international system that produces wealthy nations.... (Peattie 1981a)

The literature makes a distinction between "underdeveloped" and "undeveloped". The former connotes a structural constraint superimposed on a country and its economy. This is best seen by examining the economic impact of colonial subjugation on the colonies. The frequent assertion is that the impact was beneficial in that it caused a partial transition from a closed, primitive, agrarian, subsistence economy, to a more open economy. This assertion is usually based on the Ricardian arguments that trade is possible wherever there are differences in pre-trade prices and that invariably there are such differences due to countries having different factor endowments and consumption preference patterns (Ricardo 1817). While these arguments may well hold true in many respects, there are other important considerations that are ignored. The colonial transition, imposed by force, was invariably from self-sufficiency to an economy dependent on trade with and through the colonial center. It was paralleled by cultural, social, and physical transformations that make a return to self-sufficiency or a change to a different economy extremely difficult. Soon after World War II, most of the peripheral countries of the eighteenth- and nineteenth-century colonial empires began to achieve "independence". But this independence they gained was only with respect to governance. Most of them even after the lapse of several decades continued to be dependent on the export trade of their old colonial goods, and that too in a climate of deteriorating terms of trade. This situation is very characteristic of underdevelopment.

Resource Allocation

It is useful at this point to consider another one of the fundamental assumptions that underlies development theory. Basic in the "hidden hand" theory of the allocation of productive resources by the market are such concepts as "perfect competition" and "perfect mobility of resources". The nonexistence of these "perfect" conditions in the markets of the LMICs has been noted by many Western economists. The lack of these conditions is often referred to as "market imperfections". However, it should also be noted that it is not the markets that are imperfect in their lack of correspondence to some idealized theoretical abstraction. Others too (e.g., Qadeer 1989) have observed that policy research in the LMICs requires not only an objective understanding of local conditions but that efforts to fit reality to preconceived theories and models should be avoided. All too often the erroneous conclusion is that the markets, and indeed even the behavior patterns of the people in these cultures, should be adjusted and remodeled toward some abstraction in the theories of development. The purpose of planning theory, on the contrary, is to help understand reality so that desired changes can be effected in an optimal manner. As Peattie suggests,

> ...development was seen merely as an economic process. While society and culture were considered relevant to this process, "Social Factors" were usually visualized only as obstacles to development. (Peattie 1981b)

She goes further to raise an important question when she says:

> …All these ways of thinking about the "problems of underdevelopment" locate the relevant conditions, and the obstacles to be overcome, within the backward society itself. But suppose that the social and cultural arrangements that eventuate in low material productivity are the consequences of over-riding processes outside the particular society in question, or, if of independent origins, are of relatively minor importance, compared with more powerful forces at an international level?.... (Peattie 1981c)

Recent Revisions

The 1960s saw the beginnings of environmental awareness in the West, which was triggered by a book written by Rachel Carson and published in the United States (Carson 1962). Starting in the early 1970s, several major international conferences and "summits" on the environment have been held. Despite considerable agitation by the informed public in the West and a much greater awareness of environmental issues, the world in the early twenty-first century is far from being free even of serious chemical contamination (Lear 2002). The world's intelligentsia has also come to be aware that so many of the climate-related disasters that now plague mankind much more frequently than before such as severe storms, cyclones, tornados, floods, and droughts occurring in disparate locations on the surface of the earth are not necessarily natural events; and that many of them are now recognized as being man-made. The world is currently in the midst of multiple environmental crises of serious magnitude. All too frequently, the blame is placed on science, technology, or in faulty theories in the science of economics. But, as clearly recognized by many scholars, the problem reaches deep into a dominant philosophy in the West that emphasizes anthropocentricity (White 1967). Such modern philosophers as Arne Naess (1973) have also made this point quite emphatically (Sessions 1995). This subject area is discussed more thoroughly in Chap. 3.

While awareness of environmental issues had already begun to gain momentum in the United States, a series of lectures by 25 well-known American academics on the various aspects of economic development was broadcast by the *Voice of America* in the mid-1960s. The lectures, thought to be of special relevance to the LMICs, were edited and published as a book (Weiner 1966). The editor confidently says in his preface that these countries of concern

> …are experiencing a comprehensive process of change which Europe and America once experienced….

Despite the fact that various authors of chapters in this book deal with different but inter-related subjects, the book in essence recommends that people in the LMICs should consider shedding their respective cultures which are seen as shackles preventing progress; that they should motivate themselves through adopting cultural attitudes and acquisitive values similar to those associated with frugal Protestant Christian societies; and that they should change their inadequate work ethic and strive hard to get to and stay on paths similar to what the Western industrialized nations had already trodden in their unbridled quest for economic growth and development. That this would involve the continued exploitation of the earth's resources and despoil the environment on even a much grander scale than already done by those same Western industrialized countries, some for more than two centuries, was not recognized anywhere in the book. These academics do not seem to have realized even in the late 1960s that a powerful wave of critical revision in attitude toward the means and consequences of achieving material progress had already begun in the West and was being spearheaded in their own country.

References

Black CE (1966) Change as a condition of modern life. In: Weiner M (ed) Modernization: the dynamics of growth. US Information Agency, Washington, DC, p 18
Boeke JH (1953) Economics and economic policies of dual societies as exemplified by Indonesia. International Secretariat of the Institute of Pacific Relations, New York
Carson R (1962) Silent spring. Houghton Mifflin, New York
Dahrendorf R (1968) Essays on the theory of society. Stanford University Press, Stanford, CA, pp 126–128
ESCAP (1979a) Guidelines for rural centre planning. United Nations, New York, p 27
ESCAP (1979b) Guidelines for rural centre planning. United Nations, New York, p 28
Frank AG (1969) The development of underdevelopment. Latin America in underdevelopment or revolution. Monthly Review Press, New York
Gunaratna (1996) Development: the Concept and its Basis in Science. Sri Lanka Association for the Advancement of Science, Sri Lanka
Kanabur R et al (eds) (2014) Inequality in Asia and the Pacific: trends, drivers, and policy implications. Routledge, Oxford
Lear L (2002) Introduction. In: Carson R (ed) Silent spring, New edition. Houghton Mifflin, New York
Lee E (1981) Basic needs strategies: a frustrated response to the development from below. In: Stohr WB, Taylor DRF (eds) Development from above or below. Wiley, New York, pp 107–108
Mehmet O (1999) Westernizing the Third World: the Eurocentricity of economic development theories. Routledge, London
Naess A (1973) The shallow and the deep, long-range ecology movement. Summ Inq 16(1):95–100
Nelson RR (1995) Recent evolutionary theorizing about economic change. J Econ Lit J 33:48–90
Peattie L (1981a) Thinking about development. Plenum Press, New York, p 45
Peattie L (1981b) Thinking about development. Plenum Press, New York, p 37
Peattie L (1981c) Thinking about development. Plenum Press, New York, pp 45–47
Qadeer MA (1989) The international dimension is urban policy research. Third World Planners Newsletter
Rhodes RI (1968) Disguised conservatism in evolutionary development theory. Sci Soc J 32: 383–385
Ricardo D (1817) The principles of political economy and taxation. In: Staffa P (ed) The work and correspondence of David Ricardo. Cambridge (1966)
Rostow WW (1971) The process of economic growth. Norton, New York
Sauer CO (1969) Agricultural origins and dispersals. MIT Press, Cambridge, Massachusetts, p 3
Sessions G (ed) (1995) Deep ecology for the 21st century. Shambhala, Boston
Skinner BF (1971) Beyond freedom and dignity. Knopf, New York, pp 139–142

References

Weaver C (1981) Development theory and the regional questions: a critique of spatial planning and its detractors. In: Stohr WB, Taylor DRF (eds) Development from above or below. Wiley, New York

Weiner M (ed) (1966) Modernization: the dynamics of growth. US Information Agency, Washington, DC

Wellisz S (1968) Dual economies, disguised unemployment and the unlimited supply of labor. Econ New Ser J 35(137):22–51

White Jr TL (1967) The historical roots of our ecological crisis. Science 155:1203–1207 (reprinted in: ecology and religion in history (1974) Harper and Row, New York)

Chapter 3
Sustainable Development: Some Philosophic and Ethical Concerns

Abstract Starting in the 1960s and progressing through the 1970s, an important revision had begun in regard to the advocacy of unbridled economic growth and industrialization. The need to pay heed to environmental concerns in any process of economic progress was beginning to be recognized during this period. The greater awareness of the ecological consequences of economic growth has, with time, led to the current promotion of development in the LMICs as qualified by the word "sustainable". Noting that multiple environmental crises confront the world now with consequences that could, in the extreme, even threaten all life on earth, it is sought here to address at least briefly some of the environmental challenges facing the LMICs. The philosophical concerns that arise within the new paradigm of "sustainable development" are also examined. The contention of some Western scholars now is that at least in the past few centuries, anthropocentrism with its many philosophic references to the roots of Western civilization in ancient Greece has become a dominant attitude in the Western world and that attitude stands in the way of a sustainable approach to progress. However, it is also recognized that non-anthropocentric philosophy is already entrenched in many Asian cultures.

Preamble

Since the Meiji restoration in 1868, Japan an Asian country adopted substantially the Western path to material progress through industrialization. They were unaware at that time of what most educated people recognize now and that the consequences that would follow will surely include adverse impacts upon the global environment. It is now quite well established especially among the scientifically literate that the entire world is currently in the midst of multiple environmental crises. Indeed these are among the most serious of all the present challenges before mankind today. There is therefore now a clear recognition among many leading Western scientists, economists, and planners that if the LMICs proceed to follow the same path to progress as that taken by the industrialized countries without adequate safeguards against environmental impacts, there could be very serious global consequences.

Thus, attempts are being made more recently through international agencies and bilateral arrangements to advice and encourage economists, planners, and decision-makers in the LMICs to move toward what is now being called "sustainable development".

On an initiative of the United Nations, 17 Sustainable Development Goals (SDGs) have been identified and many countries have agreed to reach for these goals and hopefully achieve them by the year 2030. Another such attempt, which is currently being funded by the European Union and which is focused on Asia, intends to help develop national policy in some Asian countries on sustainable consumption and production. It was commenced as a 4-year pilot project in a South Asian country (Switch-Asia 2015).

Despite the high aspirations and good intentions in all these efforts, the question arises as to how realistic these goals are for realization in the current context. Some thinkers within the industrialized countries themselves are raising the question as to whether the real cause of the environmental crises is the prevalent and dominant ethic—an ethic which encourages the quest for economic advancement to enable continuing increases in consumption with no regard for local or global environmental consequences. The environmental challenges faced today by the LMICs are not easily addressed by those countries alone within today's global context. This chapter is an exploration of some of the philosophical and ethical issues that bear upon the pursuit of socioeconomic progress consonant with sustainable development in the LMICs in general and South Asia in particular. In this regard, it should be recognized that there can be no sustainability in the progress of a country without that progress being equitably distributed among its people.

Some Philosophic Concerns

There is a body of twentieth-century Western literature based on disillusionment with the anthropocentric cultural view as it impacts on global environmental issues. These concerns are said to have been first voiced in the West by Rachel Carson when the chapters of her book "*Silent Spring*" were serialized by the well-known weekly journal *New Yorker*. The book was published later that year (Carson 1962a). It has been responsibly stated that this particular book initiated a nationwide discussion and debate on the use of chemical pesticides and the responsibilities that scientists must bear in regard to the implications of technological progress. These debates in turn led to a greater public awareness of the need for interdependence between human beings and their natural environment (Lear 2002). Carson's book is recognized as having been primarily responsible for the launching of the popular concern with ecology. It is also recognized to have alerted an entire generation to the seriousness of the effects of industrial wastes, pesticides and air pollution on human survival (Wines 2008a).

Carson's own disillusionment with anthropocentrism is clear and quite explicit when she stated:

...the "control of nature" is a phrase conceived in arrogance, born of the Neanderthal age of biology and philosophy, when it was supposed that nature exists for the convenience of man. (Carson 1962b)

The formidable impact she had, despite concerted efforts by some to discredit her, is undeniable. In point of fact, it led Americans to celebrate the first "Earth Day" in 1970 and to passing of the "National Environment Policy Act" by the U.S. Congress. Following a proclamation signed by the UN's Secretary General, "Earth Day" is now celebrated extensively and the pro-environment movement has since spread worldwide.

Scientists and public opinion in some European countries as Sweden, for example, were well ahead in their awareness of environmental concerns and the need for international controls. This is at least partly due to their early recognition as to the real cause of the "deaths" of their many thousands of their lakes; a recognition by their scientists that the cause was the severe air pollution generated over a great many decades by British industry which had been blown across the sea and over their country for many decades to fall as acid rain upon their lakes. The first Conference on Environment and Development was hosted in the Swedish capital Stockholm in 1972 under the auspices of the United Nations.

A well-known group of Western scientists who called themselves the "Club of Rome" published the book "Limits to Growth" (Meadows and Randers 2004). More international conferences and "summits" have since been held over the many past decades, one in Vancouver (1990) proceeding to Rio (1992). More recently, important UN-backed conferences focused on climate change were held in Kyoto (1997), Copenhagen (2009), and Cancun (2011). Rio was again the venue for the UN Conference on Environment and Development in 2012. Despite the much greater environmental awareness today, needed positive action based on a binding global agreement has been hard to come by. The world has still to be freed from continuing environmental damage and chemical contamination (Lear 2002). An international conference on climate change was held in Paris (France) at the end of 2015. A historic agreement was finally and unanimously reached there. However, it is still to be seen whether some of the industrialized and rapidly industrializing countries which are among the main culprits will limit and reduce their contributions to environmental degradation to the agreed extents and in accordance with the specified and agreed time frame. Such agreement is considered as being absolutely essential by the consensus of scientific opinion, if the world is to avoid a catastrophic escalation of the current environmental crises.

The world's intelligentsia has come to be much more aware today that so many of the climate-related disasters that now plague mankind much more frequently than before, such as severe storms, hurricanes, cyclones, tornados, floods, and droughts occurring in disparate locations on the surface of the earth and which were often assumed to be of purely natural origins, are in fact being caused by the agency of man himself. An American scholar may be seen to summarize the situation when he states that by the early 1990s people of most nations rich and poor began to personally experience unusually severe climatic and other environmental conditions such as heat waves, droughts, oil spills, pollution of the soils, and an unusual incidence of disease; that through the information revolution a larger proportion of the global population began to recognize that there indeed were threats to do with the environment which scientists had been predicting; that the world community began to see that the sacrifices to be made and the penalties to be paid would be far easier to bear than the prospect of the risk of total extinction; that because of the still remaining environmentally destructive residuals of the 1980s a cohesive global ecology movement committed to a unified course of action has not yet become a reality; that conservatism in economic and political agendas are the main obstructions to progress but that governments are being placed under considerable pressure through the activities of green parties and grass roots movements and activists; that this is happening all across Europe where these green parties are participating in the political processes and are winning ground; that the environmental advocacy societies have very greatly increased as compared to what was the situation in the 1970s; and that their memberships have vastly increased. He proceeds with his summary by saying that what was most encouraging of all was that:

> ...a recent Gallup poll indicates that 77 percent of adult Americans define themselves as pro-environment...Other areas of progressive activity in the green revolution have been related to the fields of philosophy and eco-psychology...(there is a)...widening philosophical and scientific conviction that, if the technological world persists in its seemingly irreversible expansion of consumerism and its measure of all success in terms of financial rewards alone, the end may be nearer than we think. (Wines 2008b)

As clearly recognized by such scholars of history in the mid-1960s as Lynn White, the problem seems to have much more to do with a current dominant philosophy that emphasizes anthropocentricity (White 1967). Such modern European philosophers as Arne Naess have made this point quite emphatically (Naess 1973). It has thus to be recognized that the roots of this situation may lie not in the disciplines of science, nor in faulty theories in the science of economics nor indeed in technology per se but reach much deeper into the philosophies and related ethics that underpin the cultural and legal frameworks in today's economically dominant societies. The question also arises as to whether the practices of scientific disciplines have their own codes of ethics which could be relied upon to restrain such extreme antisocial activities.

When "progress" is desired in a country, the societal processes that need to be set in place must necessarily be those that will lead to changes for the better. Such changes toward desired goals must essentially be defined by standards based on ethical concerns. Science cannot define them, as science in both the Classical and Modern versions is value-free and clearly has no built-in ethics. Nevertheless, science does provide humankind with theories and methodologies through which humans can strive to comprehend the world and the various phenomena experienced. Technology on the other hand can provide the means available for human interaction with the environment. Which particular phenomena is chosen to be explored and how, with what intent, and to what extent that interaction shall modify the environment are concerns which should be driven by societal needs and ethical concerns. Such pursuits are usually governed by culturally derived dictates specific to the particular society.

There is now a body of twentieth-century literature which has originated in the West based on disillusionment with the anthropocentric cultural view as it impacts on environmental issues. These writings, as discussed earlier, seem to have begun with the work of Rachel Carson in 1962. The disillusionment is clear and quite explicit. Another early example of this disillusionment from a different source is to be found in a lecture entitled "The Historical Roots of Our Ecological Crisis". It was delivered in 1966 to the American Association for the Advancement of Science by Lynn T. White and published in the following year (White 1967). One of his main assertions was that the industrial revolution was a turning point which reinforced the mentality of ethnocentricity that now prevails in the West; the mentality which had its origins in the entrenched cultural attitudes of medieval Europe and even before which now, according to him, invariably encourages environmental degradation.

Among the other important writers on the subject was the Norwegian philosopher Arne Naess who inspired and influenced the establishment of the "Deep Ecology" movement and whose collected works have been published in ten volumes (Drengson et al. 2011). Naess believed that there are no quick technological "fixes" to the gathering environmental crises. It is said that he used the term "shallow ecology" to refer to the then growing popularity, especially among the youth of that time, of superficial opposition to pollution and resource depletion within the industrialized countries. He was apparently of the view that it was necessary to penetrate into the underlying philosophy that permitted such environmental waste and degradation—hence, his promotion of what he termed "Deep Ecology". His own summarized views have been published (Naess 1973). In a useful collection of writings carefully edited into a book, one writer states that the platform at the base of Deep Ecology which contains claims that are both factual and normative about the relationship between humans and the natural world that surrounds them. He proceeds to say that the:

> …platform was intended as a description of a Deep Ecology social movement and a basis for a larger unity among all those who accept the importance of non-anthropocentrism and understand that this entails radical social change. (McLaughlin 1995)

It would do well for planners who are concerned with development theory among those in the LMICs to take serious cognizance of the writings of these recent Western thinkers and philosophers. Through the centuries, anthropocentrism with its many philosophic references to the roots of Western civilization in ancient Greece has become a dominant attitude in the Western world. However, non-anthropocentric philosophy is firmly entrenched in most of the Asian cultures, which has happened through many centuries of Hindu and Buddhist cultural influences. Some recent penetrations of these influences into Western intellectual circles are also evident. In regard to environmental concerns, notable Western scholars have seen Buddhism and Taoism as being such influences (Callicott 1987). The beginnings of some recent penetration of these influences into Western intellectual circles are also evident. In regard to current environmental concerns, Wines (2008c) and also the "Deep Ecology Platform" (Glasser et al. 2005) clearly acknowledge such influences.

It is good to note that in a book published recently in the United States, yet another group of American scholars, having reflected on the consequences of runaway global warming, find themselves compelled to convey that in their view:

> ...this is not merely a problem of rules and regulations that can be solved by a simple technological fix. It is at base a deeply moral problem that challenges our humanity and ethical integrity. The fact that billions of human beings on this planet, as well as countless forms of non-human life, have to bear the brunt of misery caused by the irresponsible behavior of a small number of nations – those that contribute most to global climate change – presents us with an ethical crisis that sears our conscience. This is particularly the case because the populations most likely to be hit hardest by the effects of global warming are those already living in poverty: the people of sub-Saharan Africa, where droughts will get worse; the inhabitants of Central and South Asia, where crop yields could drop by 30 percent; the populations whose island-nations would be swallowed by the sea; and the residents of the Asian mega-deltas where billions will be in danger of floods. Additionally, if temperatures rise 1.5 -2.5° C, a quarter of all plant and animal species are at risk of extinction. (Stanley et al. 2009)

A non-anthropocentric and explicitly Asian response to climate change in its ethical dimensions, with views presented by several Asian and Western notables, has been published recently in the United States (Stanley et al. 2009). If it has applicability to the countries of the West, it should have equal and perhaps even more relevance to all industrialized and rapidly industrializing countries in Asia. It must therefore be observed as mentioned at the outset here that Japan an Asian country did adopt and follow the Western path to industrialization. Today, India and China are two of the three very large and rapidly industrializing countries that are on the same path to high growth despite serious externalities. These Asian countries, Japan, India, and China have strong philosophic affiliations to a non-anthropocentric culture. Regardless of whatever justifications that may be proffered by their respective captains of industry and some of their political leaders, these countries are in danger of accelerating their respective economic advancements in unsustainable ways. If such were to happen, it would clearly be a grave misfortune for the world at large. It would also be a poor reflection on Asian scientists, policy planners, advisor, and indeed their modern philosophers for not striving hard enough to find appropriate and politically acceptable paths to rapid national progress consonant with their great cultural heritage.

References

Callicott JB (1987) Conceptual resources for environmental ethics in Asian traditions of thought: a propaedeutic. In: Philosophy east and west, vol 37. Environmental Ethics, University of Hawai'i Press, Honolulu, pp 115–130

Carson R (1962a) Silent spring. Houghton Mifflin, New York

References

Carson R (1962b) Silent spring. Houghton Mifflin, New York, p 297

Drengson A, Devall B, Schroll MA (2011) The deep ecology movement: origins, development, and future prospects. Int J Transpers Stud 1–117

Glasser H, Drengson A, Devall B, Sessions G (eds) (2005) The selected works of Arne Naess. Foundation for Deep Ecology, Sausalito, CA

Lear L (2002) Introduction. In: Carson (ed) Silent spring, New edition. Mariner, New York, p xviii (1962)

Meadows D, Randers J (2004) Limits to growth. Chelsea Green Publishing, White River Junction, Vermont

McLaughlin A (1995) In: Sessions G (ed) Deep ecology for the 21st century. Shambhala, Boston, MA

Naess A (1973) The shallow and deep, long range ecology movements: a summary. Inq Interdiscip J Philos J 16:95–100

Stanley J, Loy DRL, Dorje D (eds) (2009) A Buddhist approach to the climate emergency. Wisdom Publications, Boston, MA, pp 161, 162

Switch-Asia (2015–2017) A pilot project being funded by the European Union through the Ministry of Mahaweli Development and Environment, Colombo, Sri Lanka

White LT Jr (1967) The historical roots of our ecological crisis. Sci J 155:1203–1207 (USA)

Wines J (2008a) Green architecture. Taschen, Cologne, pp 25, 26

Wines J (2008b) Green architecture. Taschen, Cologne, pp 27, 28

Wines J (2008c) Green architecture. Taschen, Cologne, pp 56, 57

Chapter 4
Climate Change: The Scientific Consensus

Abstract Following the Rio Summit of 1992, two international organizations namely the Intergovernmental Panel on Climate Change (IPCC) and the UN Framework Convention on Climate Change (UNFCCC) were empowered to perform special tasks. The former was to gather scientific information on climate change and the latter to facilitate consensus among countries to stabilize greenhouse gases (GHGs) in the atmosphere so as not to further aggravate global warming. Carbon dioxide constitutes about 75% of the GHGs, the rest being composed of three other types of gases. It is now well recognized that no country will be immune from the impacts of climate change. The most seriously affected will be the LMICs. Sea level rise will impact adversely upon small islands and river-delta regions. Increases in tropical cyclones and in drought conditions in arid areas of the tropical LMICs will be experienced frequently. Major flooding can be expected with greater frequency which will not only affect food supply but also cause disease epidemics. Increased acidification of ocean waters will cause damage to marine life and consequently to livelihoods and food supply. Furthermore, there would be large shocks to agriculture to even disrupt and dislocate populations. It has taken all of 24 years and many major international conferences for the countries of the world to voluntarily come to an accord as to their respective commitments to reduce pollution so as to diminish global warming and climate change. Whether this accord will be binding on all is still to be seen.

Preamble

There have been several international conferences where greenhouse gas emissions and global warming have been discussed as being the integral causative factors of climate change. This series of conferences started with the Rio Earth Summit of 1992 and followed by other conferences, e.g., at Copenhagen in 2009, the Cancun Conference in Mexico in 2010, the Kyoto conference with its protocol defined and arrived at in Japan in 2011, and thereafter, in Paris in 2015 where an accord was reached. Whether the commitments made in Paris will be honored by all is still to be seen. But greenhouse gas emissions and global warming have come to be recognized much more as critical issues worldwide.

Following the Rio Summit of 1992 which took into account the gravity of climate change confronting humanity, two international organizations were brought together for a specific identified purpose. The organizations were the World Meteorological Organization (WMO) and an arm of the United Nations and the UN Environmental Programme (UNEP). They were expected to initiate the establishment of the Intergovernmental Panel on Climate Change (IPCC) and the UN Framework Convention on Climate Change (UNFCCC), which they did. The mandate of the former (WMO) was to gather the scientific information available on climate change and to assess the impact of climate change and prepare necessary strategies to respond and arrest the worsening of the crisis. The latter (the UNFCCC) was expected to facilitate consensus among the countries to achieve stability in the concentrations of greenhouse gases in the atmosphere at a level that would not aggravate further global warming (Ratnasiri 2011).

The Scientists' Views

Based on scientific opinion, international agencies have consistently taken the position that the causes of global warming and climate change are of human origin. One such agency, the IPCC, is quite categorical that the earth's climate system is warming especially since the 1950s, that the cause is mainly attributable to greenhouse gas emissions through human activity, which as such is unprecedented (IPCC 2014a, b, c). Thus, **climate change** is frequently defined as "Change of climate which is attributed directly or indirectly to human activity that alters the composition of the global atmosphere and which is in addition to natural climate variability observed over comparable time periods" and **global warming** is generally defined as "an increase in the earth's atmospheric and oceanic temperatures widely predicted to occur due to an increase in the greenhouse effect resulting especially from pollution". Nevertheless, there has been a view prevalent for some time among some groups of people, even after clear scientific evidence has been published and made available, which denies that climate change is of human causation. This view is also held by some important political voices in the United States. In this context, it would be useful to recognize the consensus in regard to "climate change" that exists among some of the most prominent scientific organizations within the United States itself. This consensus may be readily seen from the following quotations:

> The scientific evidence is clear: global climate change caused by human activities is occurring now, and it is a growing threat to society. (AAAS 2006)

> Comprehensive scientific assessments of our current and potential future climates clearly indicate that climate change is real, largely attributable to emissions from human activities, and potentially a very serious problem. (ACS 2004)

Human-induced climate change requires urgent action. Humanity is the major influence on the global climate change observed over the past 50 years. Rapid societal responses can significantly lessen negative outcomes. (AGU 2013)

Our AMA … supports the findings of the Intergovernmental Panel on Climate Change's fourth assessment report and concurs with the scientific consensus that the Earth is undergoing adverse global climate change and that anthropogenic contributions are significant. (AMA 2013)

It is clear from extensive scientific evidence that the dominant cause of the rapid change in climate of the past half century is human-induced increases in the amount of atmospheric greenhouse gases, including carbon dioxide (CO2), chlorofluorocarbons, methane, and nitrous oxide. (AMS 2012)

The evidence is incontrovertible: Global warming is occurring. If no mitigating actions are taken, significant disruptions in the Earth's physical and ecological systems, social systems, security and human health are likely to occur. We must reduce emissions of greenhouse gases beginning now. (APS 2007)

The Geological Society of America (GSA) concurs with assessments by the National Academies of Science (2005), the National Research Council, and the Intergovernmental Panel on Climate Change that global climate has warmed and that human activities (mainly greenhouse-gas emissions) account for most of the warming since the middle 1900s. (GSA 2010)

The scientific understanding of climate change is now sufficiently clear to justify taking steps to reduce the amount of greenhouse gases in the atmosphere. (USNAS 2005)

The global warming of the past 50 years is due primarily to human-induced increases in heat-trapping gases. Human 'fingerprints' also have been identified in many other aspects of the climate system, including changes in ocean heat content, precipitation, atmospheric moisture, and Arctic sea ice. (USGCRP 2009)

In its Fifth Assessment Report of the IPCC a group of 1,300 independent scientific experts from countries all over the world under the auspices of the United Nations, concluded there is a more than 95% probability that human activities over the past 50 years have warmed our planet. The industrial activities that our modern civilization depends upon have raised atmospheric carbon dioxide levels from 280 parts per million to 400 parts per million in the last 150 years. The panel also concluded that there is a better than 95% probability that human-produced greenhouse gases such as carbon dioxide, methane, and nitrous oxide have caused much of the observed increase in earth's temperatures over the past 50 years (IPCC 2014a, b, c).

The Greenhouse Effect

The heat rays from the sun can be absorbed or reflected by the earth depending on the color and texture of the receiving surface. When absorbed, that heat can be released into the earth's atmosphere. This heat energy can be absorbed by such gases in the atmosphere as water vapor, carbon dioxide, methane, nitrous oxide, and ozone which are known as "greenhouse gases" (GHGs). These GHGs act as a blanket and prevent the loss of this heat into space thus making the earth warmer than it would be otherwise. There have been emissions of these gases into the atmosphere over long periods in the history of the earth. However, since the Industrial Revolution in the late eighteenth century, there has been a rapid and intensive buildup of GHGs in the atmosphere especially through the burning of fossil fuels and biomass in a large scale. There are also a range of gases called fluorinated gases ("F-gases") which are emitted in large quantities in recent times which can remain in the atmosphere even for centuries. These add to the greenhouse effect. The sources and proportions of the key greenhouse gases at the global scale are as follows:

Carbon dioxide (CO_2): The combustion of fossil fuels is the main source which creates carbon dioxide. Deforestation and land clearing for agriculture can also produce this gas (Approx. 65%).

Methane (CH_4): The burning of biomass and some agricultural activities produces methane gas (Approx. 16%).

Nitrous oxide (N_2O): The combustion of fossil fuels and some agricultural activities such as the use of chemical fertilizer result in the production of nitrous oxide (Approx. 06%).

Fluorinated gases (F-gases): Refrigeration, air-conditioning, some consumer products, and industrial activities produce these F-gases (Approx. 02%) (IPCC 2014a, b, c).

A Report Commissioned by the World Bank

A report (PICIR 2012a, b, c) prepared for the World Bank by an independent agency known as the "Potsdam Institute for Climate Impact Research" states as follows: that all nations will be impacted by climate change and that the severity of its impacts will inherently be unequal across those nations with the worst affected being the poorest countries which have the least capacity (institutional, scientific and technical) to cope and adapt. The report proceeds to mention the following examples:

> Even though absolute warming will be largest in high latitudes, the warming that will occur in the tropics is larger when compared to the historical range of temperature and extremes to which human and natural ecosystems have adapted and coped; The projected emergence of unprecedented high-temperature extremes in the tropics will consequently lead to significantly larger impacts on agriculture and ecosystems; Sea-level rise is likely to be 15 to 20 percent larger in the tropics than the global mean; Increases in tropical cyclone intensity are likely to be felt disproportionately in low-latitude regions; and, Increasing aridity and drought are likely to increase substantially in many developing country regions located in tropical and subtropical areas. (PICIR, Executive Summary p. xiii)

The report goes on to say that one of the very adverse consequences of having a high concentration of carbon dioxide in the atmosphere is that some of the gas dissolves in the oceans resulting in acidification; and that it has been observed that ocean acidity is much greater now than it was in the preindustrial period; and also that there is now much evidence of the adverse impact of acidification on marine life, organism, and ecosystems (PICIR, Executive Summary p. xv).

The same report continues to discuss the subject in the context of a debate as to what level of global warming could be tolerable and in what period of time this level should be reached. In this context, the report proceeds to state that a 4 °C increase in the worldwide temperature

> ...is likely to be one in which communities, cities and countries would experience severe disruptions, damage, and dislocation, with many of these risks spread unequally. It is likely that the poor will suffer most and the global community could become more fractured, and unequal than today...The observed and projected rates of change in ocean acidity over the ...(i.e. 21st)... century appear to be unparalleled in Earth's history. Large-scale extreme events, such as major floods that interfere with food production, could also induce nutritional deficits and the increased incidence of epidemic diseases. Flooding can introduce contaminants and diseases into healthy water supplies and increase the incidence of diarrheal and respiratory illnesses. The effects of climate change on agricultural production may exacerbate under-nutrition and malnutrition in many regions—already major contributors to child mortality in developing countries. Whilst economic growth is projected to significantly reduce childhood stunting, climate change is projected to reverse these gains in a number of regions: substantial increases in stunting due to malnutrition are projected to occur with...(an increase of)...warming of 2°C to 2.5°C, especially in Sub-Saharan Africa and South Asia, and this is likely to get...(much worse an increase of 4°C)... Despite significant efforts to improve health services ...significant additional impacts on poverty levels and human health are expected. Changes in temperature, precipitation rates, and humidity influence vector-borne diseases... "The projected impacts on water availability, ecosystems, agriculture, and human health could lead to large-scale displacement of populations and have adverse consequences for human security and economic and trade systems..." (PICIR, Executive Summary, p. xvii)

Discussing rising sea levels and coastal inundation, that report points to the following likely conclusions if there is global warming to the extent of 4 °C: that by the year 2100 the sea level may rise somewhere between 0.5 and 1.0 m; that the rise will be higher in the tropics and lower in higher latitudes; that the ocean waters will gravitate toward the equator; that cities in such countries as Mozambique, Madagascar, Mexico, Venezuela, India, Bangladesh, Indonesia, the Philippines, and Vietnam will be highly vulnerable; and that there would be severe consequences when cyclones and loss of reefs due to acidification and increases in temperature due to increased warming add to sea level rise in river deltas and small island states.

The same report discusses the disruptions and displacement of populations that are likely to occur due to impacts of climate change on water availability; ecosystems; agriculture; human health; and trade systems. The report also suggests that with increases in global mean temperature the total impact would be compounded; that extreme temperatures across many regions along with substantial pressure on water resources and changes in the hydrological cycle could deliver a large shock to agriculture and result in a serious impact on human health and livelihoods; that atoll countries would experience difficulty in adapting and could suffer malnutrition and other health issues; that the available health systems would be unable to cope and that dislocation would be forced upon them; and that the adverse impacts of global warming and sea level rise will spread very unequally across the world with the poor suffering the most. The report concludes that global warming of even 4 °C by the year 2100 should be avoided at all costs (PICIR 2012a, b, c).

Some Benefited Nations

According to a responsible synthesis report, the last 30 years has been the warmest in past 1400 years and that most of this heat energy has been stored in the oceans (IPCC 2014a, b, c). The Arctic region is said to contain a considerable extent of the world's undiscovered reserves of oil and natural gas. The estimates are 13 and 30%, respectively. Global warming and the consequent melting of icebergs will make these reserves far more accessible. Also, shipping through the Arctic seas will be far more feasible. While the adversities of climate change will seriously impact upon the tropical regions which contain most of the LMICs, there will be a few nations which have some of their territories in the Arctic region stand to reap considerable benefits. These nations include Russia, Canada, Norway, and the United States. The icy wasteland that has been Greenland is likely to dramatically change. It is a self-governing territory of Denmark who may also become a beneficiary of climate change in the not too distant future (Chilcoat 2014).

The facts and warnings have been presented by responsible and concerned scientists over all of 24 years since the Rio Summit of 1992 and many other subsequent major international conferences. These major efforts have been made to enable the polluting countries of the world to agree upon some basic commitments for each to reduce their pollution so as to diminish global warming and climate change. It is clearly apparent to all who are willing to accept the consensus of scientific opinion that the most severe impacts are on the LMICs of the tropics and that the nearest to an acceptable agreement was reached at the Paris Accord of 2016. However, the disappointing fact is that there is still no certainty that all the worst polluting countries will honor that accord. In this context, it may be useful to see how and why the Montreal Protocol became a success story.

The Montreal Protocol

The conference held in Montreal in 1987 concerned the ozone layer which is positioned about 15–30 km above the earth's surface. It forms a blanket around the planet which was in the past substantially reducing the penetration of high-frequency ultraviolet (UV) solar radiation from reaching the earth. It is known that excessive doses of these UV rays can cause skin cancer and cataracts in humans and also be harmful to other forms of life. Since around the 1970s, there were scientists who were concerned that the ozone layer could be damaged by chlorofluorocarbons (CFCs). These synthetic chemicals which were being commonly used in refrigerants and hairsprays can persist for decades and rise into the upper atmosphere to interact with ozone which is composed of unstable molecules. A British Antarctic Survey discovered in 1985 a large hole in the ozone layer over Antarctica. This discovery shocked the scientific world and led to a major UN-sponsored conference in 1987 which was held in Montreal. A very successful pact was reached which was referred to as the "Montreal Protocol". It was aimed at restoring the ozone layer through the phasing out of the use of CFCs. This is said to be the very first UN treaty which surprisingly reached unanimous ratification. Its implementation has resulted in an improvement in the ozone layer which is now expected to return to the status it had in the 1950s (Handwerk 2010).

In the mid-1980s when the hole in the ozone layer was being discovered, there were many cases of skin cancer diagnosed especially in the West. UV radiation as being a probable causative factor was well understood. The need to deal with ozone depletion as an urgent requirement in the Western world was obvious to their relevant medical and other scientific personnel (Study 2016). The promptitude with which the historic accord was reached at Montreal in 1987 and meaningful action taken thereafter to deal with ozone depletion is in stark contrast with the prolonged delays in reaching some consensus on urgently needed action in respect of climate change. Why there should be such a contrast is a matter to be pondered.

To conclude, it may be noted that there has been an unprecedented rate of global warming especially since the 1950s. Many international conferences have been held during the last quarter century to discuss and find ways of dealing with the adversities of climate change. While human causation is clearly recognized by the scientific community, influential political voices in at least one polluting country are in denial. There are a few nations who have territories within the Arctic region who may share some benefits. Nevertheless, it is recognized that, in the main, all countries will be adversely affected by climate change with the most serious impacts likely to be experienced in the tropical LMICs. An international consensus has finally been reached after deliberations over many years on the strategy needed to deal with the serious adversities of climate change. However, there is at present no unanimous commitment to implement remedial action.

References

AAAS (2006) Board statement on climate change. American Association for the Advancement of Science. www.aaas.org/sites/default/files/migrate/uploads/aaas_climate_statement.pdf. Accessed 17 July 2017

ACS (2004) Public policy statement: climate change. American Chemical Society. https://www.acs.org/content/acs/en/policy/publicpolicies/sustainability/globalclimatechange.html. Accessed 17 July 2017

AGU (2013) Human-induced climate change requires urgent action. American Geophysical Union. http://sciencepolicy.agu.org/files/2013/07/AGU-Climate-Change-Position-Statement_August-2013.pdf. Accessed 17 July 2017

AMA (2013) Global climate change and human health. American Medical Association. https://assets.ama-assn.org/sub/meeting/documents/i16-resolution-924.pdf. Accessed 17 July 2017

AMS (2012) Climate change. Information Statement of the American Meteorological Society. https://www.ametsoc.org/ams/index.cfm/about-ams/ams-statements/statements-of-the-ams-in-force/climate-change/. Accessed 17 July 2017

APS (2007) National policy on climate change. American Physical Society. https://www.aps.org/policy/statements/15_3.cfm. Accessed 17 July 2017

Chilcoat C (2014) Who stands to benefit from climate change? http://oilprice.com/The-Environment/Global-Warming/Who-Stands-To-Benefit-From-Climate-Change.html. Accessed 17 July 2017

GSA (2010) Position statement on climate change. The Geological Society of America. https://www.geosociety.org/gsa/positions/position10.aspx. Accessed 17 July 2017

Handwerk B (2010) Whatever happened to the ozone hole? http://news.nationalgeographic.com/news/2010/05/100505-science-environment-ozone-hole-25-years/. Accessed 17 July 2017

IPCC (2014) Mitigation of climate change. Intergovernmental Panel on Climate Change. https://www.ipcc.ch/report/ar5/wg3/. Accessed 17 July 2017

IPCC (2014) Climate change 2014 synthesis report. Summary. https://www.ipcc.ch/pdf/assessment-report/ar5/syr/AR5_SYR_FINAL_SPM.pdf. Accessed 17 July 2017

IPCC (2014) Fifth assessment report: summary for Policymakers. https://www.ipcc.ch/pdf/assessment-report/ar5/wg3/ipcc_wg3_ar5_summary-for-policymakers.pdf. Accessed 17 July 2017

PICIR (2012) Turn down the heat. A Report for the World Bank by the Potsdam Institute for Climate Impact Research and Climate Analytics. World Bank. http://documents.worldbank.org/curated/en/865571468149107611/pdf/NonAsciiFileName0.pdf. Accessed 17 July 2017

PICIR (2012) Executive summary, p. xv. Turn down the heat. A Report for the World Bank by the Potsdam Institute for Climate Impact Research and Climate Analytics. World Bank. http://documents.worldbank.org/curated/en/865571468149107611/pdf/NonAsciiFileName0.pdf. Accessed 17 July 2017

PICIR (2012) Executive summary, p. xvii. Turn down the heat. A Report for the World Bank by the Potsdam Institute for Climate Impact Research and Climate Analytics. World Bank. http://documents.worldbank.org/curated/en/865571468149107611/pdf/NonAsciiFileName0.pdf. Accessed 17 July 2017

Ratnasiri N (2011) Challenge of climate change. National Science Foundation, Sri Lanka Journal J 39(2):95–96

Study (2016) American Academy of Dermatology (July Issue)

USGCRP (2009) Global climate change impacts in the United States. US Global Change Research Program. https://nca2009.globalchange.gov/. Accessed 17 July 2017

USNAS (2005) Understanding and responding to climate change. US National Academy of Sciences

Chapter 5
Science, Ethics, and Development

Abstract During the Renaissance, unlike in the previous era in European history, the individualistic pursuit of knowledge and economic power overrode the moral law in human conduct. It was a secular and dynamic age which eventually led some countries to the industrial revolution. In the latter part of that period, scientific and professional disciplines began to develop their own codes of conduct. However, there was no strong overarching ethical code that could govern the whole scientific endeavor. Although technology has been used in warfare throughout history, industrialized production begun in the First World War greatly escalated during the Second World War. The manufacture of weapons of mass destruction led military technology into a much more dangerous level. Despite the horrors of nuclear weapons witnessed at the end of the latter war, an alarming arms race began during the "Cold War" that followed between the "Western Powers" and the "Eastern Bloc". Far more dangerous weapons were developed and stockpiled by both sides. The participating scientists had no code of ethics strong enough to resist their own bellicose politicians. A similar ethical situation confronts scientists and planners in dealing with the externalities of economic growth in some of today's industrialized countries. No less a daunting task is faced by the LMICs with the prospect only of grossly iniquitous progress being achieved and that too amidst environmental crises. If impending disasters are to be averted and genuine prosperity is to be seriously sought to benefit all, scientists and planners should have major parts to play.

Preamble

The InterAcademy Council (IAC) was created by the world's prominent science academies in the year 2000. It was to mobilize the best scientists and engineers worldwide to provide high-quality advice to international bodies and other institutions. The IAC recognized from the outset that all nations and societies will

---

Based on my Kotegoda Memorial Oration delivered in 2002 at the invitation of the Sri Lanka Association for the Advancement of Science.

© Springer Nature Singapore Pte Ltd. 2018
K. L. Gunaratna, *Towards Equitable Progress*, South Asia Economic and Policy Studies, https://doi.org/10.1007/978-981-10-8923-7_5

continue to face many major challenges that would require the application of science and technology for their resolution. They moved soon to appoint a study panel of eminent scientists to report on promoting Science and technology worldwide to confront the challenges of the twenty-first century (Alberts and Mehta 2003). The Study Panel's report as finalized after a thorough and appropriate external review process was received and strongly endorsed by the original governing scientific body now known as the "Global Network of Science Academies". In doing so, the heads of the latter Global Network stated inter alia that:

> scientific and technological capabilities must become integral to all nations if humanity is to confront effectively the significant challenges of the 21st Century. (Quere and Zhu 2003)

Scientific opinion at the highest levels would thus appear to be quite clear that if the low- and middle-income countries (LMICs) are to progress, they would require a strong commitment to science and technology in their planning efforts aimed at development.

When countries advance through the process that has come to be known as economic development, there invariably are externalities. Whether their progress, generally defined by indices of economic growth, will be equitable and sustainable from the environmental standpoint will depend at least partly on ethical concerns and on decisions as to the kind of technology utilized for production processes and energy supplies; and partly on whether the likely rising internal demand for consumption goods can be maintained at modest levels, if that is at all possible. Most industries under private or public ownership and management would not be concerned by the externalities and will quite naturally aim to maximize their profits. Also, most governments would prefer to see increased economic growth even at the real risk of some environmental damage, especially if there is an insistent popular demand for more consumption in the respective countries. There are also the spatial concerns as to where within these countries development will take place; which areas will be adversely affected by environmental degradation; where prosperity will or will not result; and which population segments will or will not benefit. Thus, the ethical issues along with environmental sustainability have to be treated as part and parcel of the externalities of development. It should therefore be clear that the environmental and ethical issues are invariably intertwined.

Governance in the LMICs and as indeed elsewhere is generally in the hands of political leaders who come to be present in those countries through democratic means or otherwise. It must, however, also be recognized that no efficient leadership concerned with their own political survival can be expected to act in ways contrary to the demands made by the interests they actually represent. These interests usually expect quick returns in the form of tangible short-term benefits to political constituents. They may also be totally unconcerned with, and sometimes even grossly ignorant of the externalities, especially about the need for long-term environmental sustainability. Such has been the case even in some of the so-called "advanced" industrialized countries. It must therefore be recognized that reliance cannot be placed on political leaderships alone to ensure equity and environmental safeguards, unless there is sufficient pressure brought to bear upon them through their respective constituencies. But, even when these constituencies have been educated and made aware of the facts, they too may not respond contrary to their own short-term interests unless otherwise impelled to respond. Even where the respective cultural contexts embody the needed ethical values, an alternative knowledgeable leadership responsive to the externalities and ethical concerns is required. Such a leadership has invariably to be from among the scientific and professional personnel, their governing institutions, and nongovernmental organizations which are strong enough to support the cause of equity and environmental protection, even at the expense of some economic growth.

This chapter of the book is primarily concerned with the interaction between science and ethics among professionals dealing with development as may be applicable in the LMICs and particularly in South Asia. It strives to carefully explore the epistemology of science. That is to see if there are or whether there should be any usable codes of ethics embedded in the technologies related scientific disciplines and professional bodies which may be brought to bear on their respective memberships so that they may assume an alternative leadership position in the interest of equity and environmental sustainability.

Some Views from South Asia

The LMICs are mostly those that were under colonial subjugation and gained independence in the middle and latter half of the twentieth century. The teaching of Science and professional education were not given much priority in those countries during colonial rule. Asian scientists who sought post-graduate and professional studies during the past century generally did so in the West. Consequently, they also imbibed a strong dose of Western culture. Thus, Western ethical standards and codes of professional conduct became quite intelligible and acceptable to them. One of these scientists states that:

> Science is an ethical or a moral construct, and therefore the practice of science is ethical per se…The scientific attitude has such a large ethical and moral element that one might say that the scientific attitude is, in its entirety, predicated on ethics. (Modder 1998)

This senior scientist discusses the process that underlies scientific inquiry which he traces from its Galilean origins, through the inductive methodology introduced by Francis Bacon, through modifications, and reformulations in consequence of the work of David Hume and by Karl Popper. The process itself, he believes, has a great many instances where ethical conduct is essential. He speaks of the "soft" virtues of kindness, love, and compassion, which he considers much less relevant to the scientist's work. He goes on to speak about the "hard" characteristics and virtues that scientists must have. These according to him should include hard-headedness, pragmatism and common sense, honesty and integrity, sense of purpose, application, and diligence. He goes further to include a kind of monasticism as a required virtue stating that a scientist should identify with his science in near-mystical fashion. He quotes the Russian Physiologist, Pavlov, as saying that Science demands from a man all his life. It is clear that this scientist, through his formal education and sensitization to Western cultural values, wide reading, and shear passion for his discipline, has assimilated and developed for himself a comprehensive ethic and a code of conduct relating to the practice of his profession. It is a self-imposed code and not one that has been made explicit and mandatory by any external professional body. The quoted scientist's views, expressed succinctly and with clarity, represent as good an example as one could find anywhere of an optimistic view of ethics in Science.

A very different view of science and ethics is presented by another senior scientist and medical educator. He is far from optimistic when he says:

> The practice of science has many areas of ethical concern...The situation is, universally bad enough to warrant the publication of books on fraud in science... complex issues occur in medicine. There is much in the Hippocratic corpus...which deals with these but it was with the tragic experimentation on prisoners in World War II and subsequent universalisation of health concerns that a redefinition of ethical norms acquired urgency. Many declarations and codes have thus been formulated...We have had a gradual diffusion of Western ethical ideas especially through colonialism. In the scientific and medical fields, this influence has been more profound because the science and medicine we practice are of Western origin. It seems to me that our consequent Western orientation has been paralleled by an ignorance of our own cultural heritage in this area. I think it is time now, therefore, to reconsider our orientation in medical ethics.... (Arsecularatne 1999a)

This scientist proposes that in Asia in general and South Asia in particular, there is a need to consider that Science in Asia should be bolstered by a more indigenous Asian system of ethics. He presents six arguments to justify his position, one of which states that there is a conflict between the indigenous morality of the very predominant majority, on the one hand, and the Western value system, on the other hand. He believes that there is a cultural resistance to the

> ideas introduced solely through the essentially Western model of medical ethics which is currently taught and which might appear alien to their own cultural values...our justification for a base of South Asian views in biomedical ethics, lies in their cultural relevance, their capability for handling 'situation ethics' and their greater focus on the community than on the individual. (Arsecularatne 1999b)

The two sets of views discussed above appear at first glance to be divergent. It must, however, be observed that the first author's views were presented as a set of personal beliefs culled from a broad education involving close contact with the West and intensive scientific endeavor over a lifetime. The second author's presentation was based on an equally rigorous and very similar background of scientific education and involvement but concerned primarily a dilemma in educating a younger generation of scientists—particularly those less exposed directly to the West and in a complex sociopolitical context of cultural change in South Asia. Seen in this light, both sets of views may be correct.

There is a third point of view which seems important to the discussion here. The view which comes from the West is evident from Aldous Huxley's novel "Island" (1962). He, as an educated dissident, is seen to recommend an attitude toward science and ethics as practiced in a fictitious tropical island called "Pala" located somewhere in the Indian Ocean. In this "utopia", English and Palanese a fictitious Sanskrit-based language are both spoken by all and Tantric Buddhism is the majority religion. Among the many aspects highlighted are a very pragmatic science policy, science education, and two categories of ethics. One category involves codes of conduct that are "specific" to particular professional disciplines and the other is "general" in that it contains a broad code of ethics, which is universally applicable to all professions. Huxley found it necessary to write a book to present his utopian vision. This points clearly to the recognition at least by concerned and educated personalities that all is not well with ethics in science as practiced either in the West or in Asia. Also, clearly recognized by at least a few eminent persons with Huxley among them is that a "marriage" between Western science and an Asian ethic is within the realm of possibility.

Science in the West

Science is manifest today in two versions which are generally referred to as "Classical Science" and "Modern Science". The accepted view is that Classical Science has its roots in the intellectual discourse in Europe in the "Age of Humanism", i.e., during the "European Renaissance". Science was an integral part of an epistemology which arose in that age for whatever reason, and broke with the Medieval Christian Church. Those European intellectuals who at that time professed and pursued Science as a system of knowledge sought and found roots for their views and attitudes not in their immediately preceding Medieval period of their history. Their thinking was clearly inspired by the works and pagan philosophies of ancient Greece and Rome. Forgotten treatises were rediscovered, and theories and principles were adopted from pre-Christian antiquity. The ancient Greek and Roman civilizations became their sources for historical reference and validation. The works of Euclid, Pythagoras, Hippocrates, and Vitruvius are merely a few examples that may be cited.

The fragments of knowledge that arose in Classical Science began to be systemized in the sixteenth and seventeenth centuries. The works of the English philosopher Francis Bacon (1561–1626) and the French mathematician and philosopher Rene Descartes (1596–1650) were important in this systematization. In the course of time, the various disparate pieces of scientific inquiry became parts of an apparently consistent and mutually reinforcing body of knowledge. The highly visible technological advances based on science that accompanied the Industrial Revolution in the West strengthened the belief in the value of science. Thus, at the beginning of the twentieth century, Classical Science offered a formidable body of literature consisting of a great many pieces of knowledge on life form and physical reality, from the invisibly minute to the cosmos.

The publication of three scientific papers by Albert Einstein in the period 1905–1907 caused a revolution in science. The "Theory of Relativity" which emerged with these published papers marks the beginning of a new epistemology in scientific thought in the West and the birth of Modern Science. This apparently new way of thinking also had its own lineage. The influence of philosophical writings particularly of Ernst Mach the Austrian Physicist (1838–1916) and David Hume the Scottish Philosopher (1711–1776) on Einstein's work is generally recognized among knowledgeable persons in this field of inquiry. Einstein's own impact on the Galilei–Newtonian Physics, a cornerstone of Classical Science, was powerful. It must, however, be observed that despite the passage of almost a century, the shock waves from the newer thinking have perhaps been felt only weakly in a few of the other scientific disciplines.

The European colonial powers exported Classical Science though only to a limited extent to their dependencies in Asia during the nineteenth and early twentieth centuries. Science was presented as a product of European origin, developed, and perfected in the West. It was this brand of science that was taught in European schools and later adopted in the schools curricula of the Asian colonies. This euro-centric view of science was of course not entirely correct. It has to be observed that there were many important Asian influences upon Classical Science, starting even during the early period of the European Renaissance. These influences originally reached Europe through the trade routes from India and China via the Middle East or Central Asia. Consider, for example, the subject of Mathematics, which is not only important by itself but is seen to be necessary to pursue the study of many other scientific subjects. Of the subdisciplines of Mathematics probably only Euclidean Geometry has a purely European lineage originating in classical antiquity. Furthermore, Europe had only the Roman Numeral System which was very primitive. The concept of "zero", a symbol for "nothing", originated in India and caused a great advance in Mathematics the world over. The resulting numeral system, which is what is used today, reached Europe via the Arabs. Algebra and much of Astronomy also reached the West from the East. It may thus be asserted that an important part of the sciences as found in Western Classical Science had Asian origins and strong subsequent influences.

Asian influences were not confined to the early development period of Science. Modern Science too is said to contain more than a trace of Asian influence. The concepts of "matter", "space", and "time" in Einstein's early work were extremely different from those in the then established Newtonian school of scientific thought. The influence of the views of Hume and Mach on Einstein on his Special Theory of Relativity has been noted. The similarities in Mach's published writings on "perception" (1886) with the position taken in the Theravada tradition of Buddhism have been commented upon. Blackmore (1972) devotes a chapter of his book on Mach to "Mach and Buddhism". Several other Western scholars (e.g., McFarlane 2002) have traced similarities and parallels in thinking between Einstein and the Buddha.

Ethics in Science

The early Renaissance was associated with the growth of mercantilism in Europe and the rise to pre-eminent power of the Italian "merchant princes". They, as for example the Sforza and the Medici families patronized the men of genius, in contrast to the sole control that the Church had over the intelligentsia in the previous Medieval age. The rules of commerce, the individualistic quest for economic power and the pursuit of knowledge and beauty, overrode the moral law in human conduct. It was indeed a secular age where the achievement of the individual over even that of the community was recognized and appreciated (Pevsner 1963). The Scholastic tradition of the previous age had within it a close inter-relationship between the pursuit of knowledge and spirituality. Ethical norms in the conduct of human affairs were an integral part of that tradition (Coomaraswamy 1956).

The new epistemology of the early Renaissance saw knowledge being pursued with no apparent connection to the quest for spirituality. There was a clear breach between science and the notion of ethical conduct that had prevailed in the preceding period. It may be recalled that Niccolo Machiavelli (1469–1527) was of that time. He rose to the position of an adviser to the powerful Florentine government at the young age of 30. The book he is famous for, "The Prince" (Machiavelli 1513), provides a good insight into the worldly ethics and the lack of a higher moral order in the quest for knowledge during that age.

It is not that the people of Europe during the Renaissance rejected Christianity. The rejection was of some of the notions of the Medieval Church and of the Church's control over knowledge. The new age celebrated the individual and individualistic achievement in the pursuit of knowledge and beauty. All this was in stark contrast to the perceptions and beliefs of the preceding age. Soon, the Church itself found it useful and appropriate to join the merchant princes in recognizing the great men of that age. The effort was not necessarily to induct them into the clergy, but to win them over to work for the Church in their personal capacities. Indeed, the Church became one of the major patrons and benefactors of many of the Renaissance men of genius. There would have been little choice for the Church but to begin a process of assimilating some of the new ideas of these men. This is clearly borne out in the work of great Architects who were commissioned to design the Renaissance churches in the city-states of Italy. The prototypical origins of the Renaissance Church are the pre-Christian temples of ancient Greece and Rome. Their geometry was Euclidean. Their philosophy was based on Plato. The visual historical references were to Vitruvius, that Roman Architect and writer whose life and work was contemporaneous with the times of the Caesars, Julius, and Augustus. There was a total rejection of even the wonderful and stupendous ecclesiastical architecture of the Medieval age. Notions of the ideal architectural form for a church as aesthetically befitting a "House of God" are quite remarkable (Wittkower 1962: 3–27). There is a close parallel between these thoughts when seen as a microcosm of the universe and when compared with the Newtonian macrocosmic view. Science continued to thrive and progress with no special links to morality and a higher order of ethics.

The consolidating impact of the Industrial Revolution on Science has already been mentioned. By the eighteenth and nineteenth centuries, discrete science-based professional disciplines had begun to emerge in the West. They sought legal recognition and status as the sole guardians of their respective disciplines. This, in the then emerging Western democratic tradition, required the provision of a guarantee by each profession that they function in the public interest. This social concern was relatively new at the time. Professions were expected to maintain standards in the discharge of their duties and their individual members were expected to conduct themselves in a trustworthy manner. Thus, in the absence of an overarching moral code that could govern the whole of Classical Science, it soon became mandatory for each professional discipline to have its own code of conduct and internal procedures to ensure that its membership would uphold the established code. These were not codes that demanded ethical behavior as required by moral precepts. Instead, the need was to deal properly with the more mundane issues that arose in the working life of a professional. There was no visible connection between these professional codes and any greater moral law. When these professions in their "Western" guise came to be known in the LMICs of Asia, they were already prepackaged complete with their respective culture-specific codes of conduct. When some of these professions did search for historical precedent in formulating codes of conduct, they sought to by-pass more than fifteen centuries of their Christian past and establish references to pagan antiquity as did the medical profession when they adopted the code that they believed was promulgated by the followers of Hippocrates (460–377 BCE) in ancient Greece.

Ethical Crises in Science

The use of available technology in warfare has been a recurring fact throughout most of recorded history. The extreme acts of militarism that accompanied European commercial endeavor and early colonial expansion into the non-European world do not seem to have raised any moral issues in Europe during most of the past five centuries. On the contrary, European Christianity and its propagation accompanied and benefited from the colonial endeavor. There were conventions that governed the conduct of wars mainly between European states. There were no such conventions on how such states dealt militarily with their colonized territories. The Dum-Dum bullet was developed by the British to quell uprisings on the Indian subcontinent. Its use was banned as being inhumane in 1899 by the Hague Convention, that happened only at the behest of the German government for fear of its use in European wars. However, the Dum-Dum bullet was used by the British in India. Industrialization and the mass production of weapons of destruction that began in Europe at that time especially with the onset of the First World War (1914–1918), began to cause some ethical concern. During the Second World War, experimentation by the Nazis on prisoners of war shocked the civilized world. Another rude shock came with the climactic punctuations in 1945 at the end of that same war, when the Americans dropped two atom bombs on the Japanese cities of Hiroshima and Nagasaki. The world at large witnessed for the first time the massive destructive capability of nuclear weapons and the prolonged and widespread horrors of "nuclear fallout".

Then, the industrialized world divided again with the Western powers led by the US on one side, and, the Soviet Union and the "Eastern Bloc" countries on the other. The so-called "Cold War" arms race began, where even more destructive nuclear weapons were being developed and stockpiled by both sides. It was in this climate that the *cognoscenti* in most countries began to realize that there was indeed an ethical crisis in Science. Governments in the technologically advanced countries were recruiting their able scientists into programs to develop ever more powerful nuclear weapons. The possibility of making hydrogen ("H") bombs was known theoretically. It was also understood that the destructive capability of an H-bomb would, quite literally, be more than a thousand times that of the "A" bombs used in Japan. Still, the Western and Soviet governments were demanding their respective nuclear scientists to develop the H-bomb. These scientists had no code of ethics strong enough to resist their own governments. Those few who, through their own moral convictions, refused to participate were sometimes subjected to extreme harassment and ostracism by their own governments. Some of their professional careers were ruined in consequence (Russell 1961a).

It was in this atmosphere in the 1950s that a few notable scientists were brave enough to band together to protest. They signed appeals and petitions and also took steps to inform the public about the utmost danger to all life on earth that would inevitably be caused by a nuclear holocaust. The famous British mathematician and philosopher, Bertrand Russell, cited four such documents which he hoped would also dispel the impression that scientists were morally to blame for the peril that nuclear weapons pose to the world. These documents included an appeal signed in Mainau in 1955 by a group of Nobel laureates from Western countries; a statement and resolution signed in London in 1955 by a group of eminent scientists and philosophers with representatives from the Soviet Union as well; a report of the Indian government published in New Delhi in 1956; and a statement and a resolution signed in Pugwash, Nova Scotia in 1955 by Bertrand Russell along with ten eminent scientists all of whom were Nobel laureates. The signatories to this last document included Albert Einstein (Russell 1961b).

It is clear from these documents that in the mid-twentieth century, a few of the most brilliant scientists were of one mind about the dangers posed by nuclear weapons. They believed that humankind, human civilization, and all forms of life on this planet were under serious threat of annihilation. What is remarkable is that even members of the educated public were not fully aware of these dangers. The dangers were often hidden from the public and denied by politicians on both sides of the Cold War. The facts came to light mainly through the courage of these few eminent scientists who were willing to express their views publicly. What is still more remarkable is that in spite of the warnings, batteries of lesser scientists and scientific workers toiled directly or indirectly for their governments to develop and produce huge stockpiles of "H"-bombs and ballistic missile delivery systems. Research and development of technology related to warfare then focused on the equally horrible areas of chemical and biological weaponry. Some significant changes have occurred in recent decades in the relationship among the Cold War contestants of the 1950s. Nevertheless, the numerous "flash points" that have arisen in various geographic locations from time-to-time since then are chilling reminders that the danger of a minor conflict escalating even into a Third World War has not disappeared. On the contrary, the danger is ever-present.

Other ethical challenges than warfare have also confronted Science in the past 50 years. A few of the more contentious issues concern recent advances in genetics, cloning, and genetic engineering, and, in those areas that have to do with human health and food production. Further ethical issues have been raised by demands from some quarters for a change of social attitude toward abortion and euthanasia. Yet, another area of contention relates to the use of animals for experimentation in science. Many are convinced today that the manner of testing new and untried drugs on animals and the widespread use of vivisection as a teaching aid often may be, on close scrutiny, unnecessary today and unconscionable. Such actions, they believe, represent a moral presupposition by some cultures that all animal life can without constraints be subordinated and sacrificed for the advancement of human species.

A similar ethical situation as that which confronted scientists and professionals during the Cold War is now before scientists and professionals in today's industrialized and fast industrializing countries in how they handle the externalities of economic growth. No less a daunting task is faced by the scientists and professionals of the LMICs with the available prospect only of grossly iniquitous progress being achieved by and within their own countries and that too amidst the likelihood of serious environmental crises. If impending ecological disasters are to be averted and genuine prosperity for all is to be seriously sought, scientists and planners of the industrialized countries and those in the LMICs have to come together, be moved by ethical concerns, and play a major part to achieve equitable progress for all humankind.

References

Alberts B, Mehta G (2003) Inventing a better future. InterAcademy Council, Amsterdam

Arsecularatne SN (1999a) Our orientation in biomedical ethics. Sri Lanka Association for the Advancement of Science, Colombo, Sri Lanka, pp 7, 8, 12

Arsecularatne SN (1999b) Our orientation in biomedical ethics. Sri Lanka Association for the Advancement of Science, Colombo, Sri Lanka, p 20

Blackmore JT (1972) Ernst Mach: his work, life and influence. University of California Press, Berkeley

Coomaraswamy AK (1956) The transformation of nature in art (First Published Harvard University Press 1934), Chapter II. Dover Publications, New York

Huxley A (1962) Island. Penguin, London

References

Machievelli N, Dunno D (2003) The prince. Bantam Dell, New York
Mcfarlane TJ (2002) Einstein and Buddha: the parallel sayings. Ulysses Press, Berkeley
Modder WWD (1998) Ethics in the practice of science and its applications in the plantation industry. In: Jayakody RL (ed) Ethics in the practice of science. Sri Lanka Association for the Advancement of Science, Colombo, p 7
Pevsner N (1963) An outline of European architecture, 7th edn. Pelican, London
Quere E, Zhu C (2003) Inventing a better future. In: Annex A: endorsement. InterAcademy Council, Amsterdam, p 101
Russell B (1961a) Has man a future. Penguin, London, p 65
Russell B (1961b) Has man a future. Penguin, London, pp 54–60
Wittkower R (1962) Architectural principles in the age of humanism. Alec Tiranti, London

Part II
Spatial Concerns

Chapter 6
Managing Climate Change in South Asia

Abstract Climate change which is caused mainly by greenhouse gas emissions and consequent global warming has been one of the main subjects of discussion at many international conferences following the Rio Earth Summit held in 1992. It has come to be clearly recognized among the scientific community that a great many of the climate disasters that occur frequently now are man-made, mainly through excessive emissions of greenhouse gases. It is also recognized that climate change impacts adversely on all countries worldwide but does so especially harshly on the low- and middle-income countries (LMICs). These latter include the massive populations that reside in South Asia—a situation worsened by the substantial presence of extreme poverty and food and water insecurity prevalent in most of these countries. Additionally, there are low-lying areas in the island nations and many other coastal areas in South Asia that are vulnerable to sea level rise. Climate change in the form of temperature extremes, altered precipitation patterns, and deficit monsoons now being frequently experienced in this region are unfortunately projected to continue and worsen causing a major challenge to social and economic progress in the region.

Preamble

There are eight countries that are regarded as comprising South Asia. They include the main independent islands in the Indian Ocean namely the large island of Sri Lanka and the archipelago of small islands known as the Maldives. Then, there are the six independent countries that are integrally within the landmass generally known as the Indian Subcontinent. The latter six are India with Bangladesh in the east, Pakistan in the west, Afghanistan in the far west, and Bhutan and Nepal both in the northern mountainous region (Fig. 6.1). These countries contain among themselves the tropical coastal areas, major rivers, flat river delta regions, vast plains, deserts, much hilly terrain, and some of the highest mountains in the world. They contain as varied a geographic mix as could be found anywhere on earth. These extreme variations preclude any easy generalizations as to the climate of

South Asia. There is however one phenomenon which influences the climate of the region but impacts differently on the many subregions. That phenomenon is the monsoon which usually appears at regular annual intervals. These annual monsoons are in fact strong winds seasonally generated in the Indian Ocean which impact upon South Asia in combination with the varying geographic conditions. They blow from the southwest in the summer and from the northeast in the winter. They invariably bring with their strong winds heavy precipitation in the form of rain over most of the region and snow in the northern and mountainous areas.

This sixth chapter attempts to identify the impact of "climate change" upon socioeconomic progress in the countries of South Asia. Afghanistan has been seriously affected by war for almost four decades starting in 1979 with only a short

Fig. 6.1 Map of South Asia

break which is now over. The situation of being caught in the midst of war still continues with no end in immediate view. Afghanistan was therefore excluded from this study as relevant statistical data relating to that country is likely to be unreliable. Thus, this chapter briefly and generally examines each of the other seven South Asian countries noting the climatic zones that characterize them, the basics of their individual climatic features in terms of temperature and precipitation, their main economic activities and their dependence on weather patterns.

There are many schemes by which geographic definitions of climatic zones applicable worldwide have been made. Many of them are variations of Wladimir Koeppen's work published first in 1900, refined in 1918 with several later minor revisions. The basic scheme that has been applied in the Indian subcontinent and is currently being used today in India and Pakistan is attributed him. It is also referred to alternatively as the Köppen–Geiger–Pohl climate classification (Koeppen 1918; Peel 2007). The following sections present country-specific summaries of the geographic and climatic conditions of these particular countries with an attempt to identify the adverse impacts of climate change upon their progress.

Climate Change and South Asian Countries

Sri Lanka

Sri Lanka is an island in the Indian Ocean. There are a few ways in which climatic zones within Sri Lanka are defined of which two are frequently used. One defines a Wet Zone in the southwestern quadrant of the island including the central hills where the major rivers originate, a Dry Zone which are mostly plains covering about two-third of the total land area of the island, and an Intermediate Zone which occupies a small geographic area in-between. The other frequent delineation has only two zones: a larger Wet Zone which combines the earlier described Wet and Intermediate Zones and a Dry Zone which is the same as was defined in the earlier scheme.

Climatology studies indicate: that average temperatures throughout the island have been increasing in the recent past; that annual rainfall has been decreasing; but, that the intensity of that rainfall has been increasing. This situation has led to multiple problems such as crop losses, increased flood frequency, soil erosion, and more damage to dwellings and properties through the occurrence of landslides in the steeper slopes of the Wet Zone hills, and frequent droughts. The adverse impacts have not only been to agriculture and water resources but also to human health, human settlements and infrastructure, tourism, forestry, wildlife, and biodiversity (Silva 2009).

A comprehensive study, while identifying the same issues as already mentioned, also discusses in detail the adverse impacts of climate change on the plantations of tea and coconut, on hydropower generation and consequently on the country's energy supply, economy and also, very importantly, the negative impact on the prospect of achieving inclusive growth. Sri Lanka has a relatively low-lying and flat coastal region which is susceptible to serious damage by changes in sea level—a fact which was made abundantly clear during the 2004 tsunami. The coastal areas are populated and contain within it people involved in the activities of ocean fishing and much of the country's tourism which are vitally important to the national economy (IPS 2013).

Another comprehensive research project and its scientific projections finds that Sri Lanka's vulnerability to climate change will continue to be high and that climate change will impact upon the island in different ways.

> …Raised temperatures and unpredictable monsoon rains are already affecting the country's food production and water resources… Hydro-meteorological hazards like floods and droughts can disrupt public life and damage property and crop harvests… In the longer term, rising sea levels can impact the island's highly populated coastal areas, threatening human settlements, infrastructure and coastal/marine ecosystems… (NSF 2016)

Maldives

The Maldives is an archipelago of very small, closely clustered, and low-lying islands. The entire archipelago may be treated as one climatic zone. The main weather event it experiences is the Southwest Monsoon which in the past regularly occupied a few months of the May–September period. The economy of the Maldives is primarily based on fishing and tourism. The main attractions to tourists are its pristine white beaches, the blue, usually calm ocean and underwater exploration of its coral reefs and rich aquatic life.

A recent report on the impact of climate change upon the Maldives states that the geography of the country, being a land-scarce low-lying archipelago, has made it

> …especially vulnerable to the consequences of climate change…the country is exposed to the risks of intensifying weather events such as damage caused by inundation, extreme winds, and flooding from storms…the Maldives is also exposed to the risks of sea level rise. Future sea level is projected to rise…which means the entire country could be submerged in the worst-case scenario. (World Bank 2010)

Bangladesh

Much of the land in Bangladesh is flat, low-lying, and located within the delta region between two very large rivers—the Ganges and the Brahmaputra—a delta which is one of the biggest in the world. This area is subject to flooding annually but is fertile with regularly replenished alluvium deposits. There is some hilly terrain which is barely one-tenth of the total land area. These hill areas are located near the eastern border with India and also close to the border with Myanmar in the southeast. Being one of the wettest countries in the world, the entire country receives high rainfall.

Bangladesh is a densely populated country having more than 160 million people. It is often subjected to devastating cyclones that form in the Bay of Bengal. These cyclones regularly bring with them serious devastation to property and loss of lives often amounting to many thousands. The climate is that of a subtropical monsoon type. The monsoons are usually experienced from the southwest bringing most of the heavy rains in the June–September period. The summers are generally hot and wet while the winters are cooler and dryer.

It is said that about two-fifth of the world's storm surges directly impact upon Bangladesh annually.

> Two-thirds of the country is less than five meters above sea level, and floods increasingly inundate homes, destroy farm production, close businesses, and shut down public infrastructure. Erosion leads to an annual loss of about 10,000 hectares of land and weakens natural coastal defenses and aquatic ecosystems…Fresh water has become scarcer in Bangladesh's drought-prone northwest and in southwest coastal areas where about 2.5 million profoundly poor residents regularly suffer from shortages of drinking water and water for irrigation. Further, their coastal aquatic ecosystems have been severely compromised.

It is also recognized that this country's economy is more at risk to climate change than that of any other country (World Bank 2016).

Other adversities of climate change upon Bangladesh include the damage caused to groundwater assets, irrigation, fisheries, and industrial production. Furthermore, health problems result from waterborne diseases through frequent flooding. In regard to the direct impact of rising ocean temperature upon Bangladesh, a published research paper, quoting readings from a calibrated numerical hydrodynamic model, describes the predicted extent of cyclonic storm surge flooding that would arise due to sea surface temperature (SST) rise, states that:

> …for a storm surge under 2 °C SST rise and 0.3 m SLR, flood risk area would be 15.3% greater than the present risk area and depth of flooding would increase by as much as 22.7% within 20 km from the coastline. Within the risk area, the study identified 5690 km^2 land (22% of exposed coast) as a high-risk zone (HRZ) where flooding of depth 1 m or more might occur, and people should move to nearby cyclone shelters during extreme cyclonic events. Predicted area of HRZ is 1.26 times the currently demarcated HRZ. It was estimated that 320 additional shelters are required to accommodate people in the newly identified HRZ… (Karim and Mimura 2008)

India

There are a few alternative schemes that attempt to define the climatic regions in India which are, mostly all, based on monthly records of temperature and precipitation. There are many schemes by which geographic definitions of climatic zones have been made. Most of them in one way or other are variations of Koeppen's work. It defines the following nine zones: (1) Monsoon type with short dry seasons; (2) Monsoon type with a dry season in summers; (3) Tropical savannah type; (4) Semiarid steppe climate; (5) Hot desert type; (6) Monsoon type with dry winters; (7) Cold-humid winter type with short summers; (8) Tundra type; and (9) Polar type (Koeppen 1936).

In regard to the impact of climate change upon India, analyses of meteorological data across India, gathered over the past quarter century suggest marked increases in temperature but these vary by seasons and by regions. Serious implications for the vast Indian population of 1.311 billion (in 2015) are seen in the impacts of these changes on agriculture and human health (Dash and Hunt 2007). An ultrahigh-resolution model to study climate change predicts extremely hot events over the whole of India by the end of the century. The model has also helped to predict in the same time frame extreme rainfall over most parts of the country and scarcity of rain over the west coast.

> ...The close correspondence between changes in seasonal mean rainfall and extreme rainfall events points out that the contribution of high percentile rainfall events to seasonal rainfall is also likely to increase in future over the country. For the west coast, the increase in temperature, coupled with a decline in rainfall, will have drastic consequences on the production of crops. This will exacerbate existing vulnerabilities of the people who depend on agriculture. On the other hand, decrease of moderate precipitation can lengthen dry spells and increase the risk of drought because light and moderate precipitation is a critical source of soil moisture as well as groundwater. Over other regions, increases in heavy precipitation can increase surface run-off and lead to intense floods and landslides. (Rajendran et al. 2013)

Pakistan

Pakistan occupies a large landmass to the west of India. It extends from the subtropical Arabian Sea in the south to the Himalayan mountains in the north. The second highest peak in the world, Karakoram (popularly known as 'K2'), is in that mountain range. The highlands of the north, the Indus River basin and the plains, and the Balochistan Plateau comprise the three major geographic regions. Balochistan covers an area of almost half of the land area of Pakistan. It has a low population due to water scarcity and its rugged terrain. The country contains some desert areas as well.

Pakistan has four climatic seasons which vary according to location. Its winters lasting between December and February are generally cool and mild. The spring from March through May is usually hot and dry. The southwest monsoon is experienced in the summer months from June through September making it a rainy season. The fourth and last season sees the retreat of the monsoon. The north and the west experience frequent and severe earthquakes. Heavy rains when they do occur cause landslides in the mountains of the north and severe flooding of the

Indus in the July–August period. The silt from the Indus has, over the centuries, formed the fertile plain which has been host to an agricultural civilization for at least five millennia.

The Koppen–Geiger classification is often used to define the country's climatic zones, which are classified as: (1) hot desert; (2) humid subtropical; (3) hot semiarid; (4) cold desert; and (5) hot-summer Mediterranean type. Of these the most common to be found are the first three (Climate-Data.org>Asia>Pakistan). Accordingly, hot dry summers and damp winters are experienced in the north and arid climates in varying degrees characterize the west and parts of the south.

A research paper published in a specialized journal mentions that annual mean surface temperature shows "a consistent rising trend since the beginning of the twentieth century" and that in the arid coastal and mountainous areas and in the hyperarid plains, there is a rise in mean temperature but a decrease in rainfall in both winter and summer in the coastal belt and hyperarid plains; that there is an increase in rainfall especially in humid and subhumid areas of the monsoon zone; that a decrease in relative humidity is observed in Balochistan; that there is an increase of solar radiation in the southern half of Pakistan; that there is a decrease in cloud cover but an increase in sunshine hours with increased temperature in the central parts; and that there is an increase in net irrigation water needs. Mention is also made of the expanding aridity in the north outside of the monsoon range and that there is an increased frequency over the last 50 years of depressions and cyclones including those that occur in the Arabian Sea; and that low temperature winds which blow in January into the southern plains from the northwest cause some other extreme events. The paper goes on to say that heat waves and high temperatures occur in the large urban areas and megacities exacerbated by the urban heat-island effect and air pollution (Farooqi et al. 2005).

A report of a Guest Lecture delivered to a policy research institute in Pakistan states: that climate change is a serious threat to the country; that extreme weather events such as erratic monsoon rains, intense floods, droughts, and heat waves are now being experienced far more frequently than in the 1950–1990 period; that sea level rise threatens the coastal areas and has resulted in the displacement of large numbers of people; that ocean acidification will affect the fishing industry; that water availability in a country which has been described by the World Bank as being "water stressed"; that the variability of the monsoons has impacted on river flows and a consequent decrease in agricultural productivity and an increase in water demand for irrigation as well as for hydropower and for the cooling need of thermal power plants and the consequent reduction of efficiency of those plants; and that food insecurity has risen.

The report mentions that human health is also adversely affected by climate change and that heat-related mortality is being experienced in Karachi. Mention is made of the greater probability of vector-borne infectious diseases such as dengue fever in the context of increased air and water temperatures which are favorable to the reproduction of disease-carrying mosquitos and like insects. The report goes on the state that

The country has suffered heavy losses because of floods owing to climate change…The German Watch has ranked Pakistan among the ten most vulnerable countries consecutively since 2010. The negative impact of climate change is likely to steer public emotions leading to street disturbances… Indirectly, it has the potential to be a security threat: a "terrorism multiplier" triggered by climate refugees and economic deprivation. The climate change can also become a source of cross-border conflict owing to shared water resources coming under extreme stress…. (Ijaz 2017)

Bhutan

The land area of Bhutan is sandwiched between India and China, close to and east of Nepal, north of Bangladesh and northwest of Myanmar. Part of the Himalayan range occupies the north which borders China. That part of the country experiences severe cold weather conditions making it uninhabitable. The highlands occupy the rest of the country. Their valleys are home to most of Bhutan's small population. The country has many streams and rivers which are tributaries to India's Brahmaputra. Almost 70% of the land area has forest cover with conifers in the north and broadleaf forests in the south. There is a small strip of land in the extreme south bordering India which is a tropical plain where agriculture is practiced and rice is produced. It is a country which is cold in the winter and warm in the summer.

Precipitation is low in the north and takes the form of snow. The central parts experience a relatively dry winter after which much more precipitation is received but in the form of rain. There are pre-monsoon rains usually in late June. The summer monsoon rains from the southwest are heavier and are accompanied by high humidity. These rains are experienced mostly in the period between late June and September. The slow melting of the glaciers in the north is a resource which adds freshwater annually to the streams and rivers. Coupled with heavy monsoon rains, the rivers sometimes tend to cause flash floods and landslides. These situations often result in damage to agriculture in the southern plains.

The impact of climate change is being felt in Bhutan mainly through global warming and the rapid melting of glaciers. A UN-sponsored report states that

…due to rising temperatures, glaciers in Bhutan were retreating at a rate of 30–40 meters per year, poised to make many lakes burst their banks and send millions of gallons of floodwater downstream.

The situation can be aggravated by high and unseasonal monsoon rains that could swell the rivers. Some regional bodies have come together to diminish some of the hazardous outcomes of this situation (Tirwa 2008).

Nepal

Nepal is a small, landlocked country of diverse physiography of plains in the south known as the Terai, the high mountains in the Himalayas which include Mount Everest in the north and hilly rugged terrain in-between. These form different geographic zones with the Terai being hot, the hills being cool and the mountainous zone being a cold and icy environment. Precipitation is greatly influenced by the Asian monsoon system. The country relies on its natural resources for its economy and the livelihoods of its people. Its economy is based mainly on rain-fed agriculture which is dominated by the monsoons. Adventure tourism in high altitudes also plays an important additional role in its economy. The country has hydropower potential which has been tapped at present only to 0.75% of its potential. The better utilization of this natural resource can greatly benefit the country in the future (Shrestha and Aryal 2011).

A paper published in a specialized journal states that there is a disproportionate impact of climate change upon Nepal considering its size and its own negligible contribution toward global greenhouse gas emissions. It mentions that, nevertheless, it cannot escape the increasingly adverse impacts of climate changes especially due to its geographic location between the fast-growing economies of India and China. It goes on to say that:

> The rapidly retreating glaciers (average retreat of more than 30 m/year), rapid rise in temperature (>0.06°C), erratic rainfalls and increase in frequency of extreme events such as floods and drought like situations are some of the effects Nepal is facing during the last few years. Most of the big rivers of Nepal are glacier-fed and its main resources of water and hydroelectricity will be seriously affected due to the ongoing changes in glacier reserves, snowfall and natural hazards. Nepal has to prepare itself to try and mitigate these effects if possible and if not adapt to them to reduce their impacts…current indications are that the mountain regions are more vulnerable due to increased warming trends as well as extreme changes in altitude over small distances. These alarming trends not only make Nepal's major sectors of economy such as agriculture, tourism and energy more vulnerable but also endanger the health, safety and wellbeing of Nepali people. Biodiversity - the other important resources of Nepal is also being affected as invasive species will spread fast and useful medicinal, food and nutrition related plants may disappear…The globally accepted strategy to contain disastrous climate change impacts is Adaptation and Mitigation. For a least developed country such as Nepal, adaptation should be the priority.

Yet another research paper on flooding caused by instability of glacial lakes, mentions that:

> Glacier thinning and retreat in the Himalayas has resulted in the formation of new glacial lakes and the enlargement of existing ones due to the accumulation of meltwater behind loosely consolidated end moraine dams that had formed when the glaciers attained their Little Ice Age maxima. Because such lakes are inherently unstable and subject to catastrophic drainage they are potential sources of danger to people and property in the valleys below them. The torrent of water and associated debris that sudden lake discharges produce is known as a glacial lake outburst flood (GLOF). Recent surveys have shown that many glacial lakes in Nepal are expanding at a considerable rate so that the danger they pose appears to be increasing. (Schild 2011)

General Observations

The following two sets of observations summarize the conclusions that may be drawn in regard to the impact of climate change upon the South Asian region taken as a whole:

> The impacts of CC in South Asia are beginning to be felt in a number of ways, but most critical are likely to be those impacts that are affecting water resources, which directly affect agricultural systems and food security. There is an abundant water supply in the region, but because it is so unequally distributed, both spatially and temporally, agricultural productivity is low, inconsistent and severely dependent on weather patterns. As anticipated changes to the timing of the monsoon and expected adverse effects of CC begin to be felt on a wider scale and in a variety of ways (including increasingly frequent disaster events, more extreme storms and prolonged droughts, and an increasingly variable water supply), massive pressures will be levied on ecosystems, from water bodies to forests and agricultural lands, further limiting agricultural productivity in the region. In addition to these climate factors, socioeconomic aspects like high levels of poverty, migration and increasing population growth will also place an even greater pressure on agricultural system capacity and productivity… (Bartlett et al. 2010)

Another important journal publication states that the South Asian countries find climate change to be a critical issue not only for reasons of its geographic configurations but also due to the vulnerability that arises through the prevalence of much poverty and the presence of many undernourished people in the context of food insecurity. It proceeds to elaborate that:

> The rivers of the region are the lifelines of the economy providing water to more than half of the world's population. The increased occurrence of temperature extremes, altered rainfall patterns, rise in frequency of deficit monsoons, and heavy precipitation events observed in the region are the outcomes of climate change. Regretfully, these trends are projected to continue challenging the growth and development in the region, thereby necessitating cooperation among member countries. In this context, an analysis of the food and water security situation is undertaken, along with the expected impacts of climate change on the same…" Recommendations are also made in conclusion on the need for policies that should address cooperation on water issues, public investments in agriculture and the need for regional food stocks. (Kaur and Kaur 2016)

Climate and Culture

The appearance of settled agriculture is inevitably the feature that signifies the beginnings and progress of ancient civilizations. Two of the six river valleys which are best known as having fostered settled agricultural civilizations for more than five millennia are the Indus and the Ganges river deltas, both of which are in South Asia. An American Anthropogeographer being of the "New World" and breaking with set "Old World" beliefs of European origin, has suggested that South East Asia was probably the original setting of earliest agriculture and that the spread of that innovation depicted by him through a diagrammatic map was first to South Asia. In his words,

> ...the Cradle of our race may well have lain in what would still seem to us as pleasant places, of mild weather with alternating rainy and dry seasons, of varied woodlands, shrubs and herbs, a land of hills and valleys, of streams and springs, with alluvial reaches and rock sheltered cliffs. Our place of origin was one of invitation to the wellbeing of our kind...the earliest Neolithic farmers lived at the time when the sea had risen to about its present level, that is, when a balance had been struck between ice formation and ice melt...Agriculture did not originate from a growing or chronic shortage of food...The improvement of plants by selection for better utility to man was accomplished only by people who lived at a comfortable margin above the level of want. (Sauer 1969)

Settled agriculture requires a close relationship between people engaged in its activities and the climate within which they live and work. There has to be a clear recognition of the prevailing weather patterns, their predictable variations and particularly their regularities that lead to the possibility of marked cultivation seasons. There would have been some unforeseen and unpredictable freak weather events to affect the region or parts of it from time to time. Some of these events that have led to natural disasters have been chronicled. However, the predictable weather patterns have prevailed over time. The recognition within South Asia of its monsoon climate experienced over a great many centuries and of the regularity of variations in its weather patterns has invariably led to their translation and utilization as marked cultivation seasons. Whatever be the correctness of Sauer's theory of its origins and details, we may indeed accept with considerable certainty that South Asia was one of the main early hearths of settled agriculture; and also that the civilization of the region in all it cultural variety and richness was based upon the adoption and practice of agriculture. Recognizing the vagaries of climate in this region has clearly not led to attempts to dominate nature but to work in harmony with it. The adaptation to climate and the development of a harmonious relationship with the natural environment, sometimes through complex innovations, is a hallmark of South Asian cultures. An example from Sri Lanka is presented and discussed briefly below.

Sri Lanka has two main climatic zones referred to as the Dry Zone and the Wet Zone (Fig. 6.1). During the ancient period of Sri Lanka's history, the economy was mainly based on agriculture. There was trade with the outside world but on the whole, production was for consumption. Most of the people lived in the Dry Zone of the island which constitutes two-third of the land area. They farmed the land with boldly conceived irrigation systems consisting of numerous reservoirs and canal networks. Archaeological remains indicate that the large cities were located in the central plains of the Dry Zone and that the Wet Zone and its hills were deliberately left under forest cover and largely unpopulated. This was ecologically very sound because the forest cover in the Wet Zone hills protected the upper catchments of the main rivers that flowed through the Dry Zone and fed the network of the man-made reservoirs and irrigation systems. This clearly indicates a beneficial and harmonious relationship with the climate in particular and nature in general. Even the voluminous excess water from unseasonal and heavy rains which occasionally and unpredictably descended upon the river upper catchment areas of the Wet Zone were to a great extent absorbed by the forests avoiding rapid runoff and only slowly released into the streams. Thereafter, the resulting flows of water were captured downstream in the network of purpose built reservoirs and reservoir cascades of the Dry Zone. Thus, water was stored for use and major floods were often averted.

The economy, land use, and population distribution changed dramatically during the four and a half centuries of colonial rule first by the Portuguese in 1505 AC, then by the Dutch in 1658 and finally by the British (1805–1948). Agriculture for domestic consumption gave way gradually to plantation production for "empire" exports. By the time of the British period, the bulk of the population had shifted from the Dry Zone to the Wet Zone where most of the colonial plantation activities had become concentrated. Meanwhile, the ancient cities and the irrigation systems in the Dry Zone had gradually gone to ruin.

The British colonial government provided substantial encouragement to their adventurous "Planters" to clear the dense primeval forests in the upper catchments of the main rivers. This was to gain control of large extents of land for establishing plantations first for coffee and later for tea. These forests were also the habitat for many species of animals. Much encouragement was given to the pioneer British planters to hunt and slaughter these animals. Elephants in particular were treated as vermin.

The tea plantations in the upper catchments of Sri Lankan rivers were established by the British through the destruction of primeval forests along with the animal life within them. Their establishment represents a clear case of economic exploitation with a wanton disregard for environmental consequences. Tea is grown now in the lower reaches of the Wet Zone hill country as well. But the continuing existence of well-established and lucrative tea plantations located in the upper reaches causes a plethora of problems and presents the country with many dilemmas. The problems include serious damage by frequent floods and landslides in the hill country. Furthermore, heavy unseasonal rains are far more common now with climate change. Reforestation with appropriate species of trees in the upper catchment areas would go a long way towards a solution. But, such a solution is strongly resisted for reasons of short-term economic gain, led not surprisingly by a lobby of commercial interests.

Public debate in the West about environmental concerns had quiet beginnings in the 1960s and in due course began to build up gradually, as discussed in Chap. 3. It is interesting to note that an important Sri Lankan politician, some three decades earlier, had the following to say in a book he published in 1935 about a preferred path to progress for his country which was then under British colonial rule:

> With the evidence daily accumulating of the wisdom of our fore-fathers we need scarcely doubt that it was not merely the idea of making the mountain country difficulty to approach by the foreign invader that caused them to preserve unfelled and un-cleared the dense vegetation of their mountain slopes. We may readily believe that they deliberatively left these untouched in order to provide that abundant supply of water in which they might draw for the benefit of man … (Senanayake 1935)

The statement represents as clear an understanding as one could expect of the environmental issues raised by high-grown tea plantations. The author quoted above was not someone with a strong background in the Science of Ecology which was a discipline hardly known then. He was a politician with a general education gained in the form provided by the Colonial British Government to their subjects. It has to be recognized therefore that the ecological awareness that his views published in 1935 points to is a source other than general education and casual reading. It would not be unreasonable to suppose that the source was derived from deep-seated cultural awareness which was prevalent and perhaps still exists in South Asia.

Unpredictable Events

There are climatic events that are predictable as well as those that cannot be predicted well in advance, which latter may be thought of as being unpredictable events. Some of these are "natural" in that they are caused by natural phenomena. A few examples of these are cyclones, lightning strikes, earthquakes, and tsunamis triggered by earthquakes. Some, as defined by scientific interpretation, are caused by human activity and interventions. These latter events are almost always unpredictable and are usually now, for good reason, associated with "climate change". These events invariably result in disasters of varying magnitude.

The immediate responses to such unpredictable disasters in South Asia and also in many of the other LMICs have invariably to be from the distressed local communities. And, their local-level bureaucratic machinery whose capacity to deal with such extraordinary situations in these countries is weak. Thus, the secondary response usually involves appeals to some specific central body established in the particular country. Such bodies have usually been endowed with some limited facilities and funds and these agencies do get galvanized to take action as promptly as possible to provide relief to those most affected. These facilities are usually quite inadequate to deal with large-scale disasters. The respective governments in such circumstances then appeal to international agencies, for bilateral assistance from other countries, and to international nongovernmental organizations (INGOs) dedicated to deal with such situations.

Response to Disasters: Two Examples

It will be useful at this stage to examine here some examples of action taken in consequence of such large-scale disasters in a South Asian country—the specific country being immaterial as the experiences among these countries are often quite similar. Two examples of disasters are discussed here. The first relates to the severe cyclone which hit Sri Lanka in 1978. Such cyclones usually originate in the Bay of

Bengal. Many often come close but veer away from the island and often end up causing serious damage in Bangladesh. However, the cyclone of 1978 which is to be discussed here first, entered the East Coast of Sri Lanka and traveled across the island wreaking considerable destruction to life and property particularly in the Eastern and Central parts of the country which fall within the Dry Zone of the island.

A frequent occurrence observed in the destruction caused by this cyclone was that the roofs even of substantial buildings were blown away, sometimes even carrying parts of the structural elements they were connected to. Some of these buildings were relatively recent structures constructed by public and also by private sector agencies. There were also many villages of peasant farmers which were destroyed. However, what was less noticed and generally ignored was that a few small traditionally built huts in the local vernacular architecture serving as homes for poor peasant families had in fact survived! After much effort in the immediate rehabilitation and reconstruction work that followed the cyclone, there were organized exercises in extracting lessons from the disaster. Participants included local and foreign experts and specialists with a few being drawn through foreign aid programs. The various fields they represented included climatology and the civil and structural engineering professions with many having relevant experience gained abroad, and military personnel called upon to help in the emergency. It was recognized that there were records of many cyclones before in Sri Lanka and that there would be more such events still to come.

One very useful outcome from among many in this learning exercise was the preparation of a new map. It demarcated zones within the island which in all probability were prone to varying degrees of the cyclone hazard. This map led to the drafting of some new building regulations aimed at resistance to cyclonic conditions applicable in the danger-prone areas. Almost four decades on, these regulations are still followed in the public and private sector building activities in these particular areas and have proved to be useful. But, these regulations are neither practical nor affordable in the construction of shelter for the rural poor which by far is the vast majority of buildings that must concern us. There have been neither analyses nor even basic studies done of the peasant huts that did survive the cyclone of 1978. The conclusion here is not that we should all now go for steeply shaped straw thatch roofs with low eaves, as was distinguishable in the peasant built structures that survived. What has to be recognized is that there is traditional wisdom residing among the peasant families in regard to building in cyclone-prone areas. These are areas in which some of these families have lived for generations and experienced cyclones before. This knowledge of their survival could be translated through science into modern technology. It is not only the hard engineering sciences that we must rely upon. There are also the social sciences along with architectural expertise that must be utilized to understand the realities of life experiences in this South Asian part of the world, and perhaps in other LMICs as well.

The second example of a major disaster concerns the "Boxing Day Tsunami" of December 2004. It caused chaos and severe destruction in many coastal areas in

South Asia including those in Sri Lanka as indeed it did in some Southeast Asian countries as well. This tsunami was triggered by a massive (9 on the Richter scale) megathrust earthquake which occurred beneath the Indian Ocean some 160 miles west of Sumatra. It is considered to have caused at that time perhaps the worst tsunami damage in recorded history and is estimated to have killed more than 38,000 people and displaced many more in Sri Lanka alone (New Scientist 2005). Immediately following the event, there was very positive support that was received not only from the local people and the various agencies of the government but also a massive and favorable response from abroad. This latter originated with foreign governments and arrived both directly and through international agencies, INGOs, and expatriate Sri Lankan sources.

As happened before with the 1978 cyclone, along with the rehabilitation and reconstruction work that followed the tsunami, there were organized exercises in striving to extract lessons from dealing with the disaster. Participants as before included local and foreign experts including various specialists with many drawn through aid programs. The fields they represented also included as before, climatology and the civil and structural engineering professions, military personnel called upon to help in the emergency, and many having relevant experience gained abroad. One most valuable outcome was the unanimous insistence on the need for early warning systems relating to "unpredictable" disasters from the time their onset is perceived. This need is being satisfied to a great extent through the establishment and/or strengthening of appropriate institutions with the ready cooperation of international and regional governments and their relevant agencies.

However, this useful exercise of learning from the experience of the tsunami disaster, as before with the 1978 cyclone disaster, was being expected to lead to the drafting of some new building regulations aimed at resistance to tsunami conditions applicable in the low-lying coastal areas. Seminars and workshops were initiated by well-meaning local professional bodies and funded by foreign governments and INGOs with such expectations. But, such regulations as were outcomes in draft were relevant to major construction projects such as tourist hotels and institutional buildings. They are neither practical nor affordable in the construction of shelter for the poor who live and work in these vulnerable areas. The kind of construction needed to withstand a tsunami is way beyond the reach of the poor. Furthermore, the numbers and quality of personnel needed to ensure adherence to such regulations in extended low-income coastal housing simply do not exist in Sri Lanka nor perhaps in most LMICs.

Needed Responses to Climate Change

The main attempt in the international climate change conferences such as in those that led to and included the one held in Paris in 2015 was to arrive at an agreement with commitments merely to reduce the rate of increase in global warming. It was hoped to reach agreement internationally to ensure the increase in global warming would be brought down to 2% or less than the preindustrial level by the end of this twenty-first century. The present rate of increase is in excess of 3%. It is reckoned by responsible scientist that an increase of 4% or more by the year 2100 would lead to irreversible catastrophes worldwide. The most adversely affected, as is already the case, will be the LMICs. The current experience of climate change in South Asia includes sea level rise in the coastal areas, increased glacier melt in the mountainous regions and, generally across the region, the experience of more unseasonal weather patterns with an overall reduction in precipitation but an increase in its intensity. Some of these often result in a succession of floods, droughts, and food scarcities. These climate events are getting harder to predict and their impacts are much more difficult even to ameliorate.

Due to the geographic and other variations found among the countries of South Asia, the strategy that may need to be adopted in one country may not be directly applicable in another. The responses generally recommended by the internal agencies involve taking measures to mitigate the adverse impact and/or to adapt to them. Some South Asian countries have little choice but to adapt. It has to be anticipated that the impact of climate change will worsen with time. This may happen in different ways in the seven separate countries discussed here and even within each of them. How will all these many separate communities adapt? How can the respective governments help support adaptation? These are serious questions that need answers and these answers will not be easy to find. In this context, there is perhaps one strategy that may be applicable in most of these countries and their diverse circumstances. This common strategy involves moving the most vulnerable families out of harm's way which inevitably requires reliance on spatial planning. It may thus be useful to examine spatial planning approaches that are being tested.

One such strategy that may be studied could be the proposed spatial planning exercise at national level in the Case Study based in Sri Lanka as presented in Chap. 10 of this book. It identified two "fragile areas" in the country which are most vulnerable to disasters of different kinds. These identified areas are two populated parts of the country, one in the upper reaches of the Wet Zone highlands particularly where unstable hillslopes exist. The hazards to be expected there are landslides, rockslides, mudslides, subsidence of the soil, and such like. The other identified fragile area consists of low-lying coastal lands which are exposed to erosion by the sea, sea level rise, severe storms and cyclones and such like events—natural and predictable or otherwise. These events can be expected more frequently especially with unseasonal and heavy rainfall intensity which is now part and parcel of the climate change impacts already being experienced. The best solutions in both identified "fragile areas" involve spatial planning exercises of resettling the vulnerable families elsewhere ahead of impending disasters. Where the resettlement is voluntary on the part of the families at risk, the problem is much easier provided alternative land is available. In the case of farmers living in vulnerable locations in the Wet Zone highlands of Sri Lanka, appropriate alternative land parcels can be found and made available if there is political will to do so. These lands may be in new irrigated agriculture projects in the country's Dry Zone. In such circumstances, the relocation could often be voluntary and welcomed provided appropriate incentives are made available to the families to be resettled. Such resettlement programs are not likely to be welcomed in the case of families engaged in ocean fishing as a livelihood in the vulnerable coastal areas. Here, a different strategy needs to be identified and developed.

References

Bartlett R, Bharati L, Pant D, Hosterman H, McCornick P (2010) Climate change impacts and adaptation in Nepal. International Water Management Institute, Colombo, Sri Lanka

Dash SK, Hunt JRC (2007) Variability of climate change in India. Curr Sci J 93(6)

Farooqi AB, Khan AH, Mir H (2005) Climate change perspective in Pakistan. Pak J Meteorol J 2(3)

Gosain AK, Rao S, Basuray D (2006) Climate change impact assessment on hydrology of Indian river basins. Curr Sci J 90(3)

http://www.ipripak.org/post-event-report-of-guest-lecture-on-impact-of-climate-change-on-pakistans-national-security/. Accessed 3rd Oct 2017

https://www.pmfias.com/climatic-regions-of-india-stamps-koeppens-classification/. Accessed 20 Aug 2017

Ijaz A (2017) Post-Event Report on a guest lecture by Akif SAA, Irfan Tariq MA: impact of climate change on Pakistan's national security. Islamabad Policy Research Institute, Islamabad, Pakistan

IPS (2013) Climate change issues in Sri Lanka. Institute of Policy Studies, Colombo, Sri Lanka

Karim MF, Mimura N (2008) Impacts of climate change and sea-level rise on cyclonic storm surge floods in Bangladesh. Glob Environ Change J 18(3):490–500

Kaur S, Kaur H (2016) Climate change, food security and water management in South Asia: implications for regional cooperation. Emerg Econ Stud J 2

Koeppen W (1918) Köppen climate classification. In: Encyclopædia britannica. https://www.britannica.com/science/Koppen-climate-classification. Accessed 20 Aug 2017

Koeppen W (1936) Climatic regions of India—Stamp's, Koeppen's. In: PMF IAS

NSF (2016) National thematic research programme on climate change and natural disasters. The National Science Foundation, Colombo, Sri Lanka

Peel MC et al (2007) Updated world map of the Koppen-Geiger climate classification. In: Hydrology and earth systems sciences. https://www.hydrol-earth-syst-sci.net/11/1633/2007/hess-11-1633-2007.pdf. Accessed 22 Aug 2017

Rajendran K, Sajani S, Jayasankar CB, Kitoh A (2013) How dependent is climate change projection of Indian summer monsoon rainfall and extreme events on model resolution? Curr Sci J 104(10):1417

Sauer CO (1969) Agricultural origins and dispersals. MIT Press, Cambridge, MA, pp 5, 6, 19, 20, 21, 24

Schild A (2011) Glacial lakes and glacial lake outburst floods in Nepal (Foreword). International Centre for Integrated Mountain Development, Kathmandu, Nepal

Senanayake DS (1935) Agriculture and patriotism. Lake House, Colombo, Sri Lanka

Shrestha AB, Aryal R (2011) Climate change in Nepal and its impact on Himalayan glaciers. Reg Environ Change J 11(1):65. (Springer)

Silva A (2009) Climate change and Sri Lanka. Ministry of Environment and Natural Resources, Colombo, Sri Lanka

Tirwa B (2008) Managing health disasters. In: Bhutan observer online. Accessed 27 Mar 2011

World Bank (2010) Climate change in the Maldives. Washington, DC

World Bank (2016) Bangladesh: building resilience to climate change. Washington, DC

Chapter 7
Managing Urbanization

Abstract The countries that underwent industrialization during the nineteenth century did experience economic growth coupled with rural–urban migration. Later, the extensive mechanization of agriculture over the years in some of those countries also provided a further impetus to urbanization in their respective populations. Thus, economic growth has come to be closely associated with urbanization. The conditions that generated urbanization in the West are not necessarily the same as those that cause urbanization in the LMICs today. Furthermore, the colonial impact did cause urbanization in the LMICs but the prosperity it generated benefitted only some of those who were subjugated. It also appears to have caused some serious spatial disparities. There was an important spatial planning approach that arose in the West to deal with urbanization. It was based on some visionary "utopian" concept that arose in Europe toward the end of the nineteenth century and had gained much credence in the past. That approach was perhaps appropriate to those contexts then but its relevance to the LMICs today needs to be questioned. The scale of urbanization being experienced today in the LMICs including those in South Asia is much greater in magnitude than what was experienced earlier in the West. Furthermore, the impacts upon LMICs of ongoing globalization, popularization of scientific developments, and technological innovations including those of ICT need also to be recognized. Thus, it should be expected that the planning approaches and spatial results in most LMICs including those in South Asia are likely to be very different.

This chapter is based on a paper by the author titled "Managing Urbanization in South Asia: Towards a Rational Theoretical Base", published in the Sri Lanka Economic Journal, Vol. 13 No. 2, 2012. Certain sections are also an extension of a newspaper article "Megacities and urbanization in South Asia" of the author which was published in Sri Lanka Daily News of 30th November 2015.

Preamble

The scale and pace of current urbanization is recognized as being unprecedented in human history. It is reported that the urban share of the global population could reach 60% by 2030 and 67% by 2050 (Bloom and Khanna 2007). The bulk of that growth is expected to come from the low- and middle-income countries (LMICs) which are likely to double from 2.6 billion in 2010 to 5.2 billion in 2050. Clearly, urbanization and its consequences are most prominently manifest today in the LMICs. *The Global Network of Science Academies* recently placed population growth coupled with unplanned urbanization among the ten most serious global concerns. That important apex body of worldwide scientific institutions identified the necessity to develop and implement urban planning policies that internalize consumption needs and demographic trends to reap the benefits of sustainable urban living (IAP 2012).

This chapter focuses on urbanization in the LMICs and particularly on the experience of the phenomena within the South Asian countries. Recognizing its benefits and adversities, there is a critical examination of some of the main approaches being taken to deal with it. In this regard, an attempt is made to identify and examine the main spatial planning approaches being taken and also those theories based on science that may be more relevant in the effort to deal with the subject in the geographic context of concern.

Discussion

The gravity of urbanization and its impact on human habitat in the LMICs had been anticipated even in the 1960s by a few eminent scholars. A landmark book was published on the subject (Abrams 1964). Despite considerable efforts to confront the adversities of urbanization, the LMICs have seen no tangible breakthroughs. The rapid growth of urban populations in the LMICs is the result of natural increase and also, importantly, rural migrations to cities. The entire urbanization process is often seen by some scholars as one that helps the emancipation of underprivileged rural migrants and also supports economic growth through the provision of labor for industrial production. The migratory targets of the urbanization process in these countries are usually those larger urban areas many of which already are, or likely to become "megacities".

Rural–urban migrations in the LMICs are a consequence of extreme rural poverty coupled with the very poor access that most of these rural folk have to basic needs and social infrastructure. The fact however is that rural migrants face serious problems even in their urban destinations. These problems include the inadequacy of shelter, access to basic services and appropriate employment opportunities, though perhaps to a lesser extent than they experienced in their original rural habitats. Also, they, by their increasingly large urban presence, cause severe and unabated stresses on the limited infrastructure facilities available to other city dwellers.

Discussion

It has been noted that

> A key trait of urbanization is that so-called agglomeration economies improve productivity and spur job creation, specifically in manufacturing and services, and indeed those two areas now account for more than 80 percent of the… (South Asian)… region's GDP. (World Bank 2016)

But, it has also been significantly noted by another important recent study sponsored by the Asian Development Bank that

> The process of urbanization reinforces the inequality effects of agglomeration. Our analysis shows that in many Asian countries, about 30–50% of income inequality is accounted for by spatial inequality due to uneven growth.

The same authors go further to say that

> …the drivers of growth are also magnifying the effects of inequalities in physical and human capital, leading to rising income inequality. These forces require Asian policy makers to redouble their efforts to generate more productive jobs, equalize opportunities in employment, education, and health, and address spatial inequality. Without such policies, which will enhance growth further, Asia may be pulled into inefficient populist policies, which will benefit neither growth nor equity. (Kanbur et al. 2014)

There is evidence of much dissatisfaction with conventional urban planning as practiced in the LMICs. A chapter in a recent comprehensive study done at Harvard University entitled "Deficiencies in How Urban Planning is Practiced Today" states as follows:

> The conduct of planning as it is commonly found today in low- and middle-income countries is wanting and results in growth that exacerbates environmental damage, increases traffic congestion and auto dependency, increases carbon emissions, leaves many areas inaccessible to employment and opportunity, perpetuates older informal settlements even as it places some of the best situated slums under redevelopment pressure, and spawns new informal settlements. (JCHS 2013a)

The relevant writings tend to lay stress upon the urgent need for "radical planning" to support participation by often large, disenfranchised segments of urban and urbanizing populations. This concern was seen even many decades ago, for example, in the discussions on squatter settlements in Latin America by Turner and Fichter (1972). It reappears more recently in, for example, the anti-eviction campaigns within the Western Cape in South Africa (Miraftab 2009); and still more recently with discussions on the "stubborn realities" of informal settlements in the global south (Watson 2012). This particular focus, from its radical beginnings in the 1960s and early 1970s, has clearly moved now to be mainstream thinking at least among informed planning circles concerned with planning for the urban poor in the LMICs. This shift is exemplified in the content of the already quoted recent study at Harvard (JCHS 2013a).

There still remains much resistance in some of the LMICs among the conventionally trained and conservative urban planners who are often blind to the more appropriate techniques of planning for the urban poor. There was a cited case in Mumbai, India, where local architects and planners had worked together with a slum dweller community in *Dharavi* to prepare a sound redevelopment plan to install infrastructure, increase density, improve the housing stock, and allocate space for private development. However, despite the clear benefits of the plan prepared through community participation, the government planners in charge of redeveloping the area had deliberately excluded that work from their own official plan (JCHS 2013b).

In addition to these identified inadequacies in the practice of Planning in the LMICs, it has also to be recognized that many planners grappling specifically with problems relating to rapid urbanization in those countries do not confront the subject directly and in its entirety. In many LMICs especially in South Asia when the concern is directly with urbanization, reliance is invariably placed on intraurban interventions through the various concerned professional disciplines. The solutions are consequently and inevitably based upon guiding the expansion of impacted cities in one way or other, often involving the planning and building of satellite towns in the vicinity of those cities. The predominant intellectual material which underpins the attempts to manage urbanization in this particular manner originated in the West a century ago. The fact however is that rural out-migration impacts not only on cities that receive the migrants but also upon the rural hinterlands the migrants left behind. It does so quite adversely especially in that agriculture becomes increasingly deprived of manpower and thus subject to continuing neglect.

There are studies which strive to predict the consequences of horizontal urban expansions due to rapid urbanization and their likely spatial impact on rural land. The main prediction in one such recent study which was based on the assumption of continuing current trends, suggests the tripling of urban land cover worldwide within the next three decades with a notably severe adverse impact upon biodiversity (Seto et al. 2012). That study also brought to light that the main biodiversity "hotspots" likely to be affected by these trends are in the LMICs with many being in South Asia.

There also are other adverse consequences of horizontal urban expansion. An observation in relation to Pakistan which is clearly applicable elsewhere in South Asia is that:

> …urban planning has emphasized sprawl and horizontal growth—effectively turning its cities into expansive, car-friendly suburbs. The negative consequences are many. Large and expensive residential spaces make land scarce, and price the non-rich out of the housing market. Commercial space is limited, constraining growth. Basic services, including public transit, are difficult to provide to such widely disbursed populations. And automobiles befoul the environment…. (Kugelman 2014)

A World Bank report notes that in the decade leading to 2010, there had been a substantial increase in the physical growth of South Asian cities particularly by low-density sprawl; and that this does not augur well for the future of the region which is anticipated to experience an urban population increase of 250 million people by 2030 (Kaw 2015).

This chapter presents inter alia a review of some planning literature covering the origins, growth, and development of those concepts and theories which have already had, or could have influence in dealing with urbanization in the LMICs. The publications cited in the text of this chapter are spread over the past two centuries. The search yielded two very different outcomes. One was a set of concepts which had arisen in the late nineteenth and early twentieth century which were essentially utopian in character. They form the base of most current planning approaches adopted in South Asia to confront rapid urban growth—approaches which tend to treat urbanization as inexorable. The other outcome from the literature search was a set of theories and concepts based rationally upon empirical observations. The contention in that set is that most of these latter theories, also of Western origin, could indeed underlie a far more relevant approach to the broader problems that surround urbanization in the LMICs. These particular theories are an integral part of the discipline generally known as Spatial Economics and sometimes also referred to as Economic Geography. The findings from the entire literature search will be briefly discussed in the body of this paper. The ultimate purpose of this exercise was to try to identify a rational theoretical base to effectively and holistically deal with the current problems caused by urbanization in the specific geographic context of prime concern here, namely, that of South Asia.

The Context

There were 23 very large cities worldwide in 2011, each with more than ten million people. Asia had 12 with South Asia alone having five of these "megacities". Three of them were in India, one in Pakistan and one in Bangladesh—Dhaka, which is reckoned as the fastest growing megacity among them. The South Asian total is predicted to increase from five to eight megacities by 2025 (UN 2012). The urban populations and urbanization rates may be gleaned from Table 7.1.

An important statistical study of urbanization in India states

> Urbanisation in India has been relatively slow compared to many developing countries. The percentage of annual exponential growth rate of urban population…reveals that in India it grew at faster pace from the decade 1921-31 to until 1951. Thereafter it registered a sharp drop during the decade 1951-61. The decades 1961-71 and 1971-81 showed a significant improvement in the growth which has thereafter steadily dropped to the present level…The sharp drop in urban rate during 1951-61 was mainly due to declassification of a very large

Table 7.1 Urban population figures: World Bank staff estimates for 2012

Country	Urban population	Rate of urbanization (%)
Bangladesh	44,685,923 (28.4% of total)	2.96
India	391,535,019 (31.3% of total)	2.47
Nepal	4,762,848 (16.2% of total)	3.62
Pakistan	65,481,587 (36.2% of total)	2.68
Sri Lanka	3,092,255 (15.1% of total)	1.36

Urbanization rates: CIA World Fact book estimates for 2010–2015 number of towns during that period. Rural growth has been fluctuating since 1901. The decline in rural population growth was within small range during 1981-91 and 1991-2001...Number of million plus cities...have increased from 5 in 1951 to 23 in 1991 and to 35 in 2001. About 37% of the total urban population live in these million plus... cities. As per 2001 census the newly added million plus cities are 12 in numbers, they are Agra, Meerut, Nashik, Jabalpur, Jamshedpur, Asansol, Dhanbad, Faridabad, Allahabad, Amritsar, Vijaywada, Rajkot. (Datta 2006)

This particular author proceeds to state that the basic features and problems resulting from urbanization in India can be described as: lopsided urbanization which induces growth of the largest cities; that urbanization occurs without industrialization and a strong urban economic base; that urbanization is mainly a product of demographic explosion and poverty induced rural–urban migration; that rapid urbanization leads to massive growth of slums with its inevitable miserable conditions and the overall degradation in the quality of urban life; that urbanization occurs not due to urban pull but due to rural push; that distress migration initiates urban decay; that the urbanization process is not mainly "migration lead" but a product of the demographic explosion due to natural increase; and that rural out-migration is directed toward the largest cities, i.e., Kolkata, Mumbai, Delhi, and Chennai which attained inordinately large population size leading to the virtual collapse in the urban services and quality of life in those cities. The same author states that since these cities suffer from urban poverty, unemployment, housing shortage, and a continuing crisis in urban infrastructural services, they cannot absorb distressed rural migrants who are poor unskilled agricultural laborers. Hence, this type of migration to the largest cities results in exacerbating the urban crisis.

A World Bank report notes that the share of the national population of India living in officially defined urban areas is a little above 31% while the proportion in both urban areas and areas with urban-like facilities is 53%; that the urbanization process has been relatively slow in India with its official urban share growing annually at just over 1.15%; that the peripheries of the major cities such as Mumbai, Delhi, Bangalore, Kolkata, Chennai, Hyderabad, and Ahmedabad have been growing the fastest and that these cities dominate the economic landscape.

The annual rate of urbanization in Pakistan, currently estimated at about 3%, is perhaps the fastest in South Asia. The proportion of urban population is expected to grow from its current status of being about a third to about half of the national population within the next decade. The population of Karachi would in that period increase from its current 13 million to 20 million while Lahore is likely to become a "megacity" of 10 million people. These particular rural–urban migrations of population may perhaps have been partially fuelled by military activity in the tribal regions but the likelihood of these migrants returning to their rural origins seems most unlikely (Kugelman 2014).

Most studies confirm that Bangladesh's urbanization is relatively rapid. Its urban population is said to have been growing yearly at the rate of 6% since independence, while during the same period the national population was growing annually at only 2.2%. Most of that urban growth has been in Dhaka, its capital city which has happened and still continues in its growth through rapid migration from the rural areas. The city has almost 12 million people, and is ranked worldwide as the 11th largest, as being among the most densely populated. The main contributor to this growth is attributed to rural–urban migration (Mohit 1990).

Indigenous South Asian coverage of urbanization in its demographic aspects and urban socioeconomic impacts is extensive and very competent. These studies reveal that the larger urban areas receive far more rural migrants, with the largest cities gaining the bulk. The South Asian megacities experience immense difficulties. A few scholars, e.g., Arif and Hamid (2009) are comforted that the move to cities has resulted in marginal improvements for some rural migrants. Most others, e.g., Datta (2006) and Hossain (2006) are seriously concerned that the often illiterate and unskilled rural families who gravitate to cities to escape rural poverty, eventually become trapped in squalid and insanitary urban environments of deprivation, malnutrition, and endemic disease; that their sheer numbers cause increasing and virtually unrelievable stresses on scarce urban infrastructure and services; and that those cities cannot generate employment opportunities to sustain the massive and continuing influx of migrants. This has also been keenly observed in a policy brief on urbanization and the Pakistani megacity—Karachi (Khan 2014). Thus, a clear conclusion is that these megacities are becoming increasingly unmanageable.

According to estimates by ESCAP (2011), Sri Lanka and Nepal have low proportions of urban populations, these being respectively 14.3 and 18.6%, as compared to 30.0% in India. According to the World Bank's estimates, the urban population proportions of Sri Lanka and Nepal are 15.1 and 16.2%, respectively, as compared to India's urban population proportion of 31.3%. Despite the minor variations in the two sets of figures, it is quite clear that both Sri Lanka and Nepal have comparatively low proportions of urbanized populations. The Real GDP Growth in 2012 of Sri Lanka was estimated at 6.4%, while in Nepal it was estimated at 4.6%. Rural migrants in both countries, as elsewhere, move mainly to the largest urban areas which invariably are "primate cities"—a subject to be discussed later in another chapter. Urbanization, though not an immediately pressing problem within these two countries, could indeed become so in the near future.

Utopian Visions

Industrializing Europe of the nineteenth century did see significant urbanization. Their rural landscapes changed dramatically with intensified mining, mechanized industries, and the introduction of railroads. New industrial towns quite suddenly materialized—some on agricultural land and many grew rapidly into large and ugly cities. The intelligentsia of that period could scarcely ignore the proportions that social inequality, poverty, and urban squalor had begun to assume. Divergent schools of thought on social change originated in that context from which the evolutionary school became firmly established in the West. Urban planning theories originate there (Benevolo 1971). Friedman and Weaver (1979) saw the same roots for Regional Planning.

Those thinkers in the late nineteenth century who belonged to the classical and neoclassical schools of political economy were preoccupied with some of the dominant issues of their times. However, they had no ready models to explain the causes and to deal with the unprecedented urbanization that was then ongoing, nor did they articulate appropriate responses to address the serious spatial issues that were emerging. Some of the early thinkers who did grapple with the spatial aspects of rapid urban growth were essentially utopians who were moved by deep social concerns. They concentrated on developing ideal models of social and spatial organization. With industrialization being experienced first in Britain, many of them were British. Ebenezer Howard, the leading light of the Garden City Association founded in 1897, published a book on the subject (Howard 1898). The book and the Association became very influential and the Garden City Movement spread (Pevsner 1963). Many of their adherents saw the machine as an evil invention of man. Some of them, turned away from industrialization to revive traditional arts, crafts, and ways of life. These ideas even influenced a few enlightened industrialists. Sir Titus Salt founded "Saltaire" near Leeds for a textile mill in 1853. Lever Brothers, influenced by William Morris and the Arts and Crafts Movement, began *Port Sunlight* for a soap factory in 1888. Cadbury's "Bourneville", influenced by Quaker principles, was begun in 1895 and built around a chocolate factory. Those were some among the first industrial estates planned as satellite suburbs. "Bedford Park", near London, was designed in 1875 by Norman Shaw on the same principles, but for private residential tenants of a wealthier class (Pevsner 1963).

Some of this late nineteenth century British utopian thinking also led to changes through reform movements concerned with the urban poor. These resulted in planning and building codes to ensure minimum health and safety standards in urban working class housing constructed by speculative developers. The resulting normative codes were later exported to many cities in the colonized territories where they were imposed with great fervor, regardless of their relevance to the new cultural and climatic contexts. This entire brand of planning thought was very influential even in the mid-twentieth century. The Garden City movement spread to Scandinavia, evidenced by planning work on Stockholm (Markelius and Sidenbladh 1949). It diffused to the British colonies as seen by the work of British planners in these countries e.g. Abercrombie (1949) in his regional plan for Colombo, the then capital city of Sri Lanka.

An architectural historian has stated that the conception of the garden city with satellite suburbs was in itself an escape from the city; and that the first of the architects to deal with the problems of the city recognizing the need for zoned locations for housing, public buildings and for industry was Tony Garnier in his "Cite Industrielle" (Pevsner 1963). These hypothetical proposals made by Garnier were first published in 1917 (Richards 1956). Another key figure who arrived in the Parisian scene a little later was Charles-Edouard Jeanneret-Gris better known as Le Corbusier. His book "Urbanisme" (1925) included some articles written a few years earlier by him and already published in the journal "L'espirit Nouveau". It also contained an array of plans of hypothetical projects such as "A Contemporary City of Three Million Inhabitants" displayed earlier at the "Salon L'Automne" in 1922, and the "Voisin" plan for Paris, exhibited in 1925. There was also the Bauhaus school that emerged in Germany under Walter Gropius, another architectural luminary of the Modern Movement. These, in the early twentieth century became an integral part of a new pro-industrial school of thought and action in design and architecture extending also to urban planning, a school which saw the machine as a beneficent agency for mankind. Though receptive to the emerging industrial technology, the movement in its urban planning dimensions was also essentially based upon utopian visions.

This pro-industrial utopian preoccupation with ideal models has continued, notably among some architects in the industrialized countries. The "high technology" dreams of the "Metabolists" in Japan (Kikutake 1964), and the "Archigram Group" in Britain (Cook 1964) are examples. Another utopian model from that same period but which internalized some environmental concerns as well, was Paolo Soleri's concept for an alternative urban habitat called "*Arcology*" (Lewis and Skolimowski 1977).

The vision of garden cities with satellite towns appears still as being almost the only recognized planning model used to deal with urbanization in the South Asian region. Every now and again, a new satellite town is planned and built to cope with rapid urban expansion, as for example in Mumbai. Nevertheless such efforts seem merely to provide short-term palliatives which really are ineffective, as urbanization continues unabated. A serious researcher discussing the development of New Bombay ("Navi Mumbai") which is a recently established satellite town for Mumbai observes that:

> In the 1960s and 1970s, Asian urban development policies centered on slowing down the rate of urbanization through controls on the growth of the large metropolitan cities. Satellite towns and greenbelts have been among the most widely adopted means to achieve this. However, on the whole, satellite towns have proved to be ineffectual in meeting original objectives…The development of New Bombay is a reflection of many of the problems that have beset satellite-town building in Asia. (Shaw 1995)

In discussing a paper presented by an invited participant (Ul Haque 2014) at an important symposium, the editor of the published proceedings states that:

> Pakistani cities have long been a story of sprawl. A precedent was set in the 1960s, when the new city of Islamabad was built with a "garden city" approach—one that emphasizes low-rise suburbs and large residential housing facilities. It is a model that discourages downtown development, high-rise buildings, services (from retail stores to libraries), and even office facilities—and it remains the prevailing paradigm of urban planning today. (Kugelman 2014)

Utopian visions from late nineteenth century Britain and early twentieth century Continental Europe may have given rise in the industrialized West to some useful spatial planning models paralleled by interesting architecture. But, the serious question does arise as to the relevance of those models derived from utopian visions to the particular context of concern here. The scale of the current urbanization problem in South Asia is of a different order of magnitude from its manifestation in England and Continental Europe when the popular utopian concepts were first envisioned. The estimated total population of England and Wales combined at the census in 1901 was approximately 32.6 million. Their estimated urban population at that time, being 77% of the total (Hicks and Allen 1999), was hence approximately 25.1 million. The current urban population just of India alone *grows* today by double that figure every 5 years! (Table 7.1).

Theories from Spatial Economics

As discussed earlier, those who were preoccupied with ideal models for the industrializing cities in the context of urbanization in the West beginning in Britain were essentially Utopians. The city vis-a-vis its rural setting and explanations as to their formation, growth, and change were concerns largely ignored by them. That area was a focus of attention in Germany initiated by Von Thunen (1826). He had noted a pattern of concentric rings in agricultural land use around a particular market place. The explanation he put forward from his studies became the foundations of a theory on the location of economic activities. Based to a great extent on Von Thunen's work, Weber (1909) published a theory on industrial location. Christaller (1933) also a German, examining interurban configurations, developed his theory of "Central Places". He continued his work in the United States after World War II. There was a parallel development of the theory also in the United States attributed to Losch (1941). It would appear that the former theory is perhaps more appropriate to the task here. An authority on Central Place Theory (Woldenberg 2015) reminds that both theories, though valuable, are based on highly idealized geographic conditions which may not always exist in reality. He mentions incidentally that an early version of Central Place Theory was developed by J. H. Kolb in a series of nine articles beginning in 1923 (Berry and Alan 1964) and also mentions a book by J. G. Kohl (1850) written in German.

Growth Center Theories

The intrusion and popularity of Economic Growth Theory took place during the period that immediately followed World War II. With the rebuilding of war ravaged Europe underway, this theory was adopted and applied to the LMICs beginning around 1951. It influenced the course of spatial planning in some of those countries. According to Hansen (1981a), there was a controversy in the 1950s on "balanced versus unbalanced growth". Hansen identified four relatively independent versions of the unbalanced growth theory of which three were published in the 1950s:

"*Growth Poles*" (Perroux 1955); "Cumulative Causation" (Myrdal 1957); and "Polarization and Trickle Down" (Hirschman 1958). These were propounded by economists on the subject of spatial development. Rodwin (1963) an urban planner, had proposed a strategy of concentrated decentralization for developing backward regions. Friedman, another planner, disagreed with that approach. His, is said to be the first comprehensive center-hinterland development model. Dated at 1966, it is considered to be the fourth of the important "unbalanced growth" models (Hansen 1981b).

Perroux was concerned primarily with the interaction between industrial sectors, the dominance of one economic unit over another, and their urban locations in the surrounding region. Boudeville (1972) explored the spatial implications of Perroux's theory. Myrdal believed that once a center starts to grow for whatever reason, a series of processes begin to reinforce that growth. He also talked of "spread" effects from the center to the rural hinterland and a reverse "backwash". Hirschmann's is said to be the most optimistic of the growth center models, and was perhaps therefore most influential in the original victory of the advocates of "unbalanced growth" over the "balanced growth" proponents. While there are differences in these "growth center" models, there also are many similarities. An important common characteristic is the proposal that public and private sector capital investment for economic growth of a lagging region should be made in large concentrations at a few preselected geographic points, and not be thinly spread over the rural landscape. Development would then result at these points or "growth poles". The contention was that there would then be a polarization at these places and disparities in the living standards would begin to appear between these core areas vis-a-vis their respective peripheries, referred to sometimes in the literature as "divergence". However, with time, benefits from the investment and development effort at these poles would "spread" or "trickle down" to the hinterland. Thus a "convergence" of levels would come about soon enough—so claimed the theory.

The applications and outcomes of these growth center strategies to real-life situations have since been observed closely by many researchers. The general consensus among most including, e.g., Hansen (1981c) and Lo and Salih (1981) is not at all favorable toward the effectiveness of growth centers for their intended purpose. As had been significantly concluded,

> ...These (growth center strategies)...attempt to reduce the backwash effects between peripheral and more developed regions and at the same time create spread effects to the growth centers' hinterlands. Empirical analyses indicate that this has been achieved only rarely...(and at best)... growth centers have essentially led to a shift of disparities from the interregional to the intra regional level, but rarely seem to have led to an overall reduction of spatial disparities of living levels.... (Stohr and Todtling 1977)

Scholarly reactions based on evidence against the Growth Center Theories of the 1950s began to appear in the late 1970s or early 1980s. This disenchantment led several scholars including a few like Friedman who saw some value in them before, to look for alternatives. Walter Stohr, Fraser Taylor, Niles Hansen, Clyde Weaver, Eddy Lee, Fu-chen Lo, and Kamal Salih are some of the other pioneers. They were in the search for what Stohr and Taylor (1981) called "development from below" alternatives to the "development from above" growth center paradigm. An important publication (Lo and Salih 1978) elaborates several points reflecting different aspects of the failure of growth center strategies for regional development in Asian countries. Their main conclusions are that these strategies applied in the context of current conditions and spatial patterns tend to increase, not decrease inequalities between core and peripheral areas; and that they fail even in providing the basic needs of local people in the peripheries, whereas the requirement in the peripheries is for strategies that encourage greater autonomy and self-sustained rural development.

After much study in India, the Council for Social Development in collaboration with the Ford Foundation brought out a manual intended for use by planners and field officers to assist them inter alia in the rational distribution of infrastructure for integrated rural development (Roy and Patil 1977a, b, c). The studies covered the theoretical issues. They also gathered and assimilated a considerable volume of field level experience. The project went through a number of stages beginning in 1968 when the Indian Ministry of Community Development proposed a pilot study to establish the basis for viable rural communities. The scheme eventually had twenty research cells located in eighteen states with direction and coordination by a Central Research Cell. By 1970, the Project was designed to have five objectives of which the first was to identify growth centers and the villages within their service areas (Roy and Patil 1977a, b, c: 5). The theoretical studies carried out included a review of Western literature on the growth center concept (Roy and Patil 1977a, b, c: 24). It is both interesting and noteworthy that after 8 years of research experience gained by the Project, the term "Growth Centre" was quite deliberately dropped and replaced by the term "Service Centre" (Roy and Patil 1977a, b, c: 6). Thus, it may be seen that an important research project that harnessed and exercised competence, capability, and commitment to study the spatial issues in depth, both in theory and in the field, rejected the "growth center" concept as being irrelevant to rural and regional development in India.

There is a fundamental divergence between policies based on the "growth center" concept and the "service center" concept. The discussion has mainly to do with the types and target locations of development investment. In the former, capital is invested in existing or proposed urban areas which are then expected to experience growth and development and to spread the benefits to their rural hinterlands. In the latter, most of the development investment is made directly in the rural hinterlands so that development would result there first. The towns are expected to provide the basic goods and services for their respective surrounding rural population to facilitate rural development. Some investments would therefore have to be made in the towns themselves, but these would be aimed at introducing or upgrading socioeconomic infrastructure for the benefit of the hinterland population.

The Theory of Duality

A school of thought traceable to Boeke (1953) sees an LMIC's economy as being a duality consisting of a backward, tradition-bound agriculture sector on the one hand, where capitalism is not indigenous and therefore retarded; and on the other hand, a small, urban industrial sector where capitalism has been imported full-blown from the West. Development was thus seen as a process by which the latter progresses rapidly to overtake and dominate the former. These scholars consider urbanization as being essentially a beneficent process. Many of them believe that rural folk in the LMICs are so poor and backward that migration to cities is almost their only available process of emancipation from poverty and ignorance. The roots of such beliefs may be embedded in the cultural alienation that often exists between Westernized urban elites and indigenous rural populations. The dual economy argument is also sometimes bolstered by a theory, critically discussed by Wellisz (1968), which suggests that the marginal productivity of labor in agriculture is zero and therefore the rural sector can become an unlimited source of labor supply for urban industry without a corresponding reduction in agricultural product.

However, there were notable others who may be seen to strongly differ. Johnson was among the earliest of Western researchers to recognize that a dual economy and polarized urbanization in the LMICs may not be beneficial but even be seriously detrimental. In his view, rural–urban migration is a

> …cruel process of disorderly change…(which)…has frustrated and counteracted any prospects of a diffused type of orderly urbanization whereby a vitalization of rural landscapes could be set in motion…It has allowed the nations that most need an organically integrated regional development to weaken the links between town and country and allow an unplanned dual economy to emerge…. (Johnson 1970a)

There were others too who also saw rural out-migration as a loss to agriculture of the more intelligent and able-bodied youth—a loss that would adversely impact upon the urgent need to increase and maintain agricultural production for food security in the LMICs. The views of Nobel Laureates Theodore Schultz (1964) and Norman E. Borlaug (1970), and the very first World Food Prize winner M. S. Swaminathan (1987) may be mentioned. They strongly recommend appropriate interventions of science and technology in agriculture. Such interventions could now also include organic farming and recent advances in biotechnology, subject of course to safety protocols. These recommendations implicitly suggest that the lot of an LMIC's rural poor can indeed be vastly improved in situ while enhancing the respective national development objectives. In this context, it may be useful to give consideration to the usefulness of land reform. There may be valuable lessons to be learnt by examining the reforms that took place in Japan in the period that immediately followed the Second World War (Kawagoe 1999).

The Urban Rank–Size Relationship

A few other scholars have sought to understand whether a relationship exists between the "rank" and "size" of towns within any country, where rank refers to hierarchical order and the size of towns is determined by the numbers of residents. A particularly important study was carried out by Linsky (1965). These studies have suggested two very distinct patterns. In one, rank and size are closely correlated in a very regular and predictable manner. In such urban systems, the "rank–size rule" is said to apply. The other pattern is one in which the largest city predominates very substantially in size over the next in rank. Such a pattern is said to display "primacy" and the first ranking urban place is called a "primate city". This subject of primacy is discussed more fully in Chap. 8.

Yet another different but significant piece of work was done by a Latin American scholar (Frank 1969). He sought to establish a causal link between colonialism and the condition of underdevelopment. In doing so, he presented an explanation of the process by which the existing dendritic national urban configurations of most LMICs, often called "market systems" became highly skewed structures. The skewing process he attributed to the military and economic agencies of the respective colonial periods of those countries. His views are quite well recognized today, but not always with due credit to him. A UN publication states:

> …many developing countries are characterized by a so-called dendritic market system, which is the legacy of a colonial past and/or of persisting international dependency relations…. (ESCAP 1979a, b, c)

Johnson was one of the first among Western scholars to have understood that a national urban system, with a skewed dendritic market structure left behind as a colonial legacy in a LMIC, has little utility for national development. In his own words:

> …The thrust in such a system is outward, whether there is now any actual "colonial" control or whether a domestic capital city has replaced the external "metropole" as a trading center… This trade does nothing to integrate town and country, …the small traders have no capacity to change it; the city based merchants have no incentive to do so. (Johnson 1970b)

In other words, market forces alone cannot be expected to alter a skewed national urban system. Therefore, a clear need can be established in such an LMIC for at least some limited intervention at the national policy level to help the country free itself from this particular colonially derived structural constraint.

Small and Mid-Sized Towns

A well-founded approach bearing a strong spatial content has since begun to gain support. It began with a few influential South Asian planners agreeing at a seminar that small- and medium-sized towns have a very special role to play in the development of their respective countries (Seminar 1978). As the conclusions of this seminar are particularly relevant to urban development in South Asia, a summarized version as found in the report of the proceedings is presented in Appendix A. More than two decades later, one of the younger participants at that seminar was the lead speaker at an important and comprehensive discussion focused on urbanization in Bangladesh cosponsored by the UNFPA. The way forward he recommends includes the

> ...need for guiding the progress of the country through a national human settlements policy which will include policy on urbanization and urban development.

He states that in such a policy, special consideration should be given to decentralized urbanization by: deconcentrating growth in Dhaka city; encouraging the growth of secondary cities, small towns and the planned growth of rural towns; extending urban services to existing villages; and enhancing income-earning opportunities to reduce rural out-migration (Islam 1999).

Following the Kathmandu Seminar of 1978, two subsequent papers appeared and are discussed below. These two publications dating from the mid-1980s were not the first to break new ground in conceptualizing the subject. They are included for discussion here because the similar theme they too emphasized added more weight to the particular emerging approach which influenced academic circles concerned with urbanization and development in the LMICs.

In the first of these two publications, that author states that colonial economic policies pursued and reinforced by postcolonial economic growth strategies of the 1950s and 1960s were major causative factors behind the rapid growth of a few primate cities to extraordinary size in most Asian countries; that the emphasis in these strategies was placed on developing urban industry over agriculture and rural development; that the distributional effects and the spatial implications of investment allocation were largely ignored; and that although much effort was made to modernize some sectors of the metropolitan economy, rural regions were neglected and left poor and underdeveloped. The same author also emphasizes that in countries with dominant primate cities, few secondary mid-sized cities could grow large enough and have sufficiently diversified economies to attract rural migrants, stimulate rural economies, and promote regional development. He says in concluding the discussion:

> ...few industrial growth poles are unlikely to have much impact on relieving pressure on large metropolitan areas. But a well-developed system of secondary and intermediate sized cities might provide a stronger spatial framework for encouraging a more balanced pattern of urban development and economic growth... if secondary cities that are selected for development are not themselves to become enclaves that drain the resources of their surrounding rural areas, the economic activities fostered within them must be closely related to the agricultural economies of their rural hinterlands. (Rondinelli 1986)

The other paper mentioned above also justifies spatial programs for the development of small and intermediate urban places. The two authors of that publication had based their work on a review of over 100 empirical studies across the LMICs and also on a review of a large number of national programs for small and intermediate towns. According to them, these spatial programs

> ...can be a crucial component in attaining social and economic objectives such as increasing the proportion of national populations reached by basic services; increasing and diversifying agricultural production; and increasing the influence of citizens living in sub-national and sub-regional political and administration units.... (Hardoy and Satterthwaite 1988)

A UN publication provides some valuable observations and general conclusions for the Asia Pacific regional context (ESCAP 1979a, b, c: 87). It proceeds to state: that urban–rural inequality is a major problem in the region; that the disparities in respect of services, income-earning opportunities and wage rates have caused concern; and that many governments in the region now pay special attention to rural development to achieve a more balanced growth spatially and between rural and urban areas. The study also mentions by way of an example that the limited success of a Malaysian policy directed at decentralization of industry (through a growth pole approach) was superseded by a "regional planning approach". It further states that in the developed countries spread effects often prevail over backwash effects and that in developing countries polarization continues unabated (ESCAP 1979b). It points to the following advantages of decentralization by a regional planning approach through a hierarchy of urban and rural centers: lower cost of housing, infrastructure and other urban facilities; promotion of rural development in general and agricultural production in particular, which are considered to be prerequisites to sustained growth; reduction of social and cultural disruption by the national development efforts; and achievement of a more equitable distribution of the benefits of national development and economic growth.

More recently, one of those same authors on the subject, summarizing a publication of his on Asian urban development states that

> Most governments now recognize that diffusion of urban growth, rather than its control and suppression, is essential for economic development... Asian governments are refocusing their urban development policies on ... (inter alia)... investing in secondary cities and towns with growth potential and integrating urban and rural markets.... (Rondinelli 1991)

Even assuming a committed approach to rural and agricultural development, out-migration from rural areas for nonfarm occupations may be expected to continue, though on a reduced scale. As discussed above, the development of small towns to function as service centers for agriculture and mid-sized towns for higher order goods, services, and some light industrial activities can be valuable in fostering regional development; and the latter with nonagricultural job opportunities could greatly reduce rural migrations to the large cities. Rather than have rural migrants move to the larger cities as they generally tend to do, the more manageable and therefore preferred scenario would be one where they move to the small and mid-sized towns. In this preferred scenario, movements to the large cities would be confined to migrants from mid-sized towns. This pattern of internal migration is sometimes referred to as "decentralized urbanization".

The urban-based services and related activities to be provided in small- and mid-sized towns not only require built infrastructure but also depend upon the availability of people with special skills to be resident in those towns. As skills of this nature are not always readily available in the envisaged new towns, a proactive planned urban settlement program to provide these skills is a clear need (Gunaratna 2000).

References

Abercrombie P (1949) Regional plan for Colombo. Department of Town and Country Planning Colombo, Sri Lanka
Abrams C (1964) Man's struggle for shelter in an urbanizing world. MIT Press, Cambridge, MA
Arif GM, Hamid S (2009) Urbanization, city growth and quality of life in Pakistan. Eur J Soc Sci 10(2):214
Belsky ES et al (2013a) Advancing inclusive and sustainable urban development. Joint Center for Housing Studies of Harvard University, Cambridge, MA, p 19
Belsky ES et al (2013b) Advancing inclusive and sustainable urban development. Joint Center for Housing Studies of Harvard University, Cambridge, MA, p 32
Benevolo L (1971) Origins of modern town planning. English edition: Landry J. MIT Press, Cambridge, MA
Berry BJL, Horton FE (1970) Geographic perspectives on urban systems. Prentice Hall, Englewood Cliffs, NJ, p 66
Berry BJL, Pred A (1964) Central place studies: a bibliography of theory and applications. Bibliography Series, No. 1. Regional Science Research Institute, Philadelphia
Bloom DE, Khanna T (2007) The urban revolution, finance and development. UN Department of Economic and Social Affairs, Population Division. In: Population distribution, urbanization, internal migration and development: an International perspective, 2011, p 1
Boeke JH (1953) Economics and economic policies of dual societies as exemplified by Indonesia. International Secretariat of the Institute of Pacific Relations, New York
Boudeville J (1972) Amenagement du territoire et polarization. Genin
Christaller W (1933) Central places in southern Germany. English edition: Baskin C (1966). Prentice Hall, Englewood Cliffs, NJ
Cook P et al (1964) The Archigram Group. In: architectural association quarterly, London
Dahrendorf R (1968) Essays on the theory of society. Stanford University Press, CA, pp 107–110
Datta P (2006) Urbanisation in India. In: European population conference, Liverpool, UK, pp 24–26. http://160592857366.free.fr/joe/ebooks/ShareData/Urbanisation+in+India.pdf. Accessed 10 Oct 2013
ESCAP (1979a) Guidelines for rural centre planning. UN, New York, p 58
ESCAP (1979b) Guidelines for rural centre planning. UN, New York, p 89
ESCAP (1979c) Guidelines for rural centre planning. UN, New York, pp 87–89
ESCAP (2011) Statistical yearbook for Asia and the Pacific. UN, New York, Table 1.7, p 153
ESCAP (2012) Economic and social survey of Asia and the Pacific. UN, New York, p 25
Frank AG (1969) Development of underdevelopment. Monthly Review Press, New York
Friedmann J, Weaver C (1979) Territory and function: the evolution of regional planning. University of California Press, Berkeley and Los Angeles
Galpin CJ (1915) Social anatomy of an agricultural community. Agricultural Experiment Station Bulletin No. 34. University of Madison, Wisconsin
Gunaratna KL (2000) Accelerating regional development. In: Indraratna ADVS (Ed) A quarter century of Mahaweli: retrospect and prospect. National Academy of Sciences Sri Lanka, Colombo, Sri Lanka, pp 266–268
Hansen NM (1981a) Development from above: the centre-down development paradigm. In: Stohr WB, Taylor DRF (eds) Development from above or below. Wiley, New York, p 15

Hansen NM (1981b) Development from above: the centre-down development paradigm. In: Stohr WB, Taylor DRF (eds) Development from above or below. Wiley, New York, p 19

Hansen NM (1981c) Development from above: the centre-down development paradigm. In: Stohr WB, Taylor DRF (eds) Development from above or below. Wiley, New York, pp 33, 36

Hardoy JE, Satterthwaite D (1988) Small and intermediate urban centres in the third world: what role for government? Third World Plan Rev J Liverpool, 8

Hicks J, Allen G (1999) A century of change: trends in UK statistics since 1900 (Research Paper 99/111), House of Commons Library, London. http://www.parliament.uk/documents/commons/lib/research/rp99/rp99-111.pdf. Accessed 10 Oct 2013

Hirschman AO (1958) The strategy of economic development. Yale University Press, CT, New Haven

Hossain S (2006) Rapid mass urbanisation and its social consequences in Bangladesh: the case of the megacity of Dhaka. In: 16th Biennial conference of the Asian studies association of Australia, Wollagong, Australia, pp 7, 8

Howard E (1898) Garden cities of tomorrow. Revised edition (1985). Attic Books, Eastboune, UK

IAP (The Global Network of Science Academies) (2012) Population and consumption. Report to the Rio+20 Earth Summit

Islam N (1999) Urbanisation, migration and development in Bangladesh: recent trends and emerging issues. Centre for Policy Dialogue (in association with UNFPA), Dhaka, Bangladesh

Johnson EAJ (1970a) The organization of space in developing countries. Harvard University Press, Cambridge, MA, pp 161, 162

Johnson EAJ (1970b) The organization of space in developing countries. Harvard University Press, Cambridge, MA, pp 86, 87

Kanbur et al (eds) (2014) Inequality in Asia and the Pacific: trends, drivers, and policy implications. Asian Development Bank, Manila, pp 79, 80, 97, 98

Kaw JK (2015) Can better spatial planning transform South Asian cities? A World Bank Report. World Bank, Washington, DC

Kawagoe T (1999) Agricultural land reform in postwar Japan: experiences and issues. Development Research Group, Rural Development. World Bank, Washington, DC

Khan A (2014) The rise of Karachi as a mega-city: issues and challenges. Mahbub ul Haq Centre, Lahore University of Management Sciences, Lahore, Pakistan

Kikutake K et al (1964) The metabolists. In: Architectural design (May 1965), London, p 219

Kolb JH (1923) Central place studies: a bibliography of theory and application bibliography series number one (Berry BJL, Pred A). Regional Science Research Institute, Philadelphia, 1965

Kugelman M (ed) (2014) Pakistan's runaway urbanization: what can be done? Woodrow Wilson International Center for Scholars, Washington, DC

Le Corbusier (1925) Urbanisme, Paris. English edition: Etchells F (1971). The city of tomorrow. MIT Press, Cambridge, MA

Lewis R, Skolimowski H (1977) Arcology as an alternative urban habitat. Impact Sci Soc UNESCO J 27(2)

Linsky AS (1965) Some generalization concerning primate cities. Ann Am Assoc Geogr 55:506–513

Lo FC, Salih K (eds) (1978) Growth pole strategies and regional development policy. In: Asian experience and alternative strategies. Pergamon, Oxford, pp 163–192

Lo FC, Salih K (1981) Growth poles, agropolitan development and polorization reversal: the debate and search for alternatives. In: Stohr WB, Taylor DRF (eds) Development from above or below. Wiley, New York, p 125

Losch A (1941) The economics of location. English edition: Stopler WP, Woglom WH (1954). Yale University Press, New Haven, CT

Markelius S, Sidenbladh G (1949) Town planning in Stockholm. In: Ten lectures on Swedish architecture. Svenska Arkitekters Riksforbund, Stockholm, pp 62, 75

Miraftab F (2009) Insurgent planning: situating radical planning in the Global South. Plann Theor J 8:32–50. https://doi.org/10.1177/1473095208099297. Accessed 6 Oct 2017

References

Mohit MA (1990) Rural-urban migration in Bangladesh: an urban perspective. J Bangladesh Inst Planners J l(1, 2):41–59

Myrdal G (1957) Rich lands and poor. Harper & Brothers, New York

Perroux F (1955) Note sur la Notion de Pole de Croissance in L'economie du XX eme Siecle, 2nd edn. Presses Universitaires de France, Paris

Pevsner N (1963) An outline of European architecture, 7th edn. Pelican, London, pp 402, 403

Premadasa R (1980) Address to the UN general assembly, New York

Richards JM (1956) An introduction to modern architecture. Penguin, UK, p 78

Rodwin L (1963) Choosing regions for development. In: Friedrich C, Harris SE (eds) Public policy, vol 12. Harvard University Press, Cambridge, MA, pp 142–162

Rondinelli DA (1986) Metropolitan growth and secondary cities development policy. Habitat Int J 10(12):263–281

Rondinelli DA (1991) Asian urban development policies in the 1990s: from growth control to urban diffusion. World Dev J 19(7):791–803

Roy P, Patil BR (eds) (1977a) Manual for block level planning. Macmillan, Delhi, India

Roy P, Patil BR (eds) (1977b) Manual for block level planning. Macmillan, Delhi, India, pp 5, 6, 24

Roy P, Patil BR (eds) (1977c) Manual for block level planning. Macmillan, Delhi, India, p 6

Schultz TW (1964) Transforming traditional agriculture. Yale University Press, New Haven, CN

Seminar Proceedings (1978) Small and medium sized towns in regional development, mimeo. Quaker International Affairs Program, Kathmandu (see Annexe A)

Seto KC et al (2012) Global forecasts of urban expansion to 2030 and direct impacts on biodiversity and carbon pools. In: Proceedings of the National Academy of Sciences, US. http://www.pnas.org/content/early/2012/09/11/1211658109.full.pdf+html. Accessed 10 Oct 2013

Shaw A (1995) Satellite town development in Asia: the case of new Bombay, India. Urban Geogr J 16(3):254–271

Stohr WB, Todtling F (1977) Evaluation of regional policies: experience in market and mixed economies. In: Hansen NM (ed) Human settlement systems. Ballinger, New York, pp 91–95

Turner JFC, Fichter R (eds) (1972) Freedom to build. Macmillan, New York, London

Ul Haque N (2014) Frustrated urbanization and failed development in Pakistan. In: Kugelman Michael (ed) Pakistan's runaway urbanization: what can be done? Woodrow Wilson International Center for Scholars, Washington, DC

UN (2012) World urbanization prospects: highlights. UN, New York, p 7

Von Thunen JH (1826) Der Isolierte Staat in Beziehung auf Landwirtschaft und Nationalökonomie. Rostock, Germany. English edition (1966). The Isolated State, Pergamon, Oxford

Watson V (2012) Planning and the 'stubborn realities' of global south cities: some emerging ideas. Plann Theor. https://doi.org/10.1177/1473095212446301

Weber A (1909) Über den standort der industrie. English edition: Freidich CJ (1928). Theory of the location of industries. University of Chicago Press, Chicago

Wellisz S (1968) Dual economies, disguised unemployment and the unlimited supply of labor. Economica J New Ser 35(137):22–51

Woldenberg MJ (2015) In an unpublished personal correspondence with the author

World Bank (2016) Leveraging urbanization in South Asia. World Bank, Washington, DC

Chapter 8
Urban Primacy

Abstract The focus here is on a theory of basic relevance to the desired spatial planning approach to deal with rapid urbanization in many LMICs. It concerns the phenomena of "urban primacy" often observable in the smaller LMICs. A few scholars have examined the relationship between the rank and size of cities within the city systems of various countries. Their work suggested the existence of two distinct patterns. In one, rank and size of cities are correlated in a regular manner. In the other, the largest city predominates substantially over the next in rank. The latter pattern is said to display "primacy" and the highest ranked city is called a "primate city". One scholar, having reviewed earlier work by others, surmised that "primacy" is characteristic of the smaller "underdeveloped" countries having a colonial past. Those studies suggest: that primate cities attract a disproportionate part of available resources; that such city systems should be restructured so as to enable a more equitable distribution of resources for the benefit of their respective hinterland populations; and that doing so would greatly reduce rural–urban migration to primate cities and thereby diminish the problems arising from the impact of rapid urbanization.

Preamble

The view has already been expressed in Chap. 7 of this book that the major efforts to deal with urbanization in South Asia have relied generally upon exogenous theory and practice developed more than a century ago for very different geographic and socioeconomic circumstances. The case has also been made there, citing key intellectual sources, on the need to build a relevant theoretical base for a new approach to deal with urbanization in South Asia and perhaps also in other low- and middle-income countries (LMICs). This present chapter focuses and expands on one of the theories considered here as being of basic relevance to defining the desired new approach. It has to do with the phenomena of "urban primacy" in its observable presence especially in the smaller LMICs. These are countries that have all undergone colonial subjugation.

It may also be recalled from Chap.7 that a few scholars have examined the relationship between the rank and size of cities within the city systems of various countries. Their studies suggest the existence of two very distinct patterns. In one, rank and size are correlated in a regular and predictable manner wherein a rank–size rule may be said to apply. The other is one in which the largest city predominates very substantially over the next in rank and all other cities. Such a pattern is said to display "primacy" and the first ranking city is called a "primate city".

Linsky (1965) carried out one of the important studies on subject of primacy. He acknowledged that the concept was introduced in a paper by Jefferson written as far back as in 1939. Having briefly reviewed the literature available at the time of his paper, Linsky went on to state and test six hypotheses about the conditions under which primacy occurs. These conditions appeared to do with: the areal extent of the countries; their per capita incomes; whether they had a "colonial" history and colonially developed export-oriented agricultural economies; and, the rate of their population growth. He used a sample of statistical data gathered in and around 1955 from several countries. He then applied routine techniques to study the correlation between each of the variables and the respective degrees of primacy. His findings may be summarized briefly as follows: that primacy is characteristic especially of "underdeveloped" countries in a transitional phase of social and economic development, having a colonial past, agricultural economies, low per capita incomes, fast rates of population growth, and are dependent upon exports (Linsky 1965). A few years later another important study on primacy was carried out by Berry and Horton (1970). The usefulness of all these studies was twofold. First, it focused more light on the existence of the pattern of primacy in the hierarchical order of national urban systems within many LMICs. Second, it suggested a causal relationship between primacy and economic conditions residual from a colonial history.

As already mentioned, "primacy" is not generally found in countries that have not been subjected to colonialism. Where it is appreciable, it is in countries that have engaged in colonizing other countries. Elsewhere if it is found at all, it is generally less pronounced. The obvious question that arises about primacy in the smaller LMICs is about the relevance of these distorted city systems to the needs of their respective postcolonial economic and social development objectives, especially if they are now being very differently poised, oriented, and pursued.

An important intention here in this chapter is to examine the validity of Linsky's theoretical position noting that his conclusions were based on data mainly from a particular time period, namely around 1955. Thus, this present chapter explores the theory in the current context after the lapse of more than half a century. For this purpose, eight countries were selected for case studies from among the LMICs corresponding to Linsky's stated criteria. These countries were selected from among those geographically located in the continents of Asia, sub-Saharan Africa, and South America. Of the LMICs, China, India, South Africa, Brazil, and Argentina were excluded from the examination on the grounds that they were too large to conform to the size specification in the theory. The countries wherein their boundaries had been altered substantially in the postcolonial period were also excluded in the process of selection. Thus, the sample of countries was a random selection from among those small, predominantly agrarian coastal countries in the identified three continents. The countries selected were: Vietnam, Myanmar, Sri Lanka from Asia; Mozambique, Senegal and Ghana from Africa; and Chile and Peru from South America. It will be seen that care has been taken in this selection to also consider the impact of as many as possible of the main European colonizing countries, these latter countries being France, Britain, Portugal, and Spain.

The Case Studies

Vietnam

Vietnam became a colonial protectorate of France in 1884. It thus became a source from which the French extracted raw materials and was also a market for French manufactured goods. The North of Vietnam being better endowed with mineral resources became for the French an area for the location of some industries, while the south was identified by them mainly for agriculture. Irrigated rice cultivation which was an important activity in the South, continued as a subsistence crop in the North. Plantations of coffee, tea, cotton, rubber, and tobacco were introduced in the North by the French along with the mining of coal, iron and some other metals. Hanoi in the north became a center for industry while Saigon in the south was selected for trade and consumer goods production. Thus, the colonial economy of Vietnam came to be based on the export of such items of raw material as coal and manufactured goods from the North, and rice and consumer goods from the south. There was simultaneously the large-scale import of most other manufactured goods into the country from France (Vietnam Country Study 1987).

Table 8.1 City populations in Vietnam (2013)

Rank	City	Population (est)
1	Ho Chi Minh City	3,467,331
2	Hanoi	1,431,270
3	Da Nang	752,493
4	Hai Phong	602,695
5	Bien Hoa	407,208
6	Hue	287,217
7	Nha Trang	283,441
8	Can Tho	259,598
9	Rach Gia	228,356
10	Qui Nhon	210,338

Source www.worldpopulationsreview.com

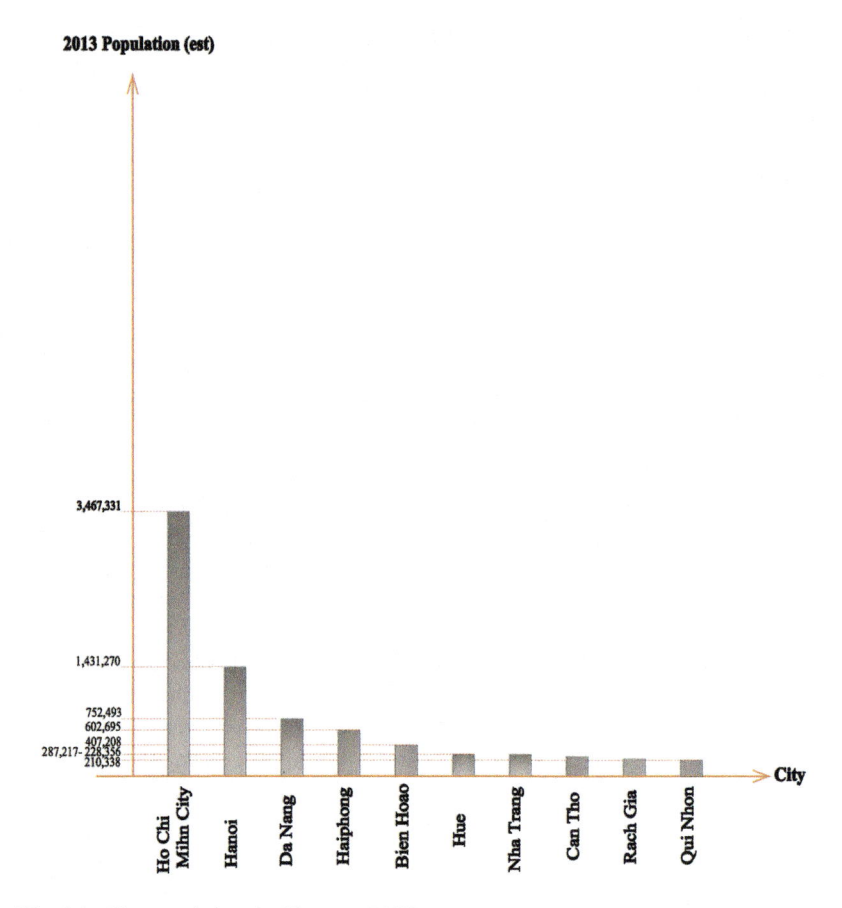

Fig. 8.1 City populations in Vietnam (1987)

Myanmar

The British fought three wars between 1824 and 1885 to gain control of Myanmar (then called Burma). Until 1937, Burma was ruled by the British as part of British India with Yangon, then called Rangoon, as the capital city. British colonial rule continued thereafter under a new constitution which was by no means acceptable to the indigenous population. Many Burmese leaders did not support the British even during World War II and some including their national hero Aung San fled to receive military training in Japan. The chaotic and violent period that ensued calmed temporarily only after that war immediately after the Aung San-Atlee Agreement of 1947. The "Union of Burma" was then established but soon thereafter General Aung San along with many of his Cabinet colleagues was assassinated. The reigns of the government were taken over then by U. Nu who was the most senior remaining member of the original Aung San Cabinet. U. Nu was ousted from power by the military led by General Ne Win in the late 1950s and the military dominance in government has continued to date.

Agriculture by peasant farm families for food self-sufficiency formed the basis of the traditional Burmese economy. The main food crop was rice. The colonial impact led to trade based on the export of rice and teak and the import of manufactured goods mainly from Britain. Rangoon, the capital, at the mouth of the Irrawaddy River was used as the main port for shipping and trade. The benefits of this colonial trade economy did not accrue to the Burmese as much as it did to the British with some spillovers to Indian merchants and money lenders. This led to a more closed economy during several decades of the postcolonial period which tended to exclude foreign businesses from participating in the Burmese economy (British rule in Burma; Wikipedia).

Table 8.2 City populations Myanmar (2012)

Rank	City	Population
1	Yangoon	4,948,920
2	Mandalay	1,620,758
3	Mawlamyine	542,017
4	Bago	278,622
5	Pathein	277,382
6	Meiktila	244,768
7	Mergui	215,636
8	Akyab	205,059
9	Myingyan	195,675
10	Monywa	194,532

Source Google Earth

2012 Population

[Bar chart showing city populations in Myanmar:
- Rangoon: 4,948,920
- Mandalay: 1,620,758
- Mawlamyine: 542,017
- Bago: 278,622
- Pathein: 277,382
- Meiktila: 244,768
- Mergui: 215,636
- Akyab: 195,615
- Myingyan: 194,932
- Monywa]

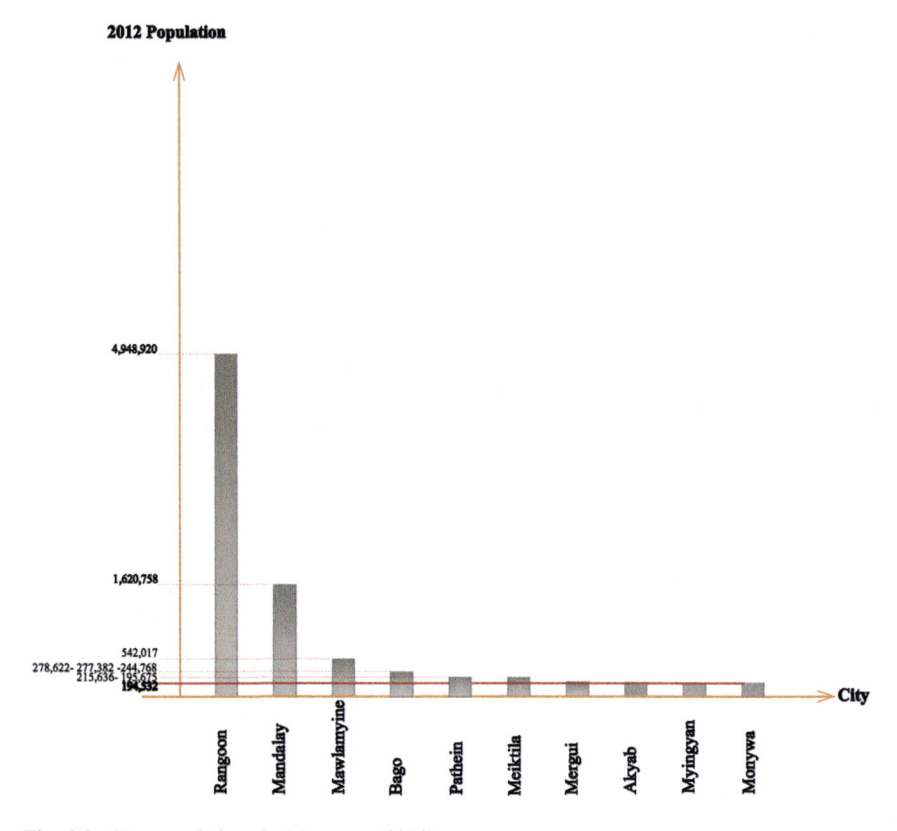

Fig. 8.2 City populations in Myanmar (2012)

Sri Lanka

Most of the external trade in the fifteenth century was conducted through Arab sailors. European colonial influence in Sri Lanka began in 1505 with the arrival of the Portuguese, continued through a period of Dutch occupation starting in 1656 till the early eighteenth century when British control ensued and extended till 1948. The Portuguese ousted the Arabs external trade. They and later the Dutch controlled in turn only the maritime regions of island with its bulk being firmly maintained and militarily defended from the hill country by the Sinhalese. Both the Portuguese and the Dutch were keenly interested in the spice trade. Thus, the imposed colonial economy involved the cultivation and extraction of spice with a special focus on cinnamon, all of which was for export mainly to Europe. The main port through which this trade traversed was through Colombo where a fort had been constructed by the Portuguese and improved upon by the Dutch. The British gained control of the hill country through a treaty and thus gained and maintained jurisdiction over the entire island. The British were more interested in agricultural produce which could be had from the heavily forested fertile hills which soon were covered with plantations of coffee and tea. Later, rubber and coconut plantations were established in the lower elevations. New transport routes and towns were developed between these plantations and Colombo generally and substantially to the exclusion of other areas. With industrialization in Britain, railroads were built to supplement the transportation infrastructure for the extraction and delivery of plantation produce to the port in Colombo for shipment to Britain. The port was substantially improved to cope with this trade. The Colombo port was ranked at the end of WW1 to be the 3rd best in the British Empire and 5th worldwide.

Table 8.3 City populations in Sri Lanka (2012)

Rank	City	Population
1	Colombo (with suburbs: Dehiwala, Mt. Lavinia, Moratuwa, and Peliyagoda)	1,238,029
2	Negombo and Katunayake	204,570
3	Sri Jayawardenapura Kotte	135,806
4	Kandy	125,351
5	Kalmunai	106,783
6	Vavuniya	99,653
7	Galle	99,478
8	Trincomalee	99,135
9	Batticaloa	92,332
10	Jaffna	88,138

Source Wikipedia (Construction; 2012 estimate)

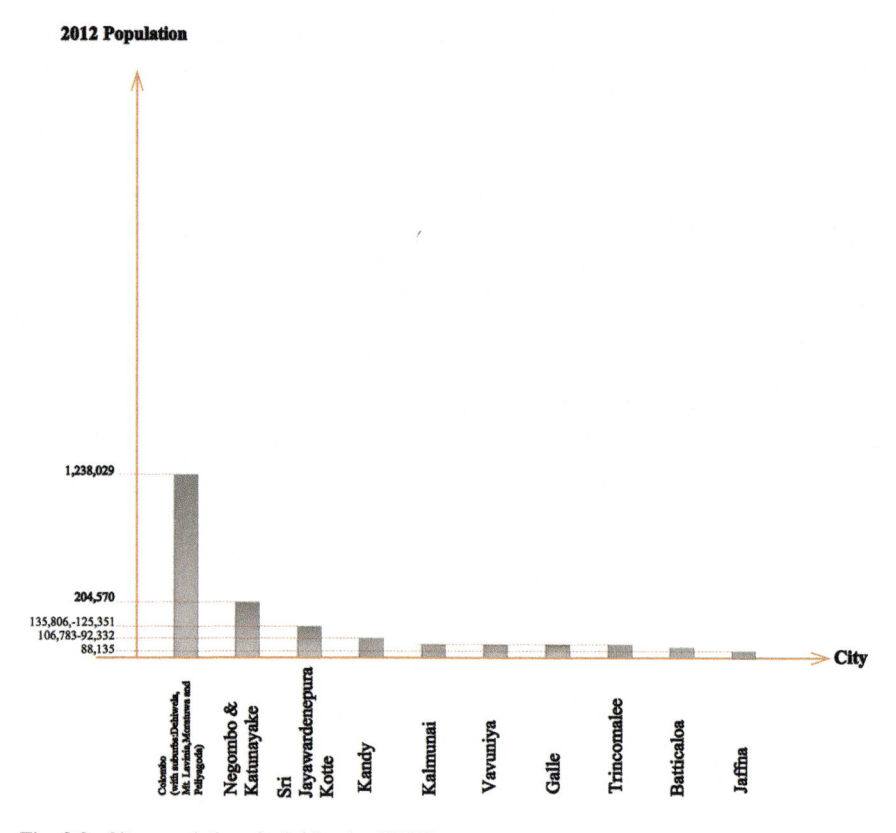

Fig. 8.3 City populations in Sri Lanka (2012)

Mozambique

Trade with the outside world had taken place in the region of Mozambique through Arab trade and their settlements on the coast till the Portuguese arrived in 1498 and gradually took over that trade. Portuguese trading posts and ports were established and began to control trade beginning about 1500. The Portuguese government based in Lisbon had greater interest in their colonized territories in the East and the West. Thus, their control in Mozambique was exercised through delegated powers to Portuguese settlers and private companies financed mostly by the British. By the twentieth century, railroad lines had been established mainly to ship local labor to British colonies nearby and to South Africa.

Even after World War II, Portugal attempted to hold on to whatever colonial possessions they had. With the economy of Mozambique continuing to benefit mainly the white settlers, anticolonial political groups formed and coalesced into a liberation front ("FRELIMO") in 1962. An armed struggle ensued in 1964 which lasted 10 years and led to a negotiated "independence" for Mozambique in 1975.

While there is an appreciable difference in size between the first two cities in Mozambique, i.e., between Maputo and Matola, the lack of a very substantial difference in population size between them makes Mozambique a little different from most other small SMICs with primate cities. An explanation may be had from the fact that in 1698 Arab traders seized Portugal's key fort on Mombasa Island. This led to less Portuguese investments in Mozambique in favor of her other colonies. This would have resulted in a reduction in their interest in continuing the use and development of the port of Moputo and thus its consequent curtailment in growth. Thus, there is lesser population size difference in relation to Matola and other Mozambican cities (https://en.wikipedia.org/wiki/History_of_Mozambique).

Table 8.4 City populations in Mozambique (2013)

Rank	City	Population
1	Maputo	1,191,613
2	Matola	675,422
3	Beira	530,604
4	Nampula	388,526
5	Chimoio	256,936
6	Cidade de Nacala	224,795
7	Quelimane	188,964
8	Tete	129,316
9	Xai-Xai	127,366
10	Maxixe	119,868

Source www.worldpopulationsreview.com/Mozambique/cities

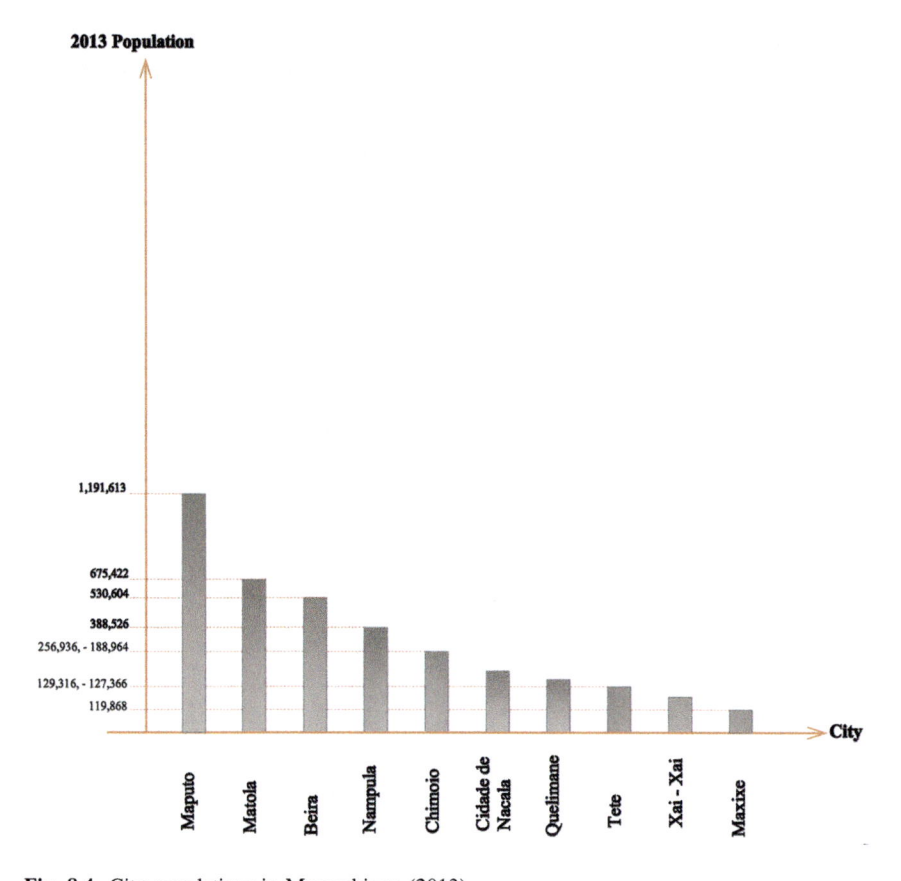

Fig. 8.4 City populations in Mozambique (2013)

Senegal

Despite competition from several other European trade interests, France came into possession in 1677 of the small island of Goree very near Dakar the present capital city of Senegal. This was an important departure point in the ongoing slave trade at that time. French extension into the mainland of Senegal took place in 1850 displacing the indigenous kingdoms. There was a merger in 1959 between Senegal and French Sudan to form the Republic of Mali which broke up within a year. Independence from France was proclaimed by Senegal and a Senagalese became their first president in 1960.

The colonial economy of Senegal was based on agriculture with particular attention to the growing transport to and from the port and capital city for the export of peanuts. Since independence, there was some diversification but state control of the purchase of all agricultural products and the growth of a "rentier class" are said to have led to the growers receiving less than the products' worth. This had resulted in the exacerbation of rural–urban migration.

Source: www.nationsencyclopedia.com.

The Case Studies 101

Table 8.5 City populations in Senegal (2010)

Rank	City	Population
1	Dakar	2,396,800
2	ToubaMosquee	620,500
3	Thies	278,200
4	Mbour	199,400
5	Kaolack	193,400
6	Saint-Louis	180,900
7	Rufisque	173,100
8	Zinguinchor	165,100
9	Diourbel	102,800
10	Louga	88,300

Source Agence Nationale de la Statistique et, de la Demographic, Senegal (web) 2010

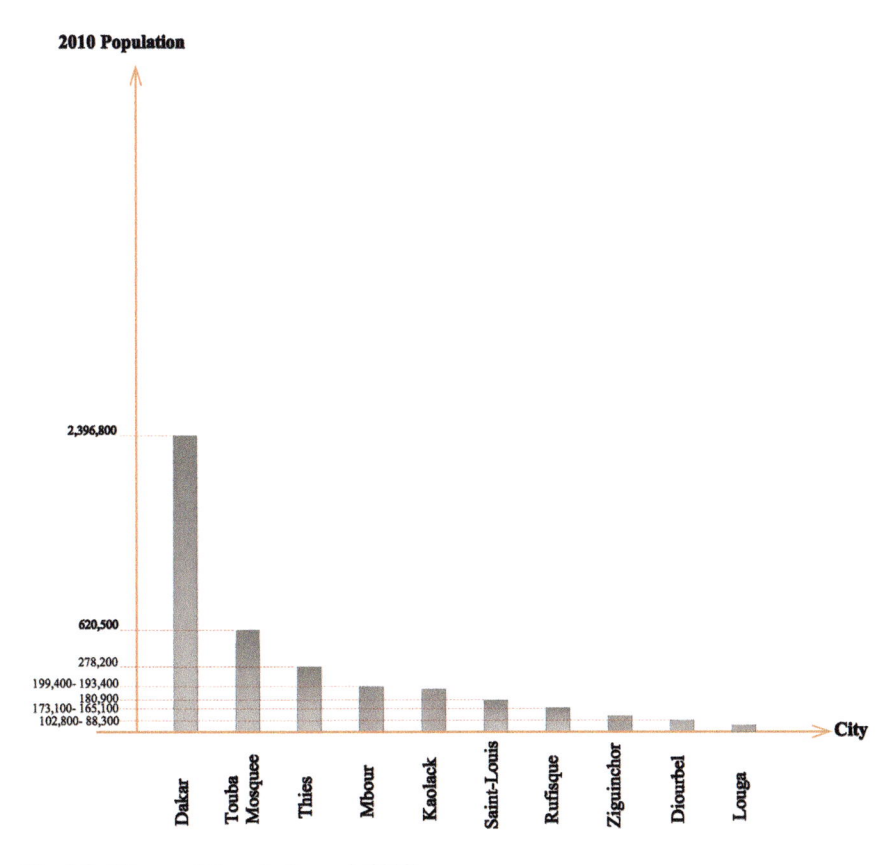

Fig. 8.5 City populations in Senegal (2010)

Ghana

Accra on the West African coast became prominent in the eighteenth century due to nearby Dutch forts and their active participation in the slave trade. Following the abolition of that trade in the early nineteenth century, the Dutch sold their forts to the British. After many battles with the indigenous peoples of central Ghana and the virtual destruction of Kumasi the Ashanti capital, Ghana was declared a Crown Colony of Britain. Accra was selected by them as Ghana's capital city. In 1908, the railway was built connecting Kumasi with Accra. Its completion in 1923 established a strong connection between the cocoa growing areas with the port in Accra. Cocoa soon became Ghana's main export. Accra's prosperity and the construction of infrastructure lead to much migration into Accra from the rural areas. The Ghanaian campaign for independence began with the Accra Riots of 1948. Independence from Britain was achieved in 1957 (Adarkwa 2012).

The lack a substantial difference in the size of the populations between the first and second ranked cities, i.e., Accra and Kumasi, is uncommon in most other studied LMICs. This therefore needs some explanation. During the colonial period after the abolition of the slave trade, Kumasi became almost as important as Accra due to the fact that it was the collection center for raw material to be exported from Accra. The construction of the railway connection between the two cities added more weight to the importance and growth of Kumasi. In the immediate postindependence development effort focused on import substitution under the leadership of Kwami Nkrumah (1957–1966), both Accra and Kumasi received almost equal importance in urban infrastructure development. The important place given to Kumasi continued even in the subsequent development strategies to date.

Table 8.6 City populations in Ghana (2013)

Rank	City	Population
1	Accra	1,963,264
2	Kumasi	1,468,609
3	Tamale	360,579
4	Takoradi	232,919
5	Achiaman	202,932
6	Tema	155,782
7	Teshi Old Town	144,013
8	Cape Coast	143,015
9	Sekondi-Takoradi	138,872
10	Obuasi	137,856

Source www.worldpopulationsreview.com

The Case Studies 103

[Bar chart showing 2013 Population by City]

- Accra: 1,963,264
- Kumasi: 1,468,609
- Tamale: 360,579
- Takoradi: 232,919
- Achiaman: 202,932
- Tema: 155,782
- Teshi Old Town: 144,013
- Cape Coast: 143,015
- Sekondi-Takoradi: 138,872
- Obuasi: 137,856

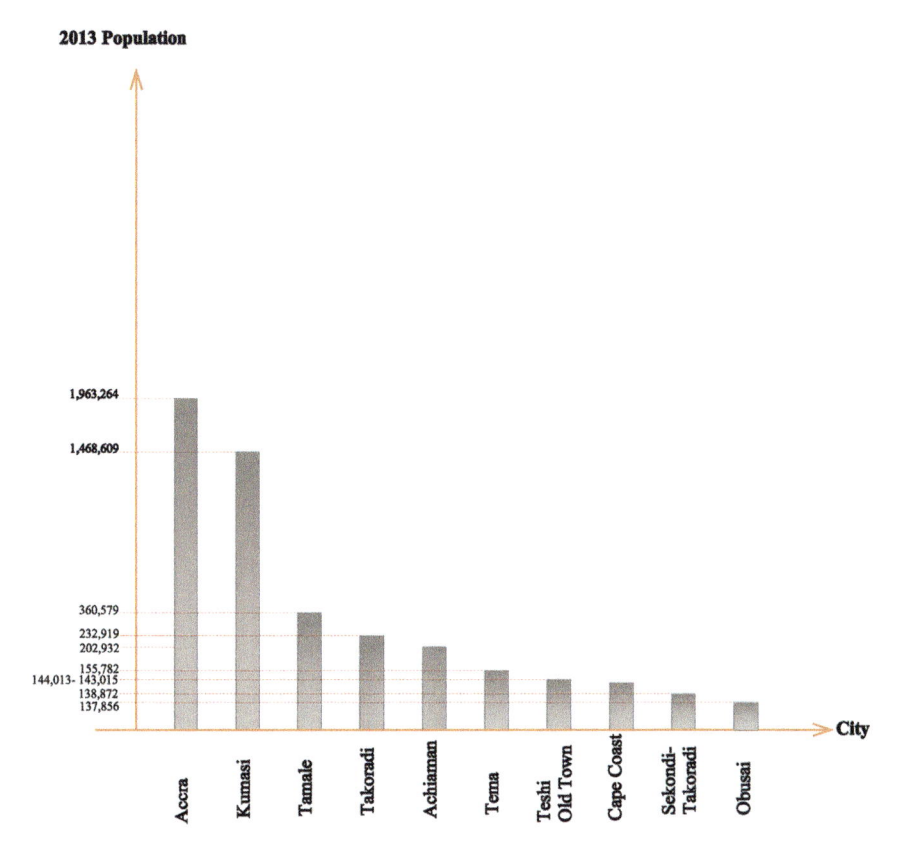

Fig. 8.6 City populations in Ghana (2013)

Chile

The sixteenth century saw the Spanish *conquistadores* active in a long coastal strip of land in the southwestern seaboard of the South American continent. That territory became a colony of Spain in 1540 and came to be known as Chile. The colonial economy was based on agricultural exports and later also on saltpeter and copper transported through the main port of Santiago. Independence from Spain, gained in 1818 led to an elitist controlled economy. After a period of turmoil when the country was sucked into Cold War politics, the country transitioned peacefully to democracy around 1990 (Wikipedia).

Table 8.7 City populations in Chile (2013)

Rank	City	Population
1	Santiago	4,837,295
2	Puente Alto	510,471
3	Antofagasta	309,832
4	Vina del Mar	294,551
5	Valparaiso	282,448
6	Talcahuano	252,968
7	San Bernado	249,858
8	Temuco	238,129
9	Iquique	227,499
10	Concepcion	215,413

Source www.worldpopulationsreview.com

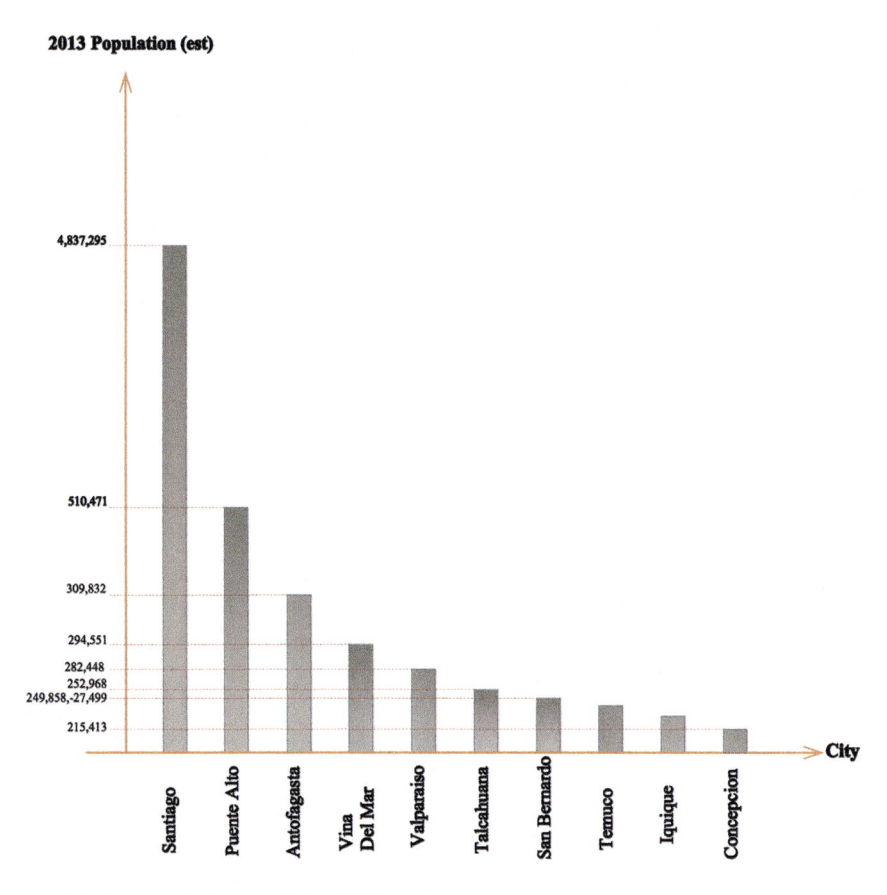

Fig. 8.7 City populations in Chile (2013)

Peru

The availability of a large indigenous population for use as labor and the extraordinary mineral wealth of Peru were very beneficial to Spain's colonial economy. Agricultural products such as sugar, textiles, and a great deal of its minerals were exported to Spain and to Europe through Lima, Peru's capital and port. Despite high growth, the War of the Spanish Succession (1701–1714) was eventually followed by economic stagnation and the marginalization of the indigenous peoples of Peru (Wikipedia).

The War of the Pacific (1879–1888) which involved Peru, Bolivia, and Chile left its toll on Peru. Despite an effort to rebuild and introduce social and economic reforms, political stability was achieved only in the early twentieth century. However, military coups and juntas continued well into the mid-twentieth century. The authoritarian regime headed by Alberto Fujimori opened up the economy and despite natural disasters and external economic impacts, the country is now receiving more foreign assistance and investments. While continued growth is likely, the matter of equity in the distribution of incomes across the country appears to remain as before. The rapid population growth in Lima is attributed mainly to rural–urban migration (De Soto 1987).

Table 8.8 City populations in Peru (2013)

Rank	City	Population
1	Lima	7,737,002
2	Arequipa	841,130
3	Callao	813,264
4	Trujillo	747,450
5	Chiclayo	577,375
6	Iquitos	437,620
7	Huancayo	376,657
8	Piura	325,466
9	Chimbote	316,966
10	Cusco	312,140

Source www.worldpopulationsreview.com

2013 Population (est)

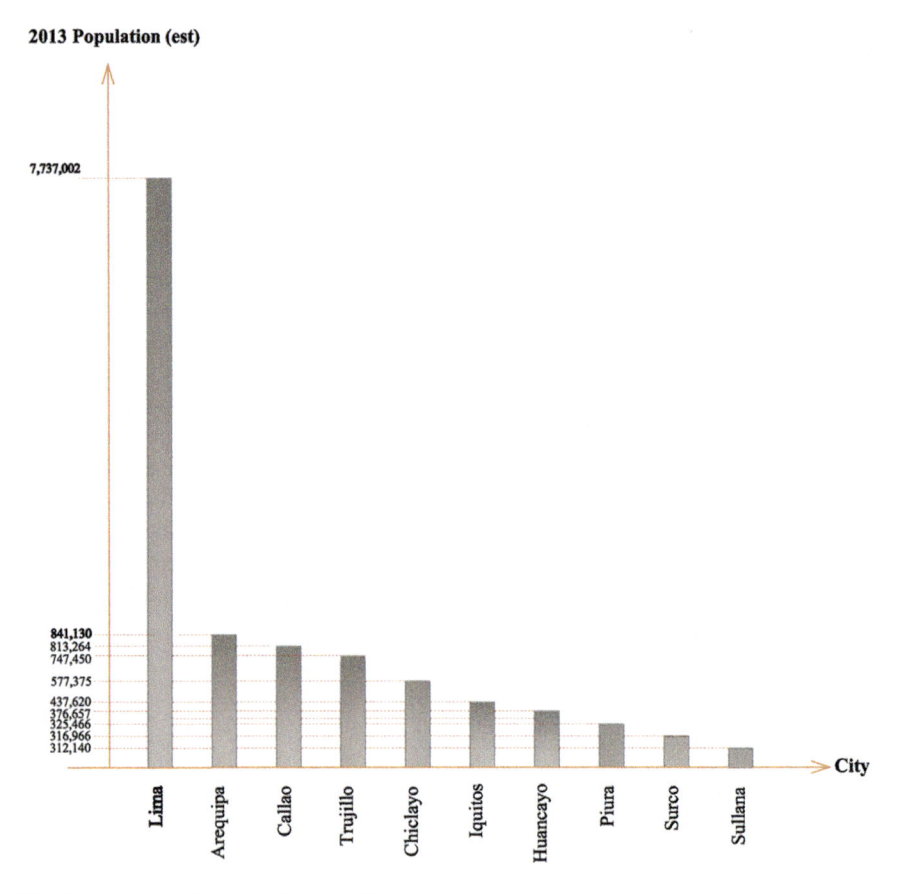

7,737,002

841,130
813,264
747,450
577,375
437,620
376,657
325,466
316,966
312,140

Lima, Arequipa, Callao, Trujillo, Chiclayo, Iquitos, Huancayo, Piura, Surco, Sullana

City

Fig. 8.8 City populations in Peru (2013)

Discussion

One of the main intentions here in this chapter was to examine the validity of Linsky's theoretical position noting that his conclusions were based on data mainly from and around one year, namely 1955. The sample of LMICs selected for study here was eight in number from among those small, predominantly agrarian coastal countries in the three continents of Asia, Africa, and South America. The statistics were recent, being taken from 2010, 2011, and 2013. The countries selected included those that had undergone colonial subjugation by France (i.e., Vietnam and Senegal); by Britain (i.e., Myanmar, Sri Lanka and Ghana); by Portugal (i.e., Mozambique); and by Spain (i.e., Chile and Peru). The graphic presentations in Figs. 8.1, 8.2, 8.3, 8.4, 8.5, 8.6, 8.7, and 8.8 are based on the Tables 8.1, 8.2, 8.3, 8.4, 8.5, 8.6, 8.7, and 8.8, respectively.

The conclusion that emerges from the analysis of data from all but one of the selected countries suggests that "Primacy" is a phenomenon common to all of them. Even in the one apparent exception—the city system of Ghana—the pattern falls into line with the others if it is recognized that the first two ranked Ghanaian cities, Accra and Kumasi, underwent rapid infrastructure development together jointly as an interconnected dual system of cities particularly in the postcolonial era.

Thus, it may be concluded that the "Theory of Primacy" may indeed be seen as being validated. Part and parcel of the validated theory is the assertion that the main associated and very likely causative factor behind the phenomena of primacy common to all these countries are the colonial economies that each of them had been subjected to. However, it may be observed that "primacy" as a phenomenon may be found in some countries that have not been under colonial subjugation. Examples in South Asia itself are Nepal and Bangladesh. Nepal was never subjected to European colonial occupation and Bangladesh was not a separate country during the pre-1947 period when it was part of British India. However, these two countries are clearly impacted by rapid urbanization and the two capital cities, Kathmandu and Dhaka, experience rural–urban migration and also they clearly are "primate" cities.

It should also be recognized that some of the city systems within the colonizing countries also evidence some degree of primacy. London and Paris are cases in point. This phenomenon may be seen as the "reverse side of the coin" of the colonial enterprise.

References

Adarkwa KK (2012) The changing face of Ghanaian towns. Afr Rev Econ Finance J 4(1)
De Soto H (1987) El otrosender. Sudamericana, Lima, Peru
Linsky AS (1965) Somegeneralization concerning primate cities. Ann Am Assoc Geogr J 55 (3):506–513

Chapter 9
Conserving Cultural Heritage Sites: A Case Study

Abstract Much work has been done since the UNESCO sponsored Lumbini conservation project was launched in 1970 in Southern Nepal near the Indian border. A Master Plan had been prepared by a famous Japanese Architect to provide a zoned spatial framework for related building activity amid conservation work. In recent decades, progress in construction and conservation has been delayed for long periods. Some serious threats have arisen in consequence. It is now considered essential that both construction and ongoing conservation work should be prioritized, better managed, and expedited. This will require more intensive use of appropriate remote sensing technology to precede and direct more accurately the conventional field excavations. A major conference of international stakeholders has recently recommended that the UN now appoint a high-level International Committee similar to one that was appointed at the outset in 1970 to safeguard the approved Master Plan and oversee the project's progress till satisfactory completion. Expert spatial planning work becomes essential to establish land use controls and relocate encroachers in carefully planned settlements nearby. This required the active support of the Government of Nepal and relevant international agencies leading quickly to reestablish the Buffer Zone to its original intended purpose. It is desirable that the guiding principles in the conservation of culturally sensitive heritage sites in Asia should be those enunciated by the *Nara Document on Authenticity*.

Preamble

In ancient times, there were many small kingdoms within what is now known as the Indian subcontinent. It is chronicled that in one of those—the Sakya Kingdom—Queen Mayadevi, wife of King Suddhodana, while traveling for her pregnancy confinement in a palanquin with her retinue from her palace to her mother's palace,

---

The text of this chapter was first presented as a paper to the Science Council of Asia for their International Symposium on 'Science and Technology for Culture' held in Siem Reap, Cambodia in May 2015 and has been published in the symposium's Proceedings.

© Springer Nature Singapore Pte Ltd. 2018
K. L. Gunaratna, *Towards Equitable Progress*, South Asia Economic and Policy Studies, https://doi.org/10.1007/978-981-10-8923-7_9

had gone into labor; and that the birth of her son Prince Siddhartha Gautama took place within a pleasant grove of trees in the gardens of Lumbini. The date of birth as recognized today was a full moon day in the month of Vaisakh in the year 623 BCE. It is said further that though Siddhartha as a young man was highly accomplished in all the expected princely skills, he abandoned the luxury of his palace home in the city of Kapilavastu at the age of 29. He had gone forth as a mendicant hermit into the solitude of the forests in search of a path to the elimination of human suffering. Years later, he came to be known as the "Buddha" the "Enlightened One".

The often cited historical artifact attesting to Lumbini as the Buddha's birthplace is a monolithic sandstone column bearing a *Brahmi* inscription marking the site. Dated at 249 BCE, it is attributed to the Indian emperor Asoka of the Mauryan Dynasty (Fig. 9.1). Some visits made over many centuries to this nativity site by pilgrims from many countries are well documented. Notable early visitors include the Chinese pilgrims Fa-hsien (c. 409 ACE) and Hsuan-tsang (c. 636 ACE). Their writings confirm the existence of many religious structures in Lumbini, some in various states of disrepair. The area had come under the control of other religious groups in and after the ninth century ACE and many Buddhist structures were neglected, damaged, or destroyed (Violatti 2013). The *Mahawansa* (fifth century ACE) is one of the important chronicles that records where Prince Siddhartha was born and lived till manhood, these being the garden of Lumbini and the city of Kapilavastu, respectively. Identifying their exact locations today needs corroboration between historical information from reliable chronicles, records of early eyewitness accounts, general agreement that these locations are within the present boundary area between India and the Terai region of Southern Nepal. Nationalist sentiments in the two countries have sometimes clouded the issue of identifying their precise locations. The fact is that in the time of the Buddha, India and Nepal were not separate nation-states as understood and defined today but were each part of a large conglomeration of relatively independent kingdoms and principalities.

A major conservation project was initiated at Lumbini jointly by the United Nations (UN) and the Government of Nepal in the 1970s. Work was to be executed within a set time frame and the spatial framework of a newly defined and widely acclaimed Master Plan. However, implementation delays have cumulatively resulted in the recent emergence of serious threats not only to that Master Plan but also to the project and its very purpose.

This present chapter attempts to briefly discuss the origins of this important conservation project, describe the main features of the approved Master Plan, and examine the implementation effort and the main threats to the project that have emerged. It is hoped that the paper will help generate more interest in the project among scientists and stakeholders especially those from the Asian region. The scope of the discussion here would also cover some possible mechanisms of collaborative studies within the region. It is also hoped that the lessons to be learnt may benefit not only the Lumbini project but also other ongoing and future projects on conserving the many cultural heritage sites in the Asian region.

Fig. 9.1 Asokan column

Conservation Work

The conservation work being executed in the area assumed to be Lumbini was underpinned by historical studies and archaeological investigations carried out in the late nineteenth century during British colonial rule in India. Dr. Anton Fuhrer, a German archaeologist engaged by the Archaeological Survey of India (ASI), received permission in 1896 to make an expedition to Rummindehi in the Terai region of the Kingdom of Nepal. That location was just outside the territorial boundary of British-held India. The exercise brought him into contact with General Khadga Shamsher Rana the Governor of Palpa in Nepal. They together are generally credited now with having "rediscovered" Lumbini the ancient site of the Buddha's birth. There is even a recent acknowledgement of this by Giri (2013).

Fuhrer's work in the Terai had received some serious criticisms in his time, of which two were from the British archaeologists Waddell and Hoey (1899). They themselves had carried out further investigations in the same area immediately after Fuhrer. He was later found to be at serious fault on some other work he had done which led to his resignation in 1898. There are even recent strident criticisms of Fuhrer's work (Allen 2010) some of which proceed to contest the locations he identified for Lumbini and Kapilavastu. However, excavations in the vicinity by Mukherji (1899) had unearthed inter alia an ancient bas-relief sculpture (Fig. 9.2) apparently depicting the nativity scene of Prince Siddhartha (UNESCO 2013a). That "find" would have added much weight to the possibility that Rummindehi is the true location of ancient Lumbini.

Later during the 1930s, some extensive excavations were carried out in the Terai region close to Rummindehi by General Keshar Shamsher Rana, a nephew of Khadga Shamsher Rana. Some further investigations were made in the early 1960s by an Indian archaeologist (Mitra 1972) through the ASI. She was quite critical of the work done there by Rana in the 1930s. Her main complaints were that scientific methodology had generally been absent in that work, that much damage had been done to the site, and that there were no proper records kept.

Discussion

The UN has taken a very special interest in Lumbini. Seven of their successive Secretaries-General, starting with Daag Hammarskjold in 1959, have made special visits to the site. A proposal to prepare a comprehensive plan to help conserve the Lumbini region followed the second visit, which was by U. Thant in 1967. He was able to rally international support and a Consultant Mission from the UN's Development Program (UNDP) followed in 1969 which led to the commencement of a major joint conservation project between the UN and Nepalese Government. A special International Committee chaired by Nepal's Representative at the UN was established in 1970 to oversee the proposed planning effort. The Committee

Fig. 9.2 Nativity scupture

commissioned the famous Japanese architect Kenzo Tange to prepare a Master Plan which was first presented in 1972 and finalized in 1978 (Fig. 9.3). With consent from the Nepalese government, it was approved by the UN in that same year. Lumbini was listed by UNESCO as a *World Heritage Site* two decades later in 1997.

The approved Master Plan contains, in essence, a 1 × 3 mile "Project Area" of three equal mile-square zones. The three are together oriented in a north-south axis

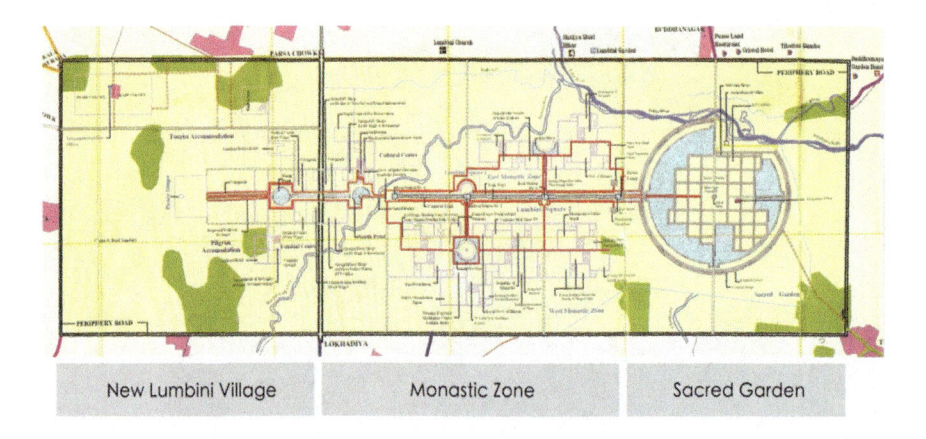

Fig. 9.3 The "Project Area" in Kenzo Tange's Master Plan

and consist of the *New Lumbini Village Zone*, the *Monastic Zone*, and the *Sacred Garden Zone*. Most visitors are expected to first enter the northern zone and progress southward gradually through an axial transport corridor created by a canal with broad footpaths on both sides (Fig. 9.4). It is by intention an increasingly quiet and peaceful progression from the secular to eventually reach the Sacred Garden. The plan also defines a "Buffer Zone" to surround and protect the Project Area, the entirety of which falls within a 5×5 mile square. The Sacred Garden Zone is central within the Buffer Zone (Fig. 9.5).

Following the approvals for the Master Plan in 1978, implementation work began with completion expected within 7 years. However, published reports evidence that progress was much slower than expected. The Lumbini Development Trust was then created in 1985 to help manage without further delay the remaining work. Political instability in Nepal in the interim and the turmoil which led to the abolition of their monarchy in 2008 would indeed have also impacted on progress. Some key planned elements in all three "zones" of the Project Area still await implementation. Of the 42 plots in the Monastic Zone delineated to construct monasteries for the various "schools" of Buddhism, six plots are still vacant. A special requirement in the Master Plan was the need for a peaceful and quiet atmosphere. The use of electrically driven transport modes and photovoltaic energy generation is minimal or nonexistent in the Project Area.

Some of the most urgently needed archaeological investigations are within the Sacred Garden Zone itself—the focal point of the entire conservation project. The main ongoing investigations are in proximity to the very site of the birth of Prince Siddhartha. The ruins of an ancient temple are being unearthed there. It is known as the Mayadevi Temple. The Government of Nepal has built a protective structure to envelop this site (Fig. 9.6). There are said to be inadequacies in this structure and consequently, an *International Architectural Competition* had been proposed to design a new structure to protect these ruins. The competition has not been

Fig. 9.4 View of the Axial Corridor

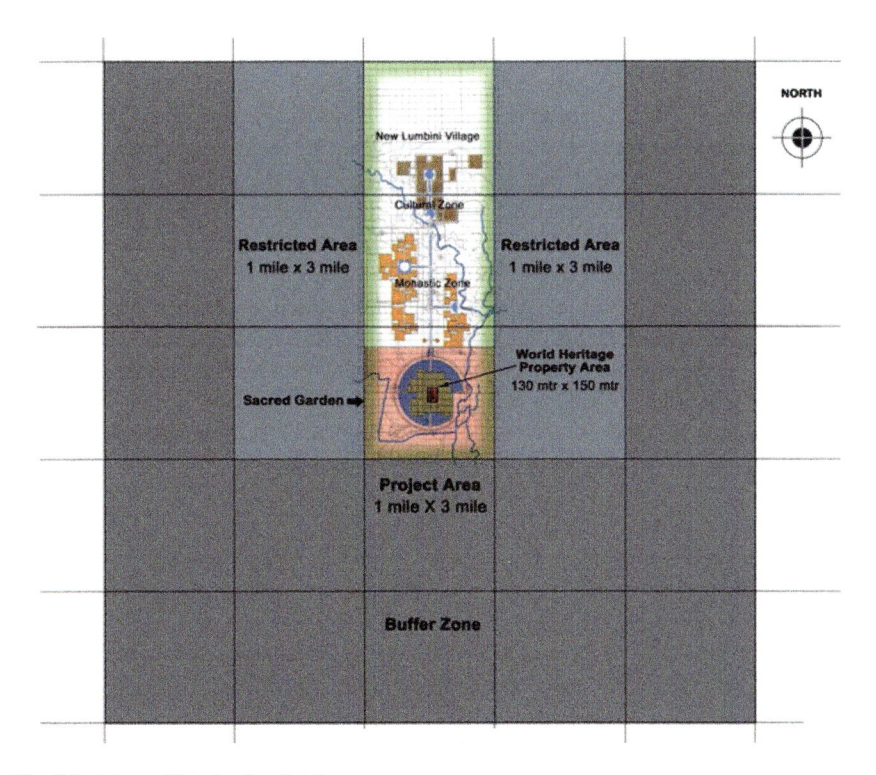

Fig. 9.5 Master Plan detail—the three zones

Fig. 9.6 Mayadevi Temple Enclosure

conducted yet. There was also an important proposal to locate an *International Documentation Centre* to preserve documents, data, and images of historical value and to facilitate their ready accessibility to researchers, students, pilgrims, and other visitors. In general, most of this work still awaits commencement.

The Greater Lumbini Area comprises the three districts of Rummindehi (also known as Rupandehi), Nawalparasi, and Tilaurakot. These three districts too contain major archaeological complexes. Considering accuracy and speed, investigations by noninvasive remote sensing techniques such as *Light Detection and Ranging* (LiDAR) which are airborne surveys, geophysical surveys by *ground-penetrating radar* (GPR), and also electromagnetic conductivity (*EM*) to inspect subsurface structures are clearly preferred to precede field surveys.

In Nawalparasi, there is a special archaeological site of great importance at Ramagrama, which has been on the Tentative World Heritage list since 1996. It is said to contain the ruins of a Stupa enshrining some relics of the Buddha (Fig. 9.7). Archaeological surveys, conservation and management plans, and improved visitor facilities are considered urgent needs there. None have been commenced. All these items of delayed work in the Lumbini Project are discussed more fully in a UNESCO report (May 2013). An *International Scientific Steering Committee* (ISSC 2013) had then been established to supervise implementation. It has eight members and is chaired by Prof. Yukio Nishimura of the Urban Design Laboratory, University of Tokyo (Nishimura, 2013).

Discussion

Fig. 9.7 Ramagrama stupa

Currently, an Archaeological team co-directed by Prof. Robin Coningham of Durham University in the UK and the Nepalese archaeologist Kosh Prasad Acharya is at work within the UNESCO project which is being funded by the Japanese Trust. According to a press conference (Coningham 2013), the team is reported to have unearthed evidence beneath the Mayadevi Temple of a pre-Asokan temple built in brick over yet another earlier timber structure. This has received wide publicity as a very important discovery pointing toward new evidence on the period of time when the Buddha lived. However, these historical conclusions have been contested and criticized by a British historian and scholar of Early Buddhism (Gombrich 2013).

A report by UNESCO (2013b) mentions that the second phase of the ongoing Lumbini project will be extending its scope to Tilaurakot in the Nepalese Terai, to search for the archaeological remains of the ancient Shakya Kingdom and the supposed relic stupa of the Buddha at Ramagrama. One important intention is clear, that being to establish Tilaurakot as the location of the ancient city of Kapilavastu. It has also been said more recently (Coningham 2014) that they will begin work on this aspect very soon. It may be noted that the district wherein Tilaurakot is located had been named Kapilavastu by the Nepalese authorities some years ago, although the location of the ancient city by that name has not been firmly established yet. It should be recalled that some archaeological work had already been done in 1971 and 1973 by others at Piprahwa and Ganwaria on the Indian side of the border.

The resulting publication (Srivastava 1980) claim that these sites together represent the possible location of Kapilavastu. This subject has also been reviewed more recently by Allen (2006). It seems therefore that locating Kapilavastu with scientific certitude would require a more balanced effort where the finds from excavations at Piprahwa and Ganwaria on the Indian side of the border are also given due consideration.

Some Serious Threats

A report on the management framework for the Lumbini project (Weise 2013) highlights inter alia the need for enforcing "Regional Planning Controls". These concern *the scale of continuing encroachment into the Buffer Zone* and *inappropriate industrial activity within*, which are creating serious threats to the project (Fig. 9.8). Even earlier, a report (Molesworth and Muller-Boker 2005) was strongly critical of the implementation delays and of the Nepalese authorities for not taking timely action to protect the Buffer Zone. An alternative Master Plan proposal to establish a *"World Peace City"* in Lumbini has been submitted directly to the Government of Nepal through another international cooperation agency. A Memorandum of Understanding (MoU 2012) had been signed on this subject. The matter had disturbed stakeholders in many countries. *A petition was prepared by a Vietnamese American Buddhist monk the Ven. Dr. Giac Hanh. It contained more than 22,500 signatures worldwide expressing strong opposition to the World Peace City proposal.* The petition had been sent to the Secretary-General of the UN. A key point made was that the new plan departs from Lumbini's main identity as the birthplace of the Buddha and thereby possibly the most important Buddhist pilgrimage site worldwide. Another was that the plan covers the entire defined Project Area and specifically encourages a population of 200,000 persons to reside within the Buffer Zone. The petition concludes by strongly urging the UN and the Government of Nepal to drop the World Peace City Plan proposal and continue to support and implement Kenzo Tange's Master Plan. The signatories have made this request expressly recognizing that Lumbini is a world heritage site and concerned people worldwide should also have a say in its future.

An International Buddhist Conference was held in Lumbini during the period November 15–18, 2014. The author of the alternative Master Plan had on invitation made a presentation of his plan. It received strong criticism there too and the Conference organizers have since appealed to the UN to intervene and to reactivate the United Nations International Lumbini Committee. UNESCO's World Heritage Committee (2014) was also clearly disturbed by the alternative Master Plan proposal. Nevertheless, the UNESCO office in Brussels hosted in November 2016 a meeting initiated by the Nepalese government to promote the establishment of the World Peace City proposal.

Fig. 9.8 One of the factories in the immediate vicinity of the sacred area

Conservation Principles

A set of guiding principles for conserving historic monuments and sites were enunciated at a special conference organized by the *International Council on Monuments and Sites* (ICOMOS) held in Venice and have been accepted by such international bodies as the World Heritage Committee and UNESCO (Venice Charter 1964). The signatories were all European with the sole exception of one, the representative of UNESCO. With the increase of Asian specialists within ICOMOS, some concern had been voiced on a possible European bias in the charter's content. This has been discussed more recently by Nagaoka (2015). An international conference to prepare a more relevant document was mooted much earlier during the long tenure of an Asian president of ICOMOS (Silva 1994). Following a preparatory meeting in Bergen, Norway, the main conference of experts was held in Japan in the historic city of Nara in November 1994. Immediately thereafter in December 1994, the outcome of the main conference, known as the "*Nara Document on Authenticity*" was circulated by UNESCO in collaboration with the World Heritage Committee. It said inter alia that:

> The World Heritage Committee is encouraged to take into consideration the principles and views contained in the Nara Document on Authenticity in its evaluation of properties nominated for inclusion on the World Heritage List. (NARA Doc. 1994)

Conclusion

There is a clear need to review the progress of work not only on the archaeological activities but also on the delays and neglect of work on implementing the Master Plan for Lumbini, which is necessary for the development of such an important World Heritage Site. It must be acknowledged that the delays and neglect have allowed many encroachments to take place into the Buffer Zone and also to allow polluting industries to be set up immediately outside. The problems that have nothing to do with the original Master Plan which was approved by the UN and all concerned in 1978. There is clearly no need to change it as is now being proposed. Therefore, what is most important is to stay firmly within the original Master Plan. A firm decision is needed not to be sidetracked by recent proposals that tend to mask the damage, legitimize and consolidate encroachments into the Buffer Zone, and even increase the population within the Buffer Zone. What is urgently needed is the serious and scientific engagement of the authorities in a spatial planning exercise to resettle families that have encroached into the Buffer Zone. This exercise which may need external assistance has to be done in an economically beneficial and socially just manner. Also needed is a clear and enforceable policy on the establishment of industrial and economic activities in the immediate vicinity so as to ensure no environmental damage is caused to the Lumbini site. Such decisions, policy, and action are necessary not only to support and expedite the continuing archaeological and conservation work to take place in the midst of an increasing multitude of pilgrims. They are required also to enrich the original intention of developing and enhancing for posterity the position which Lumbini already enjoys. It should be recognized that Lumbini is not only a major World Heritage Site but also perhaps the most important place of Buddhist worship.

References

Allen C (2006) What happened at Piprahwa. In: Proceedings of the conference at Harewood House, Yorkshire, June 2006
Allen C (2010) The Buddha and Dr. Führer: an Archaeological Scandal. Penguin, New Delhi
Coningham RAE (2013) Press conference on 7th July 2013 (UNESCO/KAT13/2013)
Coningham RAE (2014) Information conveyed by Coningham at a videotaped lecture delivered in Colombo on 28th May 2014
Fa-hsein (c. 409 CE) (2013) The sacred garden of Lumbini: perceptions of Buddha's birthplace, p 43. UNESCO, Paris
Giri (2013) Art and architecture remains in the western terai region of Nepal. New Delhi
Gombrich R (2013) Recent discovery of "earliest Buddhist shrine" a sham? J Oxf Centre Buddhist Stud (website)
Hsuan-tsang (c. 636 AC) (2013) The sacred garden of Lumbini: perceptions of Buddha's birthplace, p 43. UNESCO, Paris

References

ISSC (International Scientific Steering Committee) (2013) Strengthening conservation and management of Lumbini, the birthplace of Lord Buddha (Final Report), World Heritage Property UNESCO project FIT/536NEP4001, UNESCO Office in Kathmandu, Nepal. www.facebook.com/unescokathmandu

Mahavamsa (5th century AC) A chronological history of Sri Lanka starting 3rd century BC (compiled in Pali using Sinhala script by Ven. Mahanama)

Mitra D (1972) Excavations at Tilaura-Kot and Kodan and the Explorations in the Nepalese Tarai. Department of Archaeology, Kathmandu

Molesworth K, Muller-Boker U (2005) Local impact of under-realization of the Lumbini master plan: a field report, Nepalese studies, vol 32, 2 (July issue)

MoU (2012) Signed on 20th January 2012 by the Governments of Nepal and the Republic of Korea in respect of the alternative master plan proposal prepared by Professor Kwaak Young Hoon and supported by the Korea International Cooperation Agency (KOICA)

Mukherji PC (1899) A report on a tour of exploration of the antiquities of Kapilavastu in the Tarai of Nepal during February and March 1899. New Delhi, 1969

Nagaoka M (2015) European and Asian approaches to cultural landscapes management at Borobudur, Indonesia in the 1970s. Int J Heritage Stud. 21(3):232–249 (online)

Nara Document (1994) Nara document on autheticity, UNESCO WHC-94/CONF.003/INF.008, 21 November 1994 Original: English. World Heritage Committee. (Circulated from Phuket) Thailand December 1994

Nishimura Y (2013) Review of the Kenzo Tange Master plan for the sacred garden: Final report (Urban Design Laboratory Department of Urban Engineering, Tokyo University

Silva R (1994) A Sri Lankan who was President of ICOMOS during the 1990–1999 period

Srivastava KM (1980) Archaeological excavations at Piprāhwā and Ganwaria and the identification of Kapilavastu. J Int Assoc Buddhist Stud 3(1):103–10

UNESCO Report (2013a) The sacred garden of Lumbini: perceptions of Buddha's birthplace, p 66, Paris

UNESCO Report (2013b) Strengthening conservation and management of Lumbini, the birthplace of Lord Buddha, World Heritage Property, Paris

UNESCO (2014) Views expressed at their World Heritage Committee Meeting in Doha, Qatar (38 COM 7B.18)

Venice Charter (1964) Second international congress of architects and technicians of historic monuments, ICOMOS (International Council on Monuments and Sites), Venice

Violatti C (2013) Published under the following license: creative commons: Attribution-NonCommercial-ShareAlike (on 12 Dec 2013)

Waddell, Hoey (1899) Government of India Proceedings (Part B), Department of Revenue & Agriculture, Archaeology & Epigraphy, April 1899, File no. 6; 'Enclosure 1' (Report) of letter no. 53A, and also letter no. 41A in this file. (National Archives of India, New Delhi). This report details the results of their own (1899) excursion into the Terai

Weise K (2013) Integrated management framework: final draft N° KAT/2013/PI/H/10 CLT/KAT/2013 © UNESCO, 2013 Printed in Nepal

Chapter 10
Concerns in Preparing a National Spatial Policy: A Case Study

Abstract This chapter relates to an exercise undertaken to define a spatial policy and plan at the national level conducted in a South Asian country—namely, Sri Lanka. This work was done through a government agency which had acquired a new and special enabling legal framework for this purpose. The exercise which extended over several years was with the intent to improve the prospects for ongoing efforts to achieve economic growth but to facilitate that effort to be equitable and environmentally sustainable. The process of drafting such a policy involved much discussion to seek consensus among stakeholder institutions as well as among relevant political representatives. Since exercises of this nature are rare in the low- and middle-income countries (LMICs), the material of this chapter is presented here primarily for critical consideration by the reader.

Preamble

Sri Lanka is an island of 65,610 km^2 located in the Indian Ocean. Its location is very strategic in relation the main sea routes (Fig. 10.1). Although the land extent is relatively small in comparison with the large landmass of India, Sri Lanka has legal rights to the ocean resources to be found in the surrounding "Exclusive Economic Zone" (EEZ) demarcated under the Law of the Sea. The Sri Lankan government is in the process of justifying a legal claim to a substantial extension of this exclusive zone through the United Nations (Fig. 10.2). The claim is based mainly on sedimentation deposits from the rivers originating in the island. Exploratory investigations have already been done. Apart from an abundant variety of fish species, there is good reason to believe that this ocean zone is very rich in minerals, natural gas, and perhaps oil as well.

This chapter is based on an invited Guest Lecture delivered in 2010 by the Author to Research Fellows in the *Special Program for Urban and Regional Studies of Developing Areas* in the Department of Urban Studies and Planning of the Massachusetts Institute of Technology, Cambridge Massachusetts, USA.

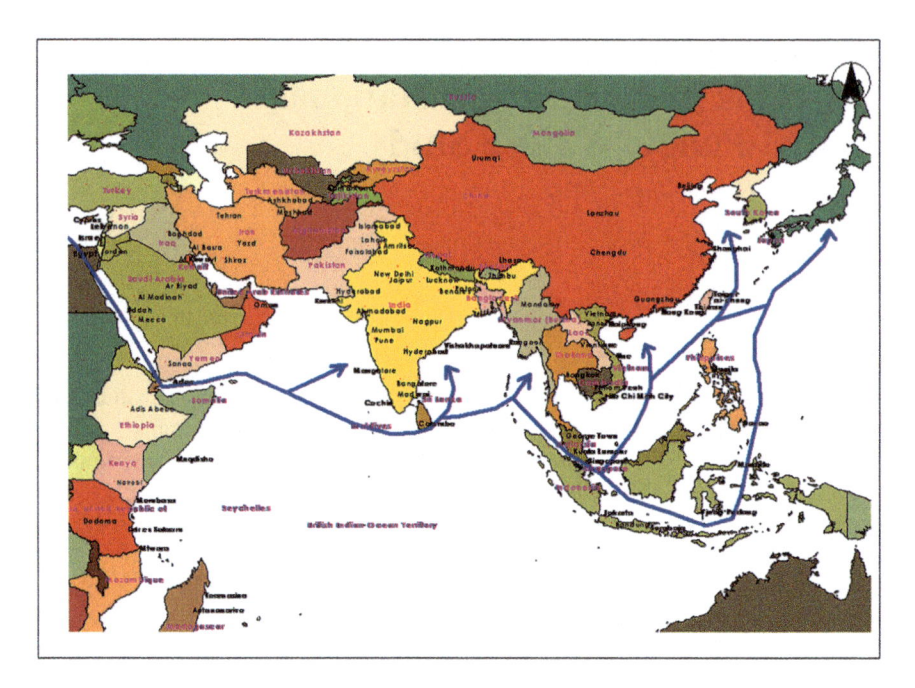

Fig. 10.1 Sri Lanka in relation to main Indian Ocean sea routes

The island's landmass contains some hills in the south central region of which the highest peak is 2,524 m above sea level. Most of the remaining land is relatively flat (Fig. 10.3). The South Western quadrant of the island receives much rain from the South West monsoons and is referred to as the Wet Zone which constitutes about one-third of the total land area. The main rivers originate in these hills and flow outward and course through surrounding flatter areas before they enter to sea. The bulk of this latter area is known as the Dry Zone which constitutes about two-thirds of the total extent of the island's landmass.

During the ancient period of Sri Lanka's history, the economy was based on agriculture although there was a considerable extent of trade with the outside world. Most of the people lived in the Dry Zone of the island. They farmed the land with boldly conceived irrigation systems consisting of numerous man-made reservoirs and canal networks. Archaeological remains indicate that the large cities were located in the central plains of the Dry Zone and that the Wet Zone and its hills were left under forest cover and largely unpopulated (Fig. 10.4). This was ecologically very sound because the forest cover in the Wet Zone hills protected the upper catchments of the main rivers that flowed through the Dry Zone and fed the numerous man-made reservoirs and irrigation systems (Fig. 10.5).

The economy, land use, and population distribution changed dramatically during the four and a half centuries of colonial rule. Agriculture for domestic consumption gave way gradually to plantation production for "empire" exports. The bulk of the

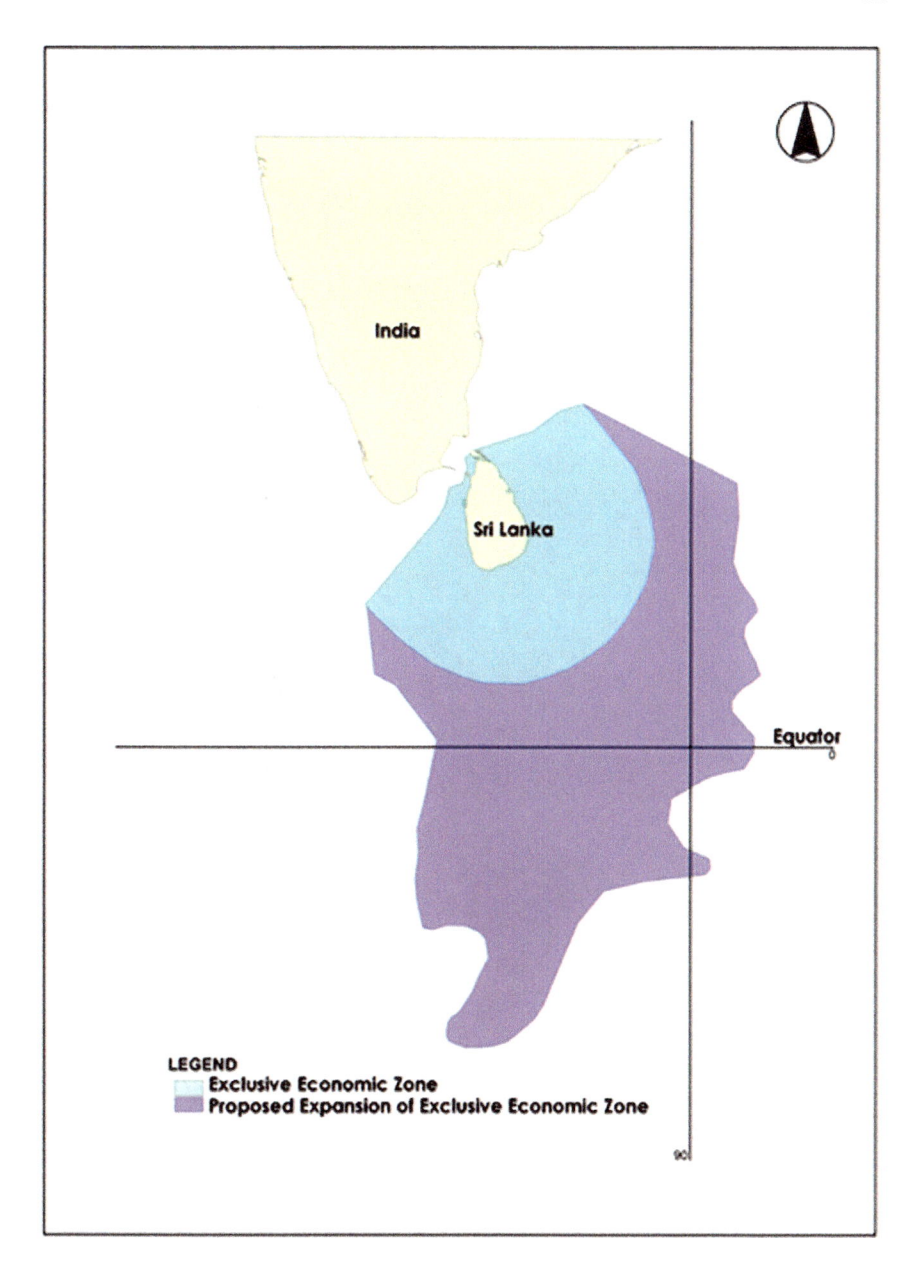

Fig. 10.2 Sri Lanka's marine economic zones

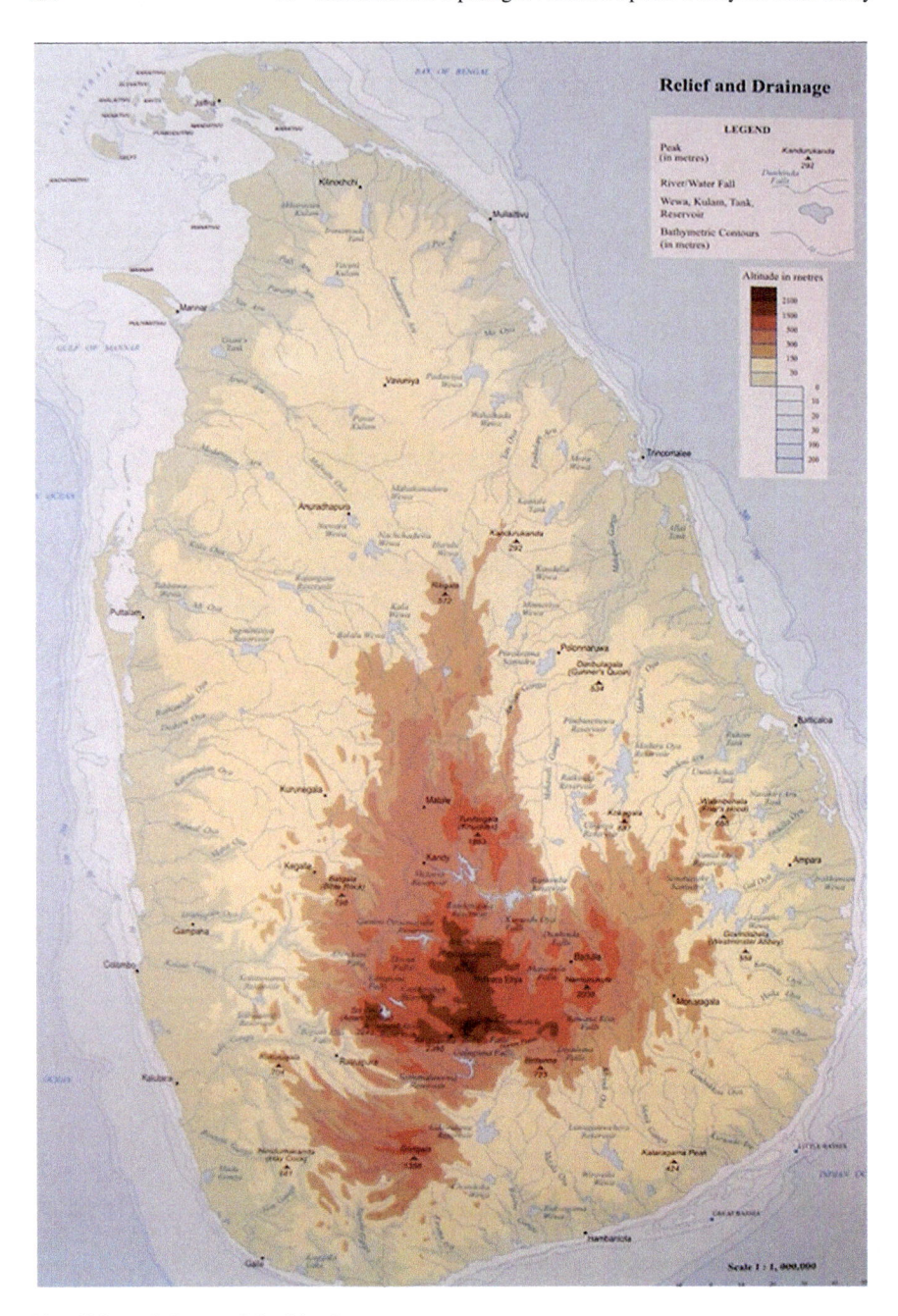

Fig. 10.3 Relief map of the Island

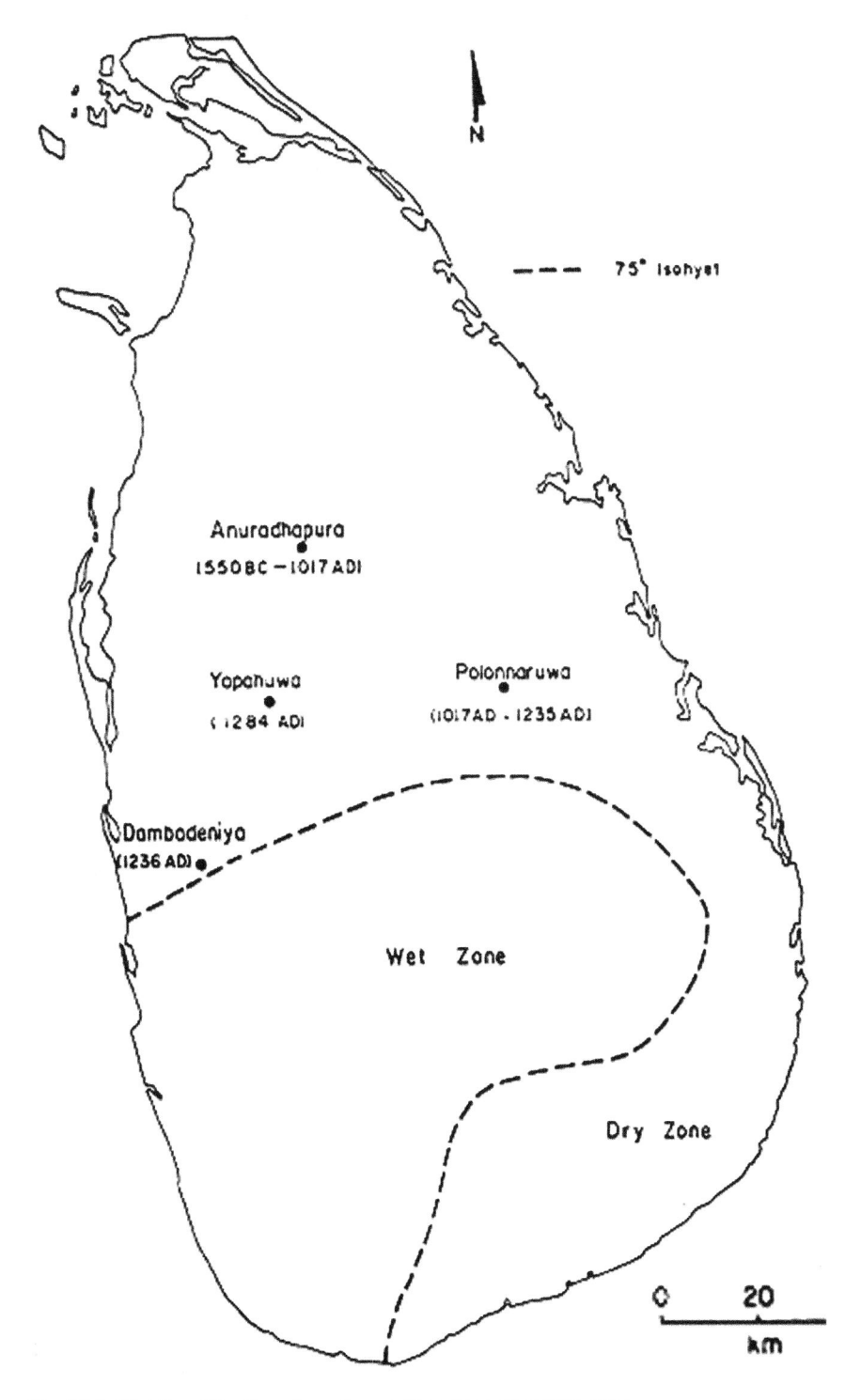

Fig. 10.4 Wet Zone/Dry Zone boundary and locations of ancient cities

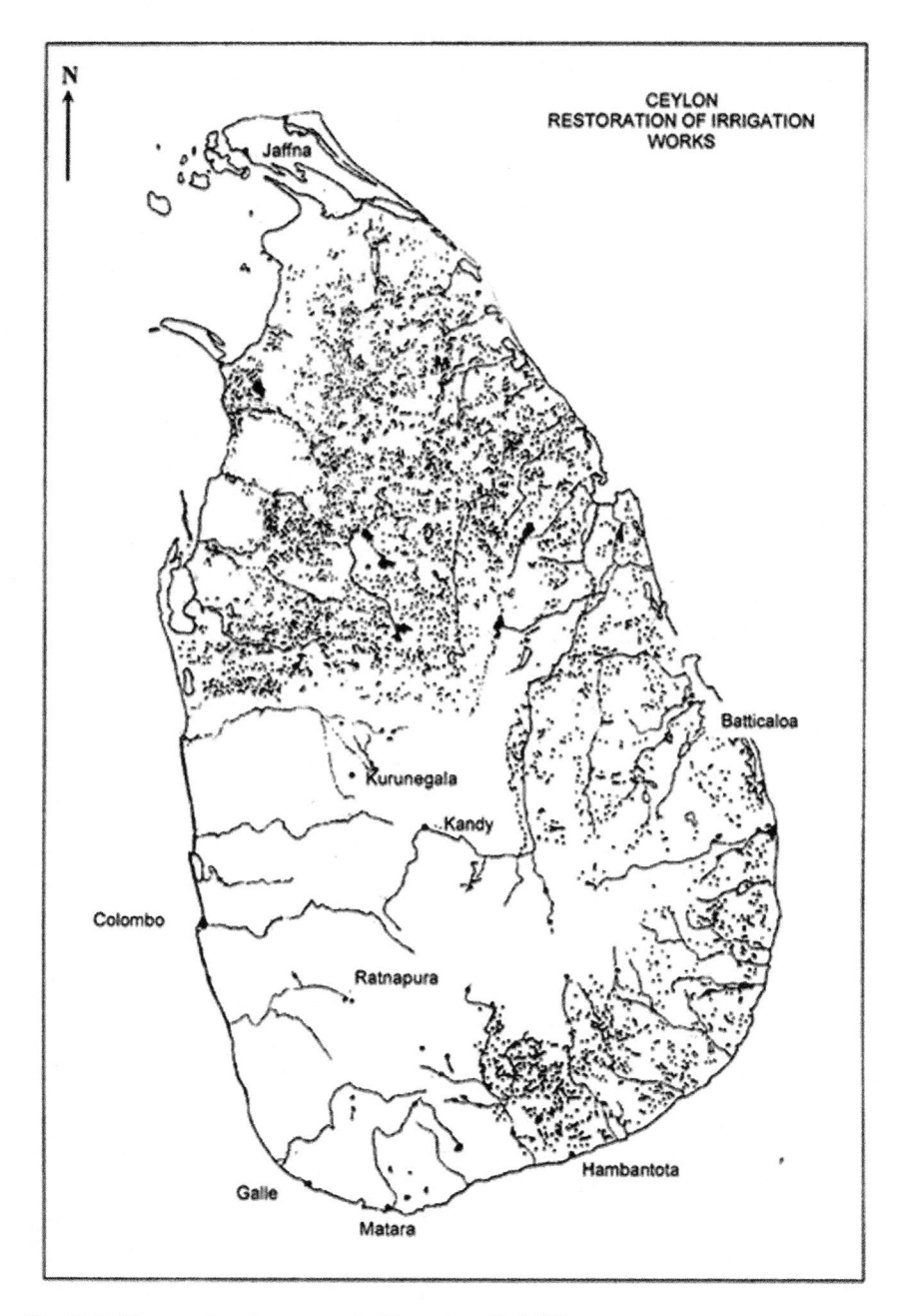

Fig. 10.5 Rivers and ancient reservoirs big and small (1905)

population shifted from the Dry Zone to the Wet Zone where most of the colonial plantation activities became concentrated. During this period, the ancient cities and the irrigation systems in the Dry Zone went gradually to ruin. A new system of towns emerged with the capital in the port city of Colombo on the South West coast. The secondary urban centers which were linked by radial communication routes to Colombo were mostly all located in the Wet Zone, leaving the rest of the country poorly served with physical and social infrastructure (Fig. 10.6).

The inheritance of this type of a spatial structure was not peculiar to Sri Lanka. It is in fact typical of many small agrarian ex-colonial dependencies and contains two special distinguishing features. One is the skewed pattern itself which is referred to as a "dendritic" structure. The other is that the commercial capital which is a port city is very much larger in population and areal extent than any of the other towns. This feature is referred to as "primacy" and has been discussed more thoroughly earlier in this book.

While dendritic structures and primate cities are common to many low- and middle-income countries (LMICs) which have experienced colonial subjugation, there is a geographic aspect which is peculiar to Sri Lanka. Infrastructure and most of the population in Sri Lanka had become concentrated under the colonial influence in the Wet Zone which contained the major hills. The colonial plantations, however, were until recently, large land holdings of foreign companies created through the felling of primeval forests in the upper catchments of the major rivers. They occupied considerable extents of Wet Zone lands. Most of the Wet Zone land in the upper elevations should have been kept in forest, while in the middle and lower elevations, the land unsuited for export-oriented plantation activities had been cultivated intensively by local smallholders with food crops for domestic consumption.

There was thus a severe population pressure on available Wet Zone agricultural land. This problem led to the recognition by some of the pioneer local political elite of the need to repair and recommission the ancient irrigation systems and resettle the Dry Zone with a farming population. This program was begun when some sense of independence was won by Sri Lankans with a new constitution promulgated in 1931. An example of the many such recommissioned ancient man-made reservoirs is one attributed to King Mahasena (ACE 274–301) at Minneriya (Fig. 10.7). The foregoing provides a brief sketch of the spatial context within which indigenous development efforts began in the early twentieth century. The main governmental agencies involved in the execution of these works were the Archaeological, Irrigation, and the Agricultural Departments.

The original agency that dealt with spatial planning in Sri Lanka's recent history was established a year prior to the achievement of Independence in 1948. It was named the "*Town and Country Planning Department*" with objectives and a legal framework similar to the then very recent enactment in Britain. Although it had powers to deal with urban as well as regional spatial planning, its focus was urban when in point of fact the national development focus was rural development. Three decades later, another government agency which had more powers to specifically

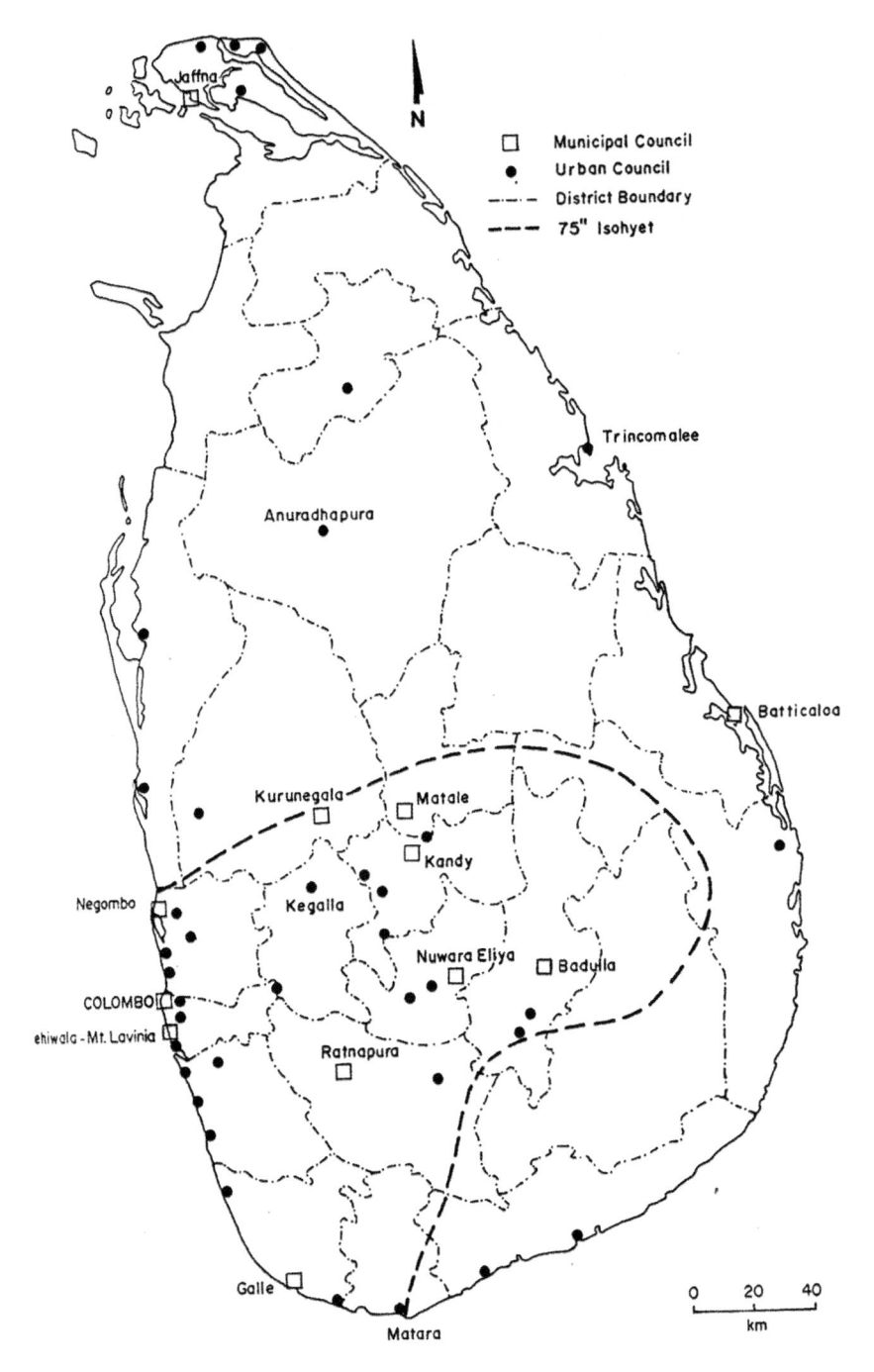

Fig. 10.6 Location of the main cities in Sri Lanka

Preamble 131

Fig. 10.7 The ancient Minneriya Reservoir

deal with urban areas and called the "*Urban Development Authority*" was established. With the availability of this new agency, it was considered by some within the country's bureaucracy that the older institution was made redundant and therefore should be closed down. The contrary views presented by concerned professionals in 1997 eventually led to the convening of a special representative committee of professionals and government officials to discuss the issue. The decision was to revamp the original agency with a greater focus on national and regional spatial planning and to draft the needed legislation for those specific purposes. The prime objectives envisaged in that draft were to provide an institutional framework to prepare a national spatial policy covering urban, regional, and rural planning, an appropriate policy approval process (Fig. 10.8), and a process for implementing related policy. These objectives were explicitly incorporated into the amended legislation governing the original agency which was renamed the National Physical Planning Department (NPPD) (Fig. 10.9).

It had taken at least two decades of concerted effort by the relevant professionals in Sri Lanka before the need for a comprehensive and explicit national spatial policy with a strong urban component was recognized. Thereafter and following the establishment of the NPPD, another decade was spent drafting a national spatial policy, getting the consensus of stakeholders, and obtaining the necessary

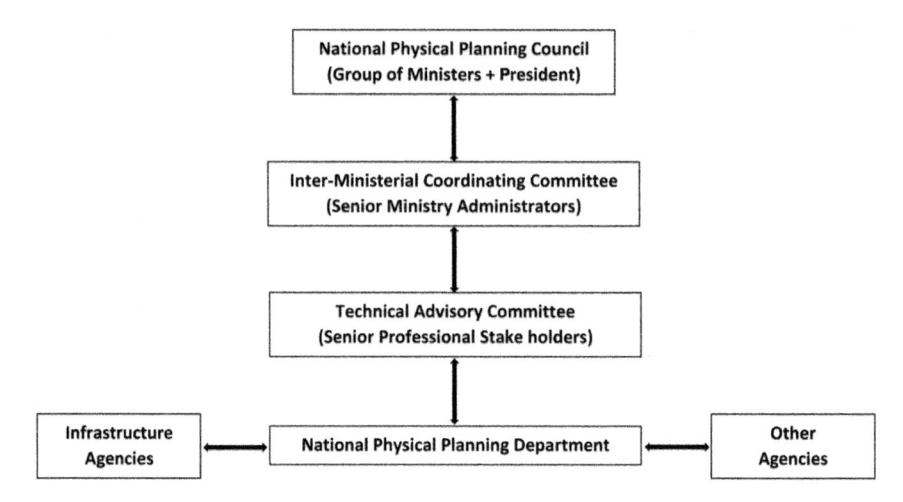

Fig. 10.8 Institutional framework for a national policy approval process

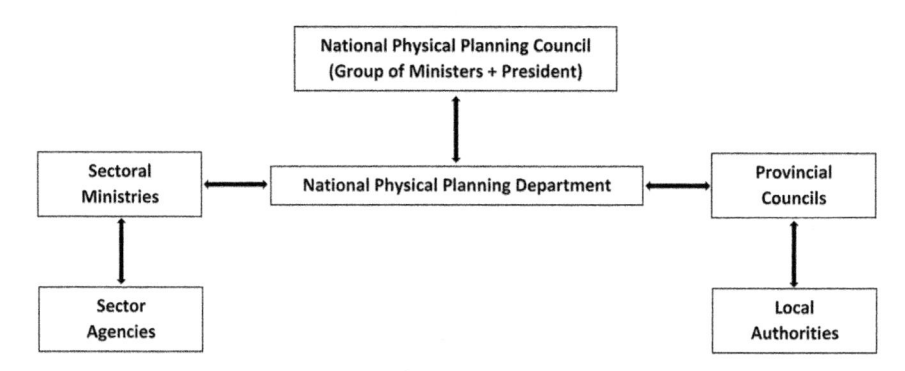

Fig. 10.9 A process for implementing a national spatial policy

approvals. The main events that led to recognizing the need for such a policy and defining and formally approving the defined policy are as set out in Appendix B.

Once revamped, the Department was expected inter alia to define a national spatial policy which would not only support and complement the country's economic development effort but also stimulate and direct change in the existing spatial structure. An unstated assumption was that without the support of state intervention in most low- or middle-income countries (LMICs), market forces alone cannot be relied upon to effect the substantial spatial change often needed to move away from the prior established colonial economy and its spatial structure and to thereby achieve spatial equity and sustainable progress. Thus, the key implicit sub-objectives that were defined were, in summary: to identify land areas where development and population growth should be encouraged and also where they should be discouraged; to anticipate and plan for an appropriate hierarchical pattern in the spatial distribution of urban places; and to identify the locations where social, economic, and communications infrastructure should be strengthened or established a new.

Since exercises of this nature are rare in the LMICs, the material of this chapter is presented here primarily for critical consideration by the reader. It is also hoped that this chapter will demonstrate that the preferred theoretical stances which emerge from some of the previous chapters in this book are indeed translatable into a national policy framework having practical applicability in the real context of an LMIC.

The Components of a National Spatial Policy

It had been responsibly predicted that the total population of Sri Lanka would stabilize at around 25 million persons by the year 2030. Some assumptions considered reasonable were that by then, 70% of that population would live and work in urban areas while the remaining 30% would be engaged mainly in agriculture or fishing in the rural and also in the non-urbanized coastal areas; and that 80% of the urban population would live in the larger and midsized cities while the remaining 20% would reside in small towns.

The spatial structure developed and defined by taking into account this population spread included the areas reserved for agricultural development, the locations to be occupied by the major cities and their command areas of their regions which latter would also contain some land for agriculture, the areas to be reserved for the District Capitals, the locations of the medium and small towns, the reservations for the network of highways, the rail network, and the seaports and airports. Being a predominantly agricultural country—a condition which was expected to prevail over at least the next few decades—it was considered necessary to minimize urban encroachment into agricultural land. The defined spatial structure also included areas demarcated as reserves for specific conservation purposes and areas which were considered as being vulnerable to serious damage through likely disasters, natural, or otherwise. While there is currently only one major city and its specific region of direct influence referred to by the NPPD as a "Metro Region" which related to the capital city and was in the island's Wet Zone, the new proposal in the NPPD's plans was for five such regions with four being located in the Dry Zone to be realized by 2030. All these five have together been referred to in the NPPD's plans as "Metro Regions", though in hindsight, the nomenclature was perhaps not the most appropriate.

There had been for many years some growing disenchantment among scholars with public sector-driven conventional "top-down" urban planning for use in many of the LMICs. From small and radical beginnings in the 1960s, a preference has grown for civil society-led community-based participatory planning interventions. This is especially where the work concerns the urban poor as the main intended beneficiaries. The situation had already been reached where it was clearly understood that the numbers living in urban slums in the LMICs was rapidly increasing through urbanization. In this context, as discussed earlier in Chap. 7 conventional urban planning was becoming increasingly irrelevant to deal with the "harsh realities" that have emerged and persist especially in major urban areas (Watson 2012). The discussion in that chapter on growth centers also shed some light on the work of several researchers, many of whom were in the search for what Stohr and Taylor (1981) called "development from below" alternatives to the "development from above" planning paradigm.

However, it has also to be recognized that the bottom-up approach, based as it has to be focused on community needs, though important as it clearly is, can sometimes be myopic and lose sight of the broader regional and/or national issues including environmental concerns. For example, poor and disadvantaged rural communities may demand and seek land for subsistence agriculture and to build shelter on steep slopes in hilly terrain where no other land areas are readily available to them. This demand could and does invariably result in the construction of unstable structures often found to be susceptible to hazards such as landslides. It also often results in the destruction of valuable tree cover where such vegetation helps to absorb rainwater, slows down precipitation runoff, and facilitates the prevention of soil erosion. Other poor urban communities, especially those among coastal fishermen, often opt to build or rebuild their meager homes on more easily accessible low-lying land. But this could expose those communities to such serious hazards as periodic flooding by adverse natural climatic events and other events resulting from climate change as sea level rise. Therefore, some environmentally predicated, top-down spatial planning at the regional and/or national level can also be seen to be very much a necessity.

Thus, while the substantial validity and successes of the "bottom-up" paradigm for appropriate circumstances must be recognized and greatly appreciated, there still are other circumstances especially in the LMICs, such as those mentioned above, for the relevance of "top-down" approaches to spatial planning. This point of view has been clearly articulated as follows:

> One inadvertent side effect of the preoccupation with planning from below...has been a lack of attention to planning at the top, which remains a critical institutional mechanism... As recent studies have indicated, the state and other institutions commonly associated with planning from the top...are critical players that can facilitate or hinder the development trajectories of newly industrializing countries...In other words, it is important to deliberate how to improve planning at the top without dismantling old mechanisms of planning... There is some evidence of the impact of efforts to either totally dismantle old planning structures, or curb the planning capacity of state planners ... rather than facilitate, institutional reforms.... (What) ... studies of such reform efforts do illustrate, however, is that the planning capacity at the top needs to be employed in a fresh way, with an awareness of institutional constraints that impede planning efforts. (Sanyal 2005)

Environmental Concerns

Protected Areas

Some of the key environmental concerns that needed to be addressed in the preparation of the national spatial policy for Sri Lanka may be summarized here as being: the current and continuing loss of rare ecosystems particularly in the Wet Zone; the loss of areas of natural beauty; soil erosion and landslides in the Wet Zone hill country; and the sedimentation of reservoirs in the Wet Zone. In view of these, a network of areas to be protected was carefully defined on a map in two categories (Fig. 10.10). This was done so as to ensure that inappropriate development activities will be curtailed and controlled within these specifically identified areas. The network consisted of the main catchment areas that provide water for domestic use, irrigation, and for the production of hydropower generation; habitats for medicinal plants, animals, birds, and aquatic life especially those that are unique to Sri Lanka; areas of natural beauty and other areas of special attraction to local and foreign tourists; and a range of land areas providing recreational opportunities. The two classified categories were as follows.

Protected Areas Category 1

This category consisted of the following: conservation forests; degraded forest areas that should be restored; areas of archaeological and historical value where development activities are not taking place at present (excluding coastal areas); areas of natural beauty and natural features of exceptional value (excluding coastal areas); environmentally important wetlands and catchments; areas where landslides and rockslides are likely to happen, for example, in land areas of high rainfall intensity with slopes that have a gradient of over 60° with highly erodible soils; and all natural and man-made watercourses, water bodies, and their reservations.

Protected Areas Category 2

This area consisted of the following: forest reserves and proposed reserves other than conservation forests identified in Category 1, such as wildlife sanctuaries and corridors; restored degraded forest areas; archaeological sites located within developed areas; tourist development areas; coastal natural habitats; sensitive areas in river basins; areas where a modest level of landslide hazard exists; utilized land in areas of high rainfall intensity with slopes that have a gradient of over 60° and with highly erodible soils; major groundwater aquifers; flood protection areas; and areas of natural beauty and natural features of exceptionally high value in the coastal areas.

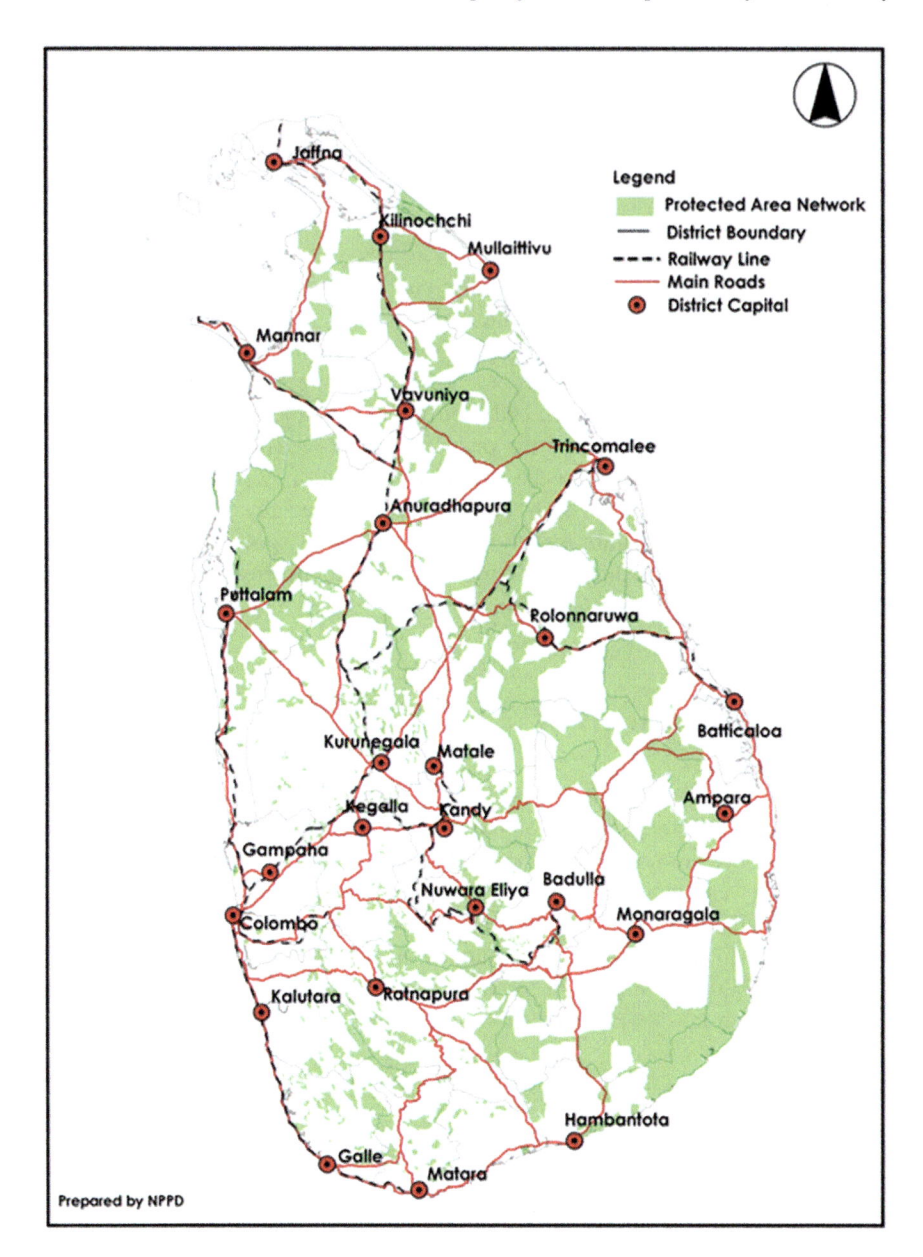

Fig. 10.10 Map of the defined protected area network

Fragile Areas

Another important classification of land areas within the island was also made taking into account the sensitivity of these areas in respect of environmental concerns. These were referred to as "fragile areas" and related to the coastal and central areas (Fig. 10.11). The Coastal Fragile Area as defined covers 4.4% of the island's land area. Though small in size, it is densely occupied by 28% of the population and contained 78% of the developed urban areas. It produced 90% of the fish catch, had 165 tourist hotels that number being 65% of the island's total, contained all the mangroves, had a large range of biodiversity, was a recreation and economic resource, and was very importantly a buffer against natural disasters such as cyclones, sea level rise, and tsunamis.

The Central Fragile Area on the other hand, as defined, covers 14,000 km^2, which is 20% of the island's total. It contains a complex and very sensitive environment including the main hills in the Wet Zone with forest cover in the upper catchments of the main rivers, that being the land area that naturally regulates the release of rainwater into streams and rivers. It contains the main plantations of tea which is one of the most important export commodities in the national economy. An ideal land use for a balanced vegetation in the Wet Zone hills, as found from among a few remaining examples of indigenous tradition, suggests that there should be forest or tree cover in the hills, human settlements in the lower slopes along with agriculture particularly rice paddy in the bottoms of the valleys (Fig. 10.12). Soil erosion results from population pressure and careless land use especially in the upper river catchments and steep hill slopes, and accounts for much of the forest degradation. These cause considerable damage in the form of floods, landslides, and rockslides. These latter, contrary to superficial appearances are in fact man-made disasters. They are common and frequent occurrences in the Wet Zone hills today (Fig. 10.13). The proposals for settlements in the Central Fragile Area included in the policy show separately those that can accommodate small expansions, settlements that cannot be expanded, and settlements that should be relocated.

Other Concerns

Some of the other concerns addressed in the draft national spatial policy included: the low levels of agricultural productivity; the weak industrial sector; the neglect of oceanic resources; the high level of unemployment; the weak international links; the slow rate of economic growth; the persistence of poverty; the widening regional disparities; the distorted spatial distribution of urban places; and the "primacy" of Colombo. Many of these problems have spatial dimensions which latter are rarely addressed by national economic development policy in most LMICs and so it was in Sri Lanka.

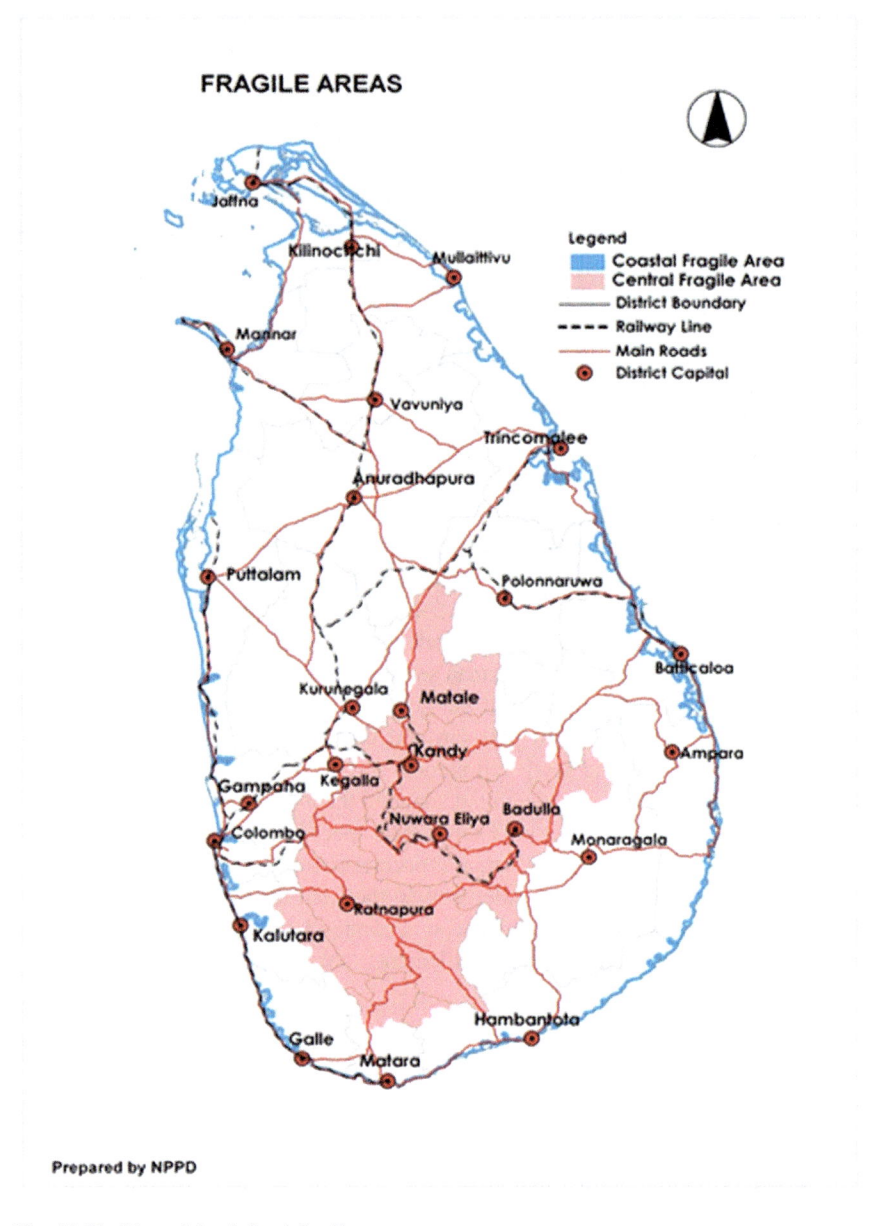

Fig. 10.11 Map of the defined fragile areas

Fig. 10.12 An example of ideal Wet Zone rural land use

Fig. 10.13 A landslide site in the Wet Zone hills

Land-Based Economic Activities

It was considered necessary to demarcate and reserve some land areas for very specific economic activities. These included areas where important mineral resources are known to be available; highly productive agricultural land areas specifically suited for tea, rubber, coconut, paddy, and livestock development (Fig. 10.14). The intention of these reservations was to discourage other activities in these land areas which would be incompatible with the identified land use. In regard to fisheries, it was considered necessary to expand, facilitate, regulate, stabilize, and protect the fishery sector by the establishment of new fishery harbors, and to provide facilities for secondary processing of fish in reasonably close proximity to the proposed coastal fishery harbors (Fig. 10.15).

Infrastructure

It was considered to be of prime importance to support the economic development effort by improving the availability and reliability of energy supplies in various possible ways. Encouraging the development and use of renewable energy sources was thought to be especially important to inter alia reduce the possibility of greenhouse gas emissions. The enhancement of information technology and telecommunications networks was also considered to be valuable especially as they would help reduce energy consumption in transport. The necessity to upgrade all District Capitals and develop a new category of urban places called "Metro Cities" was given special importance to ensure inter alia the sustainable management, treatment, and disposal of solid waste and sewerage. As noted earlier, the bulk of the current urban places are located in the Wet Zone. The new proposal is that 7 out of 8 Metro Regions identified will be in the Dry Zone (Fig. 10.16). It should be noted that these Metro Regions as geographically defined here are in point of fact land areas in which the city is centered within a defined rural area—intentionally promoting rural–urban interdependency.

In regard to airports, the need to improve domestic and international aviation linkages for passenger transport and expand capacity for air-based cargo transport was recognized, although at that time the war against terrorism was ongoing. This involved upgrading the smaller airstrips to anticipate and develop civil aviation for domestic and internal tourism-related transport. Priority was given to the importance of developing a second international airport (Fig. 10.17).

In regard to seaports, it was first recognized that there are limits to the possibility of expanding the currently used international harbor in Colombo. Of the other harbors in use, Trincomalee which is an excellent natural harbor but is away from the main sea routes was identified as being most suitable as a regional harbor and for industrial and naval purposes. Galle harbor being shallow and being adjacent to the historic Dutch Fort of considerable interest to tourists was considered to be ideal

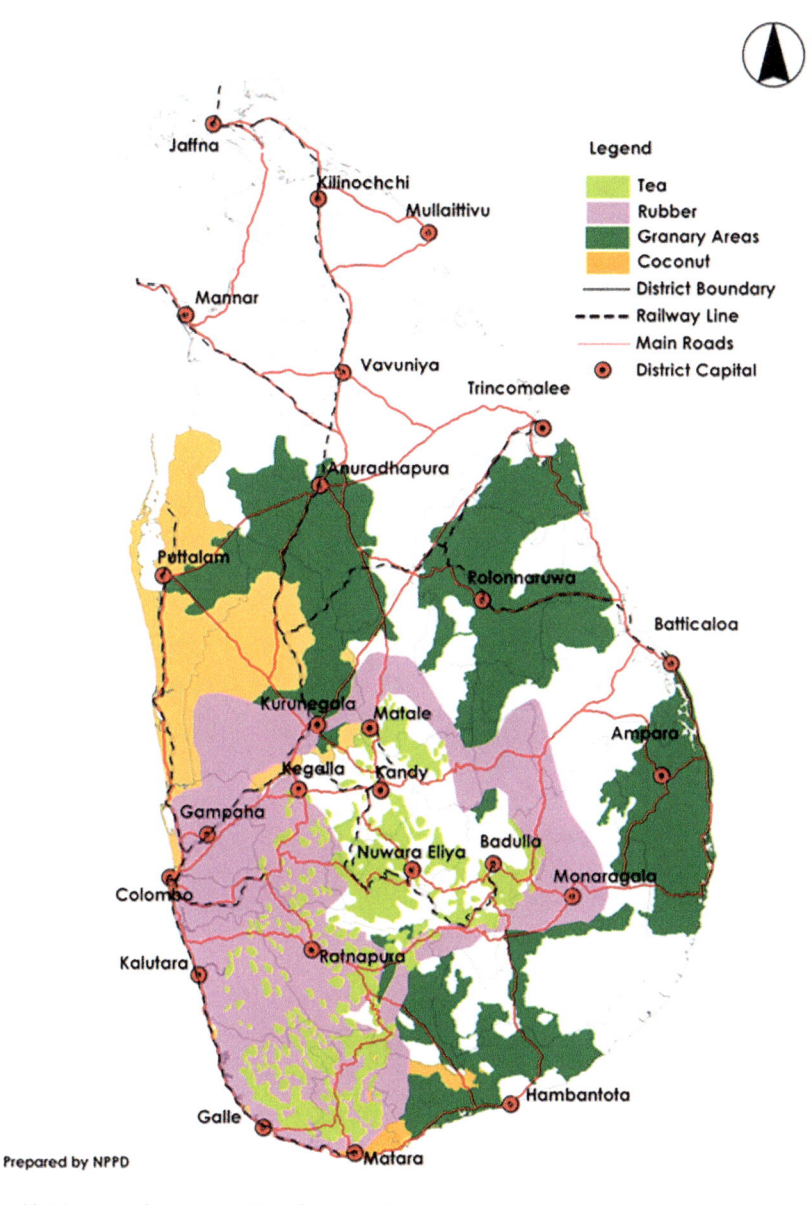

Fig. 10.14 Map of areas identified for agriculture

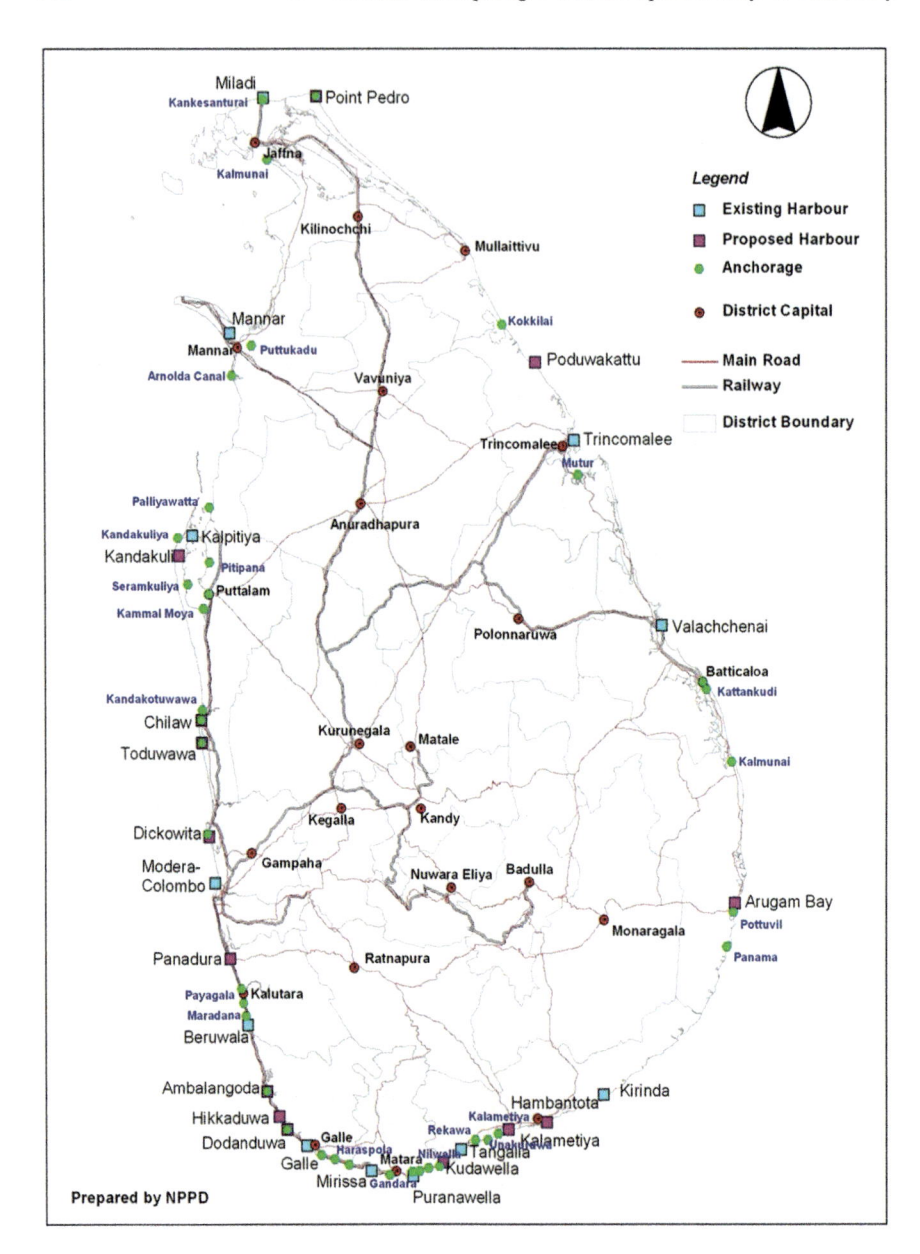

Fig. 10.15 Map of existing and proposed facilities for coastal fishing

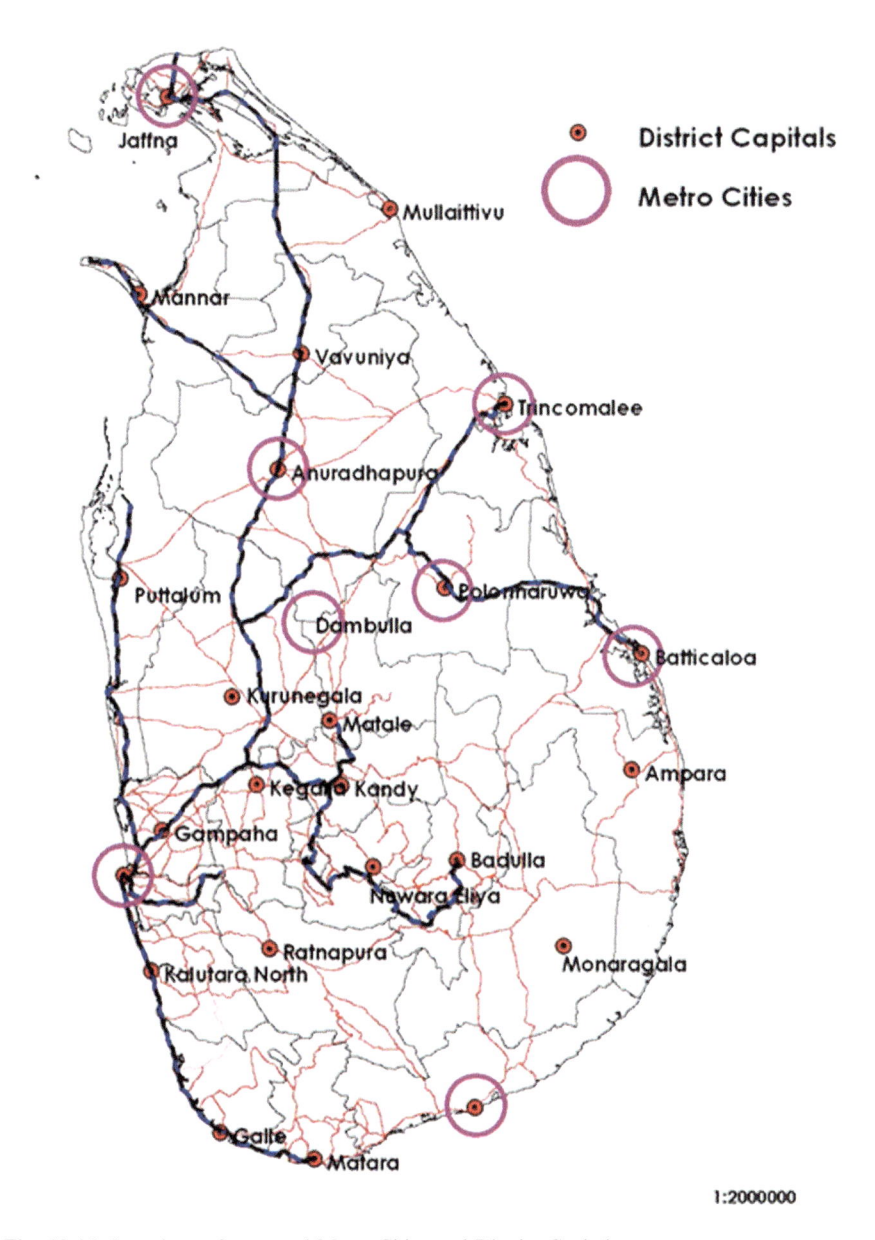

Fig. 10.16 Locations of proposed Metro Cities and District Capitals

as a marina to encourage yachting and for locating a marine museum. The bathymetry of the ocean around Sri Lanka suggests very great depths around the southern coast making a harbor in that region more easily accessible to very large vessels of deep draught (Fig. 10.18). It was thus recognized that Hambantota in the southern

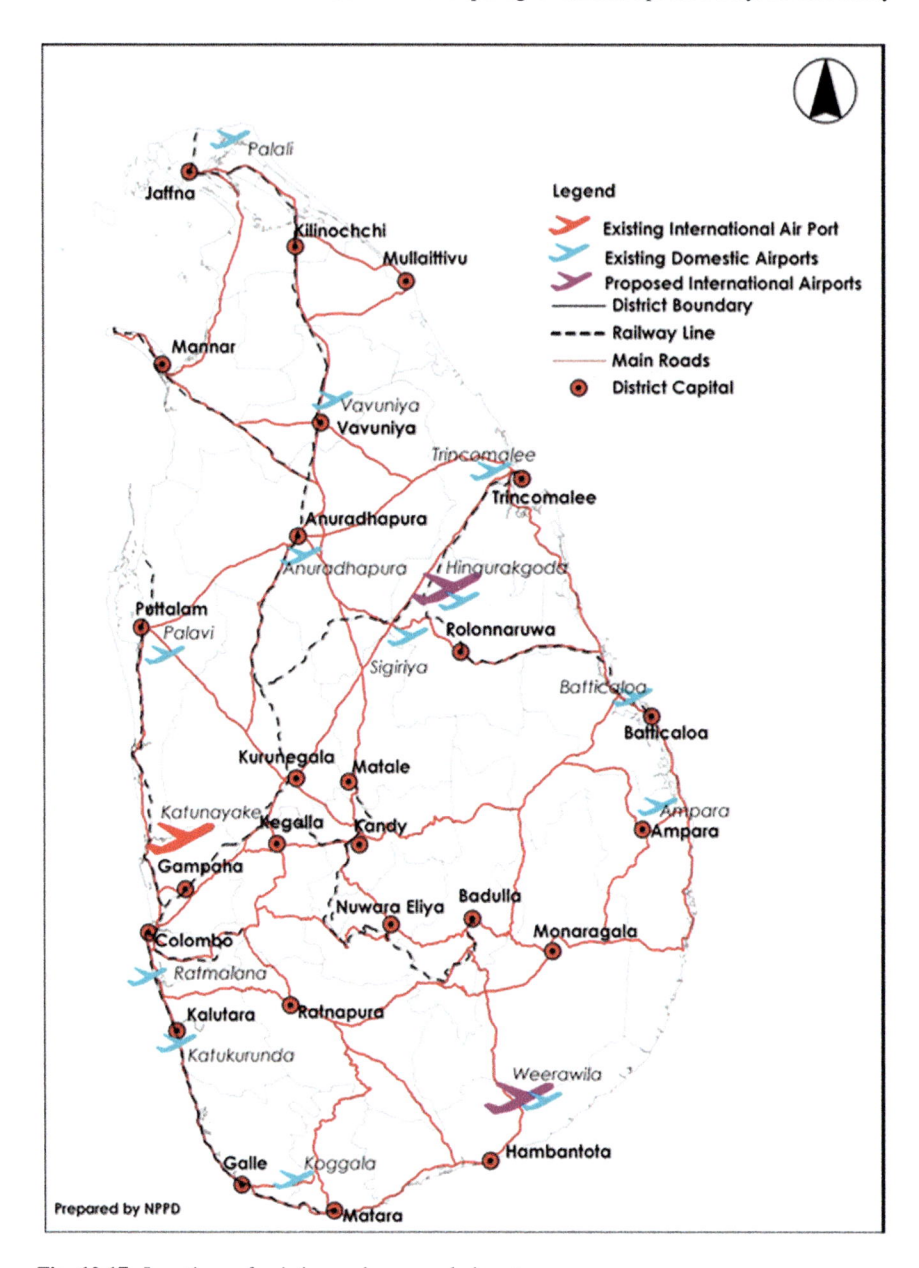

Fig. 10.17 Locations of existing and proposed airport

coast with its proximity to international shipping would be an excellent location for a new international harbor. It has therefore been included in the map of existing and proposed seaports (Fig. 10.19). Immediately southeast of Hambantota are a number of salterns. A few Sri Lankan engineers led notably by Dr. A. N. S. Kulasinghe had

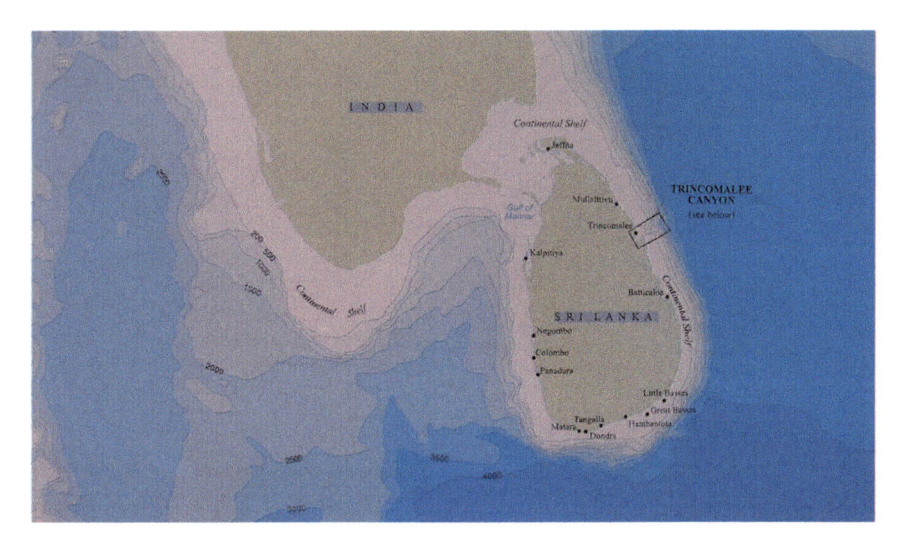

Fig. 10.18 Bathymetry of the ocean in the vicinity of Sri Lanka

suggested deepening and utilizing one of the many salterns located virtually on the coast, namely, "Karagam Lewaya" and to connect it to the sea to create the new harbor. This was seen as preferable to the very expensive alternative of extending the harbor and its breakwaters into the deep ocean. Thus, the plan developed for the harbor and the new city in relation to it was based on this advice. An artist's impression of the constructed harbor which can accommodate Post Panamax vessels and proposed new city is to be found in (Fig. 10.20).

Road and Rail Networks

The need to improve intercity and intracity connections, maintain, rehabilitate, and extend the existing road and rail networks, construct regional highways to link the District Capitals and the new Metro Cities, and also develop bus and rail networks was emphasized. These should be seen in relation to the proposals for networks of Asian transcontinental highways and railways as proposed by UN ESCAP in the 1950s (Figs. 10.21 and 10.22). It was thought necessary to include in the policy framework the need to have new highway and railway links between a proposed bridge to India over the Palk Straits at Mannar with the new harbor in the south at Hambantota and also the existing harbor in the east in Trincomalee. These particular proposed transport links as conveyed in the NPPD's plans are shown not as actual road and rail traces but as "desire lines" (Figs. 10.23 and 10.24). It was anticipated then that these links would facilitate transshipment of seaborne goods to the Indian Subcontinent and vice versa.

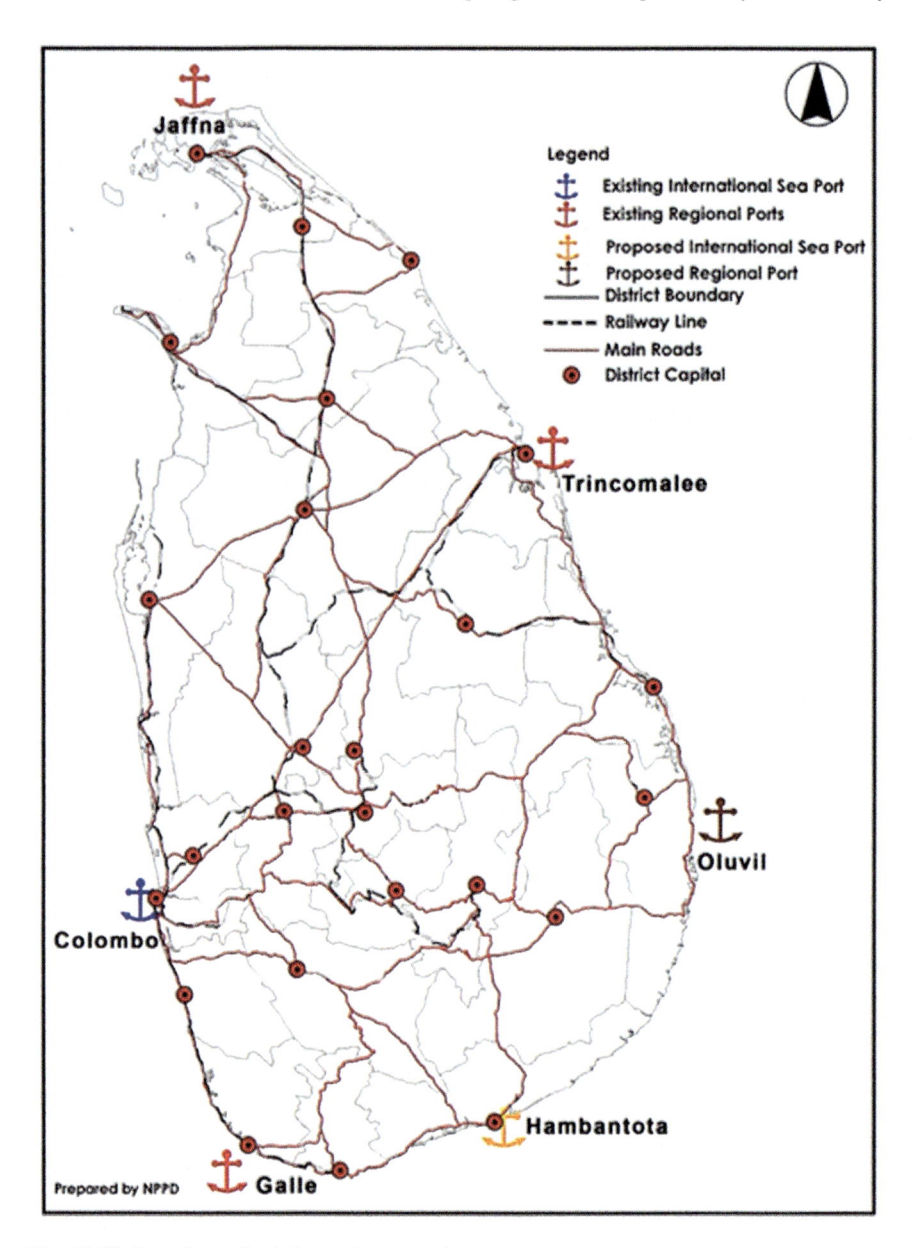

Fig. 10.19 Locations of existing and proposed seaports

Other Concerns 147

Fig. 10.20 An artist's impression of the completed Hambantota harbor

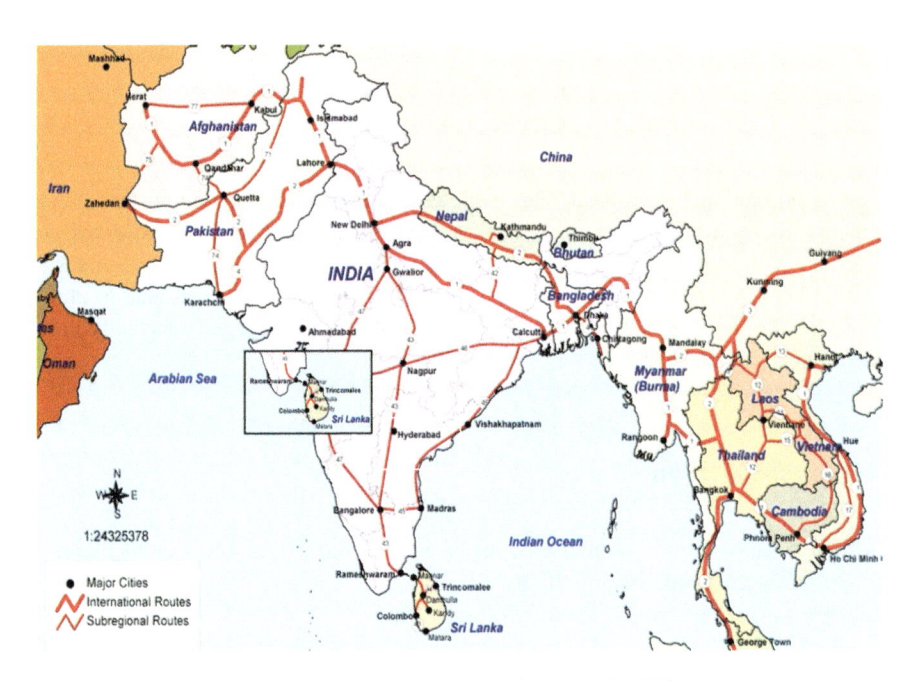

Fig. 10.21 Proposed transcontinental Asian Highway System (UN ESCAP)

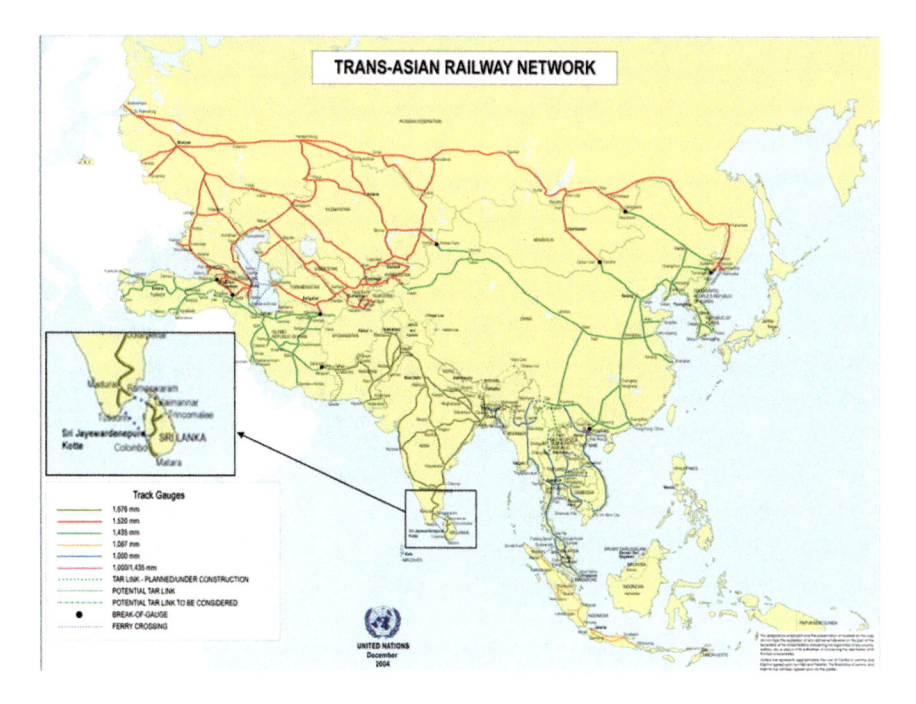

Fig. 10.22 Proposed transcontinental Asian Railway System (UN ESCAP)

Sites of Cultural and Aesthetic Importance

The important archaeological sites and also sites of religious importance, bird sanctuaries, waterfalls, peaks, ocean-based tourism, and wildlife reserves are depicted in a map (Fig. 10.25). It was proposed to protect and conserve areas of natural beauty and cultural significance more for their own sake but also to attract tourism. The development of *ecotourism* too was to be encouraged especially in the identified Fragile Areas.

A Composite Plan

A final composite plan showing as many as possible of the key spatial planning proposals is presented in Fig. 10.26.

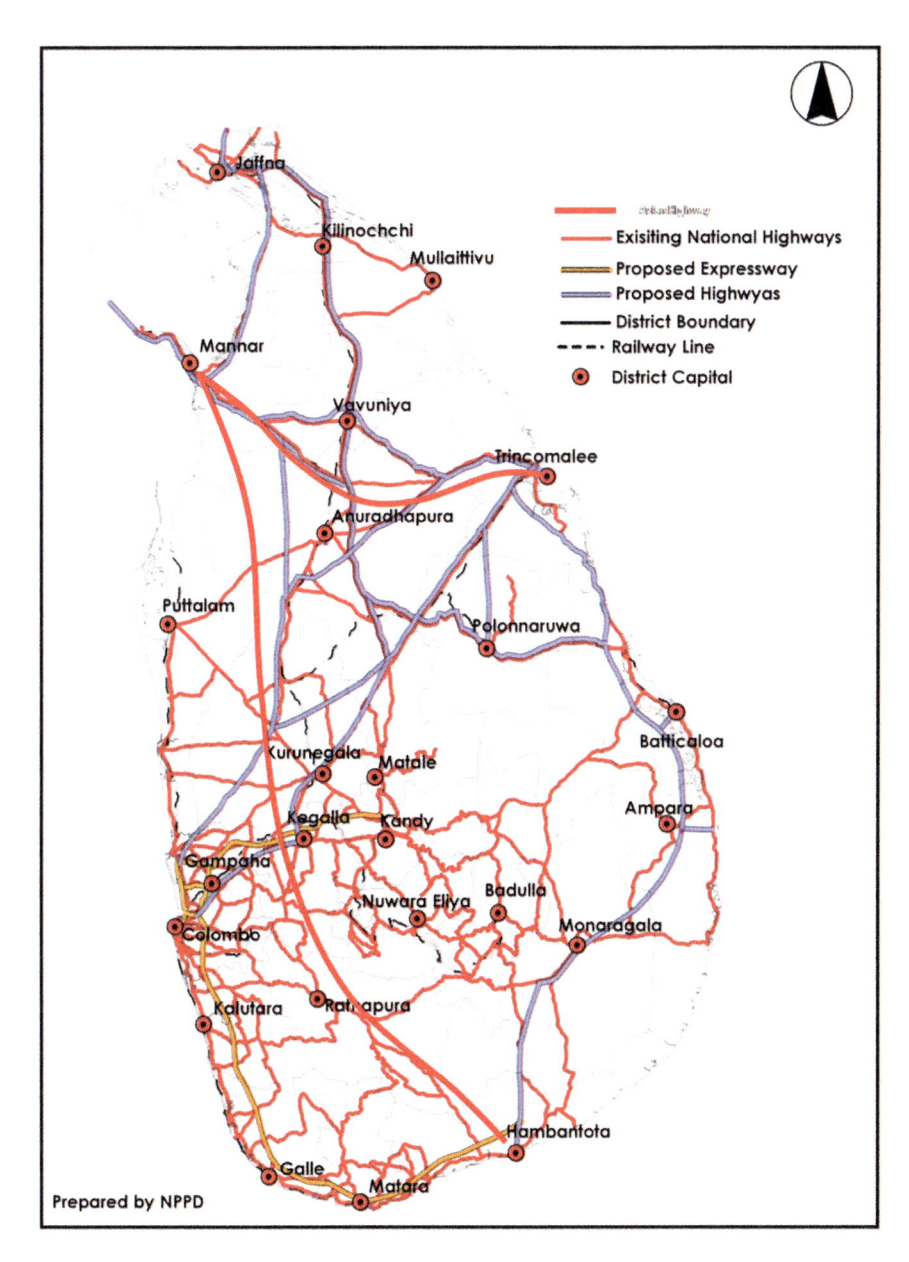

Fig. 10.23 Existing and proposed highways

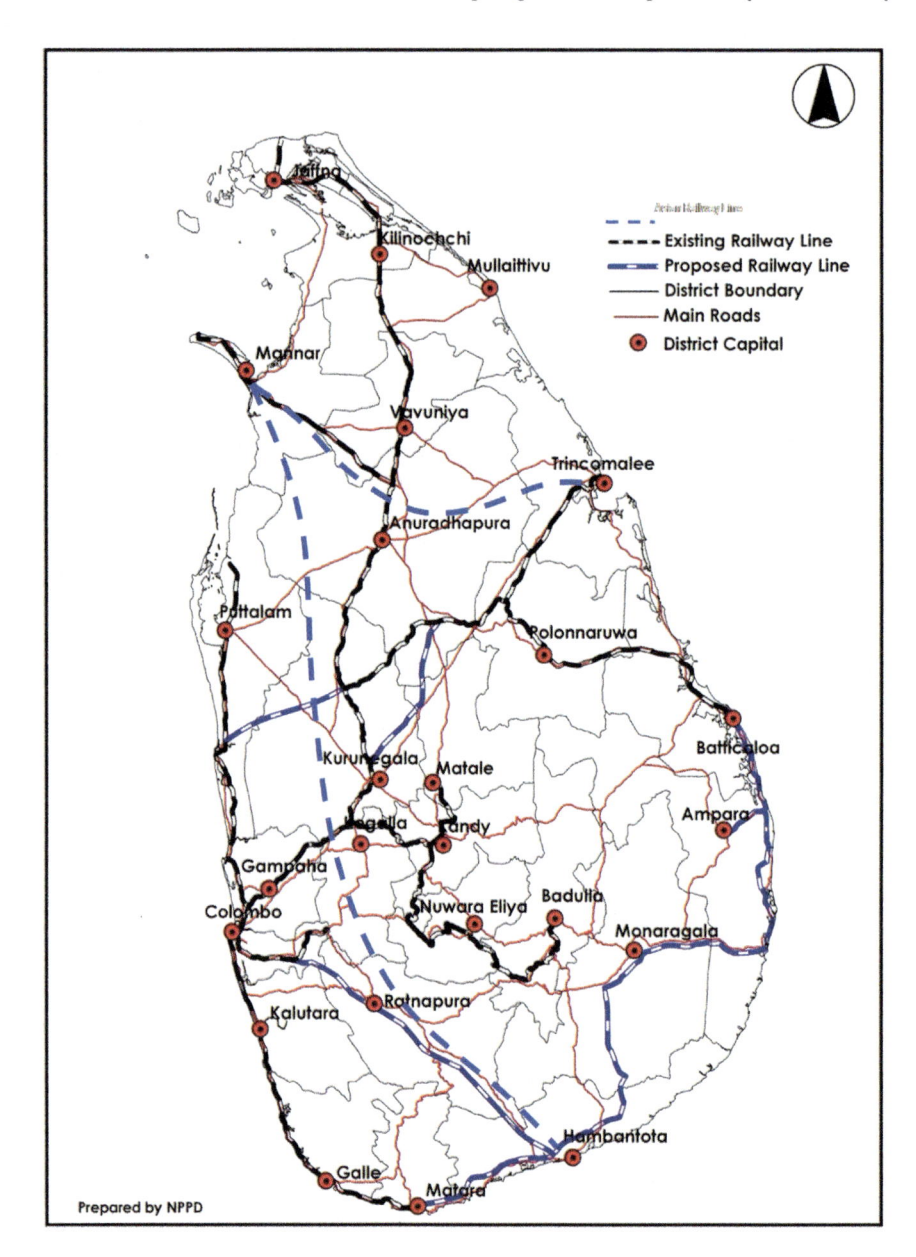

Fig. 10.24 Existing and proposed railways

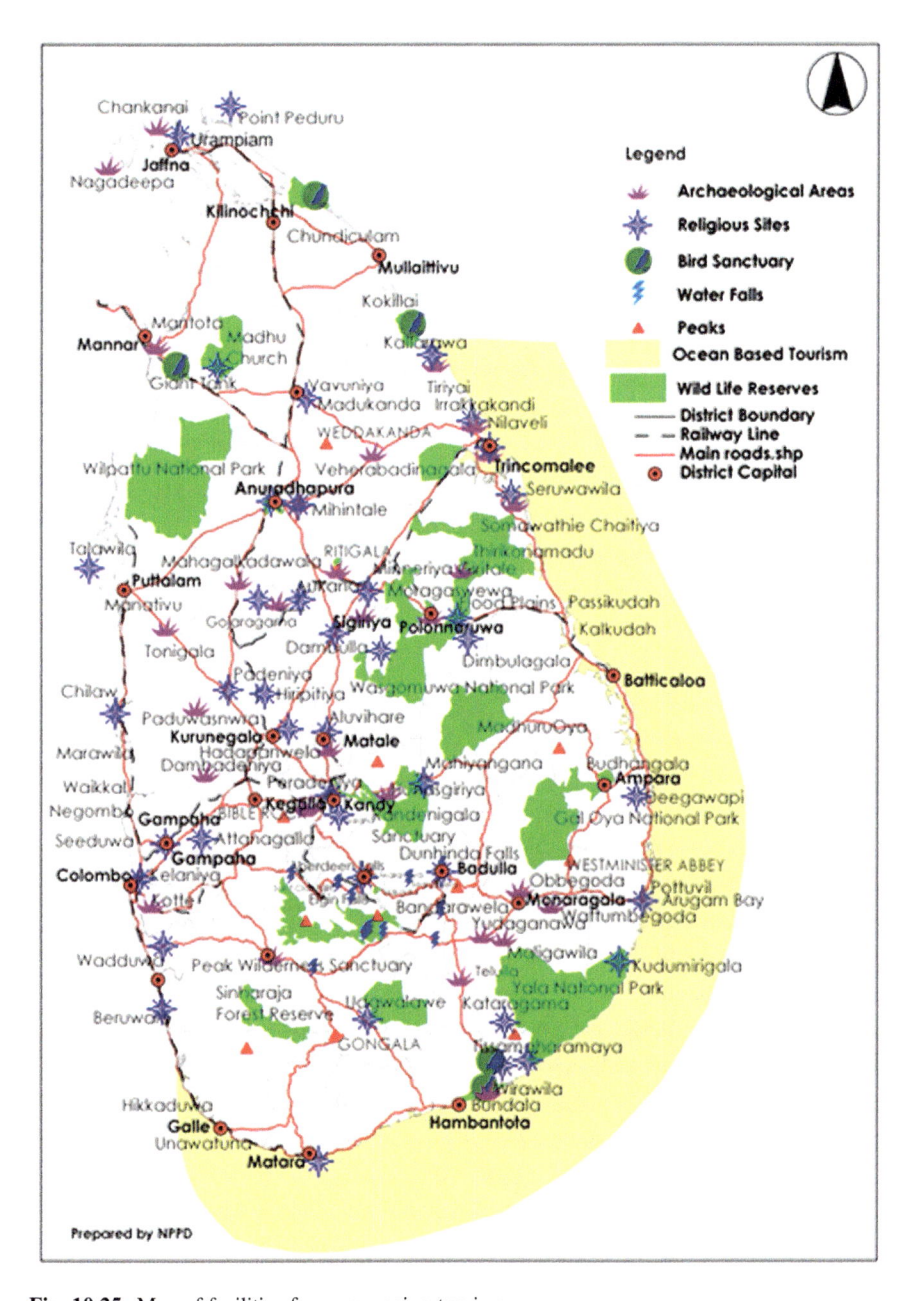

Fig. 10.25 Map of facilities for encouraging tourism

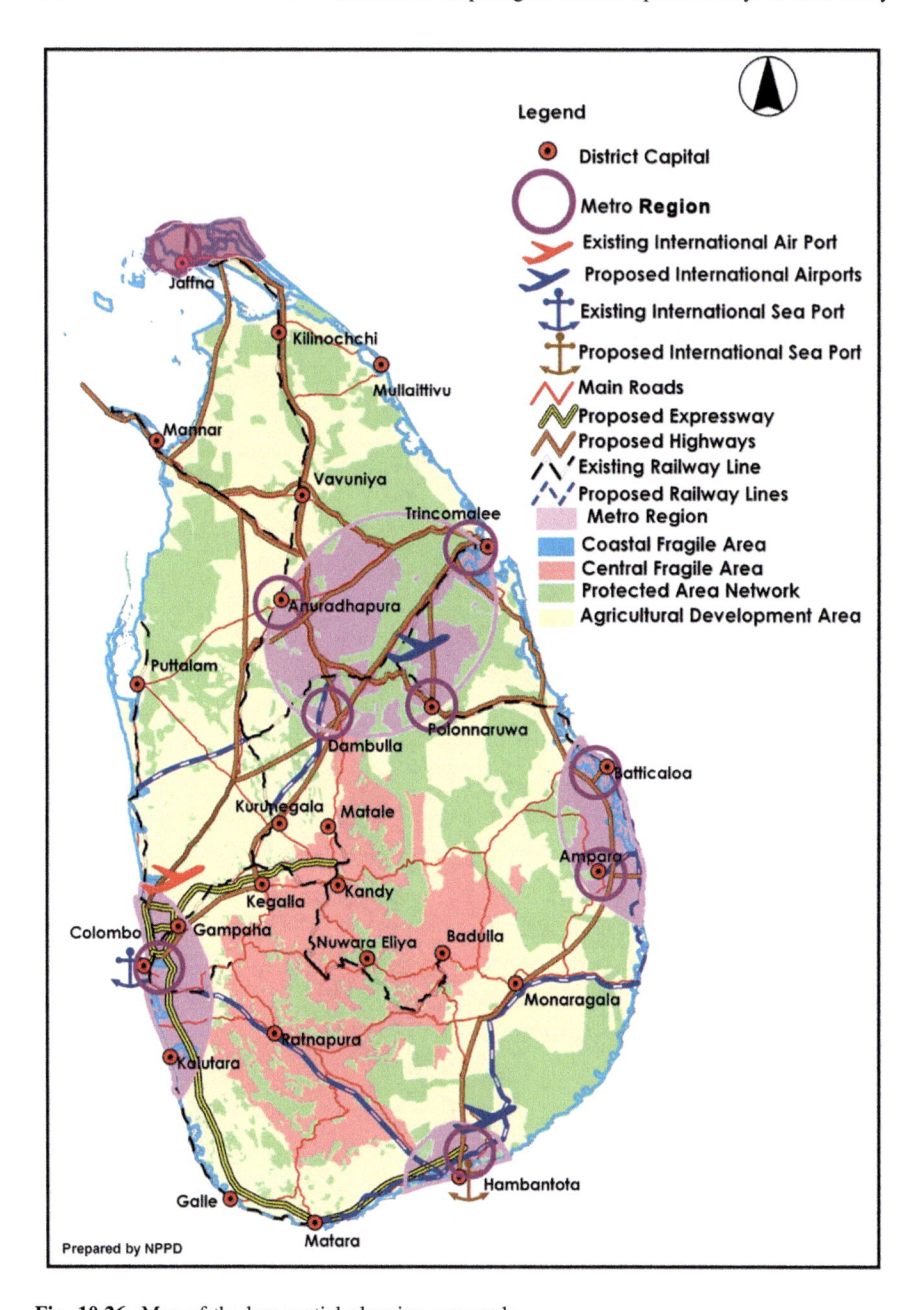

Fig. 10.26 Map of the key spatial planning proposals

References

Sanyal B (ed) (2005) Comparative planning cultures. Routledge, New York and London
Stohr WB, Taylor DRF (eds) (1981) Development from above or below. Wiley, New York
Watson V (2012) Planning and the 'stubborn realities' of global south cities: some emerging ideas. Plann Theor J 12(1)

Part III
Conclusions

Chapter 11
A Summary and Conclusions

After the Second World War, many colonized territories worldwide began to gain independence. International institutions were established along with a body of Western scholarship concerned with "development". Internalized were theories on how national progress may be fostered. Through schemes of monetary aid, loans, technical assistance, and education, the concept of development was promoted among various institutions and governments. Extraordinary funding and effort have been expended since development efforts were begun in the newly emerging low- and middle-income countries (LMICs). While some progress is evident, large numbers in many of these countries have remained illiterate, entrenched in abject poverty vulnerable to disasters, debilitating disease, hunger, and untimely death.

This chapter is a summary of the book and its conclusions. The book broadly concerns the LMICs with particular and specific reference to the countries of South Asia. It is focused on identifying more scientific and alternative approaches to the needed process of development and to the specific challenges confronting these countries. There is an emphasis here on the need for such spatial planning and changes in these countries to meet these current challenges. The first chapter of the book is the introduction. Thereafter, it is presented in three parts and their respective conclusions are included along with the summaries given below.

Part I

Part I entitled "Basic Concerns" started with Chap. 2 and contained four other chapters. Chap. 2 discussed the concept of "development" itself. It reviewed the seminal ideas and theories that form the canons which were subsequently disseminated to the LMICs. It examined these underlying ideas and theories for their scientific merit and contextual relevance. As put together and used in the Social Science literature, these theories had relatively recent origins dating from the immediate Post World War II period. The chapter noted that these economic growth theories contained metaphoric references to biologic evolution where societies, regardless of their separate historic, geographic, and cultural contexts were expected to pass through a preordained sequence of recognizable stages. This "stages" hypothesis involved the assumption that the social systems in all the LMICs must replicate in miniature the historical processes through which some of the industrialized societies had already passed. The relevant conclusions drawn in this chapter were as follows: that this was an ahistoric stance that had at its base a weak and untested hypothesis; that the hypothesis had neither any justification to substantiate a claim that it has any basis in science; nor that it has general relevance to the LMICs and to the context of special concern here, namely, the countries of South Asia.

It was noted in Chap. 3 that, starting in the mid-1960s and progressing through the 1970s, an important revision had begun in regard to the advocacy of unbridled economic growth and industrialization; that the need for environmental sustainability in such a growth process had thus come to be recognized; and that awareness of the ecological consequences of economic growth has led to the current promotion of development in the LMICs as qualified by the word "sustainable". Noting that multiple environmental crises confront the world now with consequences that could in the extreme even threaten all life on earth, this chapter also sought to address the environmental challenges facing the LMICs. It analyzed the philosophical concerns that arise within the new paradigm of "sustainable development" and focused on some of the environmental crises being faced currently by the entire world. It was noted that the contention of some Western scholars now is that at least in the past few centuries, anthropocentrism with its many philosophic references to the origins of Western civilization in ancient Greece, has become a dominant attitude in the Western world, and that this dominant attitude is a cause for serious concern. It was further noted that non-anthropocentric philosophy is already entrenched in most of the Asian cultures.

Chapter 4 was concerned with the facts as presented by scientists on the subject of climate change. It was mentioned that following the Rio Summit of 1992, two international organizations, namely, the Intergovernmental Panel on Climate Change (IPCC) and the United Nations Framework Convention on Climate Change (UNFCCC), were empowered to perform special tasks. They were, respectively, to gather scientific information on climate change and to facilitate consensus among countries to stabilize greenhouse gases (GHGs) in the atmosphere so as not to further aggravate global warming. It was noted that carbon dioxide constitutes about 75% of the GHGs with the rest being composed of three other types of gases.

It is now well recognized that no country will be immune to the impacts of climate change. The most affected will be the LMICs. Sea level rise will impact adversely upon small islands and river delta regions. Increases in tropical cyclones and in drought conditions in arid areas of the tropical LMICs will be experienced frequently. Major flooding can be expected which will not only affect food supply but also cause disease epidemics. Increased acidification of ocean waters will cause damage to marine life and consequently to livelihoods and food supply. Furthermore, large shocks to agriculture may even lead to disrupting and dislocating some populations.

This 4th chapter was concerned also with the unprecedented rate of global warming since the 1950s. It was noted there that many international UN conferences have been held over almost two decades to discuss and find ways of dealing with the adversities of climate change. While human causation is recognized by the scientific community, there are influential political voices in at least one polluting countries that are in denial. The views of some of the respected scientific organization which support human causation are discussed.

It was also noted that there are a few Arctic nations that will share some benefits from global warming and climate change. Nevertheless, it is recognized that almost all other countries will be adversely affected by these phenomena and that the worst to be affected will be the tropical LMICs. An international agreement has been reached after deliberations over many years with clear definitions on what needs to be done. However, there is at present no guarantee that the commitments made will be honored by each and all of the relevant countries.

Chapter 5 contained a foray into the epistemology of science to explore the role of scientific and professional ethics as likely factors influencing sustainable progress in the LMICs. It was recognized that a commitment to science and technology is essential for the LMICs to generate economic growth, and also that ethical convictions are necessary for that growth to be both inclusive and environmentally sustainable. One conclusion was that the success of such efforts depends on the extent of consumption of goods and services and on the types of technology and energy utilized for their production. Another conclusion was that controlling these factors is neither easy nor popular and that political leaders cannot always be relied upon to act on this matter with the needed foresight. It was thus concluded that scientists, nongovernmental organizations, and professionals governed by ethical concerns need to take upon themselves the leadership in educating the public and creating a collective ethical consciousness.

It was also noted in this chapter that Science is manifest today in two versions: "Classical Science" and "Modern Science" that the former had its roots in the "European Renaissance" and was systemized starting in the sixteenth and seventeenth centuries; that the technological advances based on science that accompanied the Industrial Revolution in the West, strengthened the belief in science; and that the European colonial powers exported Classical Science to their dependencies in Asia during the nineteenth and early twentieth centuries presenting them as being of European origin and perfected in the West. However, the fact was noted that there are many important Asian influences in Classical Science even from its beginnings and also in Modern Science.

This fifth chapter also recognized that an individualistic quest for economic power and the pursuit of knowledge was associated with the European Renaissance; that this quest even overrode the moral law in human conduct; and that by the eighteenth and nineteenth centuries, there was a consolidating impact of the

Industrial revolution on Classical Science; and thus, that discrete science-based professional disciplines which had begun to emerge in the West sought legal recognition; that this need in the Western democratic traditions required guarantees that each profession functions in the public interest; that thus, in the absence of an overarching moral code, it soon became mandatory for each professional discipline to have its own code of conduct. When these professions in their "Western" guise came to be known and practiced in the LMICs of Asia, they were already prepackaged complete with their respective culture-specific codes of conduct.

The discussions in Chap. 5 also related to the ethical concerns that arose with the industrialized mass production of weapons begun in Europe with the First and Second World Wars. The chapter noted that even much more destructive weapons of mass destruction were developed and stockpiled by the West and the Soviet Union during the "Cold War" arms race. It was recognized that the participating scientists had no code of ethics strong enough to resist their own governments; and that in this atmosphere in the 1950s and 1960s only a few notable independent scientists were brave enough to protest and to inform the public about the dangers that could be caused to all life on earth—dangers from nuclear weapons that were hidden from the public and often denied by politicians on both sides of the Cold War. Some significant changes have occurred in recent decades in the relationship among the Cold War contestants of the 1950s. Nevertheless, the numerous "flash points" have arisen and still continue to arise since then in various geographic locations from time to time. These were noted as chilling reminders that the danger of a minor conflict escalating even into a nuclear war is still ever-present.

Other important ethical challenges than warfare also confronted Science in the recent past. A serious ethical situation is before the scientists in today's environmental crises. In Chap. 4 it was observed that if impending disasters are to be averted, scientists have a major part to play; that codes of conduct behind science will have to be substantially strengthened to resonate with an overarching non-anthropocentric cultural code of ethics; that such a cultural influence is being suggested now by some Western thinkers as an urgent necessity for their own countries; and that adherence to a similar cultural influence, being more indigenous, should have an even greater relevance to all industrialized and rapidly industrializing countries of Asia including those in South Asia.

It was also observed that since the Meiji restoration, Japan, an Asian country, did adopt and follow the Western path to industrialization quite unaware at that time about serious consequential global impacts upon the environment; that today, India and China are two of the three very large and rapidly industrializing LMICs in Asia with markedly high economic growth potential. It was noted as being most unfortunate that scientists, policy planners, advisor, and indeed the modern philosophers in these Asian countries, despite strong philosophic affiliations to non-anthropocentric cultures, have not striven hard enough to find appropriate paths to rapid national progress consonant with their great cultural heritage.

Part II

Part II of the book entitled "Spatial Concerns" consists of Chaps. 6–10. Chapter 6 was concerned with the impact of climate change on South Asia. There are eight countries that are usually identified as comprising South Asia. Of them, seven, namely, Sri Lanka, the Maldives, Bangladesh, India, Pakistan, Bhutan, and Nepal, are examined in this chapter. They are as extreme a geographic variety as could be found anywhere globally. They include tropical islands and other warm coastal areas, major rivers, flat river delta regions, vast plains, deserts, much hilly terrain, and some of the highest mountains in the world. This sixth chapter briefly and generally examined each of these countries noting their climatic zones, the basics of their individual climatic feature in terms of temperature and precipitation, their main economic activities, and their dependence on weather patterns. Thereafter, the chapter proceeded to discuss the impact of climate change on these countries.

South Asia is home to half the world's population. Its special vulnerability to climate change has to do with its geography, the presence of substantial poverty, its food insecurity, and its multitude of undernourished people. Temperature extremes and altered precipitation patterns, frequent deficit monsoons, abnormally high glacial melt in the Himalayan region, and consequent swelling of those rivers, intermittent floods, and droughts all cause frequent disasters. These trends, which are expected to continue and intensify, cause a serious challenge to progress in these South Asian countries. The adverse impact upon agriculture in all these countries and thus on their economies is and will continue to be profound.

It may thus be concluded that despite the very wide geographic and climatic variations among the countries of South Asia, all of them are seriously affected by climate change. This happens due to unseasonal and unpredictable weather conditions that tend to occur. All these countries including those in the mountainous Himalayan region are now more than in the past subject to floods and landslides. Much of the adversity stems in consequence of the impact of these conditions upon agriculture in those countries. Agriculture is important to all South Asian countries not only for their food security but also as it is a key component in their respective economies. Their rural conditions, bad as they already are, are worsened, and thus, rural–urban migration is further encouraged.

Chapter 7 highlighted that the scale and pace of urbanization today is unprecedented as experienced primarily in the LMICs. It was recognized that many Western scholars have viewed urbanization as an inevitable, if not desirable product of development. Therefore, efforts have generally converged in the LMICs on mitigating resultant problems through intra-urban interventions, rather than attempting to control its causative factors to reduce their adversities. The writings on managing urbanization in this manner formed the subject matter of this chapter. It also traced contemporary spatial planning theories to their origins and critically examined their relevance to LMICs. There was also a brief mention of one of the theories concerned with the phenomena of "urban primacy" and its observable presence in the smaller among those countries. The theory was seen to be of fundamental relevance to the desired new spatial planning approach to deal with this problem in many LMICs.

Chapter 8 focused and expanded on the theory relating to urban primacy which is seen as being of special relevance to the smaller LMICs. An important conclusion is that urbanization, while it has its many benefits, also has its own serious consequences in the countries of South Asia and perhaps also in other LMICs. It tends to denude the rural areas of the younger, more intelligent, and able-bodied members of their populations and has thus an unfavorable impact upon agriculture. As mentioned earlier, agriculture is important not only for food security but also as it is a key component in the respective economies of the South Asian countries. The condition of "Primacy" is observable as a phenomenon commonly found in the smaller South Asian countries and indeed found in most other smaller LMICs as well. It reinforces marginalization of the rural populations through the strong encouragement it provides to urbanization in their respective countries.

Many LMICs have ancient monuments and sites of cultural significance. South Asia abounds in such sites. Conserving these often becomes a matter of prestige and cultural necessity receiving high priority in their respective national development programs. Chapter 9 relates to a cultural site of great importance nationally, regionally, and internationally having been declared by UNESCO as a World Heritage Site. The particular site is Lumbini, the birthplace of the Buddha, which is situated in the southern plains of Nepal adjacent to the border with India. Much work has been done since the Lumbini conservation project was launched with considerable UN assistance in 1970. A relevant and useful Master Plan had been prepared to provide a zoned spatial framework within which facilities for visitor may be located and conservation work may be pursued unhindered.

Due perhaps to the many and serious social and economic problems faced by the government of Nepal in recent decades, it is noted in this chapter that overall progress in conservation and construction has been delayed for long periods. With the consequent changes in officials and lapses in institutional memory, some serious threats have arisen. The most serious is the unauthorized encroachment and industrial activity that has been allowed to take place within and in close proximity to the Buffer Zone which could eventually jeopardize the entire project and place Lumbini's status as a *World Heritage Site* at risk. An equally serious threat is that there is an alternative proposal to create a city of more than 200,000 inhabitants with its spatial coverage over the entire Buffer Zone. The chapter notes that the urgent need now is first for social scientists to quickly study the socioeconomic conditions and the population dynamics in the Buffer Zone; that based on these studies, expert spatial planning work is put to establish land use controls, relocate encroachers in carefully planned settlements nearby with active support from the government of Nepal, and relevant international agencies to lead quickly to reestablish the Buffer Zone to its original intended purpose.

Chapter 10 makes a case for the LMICs to define and make explicit their respective national urban and regional planning policies. To help translate theory to practice, this chapter presents an environmentally predicated case study where some of the important spatial planning theories recommended in the book are embedded

—a rare attempt in an LMIC to prepare such a policy with approval by stakeholders for implementation. It is presented for its intrinsic value to concerned academics and professionals in the region.

It should be clearly evident from the chapters in Part II of this book that spatial planning is at the core of the important issues raised and is fundamental especially to the two case studies presented in Chaps. 9 and 10. These latter dealt, respectively, with conservation of cultural monuments and sites, on the one hand, and on the other, a national spatial policy. The most important conclusions to be arrived at from all the presentations made in this book relates to the overarching need for inclusive and sustained progress; and that such progress does not follow automatically through the development effort as currently practiced in South Asia, nor perhaps in most LMICs; that the progress that does arise is at best highly and invariably spatially skewed and benefits only a few segments of the population; that the particular benefited segments are in all probability already privileged groups within a major city often a "primate city" located within an already relatively privileged region of the particular LMIC; that the process, with whatever benefits it brings to the country of concern, also automatically exaggerates further the existing spatial inequalities; that it creates serious disparities in income distribution as well as in the access provided to social infrastructure; and finally, that the urbanization process which could be very beneficial is thus forced to compound existing problems rather than solve them.

It is thus an important final conclusion in this book that the entire process of development through economic growth as practiced today in South Asia and indeed in most LMICs can succeed in achieving the objective of inclusive and sustainable growth only if the effort is coupled with and tempered by an environmentally sound national spatial strategy that is aimed specifically at the provision inter alia of economic opportunities along with the necessary social and economic infrastructure to generate genuine and lasting spatial equity.

Part III

Part III of the book consists solely of Chap. 11 which is this present summary of the contents of this book and of the conclusions that may be drawn from all of its chapters.

Appendix A
South Asian Seminar on Small and Medium Sized Towns in Regional Development. Organized in Kathmandu, Nepal by the Quaker International Affairs Programme in South Asia, New Delhi. 9th–16th April 1978

Group II Report

Metro Magnets and Small and Medium Sized Towns

The group was also expected to reflect on whether small and medium sized towns do in fact have a role to play in national/regional development.

The group, after some deliberation, agreed that the statement somewhat misidentified the principle issue, which was to consider <u>what type of settlement pattern is called for in the separate countries of South Asia.</u> The group therefore proceeded to discuss this question. The main points of agreement that emerged from the discussion are given below.

1. The question needs to be studied in relation to (a) the settlement patterns or national urban systems now existing in these countries, and how they came into being; and (b) the development goals and strategies of each of the separate countries concerned.
2. There are some important similarities in the existing settlement patterns of these countries especially as regards the dichotomous nature of the rural-urban relationship. There are large primate cities on the one hand, and the rural hinterland on the other, with hardly any urban places of an intermediate scale in-between. This pattern of settlements has resulted from the nature of the economies of these countries during the 'pre-independence' period. The pattern, in general, persisted even after 'independence' because industries and other economic activities continued to gravitate to the primate cities to take advantage of the availability of infrastructure, skilled manpower, and economies of scale. Thus, these settlement systems entered a 'vicious cycle' where the rural areas continued to be drained even further of manpower and resources, and the urban centres grew exponentially to such proportions that dis-economies of scale are now being felt.

3. The development goals for these countries are concerned not only with economic growth but also social goals such as equity and justice. While in some cases development strategies call for industrialization, in all cases agricultural and rural development are given heavy weightage. There is indeed a very deep concern about the equitable distribution of socio-economic benefits among the people at large, most of who live in the rural areas.
4. The existing settlement patterns bear little relevance to the development strategies in each of the countries, are therefore not conducive to, and may even hinder the achievement of development goals. Thus, <u>intervention</u> by the national governments in each of the countries is essential to restructure the settlement patterns to make them relevant to the development strategies and facilitate the achievement of development goals.
5. In each of the countries, the re-structuring of the settlement pattern that is called for, involves the establishment of a number of urban places at an intermediate scale between the primate cities and the rural hinterland. All of these towns will not be of the same size or function. Ranking will be necessary according to the order of goods and services provided by each.
6. There can be little replicability, country to country, in the hierarchical levels of towns, or the forms the settlement systems may take. These need to be based, in each case, on such considerations <u>inter alia</u> as:

   (a) Population characteristics and spread;
   (b) Resource endowment and distribution;
   (c) Transport technology.

Also, in each case, careful attention would have to be given to establishment of the minimum levels of adequacy of infrastructure in each of the urban hierarchical levels, to ensure viability.

7. The planning of such towns as are envisaged will necessitate a much improved database, sectoral integration and popular participation that what exists in each of the countries at present.
8. The intermediate scale towns are considered essential so that (a) they may act as service centres for agriculture, (b) distribution functions can be performed (c) mutually beneficial linkages will be established between the existing urban and rural economies, and enable the diffusion of knowledge and innovation.

Appendix B
The Key Events That Led to Transforming the Town and Country Planning Department of Sri Lanka into the National Physical Planning Department

The publication of the following documents:

1. "**A Case for an Explicit National Urban Policy**"

   Economic Review, Colombo; Published: 1977.

2. "**Sri Lanka Urban Sector Profile**"

   A report prepared by the Asian Development Bank (First Draft Published in 1988).
   Manila, January 1991. This document mentions (in Section V2d p. 104) *inter alia* that the 1977 paper cited in key event 1 above recommends the establishment of a national spatial planning agency;

3. The Report of the Forum:

   "**Towards a National Urban Policy for Sri Lanka**"
   Institution of Town Planners in 1995 and the publication of its proceedings in 1997; and,

4. The report of:

   The Presidential Task Force on Housing and Urban Development: 1997
   This Task Force recommended that the Department not be disbanded but transformed to develop a National Spatial Plan for Sri Lanka.